A COMEDY OF TERRORS

Also by Lindsey Davis

The Course of Honour   The Spook Who Spoke Again
Rebels and Traitors   Vesuvius by Night
Master and God   Invitation to Die
A Cruel Fate

THE FALCO SERIES

The Silver Pigs   Ode to a Banker
Shadows in Bronze   A Body in the Bath House
Venus in Copper   The Jupiter Myth
The Iron Hand of Mars   The Accusers
Poseidon's Gold   Scandal Takes a Holiday
Last Act in Palmyra   See Delphi and Die
Time to Depart   Saturnalia
A Dying Light in Corduba   Alexandria
Three Hands in the   Nemesis
Fountain   Falco: The Official
Two for the Lions   Companion
One Virgin Too Many

THE FLAVIA ALBIA SERIES

The Ides of April   The Third Nero
Enemies at Home   Pandora's Boy
Deadly Election   A Capitol Death
The Graveyard of the   The Grove of the Caesars
Hesperides

A COMEDY OF TERRORS

A Flavia Albia Novel

Lindsey Davis

HODDER &
STOUGHTON

First published in Great Britain in 2021 by Hodder & Stoughton
An Hachette UK company

1

Copyright © Lindsey Davis 2021

Maps drawn by Rodney Paull.

A CIP catalogue record for this title is available from the British Library

Hardback ISBN 978 1 529 37429 2
Trade Paperback ISBN 978 1 529 37430 8
eBook ISBN 978 1 529 37432 2

Typeset in Plantin Light by Palimpsest Book Production Ltd, Falkirk, Stirlingshire

Printed and bound in Great Britain by Clays Ltd, Elcograf S.p.A.

Hodder & Stoughton policy is to use papers that are natural, renewable
and recyclable products and made from wood grown in sustainable forests.
The logging and manufacturing processes are expected to conform
to the environmental regulations of the country of origin.

Hodder & Stoughton Ltd
Carmelite House
50 Victoria Embankment
London EC4Y 0DZ

www.hodder.co.uk

A COMEDY OF TERRORS

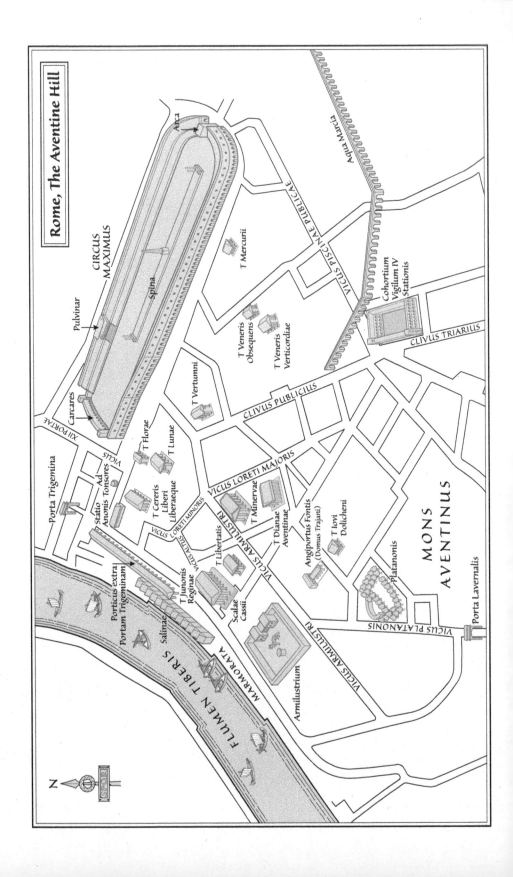

Rome, The Aventine Hill

CIRCUS MAXIMUS

Arca

Pulvinar

Spina

Carcares

XII PORTAE

VICUS

Porta Trigemina

Statio
Ad
Anonis Tonsores

Porticus extra
Portam Trigeminam

Salinae

MARMORATA

FLUMEN TIBERIS

T Mercurii

VICUS PISCINAE PUBLICAE

Aqua Marcia

Cohortium
Vigilum IV
Stationis

CLIVUS TRIARIUS

T Veneris
Obsequens

T Veneris
Verticordiae

T Vertumni

CLIVUS PUBLICIUS

T Florae

T Lunae

VICUS LORETI MAJORIS

T Cereris
Liberi
Liberaeque

T Minervae

VICUS LORETI MINORIS

T Dianae
Aventinae

Angiportus Fontis
(Domus Trajani)

T Jovi
Dolicheni

T Libertatis

VICUS ARMILUSTRI

Platanonis

MONS
AVENTINUS

T Junonis
Reginae

Scalae
Cassii

VICUS ARMILUSTRI

Armilustrium

VICUS PLATANONIS

Porta Lavernalis

N
SPQR

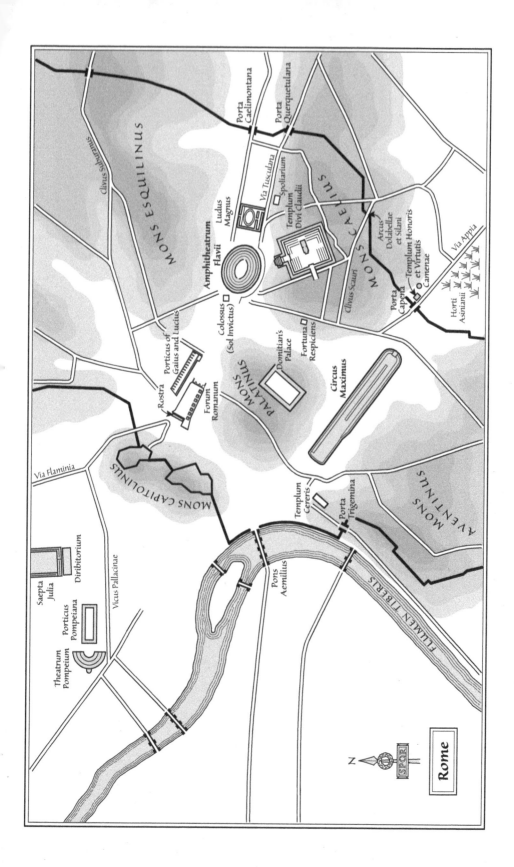

Rome, AD 89: mainly on the Aventine

The week before Saturnalia: 12–17 December

*Who can sing of these spectacles, this unrestrained humour,
this banquet with free food and lashings of free wine? . . .
How far into the future will news of this day stretch? Sacred
and ageless, your feast will survive as long as the hills of
Latium and Old Father Tiber, or your Rome, O Leader!*

Statius, *Silvae 1.6*

OUR FESTIVAL CHARACTERS

Flavia Albia	an out-of-work investigator
Tiberius Manlius	her very busy husband
Gaius and Lucius	their lucky little fosterlings
Falco and Helena	her iconic parents
Julia, Favonia and Postumus	her riotous siblings
Vitalis	unlucky tutor to Postumus
Tullius	the rich uncle, everyone needs one
Their extended (extending) household:	Gratus the smooth steward; Dromo the dim slave; Paris the cheeky runabout; Fornix the celebrity chef; Suza the hopeful beautician; Barley the dog; Mercury the donkey; Sheep the sheep; Glaphyra the new nurse
Marcia and Corellius	holiday visitors, late arrivals, one legless
Rodan	a redundant door-keeper
Titus Morellus	the Fourth Cohort's investigator, unfortunately
Pullia	his wife, deserves better, chose him, sadly
The young Morelli	their four children, lively characters
Rufinianus	retired, recalled from the reserves
Petronius Longus	Albia's uncle, not at all reserved
Maia Favonia	nor her, Albia's stroppy aunt
Cassius Scaurus	the Fourth's tribune, more bent than the villains?
Gaius Murrius	a husband, locked out, a gambler

His twins	well, there had to be some
Nephele	his wife, whose truth is truly cloudy
Berenike	her sister, a desperate fiancée
Caesius	his dangerous brother, neighbourhood benefactor
Beauty	a squawker, a.k.a. Squawker, a beauty
Terentius	the real big rissole, keeping out of sight
Greius	his trusty, a key figure, keeping to himself
Sagax	a talkative slave, true to type
Balbina Milvia	gangster's daughter, gangster's wife
Florius	her husband, a bad memory
Laetilla	a lady who lunches, apparently
Naevius	a helpful informer, looking for business
Anon	another one, a hopeless stereotype
Prisca	a businesswoman, looking for profits
Zoe and Chloe	female gladiators, with a good holiday job
Spendo	an enthusiastic dwarf, an expert
Agemathus	a statue-seller, a winning player
Victor	his brother, gone for a drink, the loser
Rosius	a defiant salesman, paying the price
Anon	another, suffering for it
Pinarius	a debtor's best friend, keeping the cash

Hieronymus	a goldsmith, owed money left and right
Zoilus	the undead ghost, a haunting regular
Xero's pies	a dubious commodity
Nuts	Io, Saturnalia!

The colourful people of the Aventine, mostly drunk and getting drunker

I

Io! Saturnalia: the year when we acquired the boys. People kept telling my husband, 'Well, this will put an end to that work of hers!' Tiberius only smiled ruefully. I stopped bothering to argue: I would continue to be a private informer because I refused to be doomed by parenthood.

The killjoys kept trying to depress us: 'And of course,' they gloated happily, 'Saturnalia will be *so* difficult for you!'

Idiots. Life would certainly hold challenges for our two nephews. From now on every December, the month when their mother died, would be sad. All of us would feel it. Tiberius would never stop grieving for his lost sister; he was that kind of man. But you cannot ignore Saturnalia, not when everyone around is heartlessly throwing themselves into the riot and, because we lived on the Aventine, the caterwauling public were keeping our two tots awake every night. Gaius and Lucius were country-born. They knew how to ignore endlessly crowing cockerels or even yokels shrieking over snail races. But the city racket of the great December holiday disturbed them. Then they whimpered into their pillows. We tried to comfort them, but they were just little boys who thought they were going to miss all the presents, jokes, cakes, and parties with ghost stories.

We were treading a fine line in sensitivity, but we handled

it as best we could. Tiberius was still grieving for his sister Fania, but we wouldn't keep these two stuck at home as if they could never have any fun again.

The other stupidity I had to endure was people assuming that I – that well-known piece of work, Flavia Albia – would have no idea how to look after the boys. Cobnuts. For a start, I knew how they were feeling because I had been an abandoned child myself, somehow lost by my birth parents in the Boudiccan Revolt in Britain. Later, when I was adopted by Falco and Helena, I too had discovered what it was like to arrive in Rome, this huge overwhelming city, and to find yourself stuck among clamorous new relatives who were not always welcoming. Even fifteen years later I felt like an outsider, though it hardly mattered since Rome was stuffed with incomers. There were more of us than them.

'How will you cope, Albia? You'll really have your hands full now!'

Oh, leave me alone. I was ready. When I came to Rome, I had had baby sisters, then later a brother. I do know how to blow a small snotty nose on a child who is wildly strug-gling to escape. I had a fair idea how to set a daily routine. We were not trying alphabet lessons yet, but when we did, I would teach them myself; we already had a set of letters because I was making our slave, Dromo, learn. In his case it was tortuous, but by the time he was ready for freedom, he would be able to run his own business. So, these two little boys would survive, if it was up to me.

Gaius and Lucius had now been here for three days. They were tentatively joining in Saturnalia; if they decided to hide away and cry instead, we found them, gently bringing them back for cuddles. We made sure they knew that, even though their loving mother was no longer here, there would be new toys. As reassurance, I had promised to take them out to buy horrible little figurines that they could give to members of our household and a few people they had decided they liked. That included my parents and sisters, though not my brother Postumus, who had scared the boys at our wedding (most people find him scary), nor Uncle Tullius, who openly loathed children.

I had to learn quickly. I shared a laugh with my own dear mama about having to provide gift-figurines secretly for Postumus and Tullius so they didn't take offence. Helena Justina was no help. Though a lovely woman in many ways, she said she had done enough of this in her time (and still had three at home, plus Father); she would just sit back and enjoy watching me go through it.

However, she did tell me which *sigillaria*-seller could be trusted with small boys: an African street hawker called Agemathus. And she warned me to choose pottery figurines, because wax ones would melt in their hot little hands when they played with them before handing them over as presents.

'Even though you explain they shouldn't, because the statues are meant for other people?'

'Oh, yes. Postumus innocently claims he is testing for hidden weaknesses, which would disappoint his recipients.'

'He knows. Some *sigillaria* hardly last a week, Mama.'

'They are made with flaws on purpose, Albia. The hawkers want you to buy new ones every year. No hiding them at the back of a cupboard for next time.'

'Next time?' Glumly, I faced the fact that I was trapped. Saturnalia stress was mine for ever: the matron in a household has to make the festival run smoothly. You cannot rely on the paterfamilias because he is probably drunk.

Who can blame him? asked my mother. She would be drunk herself, she said, only somebody has to be capable of counting the wheat-cakes. You can't run out to buy more; it's a holiday so the bakery is closed and all the street-sellers have vanished. I had a steward to monitor supplies, but Helena warned me Gratus might be tipsy too.

Even so, since the parents were holding a traditional family feast, she wanted to borrow him to help. Also, since my cook had once worked in a celebrity restaurant, she asked very sweetly, could Fornix send a batch of his wonderful cakes? Not too much cinnamon because it made Postumus sneeze.

'Anything else?' I groaned.

'You will have to find the boys a nurse, if you want to keep working.'

My mother must be the only person in Rome who assumed I would never give up. Neither of us realised how soon this would be tested.

I duly took Gaius and Lucius to buy *sigillaria*. We found the street where the recommended figurine-seller was supposed to lurk. Agemathus was nowhere to be seen.

Locals claimed the man with the tray had been around all morning, yet no one could say where he had wandered off to or when he might stroll back. If he had been lured to a bar in full festival swing, he might only surface tomorrow. The boys were becoming fretful. In the end someone told me where he lived. Needless to say, his cold hutch was a meagre room in a dark tenement off a back alley behind a street of sponge-sellers, though believe me, it was not clean.

The building where we were now having our adventure rose to about six storeys, as high as regulations permit. It

4

seemed to consist of one-room lettings from ground floor to attic, with no superior apartments lower down and no exterior streetside shops. Agemathus lived on the third floor. I homed in because he had fixed a figurine to his doorpost to advertise. I couldn't believe many people would see this by chance; already I was starting to fear the statue-seller might be scattier than Mother had promised.

Clutching the children's sticky hands, I barged into his accommodation. He was in the room, lying face down on the bed. His tray of ghastly statuettes was there too, on a wonky stool: odd little men, who might have been religious in origin. A woman with no conscience might simply have snaffled a handful for free but to reach them I would have to pass close by Agemathus. Even I shrank from that. He had clearly not passed out from festival excess: blood was soaking the back of his tunic and a knife had been plunged between his shoulder-blades.

'Oh dear!'

Oh, pigshit. And you try telling a three-year-old and a five-year-old who have been promised horrible figurines that now they can't have them.

2

For me, as a private informer, this was a familiar situation. I always seem to be stumbling upon suspicious deaths, and since I don't trust the vigiles to investigate, I often knuckle down to it myself. A woman's work is never done. I cannot abide mess and, besides, I specialise in solving problems. I have even had clients who were snuffed out by some enemy after they hired me – though more likely I would find out my client had ignored my advice and taken rash action against someone else. Many of my commissions are family affairs. People in trouble do love to snap and go for one another. As a professional, I have to warn against murder as a remedy but, let's be honest, it can be a neat solution.

The first arrival at a crime scene should carry out certain key actions. First you must stop any hysterical spouse flinging him- or herself upon the corpse in real or fake grief. Don't stand for that nonsense. Assume that they did it, until proved otherwise. The more they act up, the more certain their guilt.

Next, remove very young children. Just shove them out. It is generally assumed the sight of blood will work upon their tiny minds in a bad way. You are supposed to rescue them from that. Later, you can give them honeyed figs and interrogate them cruelly, just in case they saw anything useful.

Mine were being pretty cool about Agemathus. Coming from the countryside, full of animals being slaughtered, must have made them blasé. Also, they seemed to regard the soaking blood as a Saturnalia jape. I managed to grab them by their tunic-necks before they could run to the figurines. Thwarted, they screwed up their eyes ready for tantrums. Gaius, the five-year-old, could go red in the face at will. Lucius, aged three, watched carefully then tried to copy him.

I would have to take them home. I had automatically fired up my forensic mode, assessing the death scene and looking around for clues. I could not be distracted, not while I was conducting an examination.

Grasping their little hands again, I led them from the room. I pulled the door closed after us as best I could, though it did not fit properly and had no latch. I had got in originally by leaning on it. Had that nailed-up figurine outside helped a murderer find Agemathus?

We clattered back down two flights of a stone staircase, past the usual stinking dolium of collected urine that stood in the filthy entrance lobby – 'Oh, pooh-ee!' and 'Why isn't there one of those at your house, Albia?' – into the compara-tively fresher air outside. I paused on the threshold, wondering whether to alert anyone.

We had seen no door porter or watchful crone when we entered the tenement. It had sounded unoccupied then; it still did. I could tell that plenty of people lived here; their litter was everywhere. Something was sticking my shoe to the ground. At mid-morning the tenants must all be out working, women as well as men. Children would have been taken to grandparents, aunts or pittance-a-day minders. I doubted that any of them went to school, but the current term had already ended for the holiday.

No one in these suffocating little rooms would own slaves. Conceivably, some were runaway slaves themselves. If so, they too had gone out to beg. The Aventine was crowned with ancient temples, whose high flights of steps were sought-after pitches. My father says a cartel controls them, charging beggars a premium to sit in prime spots, even if they are genuinely blind, lame or have no arms and must hold a money-cup in their teeth. He's a gloomy theorist. Falco thinks everyone is crooked. I don't bother thinking it: I know.

This tenement was the only building on a short dark alley, with a blank wall opposite. The alley was a stub off a small crossroads piazza to which we now walked. It contained a fountain – not large, no flowing river-god statuary, just a lead pipe that dribbled sluggishly into a stone basin. Basic. Still, it was adequate. If the pipe was kept hygienic, the water would be drinkable. Fresh water came to Rome from distant hills, with very clean sludge in it and hardly any live wriggly things.

Now, as when I arrived, the piazza was filled with local slaves, one or two already wearing their Saturnalia liberty caps. They were loafing about while queuing for the fountain. Most homes on the Aventine did not possess a water supply. The Aqua Appia runs around the hill too low down for us, but higher up, a newer branch was called the Aqua Marcia, to which wealthy houses could be joined with imperial permission (you threw cash at a palace freedman, as Tiberius and I had recently done for our home). Poor people used wells. Most wells are horrible.

Where public fountains like this were run off the Aqua Marcia, householders who owned slaves could send them out with buckets. This carried risks. Every slave in Rome knew that a water fountain was their best chance to loiter, pick fights, pinch food, make noise and harass women, before dawdling home, slopping as much as possible out of their pails so they would have to be sent out again.

Four or five such characters were nattering and nudging each other. One had stuck a chipped urn under the pipe, although he was paying no attention to it. The way they sniggered together when we reappeared convinced me they had seen me go into the tenement with children, guessed why, and already knew what I was going to find in Agemathus's room. Somehow, they had learned there was a corpse. They were all waiting for me to return looking shocked.

There were too many of them for me to tackle, especially while I had the boys with me. I could see they were incipient trouble-makers. They probably came from different houses, but they all knew each other and seemed ready to gang up on a woman they outnumbered. It's best not to approach slaves like that. I made mental notes of their faces, then played deaf to the lewd comments that inevitably followed as we walked off. Low-grade slaves can be bad enough normally, but Saturnalia was giving them extra licence.

At least hauling Gaius and Lucius home gave me time to think about how to deal with what we had seen.

Tell your husband, Albia.

Oh, yes? Let a man take over? You cannot be talking to me!

At our house, my husband of four months was sitting in the courtyard with a familiar figure. They were silent, as if pondering something together. It was making them glum.

'*Io*, Morellus! How handy to find you here. I need a man from the vigiles, even a useless one.'

'We saw a dead body! It was horrible!' chorused the two boys, in brief excitement. They scampered off to stare at our new donkey. She stared back. Dromo, our slave, was astride her tail end, solemnly pretending to be riding along; he was about sixteen, with a behaviour age of seven. The donkey, Mercury, stood beside a pergola, eating a creeper. She was two but acted older; I had been promised she was steady-paced and sensible. Well, she was tolerating Dromo.

Yes, I know Mercury is a male god, but she came to us ready-named by someone who cannot have been pedantic. The boys called her Merky because they couldn't say her real name. She had no stable yet, which was one of multiple tasks that someone had to tackle around here. Instead, my husband was letting himself be distracted by Titus Morellus.

Our visitor was a podgy, shaven-headed brute in a limp red tunic, who passed for the local vigiles cohort's investigator. He was lazy and coarse, but if your house was broken into, your slave robbed in the street or your daughter raped, he would be the best on offer. Unless you hired me, Morellus was the only resource available.

Completely ignoring mention of a dead man, he reared off his stool with a joyous cry. 'Flavia Albia! Come here for a big Saturnalia hug!'

'Get lost! I am not going to be groped in my own home.' I could have added, 'With my husband watching,' but he could stand up for himself. Tiberius merely smiled. 'Titus Morellus, Gaius and Lucius are right. I took them to buy figurines, but we found the man knifed in his room.'

Morellus winced as he slumped back onto his stool. 'Ouch.'

He now deigned to acknowledge the information, though without enthusiasm. 'Who was it?'

'Agemathus.'

'Do I know him?'

'Only you can say, Morellus. Tall. Thin. African. Has touted *sigillaria* for years.'

'On the Armilustri? Yes, he's a regular. His brother must have done for him. Couple of pranksters, always vying to outdo each other with tricks, deadly competitive. It was bound to go too far one day.'

'Will you investigate?'

'No fear.'

'Oh, Morellus!'

'If somebody comes moaning to the station-house, I'll have to open a file I suppose, but I don't have time, Albia. I can't investigate every idiot whose festive treat is being stabbed by a family member. Families! Who needs them?' Morellus sailed into a practised complaint. 'Rome's a madhouse, and we haven't even reached the main day. I've had three grievous batterings already – two involving women who'd been on the drink all afternoon. Once the men are let off work for the week, the fights will really start. I'll be run ragged.'

'I see you are suffering already!' I sat on the bench beside Tiberius, then pointedly indicated piles of nuts they had lined up on a low table in front of them. 'Clearly you pair have had your feet up here all morning, making yourselves sick with snacks before the holiday even starts.'

'Work!' claimed Morellus.

'Lies.'

'Retail quality control,' Tiberius specified. To demonstrate, he tossed up an almond, caught it in his mouth and chewed.

He was in his last few weeks as an aedile, one of the magistrates responsible for testing market weights.

'Some short-changing stall-holder?' Although it sounded plausible, I was sceptical.

'We think it's a bit more than that.' He was often cagey, wanting to be sure of his facts, yet this sounded like *Don't worry your little head about men's business, lady*. I expected that from Morellus, though not Tiberius.

I could have slapped them down but I had a more important preoccupation. 'Never mind minor pistachio-diddling. Let's decide what is to be done about this *sigillaria*-seller who's had a dagger plunged into him.'

'Oh, I'm going to wait until I'm asked,' Morellus assured me again lazily, while Tiberius just took another nut from a bowl. 'Or else, since it was you who discovered the corpse, you could write up a witness report, like a concerned neighbour, Flavia? Hand it in nicely, so my clerk can file it somewhere dark?'

I was surprised. The murder was interesting. Usually they would snatch a puzzle like this away from me. 'Not my job. I work on commission, Morellus.'

'No funds for it.'

'Someone has to pay me fees. That's business – plus, in case you haven't noticed, we have a family to keep now.'

Morellus cast a rheumy eye at Gaius and Lucius, who had scrambled up our new fountain bowl and climbed onto Merky with Dromo, pulling at the donkey's long ears. 'Stop that, or he'll bite you.'

'She,' I classified. Morellus gave me his 'It would be!' glare.

'If you like,' offered the vigilis, suddenly, 'I'll take your nippers home to play with mine.'

I could never remember whether he and his rather nice wife had three or four children. It surprised me that Morellus himself kept track, though he did, because he said proudly, 'Our babby's walking now!' He made it sound as if he had brought about this feat, though I knew it would have been Pullia who did all the dandling and encouraging.

We needed distractions for the boys. Morellus must have been told their situation. Tiberius smiled thanks. I was more cautious: the Morelli were confident young characters who were bound to know all the latest terrible toys and jokes. Even the babby had probably got her chubby hands on a brand-new pig rattle, some model never seen in Rome before.

'That would be very good for them. Spare a man to go and register the Agemathus fatality, Morellus.'

'No chance, Flavia darling!'

'Don't call me "darling" – and I've told you enough times, don't call me Flavia!'

I could have left this alone, but I grabbed my note-tablets. 'All right. I'm not taking on unpaid enquiries, but I'll document the scene like a responsible witness. You munch your nuts. I'll go back there myself!'

As I stormed off to show Morellus the responsible way to register a Saturnalia killing, I heard Tiberius say darkly that nuts were not what they used to be.

3

I marched back to the scene. I took Paris, our runabout. His main job was carrying messages, though I was also training him to help in my casework. With no idea what had brought about the death of Agemathus, or who might be lurking in the vicinity with another weapon, I wanted back-up. Paris might not be hefty, but he possessed a cold stare.

We walked down the Vicus Armilustri, the main thoroughfare across our peak of the Aventine. The mighty hill has two high tops. My family lived on the rougher one. The Didii like to suffer. That's because they want to tell you about their latest disaster while they cadge a free lunch.

A side road branched off the Vicus, then a crooked lane lined with the sponge shops widdled along from that; it crossed another narrow lane at the small piazza with the water pipe, at which point the one-tenement alley protruded like a knuckle on the map. Like most, it had no name. In fact, reporting this death at the station-house would have achieved little, since the red-tunics would never have found it. The vigiles avoid a lot of work that way.

Leaving the Armilustri took us very quickly from a fairly safe environment into the dirty, lawless back entries that dominated the hill.

'Salubrious!' Paris spoke low, as if afraid of being overheard.

He came to us from the Quirinal, which believes itself highly civilised.

'Niche-living on the Aventine,' I told him. 'High rents for bad rooms, high crime, no means, no hope.' Ours was the outsiders' hill, home to freed slaves, foreigners, despised professions (mine!), temples to mainly downmarket gods, noise, smells and dirt. Its rebellious spirit went all the way back to Remus, the non-founder of Rome. He was Rome's very first murder victim. At least we all know who did that one.

Nowadays high-end provincials were tentatively buying space here; they had not yet managed to alter the character. Mansions went up with tall walls, then whoever lived in them stayed indoors. A pedlar like Agemathus never saw these wealthy types; he would be offering his goods to people who were almost as poor as himself.

On the way, I had been mentally fixing available facts. I re-envisaged his room, little bigger than a store cupboard: the short wooden bed, the single thin blanket, the stool with his tray, no other furniture. No pillow, no bucket, no personal utensils, no spare clothes. The place had not been particularly squalid, though that might be because he had nothing to make it squalid with. Every copper Agemathus ever earned must have gone on food and drink. Pedlars buy from stalls and eat in the street as they work. I wondered how he ever managed to survive outside Saturnalia; perhaps he hawked sacrificial wheat-cakes, although other festivals offered fewer opportunities. This was the big one. This was when all Rome plunged into unrestrained excess. Vendors of holiday knick-knacks could roam the streets, happily cashing in: statuettes, lights, home decorations, gifts, spiced treats, hot toddies, pointless trinkets. All trash. All eagerly snapped up, as all semblance of taste vanished.

Why had the *sigillaria*-seller come off the streets in the middle of the day, a busy time? Was he simply exhausted? Had the frantic festival commerce been too much? Or had he arranged to meet someone? His killer perhaps? So, who was it?

In my mind I placed Agemathus as I had found him in his room: face down in a neat, straight line, on top of the blanket on his bed. He looked like a tall desert tribesman from one of the southerly provinces, Africa Proconsularis or Mauretania. Polished ebony skin, black hair in crinkled curls all over. His thin arms had been bent up, cradling and hiding his face. On his bony frame he wore a long, narrow, sleeveless tunic, with frayed edges; it was in some loose-weave tawny fabric, so patched all over with other pieces that the original colour was hard to pick out. He had no belt. His large feet, hanging off the end of the bed, were in sloppy old slippers. He had appeared to have stretched out there of his own accord before someone attacked him, perhaps without him ever knowing they were there.

When Paris and I reached the end of the alley, some of the same slaves were still dawdling. They ought to have slouched off home with their buckets by now, so they must have waited around to see what happened next. When I headed off with Gaius and Lucius, it must have been clear that I was intending to ensure something was done about the murder. The slaves, giggling stupidly, now moved to the end of the alley behind Paris and me, to watch as we entered the tenement. One runabout was not enough support for me to order them to get off home.

There was still no porter. I led the way. Behind me, Paris sniffed the foul air. I sensed him bracing himself for trouble. Everywhere was silent, as if no one else had been here since

I left. I didn't bother to knock. You don't ask a corpse, can you come in, are they decent? I pushed on the top of the door, then kicked the bottom until it popped open. The room was just as I had left it – with one crucial difference.

'Oh, spit!' The body had gone.

'What?'

'He was lying on the bed. Now he's not.'

'Got up and left?' asked Paris cautiously, squeezing into the room behind me. He had not been with us long; he was being polite, yet brave enough about suggesting I might be crazy.

'The man was stone dead. No chance of him wandering off. I didn't dream it, Paris. The boys saw him too. He had a knife with a big handle sticking out of him and was covered with fresh blood.'

'Hmm!' commented Paris, as if I had just told him a joke he didn't get. He looked around, wincing at the bare space.

'Someone has moved the remains,' I insisted.

'Interesting!' Paris had mastered how to give a really irritating commentary.

'This is an outrage. Someone stole his body.'

'Undertaker?'

'Don't be daft. Pedlars never belong to a funeral club. They don't all chip in for garlands and a feast.'

'Why would someone take him away?'

'One reason. When a murdered corpse vanishes, Paris, the guilty party is trying to hide their crime.'

'So now you will need to find out who!' Paris was smiling now. As we walked here, he had been tense. Since there was nothing grim to find, he relaxed into satire. 'You want to investigate what's going on, and poor old Faustus will just have to let you.'

'It's not up to him.' In fact, by letting me come back here, I took it that Tiberius had endorsed my involvement.

'*Domina*, I am glad you made that clear!' Paris kept up the banter as he began looking around the room. 'This isn't going to keep us long – bloody hell, there's not much, no chance of clues.'

'Don't call me *domina*. Someone needs to work on this, and they need to do it fast. The culprits must be found before they can cover up the crime. The vital thing is to catch them in possession. They cannot have gone far yet.'

'You think? Doing a runner, while carrying a murdered corpse? I bet they'll be pelting away with the squits.'

Paris did then find a few rusty red spots on the floor-boards, which he grudgingly accepted as blood. He conceded I had really seen a body. But if he was right about them fleeing as fast as possible, its snatchers could now be anywhere. This would be hard to investigate. Still, what isn't? Facing up to problems never daunted me.

Since there was nobody in the building for us to question, we went back outside.

On the corner with the water pipe, those slaves were waiting to snigger about the shock Paris and I must have had. My expression made most of them slither off on urgent errands. One was too slow. We cornered him.

He tried Saturnalia role-play: 'Hands off me! I'm King-for-the-Day. I order you—'

'Don't even try to give orders to me,' I interrupted, staying calm before whatever obscenity he planned. 'Slaves won't act like kings until Jove's Day! Even if you've pulled the wizened bean in your household lottery already, you have Saturn, Sun, Moon, Mars and Mercury to go yet. So, let's have that cap of liberty off.' Paris reached, then flipped the sagging knitwear from the slave's head. 'Mind his fleas,' I warned. 'You're just a slave today. Here's your label – "I've done a runner", it's saying.' I was reading from a metal collar that had been welded onto him. To me, this said his master was a brute – which gave an idea of what to expect in a slave from such a household. 'Have you run away in the past?'

Paris pulled aside the slave's flopping hair, looking for a brand mark that would confirm he had tried to escape.

I tugged at the collar's rectangular label. 'What's here? "Take me home to Terentius for your reward." How much is this Terentius offering?'

'I bet he'd pay us to lose this runt for him,' scoffed Paris. 'What's your name, boy?' He was using 'boy' as the generic for a slave; this one was not tall, but had certainly reached adulthood. He had no fancy meek manners and prissy Greek, but was a general workhorse, probably from some household where the owners were almost as crude.

'Sagax.'

'*Intelligent?*' Paris and I fell about laughing. 'Now that is funny!'

Sagax unwisely made to bolt. Paris stuck out a foot and tripped him. He picked up the would-be escapee, then held him fast, turning his face away from ingrained garlic and sweat. 'Phew! Did no one ever tell you anyone can wash at the baths for free?'

Sagax slumped, so Paris would have to hold him up. When questioning a slave about a crime, physical torture is permitted. I left that to the vigiles. They had better equipment.

Instead, I squared up with the informer's tool: annoying rhetoric. 'You were here when I visited before, you were here when I left in a hurry, you are here now I'm back.

Sagax, you have glued yourself in situ like a snail on a dry wall. Listen – there has been a violent death in that building over there and it looks to me as if you and your horrible cronies know something about it. Now persons unknown have spirited away the corpse, so stop playing silly buggers and tell me, did you see something?'

Sagax looked vague deliberately.

'Assume that was a question expecting the answer yes – Latin is such an interesting language, isn't it? I love its barmy grammar. I reckon, Sagax, that while you were messing about here, you witnessed something going on with Agemathus the *sigillaria*-seller. Since you've been hanging about ever since, gawping, you must have seen if someone took away his corpse afterwards?'

'Don't ask me.' Another expected answer, unfortunately. Latin, the language of politicians, provides a fine medium for lies, malpractice, obfuscation and straight bamboozling. It's perfect for buffoons, inadequates and crooks.

'Try harder,' I snapped. 'Who went in and killed the African? And who then dragged, carried, drove or otherwise transported the dead body from his building?'

'Don't know what you're on about.'

'Come on – you and your horrible friends saw what happened.'

'We never.'

'Sagax, I don't want to haul you to your master and ask for permission to beat it out of you.'

'You dare try it!' he jeered, with a burst of new confidence.

'She will,' warned Paris.

'Then you don't know who Terentius is!'

'Tell me?' I offered, but something, which I supposed must have been fear of his master, held him back. I flogged on patiently: 'Anyone who went down the alley would have had to pass you slaves, hanging around the fountain instead of going home properly with your buckets. So who dropped in on the pedlar today?'

'His brother,' Sagax now admitted, forgetting to be unhelpful.

'Before I went, or afterwards?' If before, Morellus would have been right: the competitive brother was the killer.

'Just after.'

'At last we are getting somewhere. What's his name?'

'Victor.'

'Does Victor share the same room?' In Rome no one lives solo if they can go halves on rent. Their doss might be no bigger than a bedside mat – an accessory the room in question did not have – but it would be home to both Agemathus and his brother. Quite likely other people bunked up with them; further extras may even have come and gone occasionally. Sibling strife is one motive for murder; stranger danger can be worse.

Sagax stayed unresponsive until Paris shook him like a lumpy bolster. To avoid rattling teeth, the slave nodded.

'So what happened? Victor goes in and finds the corpse. Then did he run out, so upset he couldn't bear it? Or do you think he did it?'

'He just walked out like normal.' Sagax was grinning as if he was holding out on us.

'Stop giggling like a silly child. Was it Victor who carried out the body?'

'He wasn't carrying anyone!'

I kept trying to extract sense from him. 'Did he notice you and your pals loafing?'

'Must have done.'

'So did he say anything to you?'

'Nope.'

'You're lying about him.' Paris took a hand. 'Nobody would act so calm if he'd just found his own brother on the bed they shared, bloodily murdered.'

Sagax shrugged. He had the slave's airy defiance: the ways of the free were beyond him.

'Did you and your pals go in to look?' I demanded, suddenly sure they must have done.

Sagax shook his head but could not stop himself admitting he had done it. 'Brilliant!' he chortled. 'All that gory blood!'

'Never mind the blood.' I cut across his glee. 'Where do you think Victor went? Would he be heading for the vigiles to report this?'

'Of course not. He was off to the Orion's Dog for a drink.'

'How do you know?'

'That's where he always goes.'

'Stop being clever,' warned Paris. It struck me he had been a slave once, freed by his previous master not very long ago. He knew all the tricks slaves pull; in a situation like this, insider knowledge made him feel superior.

I said a drink did make sense after seeing his brother dead like that, but it still left me wondering about a body that had been spirited away by invisible forces. Sagax smirked again. He definitely seemed to know something we had missed. Still, some slaves are like that all the time.

We extracted directions to the bar, hoping Victor would be more forthcoming. Before we released Sagax, I made him provide an address for his master, the Terentius who was named on his iron collar. I checked again, but the dogtag suspended from the band merely carried the usual rubric that, if found on the loose, this slave was a runaway so hold on to him. Although it told finders to return him to Terentius, Terentius had not specified where. According to Sagax, everyone knew, but I had never heard of the man, so Paris kicked the slave until he gave me details. I wrote them down on my note-tablet, pointedly.

Paris ordered him to nip straight off home, then he and I walked to the Orion's Dog. I had no reason to suppose Sagax followed us to watch what happened, though with hindsight he must have been eager to know.

The Orion's Dog had no picture of the hunter from the starry skies, nor his cloud-treading hound. That was because there was no wall space. It was a one-counter, one-waiter cantina patronised by local workers. The frontage was so narrow that only a couple of people could lean there at the same time. Too small even to have a pot-shelf, it was sited on a slummy side-street, next to the din of a copper-beating workshop where men with muscles did vigorous planishing all the time. As we approached, we saw only two customers, both presumably deaf. One must be Victor. Rather than being in shock at finding his brother laid out in blood, he was buying a drink to cele-brate. We understood immediately. This had been a stunt: as pranks go, it was fabulous.

Paris cursed. I checked my anger. I would kick a wall later. My presence at the supposed death-bed had never been intended, but my chance arrival must have increased the brothers' hilarity.

Both men were tall, whip-thin and black. Both wore patched tunics from the same low-grade source. Their features were different, though they had to be brothers. They were close, bonded, locked in their long-running competition

23

to be wickeder, wittier and wilier. This particular trick's grinning winner had a big red stain on the back of his tunic that would never come out, though he had ditched the fake knife: today's winner was Agemathus. Absolutely alive.

Classic.

Io, Saturnalia!

4

The two brothers were almost too doubled up with mirth to pay attention to us. Intent on getting drunk at his brother's expense, Agemathus must have left his tray at home. Wryly, I put coins on the counter, then told him to bring his *sigillaria* to our house later. I hoped the money was not enough to render him incapable. Paris and I set off home for lunch.

'You'll have to learn to find jobs where there's something to investigate,' joked Paris, as he buffed aside a pushy nut-seller.

'That's an idea! How come I never thought of it?'

I was no longer in the mood. Forget intrigue. We passed a house where a man was yelling up at a window to his wife, who leaned out and yelled back. Clearly not for the first time in this exchange, she was refusing to have their front door unlocked for him. He was smartly dressed; she had her bean-meal face pack on and rags in her curls, preparing for her social life. It was nothing to do with me, though the kind of scene you watch out of neighbourly nosiness.

Before she disappeared inside, she roared that she was sick of him and that bawd from the Temple of Diana; there would be nothing for him at home, not today nor any other day. She never wanted to see him back here and she was going to throw out his smelly old mummified animal collection for anyone who wanted it. 'I don't know you! Apparently, I never did!' The old delusion. The wife must have known. One glance was enough: I had assessed the horrid chancer from his gold neck chain and his shiny pointed shoes.

Her head popped back at the window again, owl-eyed under the face mask. 'Get lost – and don't expect me to look after your first wife's children any longer! I'm not your drudge.' Then again: 'But I am keeping the parrot!'

The descent into madness had begun. Even though these people and their pet bird lived close by on Greater Laurel Street, I had no heart to offer the woman divorce advice at tempting rates. Him I would never consider as a client; I do have standards. In any case, after the festival that pair would probably negotiate a treaty. She'd give in and say he could keep a few boars' heads while he would promise solemnly that the Diana bawd would never be an issue again . . . (some hope!). So I didn't suppose they would need me, even though my brother, who keeps lists, would include misjudgement as one of my famous errors.

Reconciliation? I loathed it. What was the point of keeping families together? I needed devastated clients, insoluble rifts, frail women desperate for me to squeeze financial settlements from utter bastards whom they would never forgive. Forget compromise.

The street-seller was still buzzing around us with his tray of nuts. His persistence felt ominous. 'Not today!' I snapped, the traditional code for 'never'. Paris weakened; he picked out a hazelnut to try. He bit, then spat it out.

'Ugh! Bitter. Leave us alone, or you'll regret it. Her husband is a magistrate on quality control.'

Gurgling a festive curse, the seller slimed away.

★　★　★

When we went indoors, I learned we had acquired a sheep. Egged on by the donkey, this daft woolly thing had rounded up the dog and was penning Barley in her kennel.

'A gift to Tiberius Manlius.' My steward, the unflappable Gratus, stopped running after the sheep and explained breathlessly: the Temple of Ceres, home base of Rome's aediles, always over-ordered animals for sacrifice because Ceres was a picky goddess. This offering was deemed unsuitable for the corn lady: the poor beast had a small black mark on her long face. When Tiberius Manlius had dropped in on them for official business earlier today, the priests passed her on.

The boys would love this creature – but already my cook planned to snaffle her. I would have to send Gaius and Lucius to play with the vigilis's children again while the animal was roasted by Fornix, then I must invent a devious story that she had gone to a happy life in a field.

Just then Suza, my maid, brought home Gaius and Lucius. They were bursting to try out some trick the evil young Morelli had taught them, but instead, as soon as they saw the sheep, they rushed straight across the courtyard to fling their arms around her.

They had lost their mother. If they set their sad hearts on a new pet, what was I to do?

On cue, Fornix emerged from the kitchen in his apron, wielding a huge shiny knife, his well-honed, mutton-slaughtering snickersnee. No tug on the heartstrings affected him. I signalled him to hold off, so he stomped back indoors, his broad, sulky back saying lunch was cancelled.

'Where's the master, Gratus?' Let Tiberius sort it.

'He went out with the investigator.'

'What about his sheep?'

'He said you would know what to do.'

Oh joy. Four months of marriage was enough to turn a decent-seeming, pious, loving man into a typical husband. Given another week, I too would be a woman shouting down the street that I would not let him back in the house.

'How was he dressed?'

'The brown tunic.'

His disguise. So, while he cunningly avoided decisions at home, Tiberius Manlius had gone to mooch around our riotous district, passing himself off as a harmless pedestrian, not a magistrate who was aiming to catch people out in infringements of Rome's raft of regulations. He had three weeks left to play at this. He wanted to become the aedile with the highest record ever for on-the-spot fines.

In truth, Tiberius won that prize months ago, mainly because no other aediles in history had tried. Most preferred to swank about looking important. Even the future Emperor Vespasian, as a young office-holder, had been berated by Caligula for not having streets cleaned. Vespasian was ordered to have the folds of his toga filled with mud. This would never happen to mine: I had married a stickler. At the Temple of Ceres, delighted officials had had to buy an extra money-chest to contain the fines he collected. No wonder they had given him a festival present.

He was not such a favourite with his ex-wife. Laia Gratiana had glued herself to that temple as a do-gooder. I bet it was the jealous blonde ice-queen who suggested lumbering us with a ruminant. The next time Laia nibbled lamb chops, I hoped she would choke on a bone.

Gaius and Lucius had fallen in love with the sheep. 'Where's some grass? We need to give her grass!' The sheep and donkey, nuzzling noses, had also made lifelong bonds of friendship. Even Barley looked interested.

I was fuming that Tiberius had deliberately gone out without deciding where in our house a sheep could live or who would sweep up its droppings. If it had come from a temple, I even wondered if theoretically it was sacred . . . Good thing I had stopped Fornix butchering the creature.

'Gratus, did you happen to overhear what Tiberius is up to with Titus Morellus?'

'I think they were discussing some problem the vigiles have among the seasonal workers.'

Oh, nuts! Migrant strife. Anger and swearing in impenetrable languages. They were welcome to that.

Denied the sheep, Fornix crossly decamped to visit his brother, who lived and cooked on the Quirinal. Gratus had to pull together lunch. Caught unawares, for simplicity the steward decided to fetch a selection from Xero's pie shop.

'Pies! We are having pies!' screamed the children, delirious. Normally we enjoyed gourmet treats, prepared with skill by our one-time celebrity chef. Fortunately, Fornix had stomped off before he heard that his exquisite offerings were second-best, compared to bought-in pastry.

5

Fornix would have to live with this. Few delights can match hot meats in flaky dough, with rich gravy squelching. I only hoped the high turnover at Saturnalia, festival of excess, ensured today's pies were fresh.

Tiberius had excellent domestic timing: he returned for his lunch exactly when Gratus was laying out food on serving platters. Morellus came too. Word of a major pie-acquisition flies around a neighbourhood as if impelled on the feathered wings of Rumour, sweet-tongued herald of Olympian Jove. There was probably a queue outside our front doors. I might be the wife of a man with public duties, but I didn't look. Scroungers who claimed they needed advice from my husband were not having free lunches from me.

Our planned dining-room had no couches yet, but because of the winter weather, we piled indoors to eat. I let Dromo fix a brazier for cosiness; all of Rome's by-laws to prevent building fires concentrated on keeping water handy, though they ought to be banning hot charcoal in the hands of youths like ours. Still we had a member of the vigiles here. 'Oh, just take a chance!' was Morellus's safety advice. 'Let him enjoy himself with the flames.'

We flopped onto cushions while Gratus tried to make us pay attention to an ingredients list from the pie shop. He had scribbled it in a hurry, so had to squint to understand his notes: 'The one shaped like a rabbit is actually pheasant with almonds. The little round ones are ham with aniseed and caraway. The big cracked fellow that fell out of the basket is venison and plums, and this is mullet with ginger.'

'Do I like ginger?' little Lucius whispered, sitting close to me.

'I don't know, darling.' He looked at me darkly: I was a failure. His mother would have known. 'Just try a tiny piece and see.'

'I want to put it back if I don't like it.'

'That's fine. Give it to Uncle Tiberius. He enjoys everything in a food bowl.'

Gaius was meticulously removing every scrap of almond from a portion he had been given. Morellus scooped up these rejects in one palm, picked out pheasant bones, snaffled an entire round ham pie with the other hand, then left us. He said he had to get back to his lads in case of any emergencies; it was really because at Saturnalia the vigiles could turn up at any bar at lunchtime and be guaranteed free spiced wine.

While Gratus was out shopping, I had thrown together a dish of leeks in olive oil and fish-pickle. I served this Didius family favourite in a big shallow terracotta dish from our wedding-present dinner service. It sat on the low food table, attracting little interest. Wasted effort. We had pies. No one wanted vegetables.

As the materfamilias, I had the traditional struggle to get anything except the venison with plums, the pie nobody else wanted. Otherwise, it was a happy scrum. People leaned over, grabbing seconds and thirds for themselves or grudgingly serving others if specifically asked. Down on our cushions on the floor, we were all at the wrong height. Dromo claimed helping at lunch was not his job, so he was just grabbing for his own bowl. There was too much pushing and shoving, on top of the usual arguments that always happen over pies. The boys were livelier than normal too. That was how they stage-managed their stunt.

Suddenly Suza, my maid, a lumpish lass, let out a wild scream. She pointed to my untouched dish of leeks, then made retching sounds. Lolling in the middle of my green ragout, like an enthroned potentate, we saw a large dark brown turd.

For a beat I was fooled.

It was completely realistic. The Morellus children certainly knew good hoaxes. Only the bright eyes of two small boys, thrilling with excitement, betrayed this as a loan from their new friends.

'Great gods!' exclaimed Tiberius.

He had paused, pie pierced on a knife point, halfway to his mouth. He lowered the knife to his bowl again. The thought came to me that I had not known him long enough to be certain he would take it well. Were we about to have a furious po-faced paterfamilias? He was witty on an intellectual level, but that does not always ensure a man will embrace low comedy.

Tiberius stood up. 'Who . . . did . . . that?' he roared out slowly, making it deeply ominous. Lucius shrank up against me again, trembling. Gaius was on Suza's lap; he buried his face in her tunic. I deduced Suza had been in on the trick. She might even have positioned the spoof poo for them.

'Dromo did it!' Lucius piped up. He was the conniving one. After less than a week here, he had grasped how to sweet-talk his way out of anything by blaming Dromo.

More people joined in the accusing chorus, while Dromo gave back his stare, not seeing why he had the blame.

'Dromo!' roared Tiberius. 'You shat in the platter?'

'No, I never! Why are you picking on me?'

'Nice acting,' I murmured to my nearly-new husband. Fortunately, he winked.

Enjoying himself, Tiberius continued declaiming. 'Someone remove this repulsive object from my dining room! My wife is fainting . . .' I flopped like a smashed lily, though with care to preserve my bowl of pie. Gratus took charge of the leek platter. 'Save that evidence, Gratus. I intend to conduct a full investigation. The guilty party will be discovered – and then, by all the pantheon gods, this criminal will pay.'

Suza was mouthing to me that the Morelli would want their turd back. I nodded: the sooner the better. However, I knew my brother Postumus would dearly want to see it first. He was bound to try to make his own. He would be heartbroken if I let the specimen leave the premises before he managed measurements and working drawings. Of course, I could warn our parents what he was up to, but I would probably not do so.

Afterwards, I had another plan. I would return this proto-type to Morellus's wife Pullia, wrapped up with ribbons like a special bonbon.

Once the two nephews were sufficiently scared, we let them know we loved the joke. 'Gaius Antistius Daellius, Lucius Antistius Laellius, I pronounce both of you convicted of the hideous crime Saturnalia Too Soon!' Tiberius intoned. 'All tricks are now banned until the proper day, or there will be *no cakes*!' I muttered that I was planning to send their terrible new friends into exile.

Next, Tiberius turned himself into a jolly uncle. He

pounced on Gaius and Lucius for chasing, squealing and tickling games. Nobody ever expected me to behave like a jolly aunt, thank goodness. That meant when they spilled out into the courtyard, I had space to spoon up the last of the gravy from the demolished pies.

Gratus cleared the table, detailing the tots to help him like slaves, as if Saturnalia had really started. Then Tiberius and I finally had a quiet word together.

I told him about Agemathus playing dead. Tiberius laughed, though managed not to annoy me by enjoying it too much. Ours was a marriage of true love – at least, it was on most days – but we never strained the fabric.

'And how was your morning, O master of the house?'

'Bit of a puzzle. Morellus has asked me to help him with local street monitoring. Someone is selling bad festival nuts.'

'So this is your joint enterprise. Well, most are not eaten. They are for throwing around as holiday fun. Does it matter?'

'People do eat them. Beggars. Children. Hungry idlers. Anyone who picks them up.'

Tiberius asked my opinion. Should he agree to assist? Normally it would be me wanting his support for any doubtful new commission, but at Saturnalia everyone plunges into role-reversal. I supplied his usual questions: 'Do you want to? Is it interesting to you? Will you be paid?'

'Only in credit for being public-spirited. And an invitation to the Fourth Cohort's Saturnalia party.'

'Juno! Tell me where your will has been deposited!' Playing the sweet companion, I applied my thoughtful face. 'I can run the building firm for you, if you decide to go out sleuthing. The workmen will take a long holiday anyway. But will you have time to be public-spirited about this, darling – given the demands of your poo-dumping inquiry here at home?'

Tiberius sighed. 'You are right. It will be difficult. Morellus has bloody awful timing.' He became slightly more serious. 'I wanted to settle in the boys before anything major claimed me. I did explain that to him. But who else will take an interest in nobbling nut-scammers? It seems important to our friend, so I'll have to crunch it in somehow. Let's hope we can crack it easily!'

Thank goodness: my new husband was as light-hearted as I wished. Maybe I would keep him. If we could get through our first Saturnalia together, I reckoned he could stay.

'Some turd!' He grinned. He was very proud of his nephews. I was proud of him for the way he had offered them a home, even though their father (a parasite) was still alive. There was a third boy, who had opted to stay in Fidenae. Privately, I prophesied that when he reached his fretful adolescence he would turn up on us, wanting the easy life that he thought his lucky brothers had.

In case Tiberius thought he was in the clear, I took his hand lovingly. I smiled like his adoring bride. He smiled at me. He was a looker when he smiled, though he knew better than to rely on it.

'My darling!' I cooed. He became more uneasy. 'Now that we have a moment and you seem docile, may I open a discussion? Where are we going to house the new donkey, sweetheart – and what do you intend to do with your temple sheep?'

I loved him enough when he smiled, but when he looked guilty the man was a stunner.

6

By the end of the afternoon, Xero's pies had lived up to their reputation.

Fornix arrived home at the height of the medical emergency. I might have concealed that it was caused by a pie-purchase but Dromo, extravagantly doubled up, stupidly told him. Satisfied that punishment was in progress, Fornix pursed his lips, strutted to his kitchen and began cooking a gentle broth for our invalids. So far no one could take this nourishment. We had one worryingly sick child, Lucius. Suza, Dromo and Paris were throwing up helplessly. Even Tiberius had disappeared with a strained expression. Of the adults in our household, only Gratus and I were upright.

Then Pullia came. She was pleading for us to take her children for a few hours because Titus Morellus had also been laid low. 'I'd like to know who gave him pie!'

He had already been dangerously ill that summer; his eldest three were still affected by anxiety over it. Since Tiberius and I had been involved with the case where it happened, Pullia might have blamed us for nearly getting him killed so I could hardly refuse a favour.

The Morelli, a girl and two younger brothers, sat on a bench in their matching cloaks, looking subdued. Our Gaius perched with them, having somehow escaped the curse of Xero's. He seemed to believe all the illness had been caused by the boys' trick at lunch. Exhausted by rinsing tunics and sheets, I let him think it.

'Look after them for me while I settle the old man,' begged Pullia, though she was in no hurry to go back to her desperate husband. 'They're too scared of losing him; they won't be any trouble.'

'Really?' I eyed them, all unconvincingly quiet. It would never last, but I said nothing.

'They think you're a druid, Albia, so just give them the evil eye. Yours are right little moaners!' Pullia felt free to mention. Other than her bad judgement in husbands, she was intelligent, decent – and as outspoken as most Aventine women. Morellus had never deserved her. Perhaps he realised this, though more likely the idiot convinced himself she had a catch in him. 'I remember those boys at your wedding! Mind, I am sorry about their mother. I had a chat with her, before she started crying over her marriage – I managed to slip away while she was carrying on . . . Are they here for good?'

'Unless I accidentally kill them.' I told her how sick Lucius was, so she inspected him for me.

'He'll live – as far as you can ever tell. When they lie there looking small and pathetic, you just have to hang on, hoping. Parenting is such fun. Come and ask me any time if you want advice. I never know the answer, but you can sob on my shoulder – make sure the babby hasn't been sick on that side. But, Albia, why ever were you having bought pies?'

'Our cook went off in a huff.'

'It must be nice to have a cook!'

'It's lovely when he's here. I need to find a nursemaid too, if you know anyone reliable.'

'If I did, I'd be grabbing them myself for my lot!'

Her lot smirked. Gaius imitated them.

Pullia said she and Morellus reckoned our boys would end up in the Senate if we managed not to let them die young. I agreed: their complaining and conniving were perfect for politicians. Pullia was so sweet and straight, she thought I meant it.

Perhaps I did. But it would be twenty years before we had to find the cash to provide our little moaners with lives of civic leadership. In Rome, something as simple as a badly cooked pie could easily destroy the dream first.

Once Pullia felt Titus Morellus had been sick by himself in an empty apartment long enough, she took herself home. In the menagerie and nursery that had become my world, I struggled on. I swept up sheep droppings. I washed little faces. I pretended to be kindly. Fornix made me a beaker of mint tea. I told him it helped. He knows I think mint tea is pointless.

Tiberius recovered enough to totter through to the builder's yard, where he issued orders tetchily. Soon I could hear his workmen turning a storage shed into a stable. They were disgruntled because in the building trade in winter it was customary to be given large gifts, then to take weeks off. Being told to empty their pallet store and make a donkey's manger was outrageous.

Since they had missed our lunch, the builders enjoyed themselves exclaiming how crazy it had been to have Xero's pies during a festival, when standards slipped. I put my head around the yard door to ask, 'What standards?' I pointed out that Xero's was famous for causing upsets on any day in the calendar. Half the murder trials at the Basilica were adjourned in the afternoon because Marponius, the judge who liked condemning killers, had to go home with bellyache.

'Mind how you site the manure heap,' I offered helpfully. We had a discussion about flies. Well, I did. They stood and listened sardonically.

Muttering that they didn't seem to need him with me in charge, Tiberius came back into the house to lie down. He was well enough to carry a note-tablet upstairs with him. He planned to make a chart of who had eaten which pies, then who was ill. While he amused himself with that, I looked after Lucius, who was crying so much I could not tell whether he was genuine or playing up. Pullia was right. Feverish children were hell.

Taking a chance, I only soothed the little boy. If he died, I would blame myself for not having summoned a doctor. Even if he lived, I would feel guilty about my lack of feeling. If I did call in a doctor, it would probably make no difference, while I would curse myself for placing trust in quackery.

Fornix helped. He produced a coloured tincture; he told Lucius it contained a magic herb. The cook was big, calm, and extremely relaxed here, after many years of screaming in small hot kitchens. The boys had adopted him as their best friend as soon as they knew he could make honeyed dates.

The child sipped the narcotic, kept it down, and fell asleep. Fornix had come to us as a celebrity chef, but he knew how to stock a home with knock-out drops.

Tiberius looked in on his nephew. He told me he had worked out what was wrong with the pies. He would summon the strength to go and interrogate Xero, accusing him of tainted ingredients. He had made a chart that proved it.

Dressing for the occasion, he had changed into full togate whites, with his purple stripes as a magistrate. I agreed that this should set him up for oratory against mould. 'The nut orchards must be destroyed!'

'Oh, stop mucking about,' he said grumpily.

Since we had a donkey, Tiberius would ride. He admitted he was still queasy, so I had better come with him. We were a team; today we needed to swap roles. He would ask the nagging questions. I would have to punch the pie-maker.

I sighed. 'Can't promise that. My mother wants me to be respectable. Helena will say there are edicts for use against shopkeepers. Tiberius, can't you just fine Xero?'

'No, it's too important.'

'Giving you stomach pains?'

'He has gone too far. I intend to tackle this. Someone has to.' Tiberius Manlius was a stubborn man. He had a dogged plebeian sense of right and wrong, which could lead to a dark, intractable sense of outrage. I knew this mood from my family. You have to think of it as admirable, then wait for them to cool off. 'Xero's products are sold everywhere. If he keeps using putrid ingredients, he may slay half the city.'

'What's new?' I murmured. 'I hope he does for the half that annoys me. Those pies are legendary – for all the wrong reasons. Why ever don't people stop going there?'

'This is Rome,' Tiberius answered, shrugging. He did allow a glint of humour in those grey eyes. 'It's a festival. Colourful excess. Xero's pies are a traditional part of the joy.'

7

Can a Roman ride in a toga? No.

Am I sure? Don't argue. They rarely ride at all, but take a look at the manly images: on a horse, it is short tunic or nude. Nudity raises cultural questions that I need not explore here.

An aedile might travel in a litter, but we did not own one. Uncle Tullius did, but currently he was using it for the social side of his business life; he never said much, but everyone knew he went to meetings intending to be carried home drunk after the annual consolidation of partnerships, terms and bribes. He would not lend us his festive transport in this busy period.

The toga could have been bundled up and carried by a body slave, but Dromo was too sick to leave the house.

I refused it. Staggering through crowded streets under armfuls of wool was not in my marriage contract. I did say if Tiberius made it as far as Xero's I would help dress him. Much is discussed about Roman men and their togas. Little is said of the bigger issue: Roman wives and toga-management. Winding and making folds were my duty; I accepted that. The rest was his problem.

We settled that Tiberius would sit on the donkey, with his garment piled in front of him. We would have put it in a pannier, but Mercury was so new to us, she had no accessories yet.

While Tiberius addressed her outside our house, the donkey ignored him, turning her head back to nibble at the toga. I noticed that the air was suffused with the scent of warm spiced wine. The mood in the streets was good-humoured. That could change at any moment. But so far, even a man who was arguing about money sounded more puzzled than angry: 'I gave you the cash for safe-keeping. You know I had to stop my father getting his greedy hands on it. Where's your good faith, Pinarius? The damned goldsmith expects I'll pay him. I need it now. Hand it back, you ugly bastard!'

'Lay off me, old mate. I don't pinch from friends . . .'

These were a couple of young men-about-the-neighbourhood. I knew them by sight. The complainant was good-looking and muscular. That was about all they had going for them, in my opinion. Presuming they knew my profession, I called over that the mate could hire me to regain his loan, but he said no: Pinarius would cough up – if he didn't want his balls ripped off.

At that, Pinarius looked shifty. His mate still seemed sure he could handle this. You just can't help some people.

I had to leave anyway. Experts who like donkeys say they are eager to work with humans. Apparently so. Once Tiberius had shaken her rein enough, our new beast cantered down the Clivus Publicius so fast, people cheered. When the toga began unravelling, I ran alongside poking it back. Tiberius was fully occupied with Merky. We arrived faster than expected. This is unusual in Rome, especially in the week before a festival.

Xero's pie shop.

I had been hearing about this outlet ever since I'd come to Rome. Yes, the place was a legend, though I had never been before. Nothing I had heard was good. Our workmen, lawyers, the vigiles, Father's auction staff, they all patronised this well-known shop, and all condemned its products every time. Drax, the watchdog in our yard, never turned up his long black snout but he, poor half-starved thing, was usually sick afterwards. My Aventine grandmother, when she was alive, had whacked any child who mentioned a meal from Xero's: it was the sign of sluttish housekeeping. 'Your wicked mother is trying to kill you! I'd rather die famished than taste that muck.'

My own mother, as far as I knew, had never sent out to Xero's. She was a senator's daughter: she could not possibly know the address or understand what to order. But if ever Falco exclaimed he had dreamed of pie, Helena would say wistfully that if he got one, sharing it would only be polite.

My sisters and I were convinced Helena knew more about Xero's than she would admit. We had a bet that Falco took her. They often gave hints of secret adventures. They sneaked out of the house, becoming different people from the staid parents we were supposed to know. We were sure of it, which was thrilling, though we had never proved dates, times, or what their missions were. Or was it possible they simply bunked off to eat beef-and-mustard pasties, while enjoying peace away from home?

The pie shop, it turned out, was located right below our hill. It was hidden under the arches of the Circus Maximus, a prime location. On race days, staff carried huge trays up among the tiers of seats, but even when nothing was happening on the track, many shops in purpose-built arcades thrived down below. These shops were spacious, each easily fifteen feet wide and going back deeper inside, with handsome peperino pillars either side of big arched entrances.

Around the Circus was a very seedy area. Xero's place stood next door to a so-called manicurist, where the thin female staff did not look as if they really cut nails.

I helped my dear husband don his official drapes. In fact Tiberius, while unmarried for ten years before he met me, had learned to manage formal dress. He often still had to: Dromo would fly into tearful despair if asked to help. I had learned toga-pleating on Falco, a restless mannequin. But I was a patient daughter and a more patient wife, so we set up Tiberius handsomely in a few minutes.

I had to wait in the arcade. 'Why keep a wife and hold your own donkey?' Tiberius asked loudly. Sounding like a man of the people might have impressed the staff; they were unloading large baskets of pastries to restock the shop.

'Why keep a donkey when you can ride a wife?' joked one of the pie-porters, crudely.

'Hay is cheap,' I returned, making it amiable. Actually, in the city at Saturnalia fodder was damned dear, as we had recently discovered. Merky and the new sheep were being supplied by the local lupin-seller, who was horribly happy to do it.

Nothing was cooked at the pie shop. Ready-mades were brought here from somewhere else; being ferried across Rome in open-topped baskets explained much. The shop had shelf-racks indoors, heavy with their famous fat pies, which staff warmed up in a wood-oven if asked (you went away to buy a cabbage while it was done) or they were simply handed out cold. A waiting queue snaked down the arcade under the Circus, blocking other shops. It was a daunting line yet moved quite fast: businessmen, dock workers, slaves, fathers and sons, even a few women. Adept servers slapped orders together. People either brought their own cloths, or pies were wrapped in old pieces of papyrus discarded by libraries. Aniseed chicken in poetics and inky gravy: a Xero's classic.

Tiberius was polite, but in his official gear he always had the manner. When he demanded to see whoever was in charge, a big counter flap was lifted to admit him. He vanished into the interior.

'What's he after?' one of the staff questioned me, pretending not to care.

'Justice for the community.' I stroked Mercury's long head to distract her as she took too much interest in the pies on the counter.

'Justice? That some fancy new recipe?' he asked, as he manhandled an awkward basket.

'No, Faustus calls it traditional.'

'Faustus?' The man jumped at my husband's formal name. 'He's not that ogre who makes the market traders follow all the rules?' In Rome, obeying regulations was a loose concept.

'He does. He also rounds up stray animals and makes landlords sweep their streets.'

'Bloody hell! Doesn't he know it's Saturnalia?'

'I think that's why he came down here,' I said mildly. 'Too many people who ought to feel festive are bedridden with colic and cramps after pies they bought from here.'

'Not ours!' whipped back the porter, denying it automatically. Then he laid out traditional excuses: 'It must be their own fault. They're putting too much sauce on. Or drinking a goblet too many with it. People are plain stupid, then look for someone else to blame. You won't prove anything against us.'

It was not my duty to explain how the aedile had prepared a chart that did illustrate how, in our household, people who

45

had eaten pies containing nuts were poleaxed, while those who had the other flavours were fine. This included little Gaius, who had had the venison version but carefully picked out all his almonds, while Morellus, who had snatched a ham pie, was nevertheless suffering because he had snaffled the child's rejected almonds.

The shop manager would listen. He would realise Manlius Faustus had the power to close down Xero's. Saturnalia or not, he could order them to stop trading. When an aedile said, 'Show me your hygiene precautions,' anyone sensible jumped.

Their discussion indoors took a while. A man need not hurry while his wife is looking after his donkey. My husband would be rifling through delivery dockets to his heart's content. Meanwhile business calmly continued at the counters, with servers and porters looking unperturbed. That was him. Faustus rarely threw his weight about; he just made his point stolidly until people caved in. He had tried this on me, though rarely with success.

I stood with the donkey, contemplating how in my own work I carried no authority like his. As a woman, and as an informer, every time I questioned a witness I had to win trust, was forced to bluff, possessed no right of entry and ran personal risks. Tiberius only needed to turn up. Nobody would grope him either.

I risked that in any place where I stood around. I had been in this arcade too long. Someone tried to hire me and he did not mean for a manicure. I said if he gave me his wife's address, I would tell her how *she* could hire me to get all his cash when she divorced him.

8

Can a woman ride in a long tunic?

Yes, but it needs to be full loom-width, and even then she will have to hoick up her skirts to knee level. It will attract attention from passers-by. They love bare legs. That will annoy her husband. Mine was pretty keen on bare legs normally, although since he came back from Fidenae after his sister's funeral, his interest had been slow to rekindle. I knew this was because Fania Faustina died of a pregnancy going wrong. Whatever male guilt was interfering with my married life, I would have to stir things up again.

Tiberius had left the shop with the manager. They were now going together to another venue, Xero's bakery, where the pies were made. Tiberius was keeping his man-of-authority look in the toga, so Merky was mine. It seemed true that this donkey enjoyed working. She trotted happily around the Circus Maximus to the Trigeminal Porticus, flicking her ears at any members of the public who were admiring my legs. Tiberius muttered, though he was trying to act cool in front of the pie-shop manager.

Xero's bakery might not have been as well known as his pie shop, but there we saw the real extent of his commercial empire. Like other city bakeries it ran on an industrial scale. Bread was a key product. Feeding the people was how

47

emperors held on to power. That meant they provided free corn. Hundreds of ships arrived in Italy from the fertile growing provinces. In Rome, two hundred thousand people – men – were allocated tickets for the dole. They were supposedly from poor families, but all kinds of recipients could be observed in the queues to collect. Even senators were not ashamed to take handouts. After all, making the most of opportunities was how their noble ancestors had become rich enough to enter the Senate in the first place.

Xero's was near the dole station, under a corner of the Aventine, below the Temple of Ceres, goddess of agriculture. After bringing grain into granaries, the state tightly controlled distribution. Once people gave in their dockets and collected their measures, few could deal with it at home so they took their corn to bakers who ground it into flour and even made bread for them. It was wonderful for bakers. Oven-owners like Xero could become millionaires.

This was clear from the size and the busy racket of his Trigeminal premises. Merely being there told his story. A trader had to run a notable business to acquire space in the fancy marble Porticus. The fabled Xero was not some little pastry-fettler in a booth with an awning; he was a staggering commercial magnate. Of course, that meant he was not physically present today. Xero would be relaxing at his suburban spread where his caged finches trilled and fountains gurgled. But Tiberius had come to talk about supply-lines; Xero had a small team of account managers to do that for him.

I was left holding the donkey again.

Luckily the bakery had an open space where I tied her up. Grain was being delivered all the time, with a whole team counting in the huge amounts received. They kept lists: everything from barley for slaves' rations to spelt for fine white dinner rolls. Some official was ticking off imperial grain, as if they produced loaves for the military here, though I doubted it. They might supply the Praetorian Camp, but no one would send loaves travelling for many days to legions on the frontier, then inflict the results on soldiers. Soldiers bake their own. Trust me: I was married to an ex-soldier once. Mostly they have military biscuit. Every man can make that. Its main advantage is that the rock-hard slabs take so long to chew, troops have no time for mutiny.

I wandered further into the premises. Flour mills stood in a double row. Xero owned ten. Hades! Each tall edifice was formed from a volcanic stone cone, topped by a grinder that was powered by a donkey turning a wooden framework. The mills stood sentinel amid overpowering clouds of dust, where coughing slaves monitored progress. Grain had been carried to an upper floor, then tumbled down through pipes into the mills, delivered at carefully managed rates. The donkeys trundled. Flour spun out into panniers at ground level. It was then taken to the next stage: kneading machines. Holy moly, Fornix would love one! In each big round stone container, an arrangement of interacting metal blades chopped and mixed dough on an industrial scale. Slaves turned the mechanism. In most, water, salt and oil were added with a fermenting agent, a piece of dough 'mother'; flatbread dough omitted that, though it sometimes had rose-mary or garlic stirred in.

After a rest for rising, big warm balls of spongy dough went to tables where hardworking teams swiftly formed loaves, knocking back the elastic mixture and rekneading as necessary. They had done it so often, the workers could cut or tear off the right amount by eye, to produce very uniform loaves. Others were rolling and flattening balls of unleavened mixture to make teetering piles of flatbreads for street traders.

At the end of the line, I saw a room-sized oven with a low, round floor. It was very different from local kilns with a small door that cooked only a few pieces at a time. Here, scores of loaves were shovelled with flat paddles onto a huge revolving metal grid for firing at high temperature.

These procedures were repeated in bakeries throughout the Empire, but at Xero's they had an extra stage, his brain-wave. One branch of the kneading line turned out his notorious fatty pastry. Xero then had a range of rooms with cold marble counters, where cooks chopped meats, added seasoning and other ingredients, then rapidly formed their pies. Depending on what came into the markets, they created their sought-after pie-of-the-day, while also supplying mounds of traditional flavours and public favourites. Finishers crimped and pricked the lids then brushed on beaten egg. Xero ran a second, smaller, oven where pies were baked. Even after a household stomach upset, the scent was delectable.

In a corridor by the pie-making rooms I could see my husband talking earnestly to a couple of men in clerks' tunics, with styluses behind their ears. I retreated to donkey-minding.

Eventually Tiberius came out. He was shaking his head over something. I kept quiet. An operative must have been signalled, who dragged me to the outdoor sales counter, then loaded me up with crusty rustic loaves and little twisted rolls. I could have taken anything I wanted. The aim was to mislead the aedile's enquiries in a classic Roman way: bribe the wife with household goods. Then she will urge him to stop being ratty, and to be lenient instead – in theory.

I accepted the free gifts. You should be polite. And I am an informer's daughter.

It would take more than a sesame twist for dipping in his chickpea paste to corrupt Tiberius Manlius Faustus.

9

For Tiberius and me, the free gifts implied strongly that his questioning had hit the nail.

He said nothing until we had left the bakery and were heading home. The steep uphill climb was new to Merky; we walked on either side of her, patting her and murmuring encouragement whenever she stopped dead.

About halfway up the Clivus Publicius, Tiberius unbuttoned. He told me that Xero's staff admitted what they called 'a known problem with a limited quantity of recent ingredients'.

'That sounds as if they are planning to send you a defensive lawyer's letter.'

'Someone should tell them aediles don't listen to excuses.'

Other customers had complained. Xero's knew the score. Details of how our family had been taken ill were accepted, after which Tiberius made the staff provide an evidence trail. The source was a new supplier, who had sold Xero's a variety of nuts at knockdown prices. The pie shop was famous for skimping on ingredients. The manager told Tiberius that when these nuts were delivered, he had thought they were probably old stock. Xero's, being Xero's, used the consignment anyway.

'When I pressed him, he reckoned the nuts are last year's leftovers, which have been stored somewhere damp.'

'He accepts they are mouldy?'

'Let us say, Albiola, he does not deny it.'

'They should have been rejected.'

'I detected anxiety about sending them back.'

'Strange! What do you think?'

'I suspect it's to do with the trade problem that Morellus and I are looking into.'

'Want to explain?'

'Early days. It could be just a mad theory he has.'

'You can tell me.'

'I know I can,' said Tiberius, not troubling himself to do so.

'All right, have your secret!' I would work it out for myself, if I cared. 'Well, Xero's is a prominent outfit; they ought to possess muscle. Is Xero intending to tackle his supplier?'

'No. He should do, but it's the old tale. He wants to avoid trouble. He might seek compensation, blaming me putting on pressure, but most likely Xero's will simply drop the bad source.'

I scoffed. 'That leaves the supplier with a store of bad nuts, still liable to enter circulation.'

'It does.'

'You need to find that store.'

'Looks like it.'

Tiberius seemed terse. I finally screwed out of him that Xero's had told him where the relevant warehouse was: probably one near the Lavernal gate. It stood in a group with premises that belonged to our own uncle Tullius. He had his eye on the culprit storehouse, though he could not wrench it away from a rival we all knew: Salvius Gratus. Salvius Gratus was the brother of my husband's first wife.

Tiberius would have to pay Gratus a visit. He said he

preferred to go on his own. That suited me. Nothing would drag me over their threshold for almond fancies with Laia Gratiana. My small-talk might become crude if Laia gloated over us having been lumbered with our sheep.

Tiberius dropped off the donkey and his toga at our house, then walked away firmly over the hill. I took myself for a programme of remedial works at Prisca's bath-house.

'I've had a long hard day. I need a full body scrub, a hot soak and lashings of good moisturiser.'

'Coming up.' Prisca was a short, thin, competent proprietor who ran her baths for women only. Slapping around in wooden-soled slippers on the hot floors, she took me over. She reckoned all mothers needed the full treatment menu; when she heard I had acquired the boys, she had known I would be here, desperate. 'You can hide out with us for as long as you like, Flavia Albia. Anyone comes looking, I'll say you left us half an hour ago. I expect there is man trouble as well? What's he done, if you don't mind me asking?'

'He's working with the vigiles, but he's gone off now to see his ex-wife's brother.'

'Will she be there?'

'Bound to be.'

'Say no more!'

'You'll want to hear this, Prisca. The damned woman dumped a sheep on us.'

'Shit, Albia!'

'Exactly!'

'That's terrible. I'll give you a few shakes of this new sweet cicely oil, on the house. I recommend it. All my ladies say the scent is delicious.'

The scent was fine. It smelt like myrrh but was much

cheaper. Prisca would be selling many bottles, since the oil would make easy Saturnalia gifts. I for one bought three glass flasks, for my mother and sisters, plus one for my maid Suza, then I added another for my cousin Marcia. She was with her lover, who had gone north for medical reasons, but if he was well enough they might travel home for the holiday.

Prisca, who liked to manipulate people ('I take a friendly interest, Albia!'), then tried to fix me up with a client. She knew that when I had a case I came for thinking time and mulling things over with her; that meant I spent more money at her baths. Anyway, Prisca adored gossip.

Axilla's daughter had disappeared from home. She had taken nothing with her, told nobody, and had no known problems. 'It's a mystery. Right up your street, Albia.'

It did sound a possibility, until Axilla was whipped from the cold room and pushed onto a side bench to talk to me. A naked client (belly fat and moles) may be unnerving, but she wasn't going to be a client. She piped up that she already knew the answer: the daughter had gone off with her boyfriend, a known neighbourhood louse. He was bound to steal her savings, but that would teach her a life-lesson, and nobody thought he would beat her or anything like that. Axilla was glad to see the back of her. The girl in question was thirty; she left dirty tunics all over the floor, never pulled her weight with child-minding and contributed nothing to household bills. Axilla pleaded with me not to find her.

Undaunted, my friend the bath-house keeper hauled in another woman, Zenia. Zenia (nude, ribs sticking out, unusual birthmark) had an uncle who had been missing for three years, abroad. That warned me right off. Rome had over thirty provinces and Zenia was vague about which one her uncle wandered into last. He had always been a free spirit, but he used to stay in touch at this time of year, so it was feared he had been attracted into dangerous company and something terrible had happened to him. 'He was really sweet, never saw bad in anybody. People take advantage of his simple nature. I can feel it – he has gone. Oh, our lovely uncle is no longer on this earth!' I was finding a towel to dry Zenia's eyes, when someone ran in to tell her the lost nunc had just arrived home as a Saturnalia surprise.

Prisca and I shared a cinnamon cake.

I grumbled that all over Rome missing relatives would be turning up this month. My hope was that, after initial joy, things would go wrong. 'Incompatibility is why these people walked out in the first place. So now everybody grits their teeth and looks overjoyed to have them back during the five days of feasting, but I'm waiting for fun time. Bitter old feuds will resurface. Prime time for informers is after Saturnalia finishes.'

Prisca understood. She said there was always a rush at the baths too. The masseur had to work double shifts. 'And another thing about my mothers, Albia – they eat too much cake. You will have to watch your figure.'

Picking crumbs off my clean tunic, I said I could see why they needed it. Despondently, I ate the crumbs.

Back at home, my brother had been and gone with his tutor, Vitalis, a nervy young academic. Postumus had also brought his ferret, Ferret. Not to be outdone, the boys had let their own pet into the courtyard. 'Sheep! We are calling our sheep Sheep!'

'What an exciting idea. Did Postumus admire your turd?'

'Yes! He is going to make one, and some fake sick.'

'Lovely. It's getting dark. You need to put Sheep back in her stable.'

We still had custody of the young Morelli. When Pullia came, I assumed it was to fetch them. Instead, she wanted them to stop with us that night; she had even brought the babby as well.

'Oh, go on, Albia! It will give Titus and me some time for you-know-what. It's Saturnalia.'

'I thought Morellus was on pie-related sick leave.'

'So, he's at home, for once!'

'But is he up to you-know-what?'

'Who cares?' Pullia chortled. '*I* am!'

We did not own a cradle, but that protest was brushed aside as the excited mother deposited her infant's bone teething ring, spare loincloths, extra tunic, cute toys and spouted feeding bowl. It looked as if the babby was meant to become our permanent lodger.

'Don't let her suck the leather mouse or it goes slimy. I've brought their little potty for the others. Titus Junior has to have this rag to chew or he won't go off to sleep. You can manage without a cradle. Just put the babby in a chest with the lid up, then don't let anybody helpful come along and close it.'

Now I was literally left holding the baby. She was a nice child, oddly enough, but I passed her on. Suza and Dromo immediately vied with one another to look after her. Suza had heard some story about babies being put into mangers in stables when accommodation had been overbooked, but we agreed that would be unhygienic. Dromo, who had an odd softness for babies, fetched a basket he normally used to carry Tiberius's clothes to the bath-house.

Hysterical children ran about finding mats to sleep on.

They all crowded into one bedroom to fit out their makeshift dormitory. To quieten the noise, I ordered my staff to tell them creepy ghost stories. The children found this quite banal, though Paris had a fund of tales. Dromo and Suza ended up terrified.

It was all good-humoured. But it was not the life I had once imagined having.

Tiberius came home in a bad mood. I was glad the rest were all upstairs, so we two could talk.

'My brother-in-law is astounding. The first thing he asked was, "Has anybody died from this?" That's all he cared.'

'And do we know? Has anyone?'

'Not according to what I was told at Xero's.'

'True?'

'Who knows? I suspect a cover-up.'

Tiberius was so honest he had told Salvius Gratus there were no known casualties. Gratus reckoned any deaths among the public from nuts in his store were his tenant's responsibility. 'That doesn't help. He has no idea who his tenant is. He claims a hireling came along, squiggled initials on a rough-and-ready agreement, paid cash, took the keys, never named the principal.'

'Too casual! I hope you gave him a piece of your mind.'

'Well . . .' Suddenly Tiberius assumed a look of superiority. 'I am astonished how that man does business. He knows he has been an idiot, though I could hardly chastise him. He's my brother-in-law. I've known him fifteen years.'

I gazed at him pointedly.

'Ex.'

'That's right,' I agreed, mildly enough after the concession. 'Your brother-in-law these days is Marcus Didius Alexander

Postumus – who has just gone home from our house with a very careful diagram for making a fake turd.'

Tiberius held out for as long as he could, then we both broke into laughter. 'I know I am in love with you,' he said. 'Albiola, I fear I may end up in love with your entire family!'

The warehouse remained an issue. If this investigation had been mine, I would have sat down to eat an apple slowly, opposite the building where the mouldy nuts were. Sooner or later – quite soon, given it was Saturnalia – a man with a barrow would have trundled along to extract more sacks. This minion would have led me to the distributor.

But, being an aedile, Tiberius decided he must make a point. First, he told me that he had for once tackled his ex-brother-in-law: 'Lucius, old man, these bad nuts are hardly your fault. I won't blame you for your tenants' defects, but you do need to check whether your place has a damp problem. If you are experiencing difficulties in managing that warehouse, I am sure I can persuade Tullius to take it off your hands – though you know what he's like. It may cost you.'

Excellent! Lording it over Salvius Gratus must be doubly sweet because his sister had once imposed a hard divorce on Tiberius; also Gratus himself had tried standing for aedile this year but lacked Tiberius's popularity so he failed. I was amused at how the nut issue had brought about a shift in the two families' old power struggle.

Although it was evening, our man sent Dromo to the Temple of Ceres to fetch some of the slaves who supported magistrates in their duties. Enough were found before they dispersed to drinking dens, and they were ready for adventure with Tiberius, whom they all liked. Dromo played centurion because *he* was a slave in a private house. He marched them up the hill, shouting orders that they rudely ignored.

Under stern direction from Tiberius, the public slaves burst the locks on the warehouse. Apparently it did smell musty. Those who suffered from allergies reeled away with streaming eyes. Tiberius joked to me afterwards that even the rats had mildew.

All the foul nuts were dragged out. Tiberius then had them carried on carts to the big enclosure with the Altar of Mars, the Armilustrium. The slaves had a fine old time as the nuts were publicly burned. Dromo stayed to watch, though we could see the glow from home.

This bonfire was at the high point of the Aventine. It had grown fully dark by the time they lit it; bright flames must have been visible for a long way. Tiberius came home and announced that the nut suppliers might try to hide from him but this blaze would send them a clear message.

He was right about that. Perhaps it might have been better if he had considered how they might reply.

IO

Next morning at least we had plenty of free bread and sesame twists. Breakfast leftovers were grabbed by Morellus when he came to pick up his children. He looked chipper.

'And how is your wife today, Titus Morellus?'

He failed to pick up my allusion. Being obtuse must hamper his criminal interrogations. Luckily the vigiles work more from intuition: 'I say, you did it. Confess to me, slimeball.' This works more times than you would think.

While Morellus and Tiberius were here, I persuaded them to discuss the nut scandal. They feared territorial warfare. Nuts were traditionally thrown around by revellers and also featured in festival food. The flourishing December trade had been targeted: previous suppliers were being shoved out by aggressive new rivals, who wanted easy money. Morellus believed these were professional organised criminals. They needed to be stopped before they took too much control. He had yet to establish who they were; he had ideas, but nobody was talking.

'You need some proof.'

'Proof? What's that?'

'Something you never bother with – but it's useful for convicting people.'

'Oh, I think I heard about that crackpot idea once. Flavia,

the times when we have "proof" are always the ones when some idiot judge tosses out the case. Give me "probability" every time.'

'You make it up.'

'I know how to make things up so they stick.'

Morellus and Tiberius planned to go out patrolling the district, to canvass possible informants. This walkabout was fact-finding, they said. An in-depth investigation. I need not worry about it. That meant, don't nag us about progress.

Morellus foolishly told me to occupy myself with an easy little job, like, he said, helping a widow find birth certificates. I said I had to stay at home with our sheep. Anyway, all the document depositaries would be on their holiday closures.

Morellus peered short-sightedly at Sheep, who had been brought in for the boys to play at being shepherds. 'Albia – a domestic matron spinning wool?' He thought it hilarious. My husband managed not to grin, but gave me a wink. Tiberius knew when to suggest he was on my side, even when I could not be too sure that was true.

A slave came up from my parents' house. My brother was now annoying everyone with ceaseless pranks that involved obscene concoctions he put together in his bedroom. No one blamed Postumus; he was only twelve, yet creative, with excellent mechanical skills. His trick vomit was lurid. Everyone blamed me for giving him the idea.

My punishment was that my father had sent me the festival gift for the porter at a tenement he owned: I had to deliver it. Since the Eagle Building was to be sold and demolished, its porter, horrible Rodan, would be out of a job. Rodan knew this was coming and was very unhappy, so my errand was to pay him off finally and confirm his departure date. Then he would be even more unhappy. Thank you, Falco, devious father.

When I tried to set out to do it, I pulled open our tall front doors boldly, only to find my way blocked. A torrent of prickly green lava tried to burst in. Luckily there was so much, it held together and stayed put. The front steps were impassable under a high mound of boughs, ordered for home decoration. The carter had gone away without knocking, after he dumped his load right in our porch.

This festival treat was to be shared out between us and various relatives. Some bright spark had had the big idea of a special purchase. Top-quality material from a forest. Order early. Buy in bulk . . . Naturally that clever person would not be helping to move it.

Tiberius and Morellus had already made themselves scarce. (I bet they saw the cart coming and scarpered.) If the load stayed put, we would have no access, while people would steal our wood. Someone was already poking into the pile, pulling out branches. I yelled a classic Aventine reference to their mother's morality, while I grimly rounded up my staff for a removal job.

I refused to have all these branches indoors, blocking up the entrance hall, so everyone formed a crocodile to drag foliage along the street, around the corner and into our building yard. This was the kind of manoeuvre that haunts you later. It was dirty, scratchy, brutally hard work. There were many complaints. I had to say *we* could have first pick for decorating our house, before Father, Uncle Petro, Uncle Tullius or the waiters at the Stargazer – and, *yes, all right*, everyone could start making garlands today. I would collect the twinkly moons and stars, old family treasures, when I went to Fountain Court. Yes, I was going now. No, nobody else could come with me.

Only the dog. Barley would come instead of Suza, who wanted to begin on the decorations. Anyway, I had to be kind to Rodan, who wouldn't like people staring at him if he was very upset. Yes, he would be upset: he was going to lose his house. No, he couldn't come to live with us.

Since I had lost time during the green branch exercise, once I had washed, changed and calmed down, I decided to ride Merky. Poor Sheep bleated pathetically when the two friends were separated; I patted her long nose, with its dark mark, but she jerked away, agitated. I told Gratus to make sure Sheep was penned safely in the stable, in case she nibbled the cypress and mistletoe, which might not be good for her. I do know that I locked the door from the yard to the street; too many passers-by had seen the greenery. I won't say the Aventine was full of thieves, but if you had an interesting pimple, somebody would steal it off your face.

The Eagle Building, Fountain Court, was once known as Lenia's Laundry, though it had not functioned for years. Lenia had died. Her horrible husband had sold the place to my father, after Falco inherited money and was looking for stupid ways to waste it. The tenement had been tottering then; now it could barely stay up. We had recently sold it to a senator called Ulpius Trajanus, a Spaniard. He seemed low in the heap. He had made it to provincial governor, but in his home province. Then when he dashed to help the Emperor stop a rebellion, he arrived after another general had done all the work. To prove he was going nowhere, he bought my father's crumbling dump, intending to replace it with a new private house. He had a friend on the Aventine; his friends must be lousy too. Anyone could see this man would sink into obscurity.

64

All right. I know he has not done so. Simple mistake, Tribune. If the suggestion wasn't treason, I would hope the Dacians get him. Stick that on your column, crazy building purchaser!

Falco had lived at Fountain Court, then so did I. That was when the building only stank, creaked, rotted at the heart and echoed with misery. Nowadays the stone staircase barely held up as a skeleton. The rest slumped, rocking on temporary props whenever the wind blew. Someone had died when a balcony fell off the top storey. Any remaining tenants must be dead in their rooms too, though Father claimed he had carried out a check for bodies and only counted rats. As soon as we arrived, Barley ran off to nose them out.

'Good dog!'

Under the stairs, like one of the rats, nested Rodan. Even after he gained his pick of all the empty rooms, he kept to his foul cubicle. Once trained as a gladiator but too useless to fight, he had originally been the old landlord's rent-enforcer along with his crony, one Asiacus, who was even more hopeless, everyone said, and brutal with it. After selling up to Falco, the old landlord died of some dread disease; Pa called it disappointment at having no tenants to bully. Asiacus died in a fight, for once not of his making but one he was trying to break up. Rodan was left lonely, living on his fat, a snivelling, pustular remnant from bad times. Father felt sorry for him, though not enough to face him when he could send me instead. Because I had been a street child, a starveling, it was said I never felt sorry for anyone.

To a point people were right: I rarely did feel sorry, not even for myself. Especially not myself. Life is there. You either jump off a bridge in despair or get on with it.

I dug out the porter to give him his money. The hopeless

ex-gladiator shambled up and snatched it without bothering to greet me. 'Say thank you nicely! That's from Falco. He's sent you a big purse, Rodan. If you take care, it should last you a while. You have to be out of here by the first day of January. Trajan will own it on New Year's Day, and his agent is sending the wreckers in to clear the site immediately.'

Naturally there was an agent. My family suspected the senator himself had never seen this place.

Rodan stopped slavering over the money, as he deplored the site clearance. 'The snooty bastard just can't wait!'

'It's sensible. He can't risk squatters getting in and being hurt, then suing him.'

'I could stop them.' No, you couldn't stop a spider with a broken leg, Rodan. 'Won't his house need a porter?'

'He is bringing his own, I dare say.' Some needy Iberian, who did not pong or answer back or sleep all day. Some useful man who could, and would, keep a building secure: a door-keeper that a householder would be glad to say hello to. Not Rodan.

'So, what am I supposed to do now?'

'You know what, Rodan. Move out. There won't be a building, you will not have a job. Be grateful for all the years Marcus Didius helped you out, though we're afraid it is now over. He has given you plenty of warning.' That was true. Trajan had been a tricky buyer. Anyone might think he had doubts about the high-end piece of land we were passing off on him. 'Rodan, you great lump of lard, don't cry or I'll have to thump you.'

'You don't care!'

'I do care, Rodan. We rubbed along well enough, didn't we, when I lived here? If I hear of anything suitable, I will recommend you.'

That would not happen. Rodan's work ethic was simple: avoidance. He could be goaded into action by a very frank slew of insults, but even then he bungled it. He had never been suitable for anything.

I left him to grumble while I nervously climbed to our old apartment on the top floor. At every step I expected the dying tenement to subside into rubble under me. The deserted sixth-floor office was a sad place, not for nostalgic lingering. Most of my possessions had been taken out when I married, but in the dank bedroom I found one last casket. Stored for my parents to stop my siblings dragging it out unseasonably, it was buried under a revolting cocoon of spider's webs: the container where we kept 'gold' constellations for hanging on Saturnalia branches. Fake gold is cheap, though never as cheap as it ought to be.

A few decorations had been bought new each year, so the heavy box rattled seductively. When I looked inside, everything was smaller or duller than I remembered. Even so, I found myself reliving past times, with the ritual of hanging our moons and stars on festive branches each December. My younger sister Favonia always went down with a winter fever so she had to lie on a couch, miserably watching. Our little dog Nux would race around, teasing us by carrying off the twinkly stars. If Falco was out when we hung the decorations, we always had to save the last one for him to place . . . Now the ritual was about to start in my house. I must try to make it special for those sad little boys. Responsibility is very depressing.

I lugged the chest downstairs. There was nobody to help. Fountain Court had always been like that. Rodan heard me coming; he rolled out for another grumble. I ignored him again.

Although I had Merky, riding with a large casket in my arms would be a challenge, but I had a solution. Stepping with care, I crossed the alley. Dire in summer, in winter it was deadly. I managed not to slip over on a treacherous puddle of slurry or break an ankle in a ragged pothole, but I ended up with mule dung on my tunic hem. Classic Fountain Court embroidery.

A basket-weaver worked opposite the Eagle Building. My parents had once lived in rooms above his shop. He kept saying he intended to retire, but he was still there, still a wiry man in a tawny tunic, still reminiscing about my sister Julia as a baby (she was fifteen now), still pleasant and ready to give me a good price on a pair of panniers, which he kindly fitted on my donkey.

Barley scampered over, covered with brown smelly gunk. I biffed her nose, until she dropped the rat she was carrying. It strolled away, insouciant. The amiable dog watched as Ennianus and I hauled the casket into one of the new panniers; she immediately scrabbled up into the other, smearing muck all over the wickerwork. Ennianus, grinning, said the panniers were mine now so I could clean it up. 'Thanks, friend!'

As the dog wuffed at me to start off, I took a last look around. On the other side of the alley, gracing a damp colonnade with thin, wonky pillars, stood the same old row of dilapidated shops. The colonnade provided shelter for down-and-outs, who would come there to curse passers-by or engage in flaring fights, during which they could hurl one another like sandbags against the shops' shutters.

This sordid stretch was not part of the property Falco owned. Some tycoon was their landlord, a long-term absentee, as happened everywhere in Rome. My father knew who it was but never talked about him.

68

Ennianus suggested I might be able to buy more decorations in the Lumber Room, a far-from-suave lock-up that dolefully offered 'Gifts of Charm'. That classic dump looked a treasure trove from a distance; close to, it was piled with broken dishes, bent candelabra, mysterious metalware, dust, debris and badly damaged medical implements. Though not quite empty, it reeked of dereliction and despair. Everything inside was old and filthy, yet not antique. I barely remembered ever seeing the shop open.

'I won't bother, Ennianus. I have peered in sometimes – it's a haven of broken promises. Besides, it looks dead as usual. Does anyone ever really trade from there?'

'I noticed slaves lugging in something this week.'

'New stock? What was it?'

'I never ask. Your father always reckoned the Lumber Room was used by thieves. I'm too old to get my head bashed in for asking questions.'

That again was typical of Fountain Court. I thanked the faithful basket-weaver, then led my donkey back to the respectable haunts of Lesser Laurel Street.

Not entirely respectable, however. On arrival, I rode Merky around to the builders' yard where her stable was. The street door still needed to be unlocked, yet someone had been in before me. I went into the yard unsuspectingly, though Barley gave a knowing growl. I saw the stable's half-door standing open. The stable was empty. When I hurried through to the house, panic already raged. The two boys were wailing. I quickly confirmed the tragedy: somebody had stolen Sheep.

Gaius and Lucius were so distraught that Gratus, Paris and I walked around the nearby streets, to demand had anyone seen our beast, then to be laughed at for asking. I left Suza and Dromo, who were tearful themselves, with the boys. Fornix would supervise, though from the safety of his kitchen.

Searching was pointless. This hill had been famous for cattle-rustling ever since that myth when Geryon stole cattle from Hercules. No one kept chickens on the Aventine; even if they escaped being snatched by a fox, fear of them being stolen was too stressful. Who wants to be tantalised by the scent of their own capon braising in a neighbour's pot? A sow in a shed would be fine – if supplied with a personal bodyguard. Envious of some other cook, Fornix muttered that Sheep must be roasting by now.

I sent Paris to the station-house to make a formal burglary report. I had few hopes of a vigiles response but sheep are expensive things to lose. At least they are if you paid for them in the first place. We had not, but our beast had a temple connection, which made her special. Although I supposed my complaint was pointless, Morellus must have been told about it because he and Tiberius came home.

They took a lot of interest in how the yard door had been opened. Heads together, the two men pored over the lock, which appeared unbroken but must have been picked. I was asked several times whether I had secured it, to which I answered less and less civilly. Morellus then asked annoying questions about who held a key.

'You're talking to me as if I were a murder suspect. One for us, a spare we hid and can't find now, plus the main one for our clerk-of-works. Larcius is reliable – anyway, he's gone to his mother's for the holiday so it can't have been him. Well, he calls her his mother though we think it's a ladyfriend. I'm sure I did lock up. Face it, fellows, if you can't find a sign of a break-in and it's not that old cliché an inside job, this must be professional theft.'

Morellus glanced at Tiberius, who took note without comment. 'You've got a watchman, haven't you?' demanded Morellus.

'Trypho. He is here at night when needed.'

'Well, he was needed today!'

Trypho, who never rented a room, liked being on watch, here or at sites, because it gave him a place to stay. He came from outside Rome. 'He's away with his family, somewhere on the Campagna. Has nobody told you, Titus Morellus? This is Saturnalia! Everyone goes off to suffer with their relatives. Our men are builders. They won't reappear until January, and even then they will be sluggish.'

Exasperated, Morellus nodded at the empty chain that trailed across the yard. 'Guard dog? Was he stolen too?'

'Drax. Trypho has taken him home with him, because poor old Drax gets lonely if he's left on his own.'

'For heaven's sake, Flavia!'

'Morellus, there's nothing valuable here at the moment. Tell him, Tiberius. You have no work until the New Year, and you are not storing much.' Tiberius nodded, looking glum. 'Don't worry,' I reassured him, 'I checked your tool-store. It's still chained. All your loose materials are buried under our decorative branches, which were left alone too.'

Tiberius pulled a rueful face. I would have to quiz him about his low mood.

'What about your donkey?' Morellus persisted. Anyone would think he wanted to imply he was good at his job.

'The donkey was with me.'

'Good thing!'

'No: bad news! When we got her I was told she would provide security. Apparently good donkeys will drive off intruders.'

'Who invented that story? What about the people who lived here before you? Would they still have keys?'

'Keys again! The previous owner died. The heir is still on friendly terms with us – he rents a shop from Tiberius. Metellus Nepos would never steal our sheep, he has his own; he's a cheesemaker. He gave me all the old keys, but we changed the locks anyway.'

'If you are certain you fastened up . . .' Tiberius butted in. *That* niggle again. 'I will have to change the yard lock again.'

I was despatched to the local locksmith. Morellus gave detailed instructions as to what kind of elaborate piece to buy, while Tiberius decided I should bring it home for self-installation. Why pay for a locksmith if you were a building contractor?

'Three keys, Albia!'

'Yes, love. I worked that out.' I could also see now that Tiberius was worried that the intruders could easily have come further, into the house, where in daytime the door from the courtyard was generally left open. People indoors were at risk.

'I suppose,' sneered Morellus, 'you just have a latch here and keep the lifter beside it, handy on a nail?'

'Oh, no!' chorused Tiberius and I, though he then told me to bring a second new lock as well.

When I hurried back home, we had a new visitor: Agemathus. He had turned up as instructed by me at the Orion's Dog, now with his tray of *sigillaria*. He also brought his brother Victor as support. They must only just have arrived; they were looking nervous because Tiberius and Morellus had fastened onto them. It was not to congratulate them on their murder jape.

Upon sight of Agemathus, Lucius ran into the kitchen, shrieking that he had seen a Saturnalia ghost; he and Gaius kept sneaking out to stare, then running away again, screaming themselves silly. This did not help the efforts of Tiberius and Morellus as they tried to recruit the two Africans to provide information about nut-sellers.

'While we've got you out of public view, tell us: are the old street nutsters being pushed out?'

'No, Officer, sir. But they have to buy from the new people.'

'Does that make a difference to them?'

'Yes, because the new ones charge them more for supplies.'

'And how have the old sellers reacted?'

'They do not like it, Legate.'

'Have they fought back?'

'Too frightened, sir.' Simply talking about it Agemathus sounded scared.

Gaius and Lucius had crept from the kitchen corridor; they were walking around behind Agemathus, to see if he still had a knife in his back. Their surreptitious behaviour was making him uncomfortable, but I did not stop them. That would teach him to play dead on me.

After setting up Agemathus and his brother as possible informants, Tiberius and Morellus released them to me while they went to change the locks. I had fetched serious barrel versions. Naturally the keys were too stiff.

With one ear on cursing from the yard, I duly bought *sigillaria* from the tray. Gaius and Lucius, whose presents these figurines were supposed to be, took no interest. The Africans sold me more than I had meant to buy, then slid off elsewhere.

The new locks were problematical. I could have said they would be.

Tiberius, who deemed himself a handyman, came back into the courtyard, bringing the locks to make their keys work. Gaius and Lucius reappeared to watch him. They were standing too close, but he tried not to shout at them.

'What are you planning to do,' Morellus asked us, pinpointing the question everyone else tactfully avoided, 'when their father turns up on you, wanting them back?'

'See him off,' replied Tiberius, not looking up. The chisel he was using slipped suddenly, gouging his hand. Blood welled.

'Blood!' shrieked the children. 'Unkie is going to die!'

'Unkie is not,' I said. 'Don't call him that. You are sensible boys, not soppy cherubs. Say his name nicely. Go and ask Fornix for a bowl of warm water, please. Don't worry,' I told Tiberius. 'The wound is not as bad as when I fixed you to that table with a skewer.' Morellus looked amused.

As tension mounted over the lock problem, Morellus decided he was needed back on watch. I stuck it out until

Tiberius finally decided to take a lock apart. Time passed, with curses. While he was attempting reassembly, I happened to draw his attention to some grommet he had missed out, mentioning that if he was in trouble we could always ask the proper locksmith to come . . . Never do that. After Tiberius passionately replied, I fetched my cloak and left.

I went quietly. Now that children lived with us, I had no energy for huffs. Besides, my theory is that when a man is doing little jobs at home, either you endure the cursing or you take off to see your mother.

Mine was out. Her staff said Falco had been mending a candelabrum all morning; after a couple of hours of it, Helena had taken off to see her brother. Then Falco had walked out too, in a huff at being left alone.

It was too soon to return home. I decided to carry on to the Saepta Julia and tell my father how things had gone with Rodan.

12

Once I hit the Campus Martius, I knew my mistake. Originally a soggy field where Rome's young men played at being soldiers, the open part had shrunk right back to the first bend in the Tiber, up before the Altar of Peace and Mausoleum of Augustus. Between there and the Capitol, the Campus had been infilled with big temples, little temples, porticos filled with art and literature, theatres, baths, circuses and a gigantic sundial with an obelisk gnomon on a calibrated marble pavement. Domitian had recently built an athletics stadium and a beautiful performance odeon. The number and size of public lavatories showed how many people now visited the Campus.

At Saturnalia, the area was packed with extra stalls selling festival produce, with crowds of fraught people frantically buying things and merrymakers putting off the pain of that; wine was sloshing out of gourds or flagons. The big question is whether to spend big to hide your shabby affection or to spend small as some reverse demonstration of true love. Either way, everything was available: styli, writing tablets and scrolls; dice, dice-boxes and knucklebones; pets, from sparrows to whole squealing pigs; knives for hunting boar or murdering your partner; tweezer and ear-wax kits; balls and weights for the gym; moneyboxes; musical instruments; toys; tools; clothes; perfumes; food. As well as massed rows of *sigillaria*, there were candles everywhere to symbolise the Undying Sun. While people struggled to decide what to buy as presents, food and drinks trays were paraded around by hawkers. With people distracted by mulled wine, pickpockets worked their sly way through the crowds.

The stalls blocked any view of the paintings and statues in each elegant porticus; their fretful customers impeded my progress. I needed to struggle halfway across the Campus. Tucked between Agrippa's Pantheon and Domitian's newly glamorised sanctuary of Serapis, stood the long form of the Saepta Julia. Once used in a complicated Roman voting system, its original purpose was redundant now that our emperors generously helped us out by choosing 'elected' officials for us. Instead, the fine two-storey galleried building, not long restored after a huge city fire, was home to sinister men who sold glittery items to peculiar collectors and guilty adulterers. You could buy jewellery (both real and fake), vases (perfect or heavily restored), Greek art (original or made last week), and at the offices first rented by my grandfather and now by my father, you could acquire any of those, then organise an auction to sell all the stuff you had to clear out from your house to make space for your new goods.

At the Saepta I was disappointed. Didius Falco, the devious, swaggering proprietor, my adoptive father, was not there. Some woman who intended to surprise her husband with a divorce notice as he quaffed his Saturnalia draught was having their possessions valued. 'Falco has gone to look her over,' staff told me.

'Her belongings, you mean?'

'Oh, them too.'

'He'll be all day. I can't wait. Tell him Rodan liked the present but will be hard to winkle out. Now I'm off.'

I had come on foot. Our donkey had remained at home, saddened by losing Sheep. The auction staff let me ride theirs partway back: Patchy, a beast who was almost as antique as their stock. He and his donkey-boy could take me as far as the Forum, provided I went via the Basilica Aemilia to deposit cash with the family banker. It is best to vary your routine and Father would trust me to do it today. We needed transport to carry the money chest, though it was hard forcing a way through the crowds. Patchy got shoved around, but he shoved back gamely, showing his old teeth. When I was ogled, I showed mine.

We made it to the Basilica without either of us kicking anyone. Upstairs I duly exchanged quips with Father's banker, whose own father was nicknamed Nothokleptes, or 'thieving bastard'. It is possible his mother was respectably married but we had transferred the pseudonym to Notho's son and heir, who kept the money table now.

'Can't you drop that terrible old tease, Flavia Albia?'

'Stop moaning and give me a receipt, Young Notho.'

Though second-generation, he made an exaggerated Egyptian gesture, as if he had come straight from a temple in Thebes with a mummified monkey clasped to his pot belly. 'You don't need that nonsense.'

'My pa has banked here a long time, so he wants proof. How is yours?'

'Ready to pass on. I don't bring him out in December in case a breath of wind blows on him and he croaks. Your own dear parent?'

'Still full of life and daft ideas.'

'Business good for him?' Nothokleptes demanded narrowly, since that would mean business for him.

'As you can tell from today's bonny boodle. You must

78

have thought you'd gone to Elysium when Falco received his inheritance.'

Notho cackled happily. He questioned me whether I still banked with my Greek woman, Arsinoë; I chortled back that I needed someone ethical. Unfazed by insults, Nothokleptes swore he didn't want my custom anyway: he had had enough informer's misery with Falco in the old days. Business in Rome runs on such merry banter.

Down on the ground floor, I happened upon Naevius. He was a fellow informer, who did a lot of legal work. Since the courts were about to close for five days, most lawyers had wound down. Even so, he sat glumly on his stool by his customary pillar, in case a commission should shimmy along. He used the Porticus of Gaius and Lucius, named for Augustus's grandsons, nothing to do with our nephews; Rome may rule the civilised world, yet the noble Romans can't fix themselves up with enough personal names.

In the hundred-paces-long arcade there was a row of rooms let out for retail, but my colleague could not run to rent. He generally placed himself by one of the huge white marble pillars where at least he could stare out at the Forum while he waited around. I went over to greet him, a professional courtesy. He had affixed an advertisement to the pillar, using a long piece of rope to tie on a rather small plaque, which I cheerily admired; he knew this was irony. Naevius was eating a flatbread but immediately said he couldn't afford to treat me.

I would eat at home. I leaned on the pillar, not obstructing the advert. 'Any work on?' I asked, though the answer was obvious.

'Bugger all. You?'

'Nix.'

We gazed at the Forum Romanum. Among the mass of monuments, crowds were thinner than usual, though the atmosphere was busier. It was all festival hustling: no use to us. Dusk would soon be falling, and as temples prepared to put out lamps, the air chilled, adding to our melancholy.

I had always liked Naevius. There were informers who worked from the Saepta Julia, though I had no respect for them. One who nested in its annex, the Diribitorium, was such a dud that a client had once stopped suing his enemy and sued his informer instead; the judge awarded him extra costs for having to endure moral turpitude and bad breath. I knew Naevius was far more competent. Luckily, his work rarely put him in competition with me. He hunted down witnesses and delivered subpoenas. My uncles, both lawyers, used him when they needed evidence about shady characters (with Quintus and Aulus that usually meant background on their ropier clients).

As an informer, Naevius was no colonnade-crawler, no noser in rubbish pails, no eavesdropping spy. He always dressed carefully, today in a very clean slate-grey tunic with meticulously laced shoes. Even when slumped in despondency, he kept his feet and knees together neatly. He looked respectable enough to accompany men to argue disputed tax claims – a role he had been known to take.

He told me he had been touting for trade in all the usual bars, those being the only places where an informer could find our kind of customer at this time of year. 'I tried the lot. Don't bother, Albia. I covered the whole geography – the Athens, the Verona, the Venetia. I don't care; I even tried the Corioli.'

'You'll catch something! Had a go at the Tiger?' I asked sympathetically. 'There's usually some poor soul in there, sobbing because his master has beaten him raw with a rope's end, in need of an informer to explain for a fee that he has no protection in law.'

'Grr! No luck. I pulled a trader out of the Tiger landlord's clutches in one of his classic disputes over change – he never gets any better at fiddling – but the victim was too upset to offer me even a thank-you, let alone a genteel payoff. The Phoenix – that's really gone downhill in my opinion – the Centaur, the Porpentine—'

'The *Porpentine*, Naevius?'

'Possible misreading of the sign, dear. I was a bit bleary by that stage. I'd had a drink in most of them, which is why I'm broke. I ought to have known better. No point collecting tax-deductible expenses if you have no taxable income to deduct expenses from.' We smiled together sadly. 'It's all right for you, Flavia Albia; you married money.'

I explained that my plebeian prince had tied up his limited collateral in construction projects; it was up to me to cover home comforts and bills. Naevius shook his head and suggested I should have gone for a consul who had too many olive groves to count. Then he offered, 'There is a seek-and-find that's being hawked around, if you are interested.'

'I know that kind of job!' I scoffed. 'When an informer offers to pass on work rather than hogging it himself, he's either too busy – clearly not your situation, if you don't mind me saying so – or this job is so dire he can't face it.'

Naevius told me anyway: a priestess was trying to trace her twins, lost as babies in a shipwreck and carried off by raging waves in two directions.

'Where?'

As good Romans, we shared a Greek joke: 'Epidamnum maybe.'

'Epidaurus?'

'Could be Ephesus.'

'I think you mean Metapontum.'

'No, I say it was Corinth.'

'That's capital! When were those twins lost? How long ago was this shipwreck?'

'Twenty-five years.'

We both guffawed. She hadn't a hope. Neither of us would be daft enough to touch it.

13

Another informer wandered along the arcade and talked to Naevius. I could tell his trade from his hangdog air and the old fish-pickle down his tunic. He should ask for a comb for Saturnalia. His eyes were piggy, his belly bulging, his manner shifty. I didn't know his name. He had stopped to quiz us on whether we had work, worried in case someone else in the profession might be doing better than him.

'Overloaded!' Naevius had seemed too honest for this. I was impressed.

Taking my cue to bluff, I looked mysterious while I murmured, 'Can't give any details. Upper-crust people. Confidentiality agreement.'

Naevius shot me an admiring look; he would use that line in future. 'Aedile's wife,' he whispered to the other man. 'She has special access to the cream of the jobs.'

I simpered. 'Only until January, Naevius! Then he's at a loose end and I shall be all on my poor little lonesome again. Who knows how I shall manage?'

Naevius knew. I would never rely on my husband, or anyone else, to find me commissions; even solo I fixed myself up with a good portfolio. Continuing to tease the deadbeat, he then asked, 'How is your love-life, my old pomegranate? Making any progress?' That was enough to send the sorry specimen scuttling off into the twilight.

'An idiot,' Naevius assessed him. 'He brings me his troubles, when I have time to waste listening.'

'You are a good, consoling friend. What were you prodding him about?'

'He has his hopeless eye on a singer, smart, attractive, she even finds him a catch for some terrible reason.' I winced. 'I think he got her into bed once, but he cannot or will not follow through. She is bored and in despair of him. The first festival offer she gets, the stunning soprano will disappear for ever into someone else's life story.'

'And he will have no idea why!' I agreed.

We discussed why many investigators are hopeless with relationships. It was too easy to blame the antisocial hours, poor pay, danger, weather, stress and drink. Naevius, who was my kind of philosopher, complained, 'In our job you need empathy, staying power, understanding of people. Is it impossible to apply those skills to your own life? I don't see why every other informer fails to commit himself, fails to organise a regular home with his slippers by the bed, keeps missing promised appointments with his girl—'

'Especially if it's her birthday or it was supposed to be dinner with her mother,' I added.

'You've met these fellows! Classic mismanagement. He forgets the time, he doesn't read letters, he rushes off from meals because he's just had a clever thought about a suspect, then, worst crime of all, he is deaf to the vital question of where they should take their summer break.'

Again, I agreed. 'A lot of our colleagues never let go and take a holiday at all. But, Naevius, I've known informers who could pinpoint any suspect, all while they had a twinkle in the eye, hilarious gossip and the know-how to mend shutters. Those bright stars generally manage to sort out their lives. They're gold. Yet we both know your average private agent always falls for the wrong woman. Even if he does find a good one, he simply can't bring himself to approach her, so she slips away.'

'Don't women informers choose the wrong man too?' Naevius argued back. It was fair. Such even-handedness was surprising in a cynical man who did legal work.

'Oh, yes! Even I have picked losers enough times.'

'But you are married now.'

'So I am. I slipped out of character! The gods weren't happy – poor thing, he was struck by lightning.'

'I heard. Only you, Albia!' I really could not see why half the world said that, as if my weird choices were a Forum legend. Naevius continued jokily: 'I was surprised to see you out and about today. Rumour says you're stuck at home these days. Haven't you adopted children?'

'You keep up with the news!'

'It's the job, dear. So, what is this foolishness, Albia?'

'Husband's nephews. Poor little ducklings left motherless. They are staying with us for a while,' I said, boot-faced. 'Their father is alive, he's useless, but we have not formally adopted.'

'*Yet!*' Naevius teased, with a grin. 'You will make them a lovely mother.'

I stiffened. 'Why not annoy me properly? Do not hold back, Naevius. Tell me this will stop me being an informer. Juno, just say – in case I haven't noticed for myself – it must be the end of everything!'

Naevius, wise man, decided he *would* hold back. He sat on his stool looking calm. This must be how he reacted at difficult moments when advising clients in tribunal cases. A judge might be impressed.

85

We changed the subject. 'Have you heard any whispers about a nut-sellers' war, Naevius?'

'Not my area of expertise. But no. Surely you are too wise to mix with something like that, Albia?'

'Husband. Along with the vigiles.'

'And you are working with them?'

'No. I am waiting for them to be totally stuck. Then I want to show them how it's really done. In the meantime, they let me stay around looking ornamental. I can hand around the snacks bowls.'

'No wonder you need work of your own! Don't worry,' said Naevius. 'The crazed clients are all out there, Albia. Daft people are bitterly thinking they have had enough, while telling themselves they may as well wait until after Saturnalia, now it's here. Some may really do something about their problems in the New Year. We shall be seeing enough clients then. We always do.'

Naevius promised to tell me if he heard anything about nuts, and we parted company.

I crossed the darkened Forum, skirted the Palatine, the meat market and the far end of the Circus Max, reached the Aventine, then began to climb the hill. I could hear the hum from bars increasing, as other businesses closed and early-evening drinkers gathered. The Clivus Publicius, my route uphill, generally had a few lights showing. At least its more unfriendly dogs had been taken in. The young man I saw yesterday demanding his money back from Pinarius was still nagging him angrily in a shadowed doorway.

'I could have retrieved that cash for you by now!' I called. I don't think he heard me. He was too intent on ranting, while Pinarius continued dodging the issue.

Further up the road, outside a caupona with flares lighting

its counter, the shyster who had been locked out of home by his wife was now being harangued by a goldsmith who was owed cash for a necklace – perhaps commissioned for the wife, though more likely to give to that floozy at the Temple of Diana. I heard no mention of the parrot.

At the corner of Lesser Laurel Street, I met Dromo. He had been sent out to my parents' house to look for me; when he turned up there my mother must have returned home after the candelabrum incident. Helena Justina had told Dromo he would never catch up if he came after me to the Saepta. Besides, he might get lost (she was a good judge of slaves). She told him to go home, where I would return eventually. Although he obeyed Helena, Dromo was hanging around out of doors, kicking his heels, not wanting to go in to report he had failed to find me.

'Well, here I am, Dromo. You won't be in trouble, but I wish you had a lantern. What was urgent?'

'Tiberius Manlius only wanted me to say he has finished the lock and stopped spitting flames, so you can come home now.'

I chuckled, then set off briskly to give this interesting man a hug.

On the home approach, I had already taken off my cloak and fetched out my key when I stopped. Gratus had hung a light in the porch. Below it, something lay on our top doorstep. The thing was face up, looking at me. For a moment my brain could not take this in. An animal head. Familiar from the dark mark on the long face, it was *our* animal's, hacked off and bloody. Our disembodied friend, now with her eyes glassy in death: Sheep.

14

Though rarely squeamish, I stood there transfixed. *Sheep?* Positioning our butchered pet for one of us to find was vile. A planned assault. I was horrified.

Gaius and Lucius must have looked out and seen us coming. As children's happy voices came closer from indoors, Dromo realised I could not move. He snatched my cloak from over my arm, dropped it and gathered up the ghastly head. Almost at once the boys tumbled out to greet us, followed by Gratus, who had opened the door for them. Dromo swung the hideous bundle behind himself, acting so nonchalant that even sharp-eyed little Gaius did not spot it.

Gratus saw. 'Some terrible message to Tiberius Manlius,' I muttered to the steward. 'After his actions last night, I fear.' The boys were pulling my hands, dragging me indoors to look at decorations. Dromo flashed Gratus a look into his bundle; Gratus blenched. Less troubled, Dromo sauntered off across the courtyard with his usual dreamy attitude.

'Albia, Albia, look, look!'

Holly, a tree sacred to Saturn in his winter role, now hung above doors and was wrapped around pillars with swathes of cypress and ivy. The garlands twinkled occasionally with moons and stars. Gratus went around carefully lighting oil lamps and candles. I dutifully feigned joy. 'Ooh! Somebody did a lot of work here while I was out. Now listen, boys. Those constellations really belong to Falco and Helena, but my sisters have very kindly said they can be yours now.'

What Julia and Favonia had really screamed was: 'Eeurgh, we don't want that awful old tat, Albia! We went and bought brilliant new ones from the Campus Martius – *sooo* much more stylish!' Learning how to buy things on my parents' credit had transformed my sisters into shopping harpies.

They had warned me my brother had made some false eyes. I did not tell the boys that, since Postumus would want to jump out to scare them himself. Besides, right now the thought of eyeballs made me feel sick.

I freed myself from the children, needing to find Tiberius. However, I took a decision without him. If our house had attracted the wrong attention, we needed security. I called Dromo. 'I want you to go to Fountain Court. You know where it is, don't argue. Take your handcart; you'll be bringing someone's possessions back.'

'What is it? I don't want to go on any horrible errand.'

He was right: it was horrid.

'Dromo – *fetch Rodan!*'

15

A classic Roman townhouse turns inwards. It has high walls, generally blank or with only small, barred or shuttered windows on the outside. Its principal rooms form a semi-public space, glimpsed through the guarded doorway with its traditionally rude porter, but there is no real free access. To be invited inside is a privilege; how far visitors can penetrate is a measure of their prestige. Deliveries often arrive at the back, which can be a weak point. Burglary is a routine problem in Rome. Safety and privacy matter – as do the traditional horrors of keeping out wives' adulterous lovers, daughters' seducers, slaves' pesky light-fingered cronies and stray dogs.

Dogs are a popular home accessory, however. Often a big one with a spiked collar growls at the main entrance – or, at least, people have a jolly mosaic showing one. The fact that a black and white pictorial cur may be a house's only security measure proves Romans may be masters of the civilised arts – but it has not made them sensible.

Mind you, you have to live. The freeborn do not want to feel they live in prisons.

We had Barley, who was little more than a shy lapdog, and Drax, who barked loudly but had gone on holiday. Sometimes we were protected by have-a-go Trypho sleeping in the yard. Currently he was away too. Now we were to have a donkey with an untested reputation for seeing off intruders – and Rodan. It would not be enough. Tiberius sent Paris to find Larcius, who supervised his workforce, hoping he had not yet gone on holiday. (No, because first his ladyfriend had to despatch her husband to visit his auntie in Beneventum.) Extra masonry to raise the height of the yard wall must be built up tomorrow. Also, Larcius had to surrender the outbuilding that had been his site office, as Rodan would now live there.

Rodan turned up that evening with Dromo, then straight away went home again. Before he agreed to live with us, he would have to get used to the idea. He hadn't even brought his things.

Tiberius had dealt with him. I let the man of the house address the problem. 'Of course you can choose, Rodan. We are entirely in your hands. But you could be very happy here – warm family environment, easy work, few visitors to process, lots of back-up from Gratus and the other staff. Take it or leave it.'

Rodan chose to leave it. Unfortunately, on the way here, Dromo had told him that we also had criminals coming in to steal from us, then leaving us bloody messages in the very doorway he was supposed to guard. Rodan, the pathetic chicken, was scared to come.

Tiberius braved out the situation, assuring everyone we had good new locks. In private he confessed to me that the locksmith had said these were top-of-the-range mechanisms, but if a previous lock had been skilfully picked, the same people could get past any replacement. They must own the secret tools that locksmiths carry for opening up when feckless owners lose their keys.

Tiberius also admitted how, after I left that afternoon, he

had given up struggling and called in the locksmith. The new locks had been properly installed, which apparently was a rapid job, if you knew what you were doing. There had been nothing wrong with the mechanism: the locksmith admitted he had thought the key he gave me might be stiff. Had he come in the first place, he would have dealt with it on the spot and we need never have known there was a problem . . .

I gazed at my husband gently.

'I love you,' he said, looking meek. He knew the talk.

'I know you do, my darling. And I love you too. I shall let you tell your nephews that their precious sheep has died.'

'Do we need to say anything?'

'Their sharp little ears catch any gossip. They are bound to hear something so let's be honest.'

Tiberius scratched his ear uncomfortably, but he was a good man so he went and did it. Soon Lucius had rushed up to his bedroom, crying for his mother all over again, while Gaius buried himself in the stable; if anyone approached, he threw himself among the straw and yelled that he hated all of us. Until today we had been making progress, but now we were back where we started in the long bereavement process.

At least this meant we had our hands full; we could spare no time for dwelling on the severed-head threat. Criminals can be very blinkered. They do not grasp that a householder and his wife have neither time nor energy to respond to stupid gestures. We are fully taken up with real domestic issues: how to persuade everyone to come for their dinner, then how to get them all to bed afterwards.

Dinner, thank the gods, was mullet. No sign of mutton cheeks with onion and carrots, sheep's tongue confit, pickled eyes or brains. Bedtime passed off with no more kicking, yelling and escaping to play downstairs again than usual.

'I wonder how Cornelia, mother of the Gracchi, handled daily life?' I said to Tiberius. 'There she goes, annoying woman, primly mouthing, "These are my jewels" – but did her two jewels never act up like hysterical little monsters when they did not want to go to bed?'

He was feeling the strain. 'You are being very good about all this. I will buy you a necklace for the festival – if that doesn't make me a cliché guilty husband.'

'Don't. A woman cannot wear necklaces with children around her, or she'll end up strangled. I want hand cream, please, and a massive flask of some top-strength sleeping drug.'

Tiberius nodded. He smiled. 'Hand cream it shall be. All I need is a hint.'

So, I told him he was a lovely man and he told me to come here.

Later, when the house lay dark and silent, cocooned in bedroom privacy I found myself remembering a pottery model that had once come through Father's auction house. He reckoned its origin was Gaul. It showed a miniature bed, with a man and a woman fast asleep in each other's arms under a blanket; their dog lay curled up on their feet. Forget that tired label 'votive offering', as is often applied. It was simply a lovely object. I never saw it catalogued; I suspect Falco pulled it out for Helena.

Before that memory, I had been having more troubled thoughts: anxiety about our home being under assault by gangsters. The men who took Sheep probably knew we had children in the house: they could be threatening 'them next'.

They had been inside our property; they might come in again. No protection strategy is ever foolproof.

I felt upset, though for me fear was old news. Alone on the streets of Londinium, I had once known every terror there is. Many of them came true. But that was long ago, and in a distant province.

Even in Rome, for over a decade at Fountain Court, I lived close to danger. You do grow sadly used to it. And now I was married, married again, which brings a feeling of safety, or at least the illusion that you can cope with anything. Because you are together, you feel it will all be easier. So the sheep-stealers' threats were bad news, yet they failed to chill me as much as they intended.

They had surprised me, though. Even as a young woman alone, my life had been more discreet than this. I felt much more exposed now. Tiberius had given me the children, the animals, the whole domestic paraphernalia that made us more visible socially, identified us to the men who watched from doorways, implied to hustlers and grabbers that we would own valuables, named us to those we antagonised – set us up as possible victims.

Although Tiberius had caused our crisis, because of whatever he was doing with Titus Morellus, I did not blame him. I had come into this willingly, knowing the kind of life he wanted, seeing that he was a pious, determined kind of man. He would stand up for the wider community, taking action for good; despite that, I was sure if we ever seemed vulnerable, his first care would be for his own. So he also gave me what those Gallic lovers had: I could lie in his arms under my blanket, with the warm weight of Barley on our feet. I could be happy.

A faint small voice began crying. I listened, waiting. I

94

never left a child to grieve alone in the night. Tiberius too, though he seemed deeply asleep, had probably heard and prepared himself. He did not expect me always to respond. We both stayed quiet yet were both ready.

Someone else went to comfort the child; the sad sound stopped.

Then, although I lay still trying not to wake him, Tiberius pulled himself up from his chasm of slumber. Somehow, he was aware of my troubles. Drawing me in tighter, he kicked a little, trying to shift the dog's weight. Barley protested with a grumbling snore. Almost at once Tiberius sank back into heavy sleep. But first, perhaps without even knowing it, he reminded me of why I'd married him. On the top of my head I felt his warm breath as he murmured, 'Stop worrying.'

16

Being told not to worry ensures that you do it. I took my rest, but lightly. I woke first. I slipped downstairs, walked around the house checking, went through to the yard, placed a hand on each new door lock (acquired oil on my fingers), leaned over the stable door and stroked the donkey. Mercury pulled down strands of hay from her manger, reassuringly ignoring me. Nothing was amiss.

I liked to be by myself in the house, the only person awake. I lifted my face to the sky above the courtyard, reconnecting with the self only I knew. Grey skies, full of high, fast-moving rain clouds, were part of my old life. I would never go back to Britain, but Rome's changeable winters gave me a tug of recognition. I disliked the cold, but it was familiar. You need your past – at least, you do once you have managed to stop raving over its injustices.

The light remained gloomy, the claggy air unwelcoming. I made a jug of hot *posca*; I took some for myself, which I sipped slowly, cradling the beaker, huddled in a stole, seated alone in the courtyard, in reflective mood. When I heard movement upstairs, I did not call out. Whoever it was stayed up there. The dog came down to join me, but reproachfully – *Why are you up? I want to lie on your feet.* Still sleepy, she retreated to her kennel.

Some caller banged on our front doors. What was wrong

with the knocker? I went to squint through the grille at the man outside. Unhelpfully – or deliberately? – he had turned away while he awaited a response. Even so, his weight squeezing the seams of his tunic and his air of nonchalant dumbness were more of a pique than a threat. I lifted the big beam we kept on drop-in cradles at night, then admitted the visitor. He glanced behind at the street, which was still misty and sinister at dawn, as if he was checking it out. I was nervous the house might be watched; I urged him to hurry. With no one in sight in the silent road, he ambled indoors. At least he put the beam back for me.

I knew him. One of the vigiles. His name was Rufinianus. Well padded, not tall, his tunic too tight around his flesh. He had a square, balding head with a small mouth that he kept mostly drawn down in a straight line. His talents were basic, I knew, but his approach well-meaning. I thought he liked his job; he did not put himself out, but neither did any of them.

I led this early bird into the courtyard. 'Keep your voice down. I want people to sleep. We had some upsets yesterday.' He nodded. He had heard. When he stared at my beaker, I fetched him *posca* of his own. He said he was supposed to meet Tiberius and Morellus. While we waited for one or other of them to show up, I talked to him quietly – playing the polite hostess in order to pick his brains. 'I thought you had retired, Rufo. Can't you give up?'

'Called back for Saturnalia cover. At least I get a place at the drinks party.' This horrible booze-up was the focal point in the Fourth Cohort's calendar. They saved for it all year and needed a month to recover afterwards; those who survived the party would crawl back on duty in a week, only because their station-house offered the presence of mattresses and the absence of wives. Do not set your building on fire in the New Year.

Rufinianus looked around at what he could see of our house: respectable family property, modifications in progress, idealistic décor, pergola hung with green garlands, fountain set with festive lights on brackets that had been fixed out of reach of children.

'Flavia Albia! Who'd have thought it?' The first time I met him was some years ago when I lived at Fountain Court. Was I a different person then? I would say no, but he clearly decided so. 'I always remembered your incident. We get hundreds of home invasions, but I only know one where the perp stealing the necklaces was stopped in his tracks for ever by a young lady! I'll never forget how calm you were.'

Wrong. When I reached the Fourth's building I was shuddering so badly, I had to sit down on an upturned fire-bucket. At that point, although I was aware of how much blood I had left behind in my apartment, I had not realised the intruder had died. They only told me afterwards.

I never intended to kill the cat-burglar, probably no more than when he entered my apartment he had planned to attack me. He had thought no one was there. As soon as he saw otherwise, he decided on a full assault. At Fountain Court, people might hear screams but no one would investigate. The burglar never knew that back in Londinium, barely more than a child, I had fallen into the clutches of a sex-trader who, as part of the induction process, thought it good practice to rape me.

Never again. Stop right there, puny Aventine thief. Feel my kitchen knife going into your guts, with ten years of hate behind it. Take that for Florius: Gaius Florius Oppicus, the filthy brothel-owner with whom, if he ever returned to Rome, I planned to have my reckoning . . .

'Of course, you never wanted to finish him off,' mused Rufinianus now, remembering he had taken my statement. He had been a night-time stand-in; I had had to show him how to smooth the waxed tablet before he could start his notes. 'You just happened to be handy with a carrot knife and his liver just happened to get in the way.' He smiled, as if even after all this time I might need reassurance that their tribune would not take the business further. 'And now look at you – an aedile's wife! We'd better warn this new gang Morellus is chasing just who they are dealing with,' he told me, with amusement.

I must have been shaken by remembering the dead burglar because I said, with more passion than I meant to show, that I too would like to know with whom we were dealing. 'Who are they, the new gang?'

'Just the old gang again.' Rufo was matter-of-fact, surprised to hear I cared. 'Nothing changes.'

'What gang?'

'Hasn't your husband told you, him and Morellus, their thinking on it?' Without rancour, Rufinianus spelled out drily that, as a married woman, I would now always be trying to find out what my husband was up to.

I let him pronounce his opinion. 'They told me someone is muscling in on traders, Rufo. Is it all about festival nuts?'

'Well, no, that's only the starting point.' He set out to explain the crisis, unaware that Tiberius and Morellus wanted me to stick to scribbling shopping lists. 'Selling nuts for Saturnalia has always been a monopoly of one consortium. Now along come some would-be hard men who don't carry weapons because it's illegal – but they manage a lot with planks and broom handles. They go at the established sellers, fight them in the street, cause a riot. Well, anywhere else they would call it a riot. On the Aventine it was a mild disagreement. Just happened to occur on Dolichenus Street, though it could have been an afternoon bust-up anywhere.'

'That's a bit close to Fountain Court! Anyone hurt?'

'Planks can hurt like Hades, Flavia Albia.' Rufo shook his head. 'Never let anyone hit you with a plank, especially if it's had bloody big nails deliberately stuck in it. Nobody dead, though. Not yet. To us it's just a harp recital with a few bum notes.'

'Our sheep is dead!' I countered angrily.

'Oh, yes, I heard that.' The vigilis applied a sombre expression as if commiserating with my loss of a close relative.

'You know what the bastards did?'

'Baa-lamb's head all bloody on your nice clean doorstep. Morellus has got the lads looking out for the other cuts for you.'

'We don't want them.' I reconsidered that. 'No, my cook will. Cooks are short on feeling. He wants to come up with some delicacy, never mind that it's our pet.'

'Mutton pie?' Rufinianus chortled. 'Home-made is best! It's all over the district about your aedile having a bust-up at Xero's. He's a brave man, your fellow.'

'Manlius Faustus – absolutely bloody fearless!'

'You do choose them!' That was when Rufinianus let slip, 'Well, he must be a right lad, to be up for this – tackling the Balbinus lot.' *Balbinus?* That certainly was a dark name from the past. 'Morellus on his own would be leery. That's who we think it is now, incidentally: the rags of the old firm, having a revival. You've got connections, Albia, so you know all about these crooks.'

I nodded. I certainly did.

Balbinus Pius was an old-time, old-style mobster. Before I ever came to Rome my uncle, Lucius Petronius, managed to have him prosecuted. It had taken years of trying. Then Petro even persuaded a jury to convict. He brought jurors in from out of town.

As a free citizen, even a gang-master pinned down for capital offences had to be given 'time to depart', though his notion of that had been 'time to come back from exile incognito'. Easy to predict. Hard to prevent. But Balbinus did subsequently pass into Hades in murky circumstances, which Petro and my father used to chortle about when they believed no one was noticing. I had paid attention because their stories were always worth listening to: fine constructions of irony, suspense and metaphor. Once Falco started rattling off, his style and one-liners brought him a wide circle of admirers.

Despite their efforts, the Balbinus crime empire was never entirely extinguished. Remnants were taken over by surviving sidekicks, though there had not been many left after Petro finished. A son-in-law inherited, eagerly learning to impose fear and clutch ill-gotten money. That was Florius. The Florius who, when forced out of Rome, groomed me for his brothel in Londinium. Nobody knew where exactly he was now, but not in Britannia.

'Has Morellus decided who is behind this spurt of revival?' My heart thumped, though I made the question sound inconsequential. *Was Florius back in Rome?*

Rufinianus only pulled a face. 'Some turd who lives here on the Aventine. Been brooding here a while, but just spreading his stinking wings. We had a tip he's acquired a new sidekick to help beef up his organisation. I'm brought back to help Morellus get closer. That's all the gen so far.'

'That's enough!' I said. Then I hinted, 'The Balbinus events were before I came to Rome . . .'

Rufo assumed that, because of my heritage with Falco and Petronius, I was allowed to know. 'Old Balbinus and his key henchmen tended to live down in the valley, Albia. Their beat was the Circus originally – whorehouses and gambling dens. They were too savvy to rob temples, but they ran a lot of pavement thieves. Purse-snatchers, bangle-grabbers, even tunics from bath-houses, they were never picky. Those men were rough. If they couldn't wrench the big cabochon signet ring from a victim on the Sacred Way, they thought nothing of cutting off his finger with a dagger, then running away with the dripping digit while he stood howling.'

I was surprised. 'Isn't nut-warfare a stretch from that?'

'Nuts and the rest! You know what it's like up here,' said Rufinianus. 'You did it yourself. You've lived in an alley: no amenities.'

'No amenities?'

'The original old speculators put up tenements to bring in as much rent as possible: cram them in and cream it off. They never bothered giving people anything else, no markets, baths, temples or marble halls for literary lectures. More vitally, there were hardly any street stalls and fewer hardware shops. Well, it's all freed slaves and foreigners, isn't it? No one cares whether they eat. The new villains played on it. They started with cart wars – bringing products around to the big old lodgings, ringing a jingly little bell to say, *We're here, come and get stuff*, then selling cheap goods off the back of the cart.'

'As in cheap goods that "fell off the back of a wagon" in the first place?'

'Oh, yes. It was all tat, though. Mouldy bread and leaky lamps. Old bones you wouldn't give your dog. Greens they pinched from people's market-gardens. Working men's tunics, cloaks that are all patches, seventh-hand sandals with two left feet. Knock-offs at knock-down prices – though a high price eventually comes with it. They allowed the poor to run up massive tabs on credit, drew them in ever deeper, then they were off into loan sharking. That used to be Balbinus in the old days, putting pressure on helpless creditors, viciously beating them up to make them pay, smash your door in, set your place on fire, fatal warnings to all the others he was preying on.'

I tried not to think about Sheep. Our warning. 'Have the Fourth Cohort been aware of this for long?'

'Until recently,' Rufo told me, 'the gangsters kept everything nice and quiet. Out of sight. But come Saturnalia, the nut-sellers were going to lose too much. It's seasonal trade they were looking forward to, so they cut up rough at being pressurised. When the street fighting started, even Morellus had to sit up and take notice – he gets his corn plasters in Dolichenus Street.'

I started to laugh, just as we heard more knocks and a familiar voice shouting ruderies to demand entry: the man himself. Tiberius wanted to stop him deafening the neighbours, so he came down. Staff appeared, ready for their daily tasks or, in Dromo's case, wondering what tasks he could ritually avoid. The dog climbed out of her kennel, stretched her back and barked at the air. Little boys ran around the upper balcony with no clothes on, while exasperated people tried to fix them up with their tunics and shoes. Normal life began again.

I went into a room by myself, to do some thinking.

17

Morellus had brought his two elder children, claiming it was cover to fool observers, though I guessed Pullia needed a break from them. He said their latest trick was a fur effigy that looked like a puppy with its head trapped in a cupboard door; Morellus had made them leave it at home. Talking about it kept all the children busy, huddled together and giggling.

While the men dawdled over their business breakfast, I ran through my daily steward's meeting. Gratus was brisk, I brisker. 'You order grape-must and honey. I'll get us a door porter.' I grabbed a bread roll, summoned Dromo, then marched over to Fountain Court. From not wanting Rodan anywhere near us a few days ago, I was now determined to hire him. Whether he wanted it or not.

Hello, hello! Rodan was ready packed. Overnight he had changed his mind: from being afraid of our perilous household, he was now eager to move in. He had had a confrontation in the alley last evening, after which he was still trembling. 'I'm getting out of here. It isn't safe.'

'Rodan, you're a gladiator! You are a huge man trained in violence. Who were these scary people?'

He refused to talk about it. At Saturnalia they were probably girl garland-weavers with drink inside them. Upholstery tassel-makers have a wild reputation, and some milkmaids are notorious if you meet them in the dark. At any rate, Rodan quickly piled his stuff onto Dromo's handcart (Dromo stood watching scornfully with his arms folded, while handing out loading advice), then the porter loped along to our house.

'How long is this man staying?' asked Dromo, determined not to lose his place as the one who made us furious.

'We shall see.'

Yes, I was a mother now. I could look vague and deflect any question with bland dialogue.

At home I handed Rodan over to Gratus. They were from opposite ends of the human scale. Gratus linked his fingers, flexed them, looked as firm as he could in the face of this rebellious lump of flesh, then went into his induction talk with the air of a man drowning. Rodan single-mindedly refused to listen.

'Do I get a stool to sit on in my cubicle?'

'We can find you a stool.'

'Is there time off for eating?'

'We shall provide cover for refreshment breaks.'

'Where's the toilet?'

'Now?'

'Better had.'

'Rodan can access the builders' privacy hut in the yard,' I intervened hastily. Their facilities were a bucket surrounded by trellis; the apprentice was responsible for emptying it. Someone had better warn him. 'He may as well use the same one all the time. It will be handy for his sleeping quarters at night.'

'Indeed!' Gratus backed me up smoothly. 'The cubby-hole by the kitchen won't fit a man of your stature, Rodan, and already suffers too many queues.' Rodan prepared to argue. The steward dropped his voice to an exquisite murmur. 'Humble apologies, Rodan. House rule. The master is extremely particular, I'm afraid. We have to ensure that Tiberius Manlius is never kept waiting.'

Tiberius Manlius, mildest of men, glanced over from his meeting with the vigiles as if he could sense he was being maligned.

The first person who banged our bronze knocker after Rodan arrived had to be admitted by me. The porter had gone to the toilet. He was taking hours. This would probably be the normal state of affairs. Still, no other home in Lesser Laurel Street had an ex-gladiator to vet callers. We might be protected by sheer notoriety.

I knew the visitor: Glaphyra. I welcomed her. Life had taken an unexpected turn: my mother still wanted me to have a career. She had sent us a woman who, if she took to us, would be the boys' nurse. When Helena Justina lived in her father's house as a girl, Glaphyra had looked after her two younger brothers. She was reckoned to be good with boys, so when my parents had Postumus dumped on them by the circus lady who birthed him (do not ask: the Didii were extraordinary), Glaphyra was gifted by my grand-mother to help look after him; once he was seven, which he decreed was legally past childhood, my brother refused to have a nurse. She was passed back to Helena's sister-in-law, but Claudia had six children, which even Glaphyra found too much.

'I agreed with your mother I'll give you a try, Flavia Albia. At least we know each other.'

'Thank you,' I murmured, subdued even though we both

knew where the real power lay. She had all the options; I was desperate.

'Are they nice little boys?'

'Charming.'

'Conniving terrors?' Helena must have briefed her. 'I am told they have just lost their mother, one wets the bed, one is a kicker, and they are both unhappy souls.'

'That's about it. Their uncle and I tell ourselves nothing is their fault. We are trying to see them as having great potential for development.'

Glaphyra sniffed. She had encountered liberal ideas at my parents' and remained unimpressed. I, their eldest, only proved to her that tosh didn't work.

This darling woman had reached late middle age, a broad-beamed, impassive figure. Nowadays she was a little short-sighted, somewhat deaf, her movements creaky. But she was good at timing rewards and could mend toys, or find someone else who knew how. Since Gaius and Lucius were clever at breaking things, they ought to find her comforting.

I liked her. I couldn't say that about everyone. My mother liked her too, though Glaphyra would scoff, 'That Helena! What a little empress! I was glad I had Aulus and Quintus. I always left Naïssa to take care of your pesky mother.' That was intriguing to hear.

While this treasure and Gratus were assessing one another, like dogs in a park, Glaphyra noticed the children kicking up a racket. Her first move was to have the Morelli taken home by Paris, then Gaius and Lucius were simply picked up, placed on benches, given wooden skewers she obtained from Fornix, then started on knitting their own liberty caps. Suza, my young maid, had dreamily wafted downstairs after her customary lie-in. 'What time is this? Now hold your arms out and help me wind up the wool, if you please.'

'I have to dress Flavia Albia.'

'Albia can dress herself. She will have to, if this is the time of day you intend appearing. You need to buck yourself up, dearie, and start meeting some standards!'

Luckily Suza was eager to better herself. She eyed Glaphyra narrowly; this wide-based dame seemed an unlikely source of beauty tips but Suza was always on the lookout for a new source. I let myself be steered into a side room; there, Suza said nothing about the nurse, but bedecked me while nagging me that, in her mind at least, I had promised to send her for hairdressing lessons. I reminded her she was still on trial, adding remarks about the cost of training. Anyone could do plaits. When Suza left me at last, to take away her primping equipment, I sat quiet, while domestic life lapped around in the rest of my home.

I was very much aware that as our household increased, strife might be eased but our expenses would rocket. Two more mouths to feed today. The option to wait for a caseload after the holiday was fast diminishing. I needed work right now.

I was in the small salon where I interviewed clients, when I had any. Suddenly a loud voice startled me, redolent with cliché: 'Don't look so glum. It will never happen!'

'Rufo! Juno, your repartee is so ancient, lichen is growing on it.'

Rufinianus saw himself as a mischievous wag. He thought everybody loved him for it. So, he liked to pop up unexpectedly behind people, eager to delight them. This never goes down well with me.

'I can put a little job your way, if you're interested, Albia.'

'What?' I ought to have asked him, 'Did Morellus and my husband suggest this, to keep me occupied?' Instead, I was too annoyed because he pulled up the big chair provided for my clients. He settled himself among its cushions. The red tunic he had retrieved from some horrible chest when recalled from retirement looked as if it had not been laundered before it was put away. Or had never been laundered at all.

'There's this fellow who goes to my baths, whose his wife claims he is going mad.'

Still glaring about the chair, I added a groan. 'Oh, not the old behaving-very-strangely-these-days problem?'

That problem went right up to the Emperor. I almost hoped it was Domitian, which would certainly be thrilling and possibly lucrative. Why hadn't I thought of offering to help the Empress to dump him and go back to her father? Answer: because her father had taken a hint from Nero years before and fallen on his sword. Second answer: everyone said Domitia Longina was horrible to work with.

'Interested?' grinned Rufo.

'I doubt it. What is he, this screwy spouse?'

'A businessman.'

'Oh, very unusual! And how strange is he?'

'They are having continual rows about him not going home for lunch.'

'Oh, he's no madder than anyone, but she thinks he has a floozy? Am I supposed to get him off the hook? What's he asked you to do?'

'It's not him. *She* wants somebody, somebody clever, to find out what he's up to.'

'It doesn't need anyone clever to see whether he has a

new girlfriend.' I snorted. 'Is he combing his hair in a ghastly new way and can she smell perfume on his cloak?'

'I knew you were the girl for this! I'll send her along and you can ask her for all the clues.'

'It sounds like a mess. I am not taking the case, Rufo.'

'It's made for you, Albia. I'll send her.'

Rufinianus jumped off my client throne, so pleased with himself he was leaving before I could refuse.

18

There was no escape. She came.

When she knocked, Rodan was busy in the builders' yard, arranging his things in his new shack. After that, he took his mid-morning break, watching the builders raise the height of the exterior wall. Tiberius had caught those he could before they disappeared on holiday; since he had only got hold of the clerk-of-works and the apprentice, he himself was helping mix the mortar while they laid bricks. Dromo was watching, never thinking to fetch Tiberius an old tunic to work in. Gratus was out shopping; Fornix was in his kitchen; Paris was there too, eating; Glaphyra had taken the boys for a walk.

Suza was here. She let the woman in. I paused on my way to the salon, listening. Suza was polite, by her standards. She seated the visitor in the big armed chair, put cushions behind her, placed a footstool neatly. 'What lovely hair you have, madam! Would it be possible to tell me who does it for you? I would like to go to them for lessons.'

She of the lovely coiffure said it was done at home by her maid. That failed to shake off my brash girl. Suza replied how convenient: she would come round to their house for a maid-to-maid conference. Hearing me approach, however, she knew enough to simmer down. 'May I bring you a dish of mint tea, madam?'

Hospitality rituals might hold us up, though I generally saw this as an opportunity to settle a client while I made my first assessments. I was about to get into a Saturnalia pickle with those today, though my errors only became clear later.

Subjected to the woman's beady inspection, I was glad to be turned out with finicky plaits, face paint, fancily draped stole, the full Suza-selection of jewellery. I was facing somebody whose maid-at-home must be high-class. The hair, though not imperial-court ridiculous, was complex. There had been skincare; there was colour enhahcement. Fingers were burdened with multiple rings. The woman's outfit was expensive (silk-weave, embroidered hems, glinting fasteners), though I detected its lucky owner might be rough around the edges: a type that was familiar, especially in my clients. People who chose to use an informer tended to have humble backgrounds but to possess funds worth guarding – fear for their cash was often what brought them to me. At least it meant they could afford my fees.

I noted that my prospective client had come without the fancy maid. Failing to be chaperoned was one clue to her rough edges and I assumed that what we were to discuss was far too sensitive. Had she slipped out of the house alone, so nobody could wonder where she was sneaking off to? Something about her seemed familiar, though I could not place her.

While we awaited Suza with her titbits tray, I equipped myself with a note-tablet. 'I am Flavia Albia. And you are?'

'Terentia Nephele.' One heavily classic Roman name, one whimsical Greek: heroic but cloudy. The mixture suggested her lineage included slaves, whose names were often Greek though they would adopt extra Roman ones when given their freedom. It provided little clue to current status. She could have belonged to a boot-mender or the imperial family. She could have married her master, who could be absolutely anyone. Or if originally owned by a high-status household, with education available for polishing their slaves, it could be she who had brought culture and even money to her marriage.

Before I began my routine questions, the woman boldly took over: 'I just came along to be neighbourly. Our house is in Greater Laurel Street. Everyone has heard about the incident you had here, Flavia Albia.' She knew about Sheep. She was openly nosy. Had she gossiped with some group of women who shared borage-tea mornings? She did not seem the type; it was one thing she and I had in common. 'It sounds a nasty thing to happen. Is that worrying for you?'

Our situation was nothing to do with anyone else. 'It's either a delivery error or a misdirected joke,' I replied, breezily passing it off. If she wanted to use this incident as an excuse for calling, I could live with it. People who have never used an investigator come up with all sorts of pretexts.

'Still, you need to take care, if you are being targeted in some way!'

'I leave that worry to my husband,' I lied.

She raised a well-groomed eyebrow. 'Is your husband doing work that has annoyed someone?'

'I wouldn't know. I never ask about his work,' I lied again.

'But hasn't this frightened you all?' she persisted, eager for thrills apparently.

'No.' I cut her off. Enough of horror. 'Shall we get down to business?'

Nephele blinked and was silent. Perhaps I was being too abrupt. I spelled out that I assumed Rufinianus had recommended me. 'Oh, the man at the bath-house!' she fluttered, like someone making light of it. 'Yes, I was trying to find my husband after a tradesman had called at our house wanting payment for something I knew nothing about.'

'You think your husband is up to something?'

'He could be,' agreed Nephele, tentatively.

'Well, that is the kind of situation I often work with.'

'Is it?'

'Yes. Let me tell you my background.' I was used to reassuring clients, who are often class-conscious, so I began with status: 'My father is a wealthy plebeian, my mother from a senatorial family. My husband also has established Aventine roots and is currently a magistrate.' In case she happened to care about talent, I added, 'I have been doing this work for almost fifteen years.' It was twelve. Exaggerating your curriculum is the rule for any professional. Informers can be florid: they learn misrepresentation from their clients. 'As Rufinianus presumably told you, I am well versed in confidential enquiries.' Now Nephele was listening. 'I never use research assistants, but I have associates for consultation if a problem needs specialist advice.'

Suza reappeared at this point, carefully carrying a small silver salver with the promised mint tea, which Fornix had set out to be served from a hot jug through a pointed strainer. We did own little silver cups for dainty occasions: wedding presents. The tray was graced with a ditsy bowl of almonds. There was a neat linen napkin. It had an embroidered monogram, though we had no idea whose because it had come in a bundle of oddments from Father's auction house.

Suza was an outspoken lump, but functional; she wanted advancement, so she had learned. She served without spillage. She even asked, 'Is there anything else, Flavia Albia, or shall I make sure you are not disturbed now?'

114

I gave her a *good going!* gleam.

Now that Nephele was sipping and scalding her rouged lip, I seized back the initiative. 'So, tell me about your problem husband. What kind of business is he in?' She looked surprised, then ducked the question, as if she might not know his work. This is true of many wives. It makes me despair, but you have to go along with it. 'Rufinianus told me your man has recently, let's say, become depressed? It happens,' I reassured her. 'Let's clear away the normal reasons – has he lost money in a shipwreck recently? Buried a dear friend? Or – I am sorry to be brutal – is he trying to recover his lost youth by having a fling?'

It was at this point, I can see with hindsight, that Nephele reached a decision about talking to me. A fling, she agreed primly, was probably it.

'Who is he chasing? Have you any ideas?' When she made no reply, I suggested, 'There's a bawd at the Temple of Diana who is running through local husbands like a rat through a grain sack, I have heard.' If Nephele did belong to a borage-tea group, they were bound to know about this.

I had meant only to start speculation but Nephele banged down her cup on the salver. 'That's Laetilla!' she exclaimed, and with obvious loathing.

I blinked. 'Oh? I suppose she meets the men at the temple, then invites them back for entertainment at her house.'

'Entertainment?' queried Nephele, now seeming surprised.

'That's what she calls it. Your husband accepts invitations too frequently from this over-friendly woman? How did you realise he strays?'

There seemed to be something unconvincing here, but Nephele muttered, 'Yes, he goes there. He goes there often.'

'Do you have dates and times?'

'Well, no.'

'That's all right,' I soothed her. 'I didn't expect you to have had him tailed. If you want to hire me, that will be up to me. Well, I give you my sympathy. What is your situation at home?'

Now she spoke more easily. 'We hardly see each other. He claims he is busy. He raves that he is working very hard at the family business and leaves me all on my own, day after day. I deserve more attention. People still find me attractive.'

'I'm sure that's true. You need someone to tell you what you can do.' I sighed gently. 'These are your choices. You can stay with him – and put up with it. Or if you decide to leave him, I can help you to arrange a stress-free divorce, especially the financial side. I can ascertain by my enquiries just how badly he behaves. This will strengthen your position in demanding the best settlement. Do you have children?'

'No, thank the gods.'

'Is his father alive?'

'No.' Nephele paused. 'My brother-in-law made all our wedding arrangements. I always understood their father died abroad.' That suggested the family were involved in trade.

'Was he in the same business?'

'I believe so.'

'So is your husband legally independent?'

'Too bloody much so!' the aggrieved wife replied.

'Does he have other relatives?'

'He has family, not all horrible. His brother is the nasty one and he's daggers drawn with me, these days. In the same line – before you ask.'

Letting her rant, I asked gently, 'And is there family of your own?'

'A sister.'

'Married?'

'Not married. Not yet. There are plans.'

'You spend a lot of time together?'

'I have to talk to somebody!' The thought came to me that if Nephele's husband was of the wandering tendency he might have made a play for the sister. I did not ask, since Nephele might not yet realise. If he had schmoozed his in-law, I would let it come out in its own time.

'So, Terentia Nephele, do you want me to do what I can for you?'

'I suppose you can try.'

'Thank you.' Clients were not usually so grudging but it happened occasionally. Once I presented the evidence, her hard face would very likely crumple. 'I will send you a proposal and a list of terms. How can I contact you? Can I have your address? Then when would be the best time to call?'

'Don't come to the house!' she interrupted quickly.

It was a common fear from a client, especially one with marital problems. I advised that either she must keep visiting me, like today, or she should regularly send someone to check for news. 'I shall need details from you, as much as you can tell me about your husband's background, starting with what he is called, of course—'

'Apart from infuriating, devious and infamous? He was Gaius to me once, but Murrius is his proper cognomen. Give me a note-tablet!'

I was happy to do that. While she wrote down details, I took out the tea tray. On my return she snapped down the tablet on my goat-legged serving table. 'All you need is there. Name, age, appearance, haunts, associates and filthy habits!'

117

I resumed my seat temporarily. 'Extremely thorough! Just one thing more, Nephele. Tell me why you feel your man may be going mad—'

'I don't,' she said. Oh, thanks, Rufo!

'No depression? Confusion? Excuse me, but I must ask you: has there been any violence?'

Nephele looked at me scornfully. 'None. He is sane. Quite sane – and too wily to be anything but good-mannered towards me. He would say I have nothing to complain about. I brought him a dowry. He would never dare to bully me. He knows *exactly* what he is doing – but if I want to, I can run rings around him.'

Fighting back? Always better to be warned when a client is ready to lash out.

There was more. Nephele confessed: 'I had better mention something. I was intending to use another person to make enquiries for me, but he never got back to me.'

'Would you mind telling me who?'

'Naevius, if you know who I mean.'

'I do. A colleague. He would have done a proficient job, but I believe he is overcommitted at present and cannot take on all the cases he would like. You know how it is at this time of year. He will understand if you hire me instead. Naevius and I are on very amicable terms.'

Well, we were, until he found out I had pinched his prospect.

Why had he left her dangling? I hoped I would not end up wishing I had left her for him.

19

I took Nephele to the door, making sure she left. I wouldn't have wanted her alone with any of my staff in case she asked personal questions.

She paused on the doorstep. Once again she asked about Sheep, reprising her original suggestion that our family must be terrified. 'You do need to be careful about upsetting the wrong people!' Anyone would think the gangsters Tiberius stirred up had sent Nephele to spy on our reactions and issue further warnings on their behalf.

Could this really be another reason for her visit? If her husband was a mobster, not some ordinary price-juggling negotiator, being two-timed would be the least of her worries. But that seemed unlikely. Crime lords' wives never come out into the respectable world to complain about their treatment. And if sent as a spy, she had made a poor job of it.

Whatever Nephele was, I watched her walk off towards Greater Laurel Street, where she had told me she lived. She wrapped her stole over her head gracefully and travelled at an easy pace. I wondered if she knew the other wife I had seen that time, locking *her* husband out of doors. I would like to know whether that warring couple were reconciled or, if not, had agreed custody of the tug-of-war parrot.

While I was still in the porch, I was hailed. 'Meat delivery,

Albia!' Not funny, but I was too late to slam the doors shut in his face.

Rufinianus. Behind him, one of the slaves who worked for the vigiles was cheerfully carrying over his shoulder a headless sheep. The vigiles must have decided the woolly lump was ours, though one lifeless bloodied animal carcass looks much like another to me.

'Found it on a rubbish heap, must have been lying there all night. Morellus said bring it here.'

I drew in my skirts. 'I don't want anything that has been in the street overnight, picked over by who knows how many disease-ridden hands.'

'No one touched it.' Rufo seemed wary. 'I'm afraid that's your clue to who must have dumped it. Otherwise, Albia, there is no way good mutton would stay put on a midden. This is another warning, though aimed at a wider audience. *Look what we've done to the interfering aedile, people – so you all watch out too!* No one will touch terrorisers' messages, not even if they're starving. The Fourth've already bought a whole ox for our drinks party, otherwise we would have it.'

'Bring it in then. May as well.' I looked at Rufinianus, then past him at the slave. The carcass was being carried over the grimy youth's shoulder on his sludge-grey, fresh-off-an-unclaimed-corpse tunic. His face was pressed fondly against the dead sheep's shoulders. 'Lad, I hope you washed your hands.'

Rufinianus assured me that the slave had done – or, anyway, he would do now. I sent him with Sheep's remains to Fornix, with instructions that dishes he made for us must be disguised so our boys would not know.

While I had Rufo, I said I had taken on his proffered client. 'That's a very odd woman. She had better pay her

120

bill, or I'll be coming for it from you . . . I'm puzzled about your involvement, though. Tell me again how you know her husband.'

'He goes to the baths.'

'Murrius?'

'Is that him? I am hopeless with names.'

'Oh, Rufo! That must have hindered you, working for the vigiles.'

'Never needed to know. Morellus did all the documentation. Whoever they were, I just jumped up and down on them until they came clean. Though not if it was a young lady reporting she had stabbed a rapist dead, of course.' He kept harping on that.

'Murrius. His wife says he also answers to Gaius – or Infuriating Bastard. Such a rare species! She wants me to investigate any cheating so she can leave. But it's him who is your hot-room crony so I don't understand, Rufo, how you came to send the wife to me. Murrius would hardly say to you while he's plying his sponge on a stick in the toilet, *Oh, my wife wants a divorce. Can you suggest a good informer to help her?* She reckons he is not mad, just chronically annoying.'

'I don't actually know him,' Rufo now confessed. 'I only met the wifey. She once came to the baths trying to find him. A goldsmith had called at the house for payment for jewellery. She was furious because she knew nothing about it.'

'Nephele decided the piece must have been bought for some other woman?'

'Nephele?'

'The *wife*!'

'Oh, right! She thought the bath-house keeper was fibbing

121

when he said her man had left the place. She was causing a commotion. I was fetched to the entrance so I could talk her down. I have a knack with hysterics – they must like my easy manner.' A hysterical woman here was about to bop him, easy manner or not. 'She was so angry about the jewellery she confided in me. I told her I would talk to you because you were extremely discreet and well regarded.'

'I see. She mentioned the goldsmith, but only in passing. Still, it seems I'm stuck with her. So, Rufo, this husband – what about him? Are you telling me you don't even know what he looks like wearing no clothes?'

'Oh, no, Flavia Albia!' piped up Rufo immediately 'You can tell quite a lot from a bath-house companion. Looking at a nude, you can detect his health and his type of behaviour – it's all there. Does he eat or is he a habitual drunk? Are his hands manicured, is his hair cut well, is he fastidious with the strigil? Does he thrash in the pool for real, or toss a beanbag pretending he knows how? Has he brought a slave to the baths and, if so, is it to guard his clothes or to have it off together? Does everyone know him – is he really popular? Can he take all the time he likes, or must he rush off to dodge a creditor, find a contact, attend at his wife's giving birth, finish the argument with his brother that they started twenty years ago—'

'Spare me!' I managed to break in. 'You may have all day to ramble on, Rufinianus, but I need to start finding this quarry. You called him a businessman. What kind? Don't tell me import-export. That's meaningless.'

'Supply and demand,' answered Rufo. 'That's what the baths keeper told me.'

'Juno! Of what? I suppose your useless bath-house fellow calls it "this and that"?'

'I believe he did.'

'Why does no businessman in Rome ever simply say, "I send boots to the army," or "I make bronze cauldrons"?'

'Well,' said Rufo, 'if they did, you'd know all about them. Where's the fun in that?'

20

It was hard to envisage the crowded Aventine as it must once have been. Groves and meadows. Plane trees and the laurels that gave our street its name. The main peak, overlooking the river, offered the best panorama; an outcrop like an arx, since the remote past it had been the hill's primary religious area. Temples overlooked the valley of the Circus Maximus, dominated by Diana Aventina and Minerva, which were side by side. The shrine to Diana was among the most ancient in Rome, first established for nearby Latin towns that Rome had bashed into submission ('agreed alliance with'). Giving the Latin League the Aventine might have been because the hill lay outside the main city perimeter in those days. Up here, the excluded Latin bumpkins could offend no one with their antique language, rural habits or the smells from their alien cooking pots.

Later, all land on the Aventine was decreed public, allowing Rome's plebs to build homes on this hill. That kept them, with their own manners and smells, away from finer spots within the sacred city where the snobbish nobility lived. Finally, there came a further decline due to the Temple of Liberty, where slaves gained their freedom. Their revels were always lively, and at Saturnalia the area became hideous. Troublemakers pulled down their felted freedom caps then roamed about, looking for fights, though since they tended to be too drunk to balance, injuries were mostly slight.

The Temple of Diana stood conveniently close to us, across the road and around a corner from our house. It should have retained some privacy because of its enclosure, formed by two straight double colonnades. But drunks did lie down there for further bleary quaffing during festival periods. Also, those covered walks were an open invitation to men looking for adventure and women who helpfully offered it. All temples in Rome had a sleazy reputation; Diana Aventina was no worse, though no better either. Being the shrine of a famously chaste goddess might even have added piquancy.

For unknown reasons, Diana's temple housed a cult statue that was hewn from a trunk of wood, imported centuries ago from Gaul. Perhaps Gaul has good forests. To cover all eventualities, Diana Aventina possessed a marble one too. Nobody wants to insult a goddess who is armed with arrows. Diana bears grudges badly. Remember Actaeon! The temple contained high-minded plaques such as Rome's ancient treaty with those Latin towns and other historic stuff that had had to be housed somewhere. One snotty inscription told people how to run their own temples of Diana in case, living outside Rome, they had no idea.

The building itself gave a nod to its legendary forerunner, the Temple of Artemis in Greece, which is one of the Seven Wonders of the World. I've seen it. Ours was a high-standard, cloud-touching huge lump too. Anything Greeks can do, Rome will attempt. Approached by steep steps, our temple also had a double octastyle porch in front, plus further columns lining the sides. I guessed a loose woman would not station herself on the steps. Too obvious: she was more likely to be strolling in one of the colonnades. While she looked for flirty, dirty company, she could act as if she was there for religious purposes. Mind you, anyone who really comes for a sacrifice hurries up to do their business with the priests, then scuttles off in relief that buying off the divinity is sorted.

I arrived at the temple in thoughtful mode. I had been held up by watching a fight between a pastry-seller and a cake-tray man. I did ask a fellow pedestrian whether this was about disputed sales territory, but she said they always did it. As a special Saturnalian outburst? No, all the time. They just hated each other.

Once the men had acquired bloody noses and scattered patisserie around, I moved along. I had brought Suza. She picked up a custard that was hardly bruised. She offered me half, but I had eaten enough road grit in my life.

Suza brought me little advantage as a chaperone. I can handle dames who enjoy inviting other people's husbands home to lunch. You have to avoid interrogating them around midday, which by definition is their busy time. But Suza was curious to meet a woman with that reputation so I let her come too.

I had been right. Several speculative females were wandering through the colonnades, pretending to study architecture. Naturally, none were sketching capitals.

The one I broached looked sympathetic when I asked if Laetilla was here. 'Feeling the pinch? I can fix you up if you like.' That surprised me. I could see Suza wondering if it was exotic sexual patois.

I was not expecting the offer of a loan. True, Tiberius was struggling to pay for our courtyard fountain, and the fishmonger's bill was overdue. Fornix had bamboozled the fish man on the promise of a big holiday order, while our waterworks was the kind of installation where the architect expects to wait for his fees for many months – in our case, because the irritating shyster had pressured us into an unintended project.

This woman thought I had secretly overspent on dress pins. 'Little bit on account to keep you afloat, so the man at home never finds out?'

'Thanks, I'm all right at the moment, though I'll bear it in mind. I need Laetilla; I've brought a message from a friend.'

Even though 'message from a friend' is ever a frank lie, Laetilla was pointed out to me with no rancour.

To look at, she was as expected: surface refinement, with all the usual hints that she could be extremely unrefined at will. She would never have been so obvious as to cut open her tunic side seams – it was winter, after all. I could have prophesied the rest. Dollops of eyelash soot. Too much visible bosom, with an intriguing mole. Looping stole droop. Many neckchains. '*An ankle bracelet!*' Suza sniffed. She came from the coast but had quickly taught herself city standards.

I wondered why the men were fooled. Perhaps Laetilla could speak five languages and discuss poetic imagery. Perhaps when someone joined her for lunch at her house, her chef served up the most fabulous tripe with fennel cream sauce.

I never even managed to ask her anything.

'Unless you've come to pay a debt, piss off!' she snarled.

21

Her accent was backstreet Roman, with added-on prissy vowels. Nothing unexpected there.

Being rejected is a hazard of my trade. The first time, a novice informer may be taken aback. Best to resist the innocent urge to argue. Hard-bitten practitioners know that while you are approaching witnesses they will see at once that you are law-and-order, or the next best thing. Clamming up follows.

'Can we talk about Gaius Murrius?' I countered.

'I said, push off.'

I stood my ground. 'No, you were one degree less ladylike, though I forgive you. Nobody likes to be accosted by a stranger in the quiet surroundings of a temple, do they? I am always impressed to come upon someone who is reverential to the gods. Just tell me what I need to know, Laetilla, then I can leave you contemplating.'

This woman hardly gave the impression she spent her life attracting men, even though she came supplied with sparkly chains she might have acquired as presents. Her attitude to me was what it must always be: blunt, nasty and belligerent. This ruins your attraction, as I knew well. Men can be captivated by flattery, by gifts of multi-tools, or by promises of athletic sex, but they cannot stand bad temper.

She made no answer, walking away fast. Her shoes had high wooden platform soles, but she was so used to them she never faltered. I would have toppled and broken an ankle.

Suza was keenly watching how Laetilla kept upright, which she did with strong deployment of her muscle core. My maid (in flat, round-toe ankle boots) made a more ungainly rush after her. 'There is no need to be rude to my mistress!' One reason I was leery of bringing Suza out with me was that she had a habit of butting in. I (in laced leather with decorative cut-outs) produced a half-hearted run, then slowed and signalled for Suza to give up too.

Reluctantly, my girl came back to me. She had yet to learn patience – though she was surprisingly observant. When I happened to comment that Laetilla's get-up told us what kind of woman she must be, Suza replied, 'No, it's only her style.' I let her down stylistically, but she was always yearning to find high fashion elsewhere and itemising strangers' colours, gestures and accessories.

'Really?' I sneered. 'The open cloak to show her neck, the thumping gold chain set? She's a type, Suza. I expect in warmer weather she always has one sleeve brooch missing, so her slinky gown keeps slipping off her bare shoulder . . .'

Suza shook her head stubbornly. 'Yes, but pulling up her sleeve all the time with a graceful hand is her mannerism.'

'That's a long word!' Suza was collecting vocabulary. This was to ornament her when she found a better mistress than me. '*Idiosyncrasy*,' I suggested. 'Or *trait* is a good monosyllable.'

No one would think we had hooked Suza out of a shell-fish factory only a few weeks ago. Tiberius and I tossed her new words as if giving titbits to the dog; she was turning herself into a walking dictionary. 'She just loves shoes, Albia. Anyway, I meant I don't think she was trying for men.'

'I agree.' I backed off the argument happily enough. 'Well spotted. And that is not what we were expecting, which is interesting, Suza.'

I looked around for the woman I had spoken to earlier. Of course she had vanished. We two were alone in the colonnade. I had not noticed everyone leaving. Was it a coincidence, or had they slithered away because of my confrontation with Laetilla? (Coincidence: *accident, fortuity,* or stamp it out with monosyllables, *twist of Fate,* Suza.)

A cold wind rattled up the arcade, pushing dry leaves ahead of it. Although they rustled and scuttled like scorpions, there had been so much rain that some columns had moss growing on their bases. Occasionally puddles hung around where the stone flags underfoot needed maintenance. We started to walk home.

'What do you think, then?' asked Suza, chummily. 'What's her game, Albia?'

'Two choices. One: Laetilla was rude to us simply because we are not men. If a togate toad like Murrius arrives, looking for a light lunch and a groin-thrill, she will turn on more charm. Or two: my client is completely wrong about him and Murrius has plain fallen into debt. He will be in worse trouble if he borrows. That's a temporary fix. I think Laetilla is not his lover, she is his money-lender.'

'She could be both,' Suza suggested excitedly.

'If he is good-looking, maybe. Normally loan sharks prefer to stick with business. They don't want their dealings complicated by personal involvement.'

'She seemed a bit snap-happy to be attracted by good looks!' Suza reckoned.

'Or perhaps he merrily chats her up with sparkling wit and repartee.'

'Would *you* give a loan to someone because of his jokes, Albia?'

'Hell, no.' Hell, yes, I would! 'But Laetilla may be sick of whingers pleading at her. "*I'm in such trouble, it was not my fault, I don't know what I'm going to do, they won't give me any more time to pay, I'm thinking I'll jump in the Tiber and drown myself. Oh, Laetilla, you have to help me!*" After that, a man with a crackling silver tongue may be exactly the light entertainment she needs. She's desperate for relief from turgid misery. Given a wisecrack that makes her laugh, she may even hand out twice as much cash, with cheaper interest and longer credit.'

'You are inventing,' replied Suza, stubbornly. 'You have no evidence for this picture, Albia.'

I growled. The trouble with my growing household was that more people were there to criticise. 'Stop asking me, then. Talking over a case with you is worse than discussing it with a husband.'

Suza looked worried. 'That sounds like you have had more than one.'

'I was married once before.' We were very young; he was an ex-soldier; we had plenty of interaction – though not much of it was talk.

'Does Tiberius Manlius know?' demanded Suza, protectively. She seemed to believe he was a really good man, married to a really dangerous wife.

'It's no secret, Suza.'

'Definitely?'

'Of course he knows. We both had partners long ago.'

'Oh, he was married to that woman Laia!' Suza remembered, losing her anxiety.

'Yes. That woman.' Bloody Laia. The skinny temple-devotee, who had deviously dumped Sheep on us.

One thing I liked a lot about Tiberius, a fact he had honestly told me quite early on in our history, was that he had had the good taste to thunderously cheat on Laia.

22

Back at home, my husband was now missing, though not out cheating on me. 'Sudden site-call from the vigiles,' whistled Larcius the foreman, toothlessly. 'Dead body found.'

Since Tiberius had had to leave, while Larcius and the apprentice were still up on a trestle madly laying bricks, Fornix the cook was now mixing their mortar.

'Dromo was here. Couldn't he have helped with that?'

'He decided he ought to play escort with the master.'

'He must have guessed you had a job for him, Larcius.'

'This is nothing,' Fornix assured me. 'Like stirring a sauce with a huge spurtle. I've got the muscles. Anyone who has put in years with a pestle and mortar can spade together hydraulic lime and aggregate.'

He sounded as though he had done time on building sites. The big fellow was wrapped in his second-best apron, with his sleeves rolled up, as he really put his back into it. He was happy, so were the builders. They ought to be. When your bonding material is mingled by a celebrity chef, it will have a silken consistency, with no lumps of dry sand.

I was assembling a cluster of talented staff. It was Fornix, too, who was teaching us all to look after the new donkey ('Always approach her from the side, say her name so she feels she has friends, and wipe her down when you take the bridle off in case the leather chafes.') Gratus had wide domestic knowledge, plus a cynically varied repertoire to suit all types of visitor. Rodan could simply keep any visitor out by not answering the door. Glaphyra wiped noses, bottoms, tears or smears left on door-handles by sticky little fingers. Paris and Suza helped me. Even Dromo had his speciality: knowing the difference between the fillings in all the cakes sold at the baths.

'A dead body, Larcius? Anyone say whose cadaver?'

The messenger had been mysterious. Trust the vigiles. Unless a corpse was so important their tribune poked his nose in, death was a game to them: plucking a body off the pavement or out of the river, while helping themselves to any small change left on the corpse. This time, though, someone thought it would interest Tiberius: Morellus, no doubt. I might have to wait some time to hear about it. I decided to have my lunch.

Only well-scraped dishes remained when Tiberius came home, trailed by a disconsolate Dromo. I had even brought the builders in to eat with us, which seemed fair after they were pulled off their holiday break. Gaius and Lucius had shown us their latest trick, learned from the Morelli that morning, which involved goggling their real eyes so horribly they bulged like fake ones. Glaphyra started teaching them that the words 'That's enough of that now' could actually mean it.

Once Lucius, who lacked his elder brother's social savvy, had nevertheless shown the eyes trick to their uncle, the boys were removed. Glaphyra thought children deserved breaks from adult company. I took Tiberius to a private space, bringing a food bowl I had reserved for him.

'What about me, then?' came a sad call after us.

'It's all gone. You'll have to wait until dinner, Dromo.'

Dromo started complaining, but Glaphyra leaned over from the balcony to say that that would be enough of that too.

Dromo called her a rude word. *Cringe!*

My discussion with Tiberius stalled, while he explained to Dromo how there was to be no swearing at other staff, or else some slave boy's next job would be cleaning dead bodies' orifices for a second-rate embalmer who wouldn't provide any lamb's wool to perform the job but made assistants use their fingers . . .

It was rare for his master to discipline Dromo. I was impressed. Dromo soon managed to recover.

There are times when a wise wife sits quiet and lets her man eat his food.

If Tiberius ever lost his temper, I knew something disastrous had happened. I let him finish morosely chewing, then I tidied away his bowl, spoon and napkin, leaving them on a side-table outside the room, where Gratus would ensure they were silently collected. I sat beside Tiberius on a couch. I took his hand. I waited.

Eventually, he shook away my hand, but only to lean on the couch back with his arm around me. He pressed his head against mine, breathing slowly, taking comfort. It was safe to ask what had happened. He groaned. He told me the nut-war had been whipped up to a new level, then described the call-out. It had been shocking.

The scene-of-crime was a warehouse. A body had been discovered by a wholesaler who hired space there. The dead man was crammed into a sack. This had originally contained walnuts, which until recently were being sold by one of the traditional hawkers, acting for the wholesaler – who opened the oddly bulging sack and recognised his man.

135

This dead street-seller had doggedly refused to change. He declined to buy from the newcomers and stuck with his old supplier. Now he had been left with his limbs folded up, like a linen serviette, then tied in place with extremely tight twine. Morellus believed that while that had happened to him he was still alive. He must have realised what his final fate would be. Making him suffer was a sadistic element. The sack had been deposited in a side-room that formed a deep square bin for storing nuts. Walnuts, hazelnuts and cobnuts in heavy quantities had been piled on top, then tamped down, probably by people jumping on them, going by the number that were cracked open.

'Morellus reckoned the man had been there for three days. At some point he suffocated.'

'Bad smell?'

'Whole bad scene.'

'Dare I ask, love, did the warehouse belong to your brother-in-law?'

'No. Not him, nor Uncle Tullius, thankfully. Another small operator, a slightly disorganised absentee owner. His site-manager should have been vigilant – the whole point of warehouses is to be secure, and constantly monitored – but *he* is suffering from a bad heart, not doing his job well. When the vigiles fetched him and he saw what had happened, I thought he would drop dead from shock.'

'Could the manager tell you anything useful?' I asked.

'Not really. His regime is relaxed, to put it mildly. He admits he sometimes looked the other way if a vagrant was sheltering in a colonnade, but of course that was allegedly rare and only done out of charity during bad weather.'

'Could a rough sleeper have committed this murder?'

'No. It's plainly part of the nut-wars.'

'It's a complication, though,' I warned. 'If you ever catch the real perpetrators, they could claim a vagrant was to blame.'

'I'd like to find him anyway,' Tiberius said. 'He may be a witness.'

'You speak as if there was a special regular?'

'Yes, one frequent visitor was described to me – though he sounds feeble, a wafting character, with no flesh on his bones, who melts away if anyone speaks to him. He wouldn't have the strength or courage, let alone a motive.'

'If he saw something happen, he is bound to have run away now,' I said. 'He'll be terrified.'

'I know.' Tiberius was brooding. 'I know, I know.'

'So, back to the building manager. Does he have any ideas?'

'He reckons the killers broke in. Obvious conclusion! He cannot have been supervising on any regular basis, but that's a matter for the warehouse owner. If the manager had been going round properly, he might have discovered the intrusion while the poor victim could have been saved.'

'I expect he blames Saturnalia.'

'Indeed. Anyway, the manager knows what he has done, so Morellus isn't pushing the matter. The wholesaler is innocent, of course. Leaving this body in his rental space was a warning for him to get out of town and let the criminals take over. He is utterly distressed that a loyal member of his team has been so savagely punished. They had worked together for twenty years. You can imagine.'

'You and Morellus have spoken to this wholesaler?' I asked. 'Any suggestion who the rivals are?'

'Men in the shadows. He couldn't – or dared not – supply names, though he knows how they operate. Same as happened to my brother-in-law – deals are closed by some shifty lag, who keeps his hat pulled down. No address ever given, details later found out to be fake, paid in cash or never paid at all, operatives vanish from sight after the keys are taken. These new crooks flit in and use space for a very brief time. Their rotten stock appears on the streets, with regular hawkers bullied into taking it. The street hawkers are all too scared to say who they have been made to buy their stock from.'

'Don't warehouse owners ever ask for references from customers they don't know?'

Tiberius gave a dry laugh. 'Rarely. Tullius claims he can smell a wrong 'un. He says, if a tenant is going to cheat on him, they will provide fake refs in any case. He builds in slack to cover occasional mistakes. Besides,' admitted Tiberius, wryly, 'I think Tullius, charming though he is, has a reputation for dealing with it, if anything goes bad on him. I've seen the accounts, remember. Marked absence of defaulters!'

I would not have called Tullius Icilius charming. He had never charmed me. Tiberius and his uncle were quite different characters, although they co-existed in curious harmony. I hoped the same would happen eventually with Tiberius and his own nephews.

'So,' I pondered, 'the dead man is a street-seller who dared to stand up to bullying.'

'Yes. Suffocating him is intended to dampen resistance elsewhere. As it undoubtedly will.'

'You can't blame people, love. Who wants to be killed in a trade dispute? And now,' I summed up, 'you'll have the usual questions. Did any witnesses see when or how the victim was taken to the site? Did he go willingly to meet someone, or was he kidnapped?'

Tiberius sighed. 'Morellus thinks anyone who saw what happened will go to ground in terror. He has troops out combing the neighbourhood nevertheless, stopping people in the street, knocking on doors.'

'Waste of time.' I pre-judged it. 'So, what next, love?'

Tiberius shifted against me on the couch. 'I shall engage with it in the way you would. I'll find out if the dead man had any family or friends, then interview them myself in a different style from whatever they expect from the vigiles. Someone should know when he first disappeared, what he was doing beforehand, whom he might have met on that occasion, where he might have been snatched and who took him.'

'Need any help?' I asked hopefully.

But he shook his head. 'Better not go in mob-handed. I want to approach people quietly, trying to win trust. The intelligent method you use, Albia: show understanding, promise no harm will come to them if they talk to me, sweet-talk them.' I pulled a face. I never classify sweetness as a tool of mine. 'Anyway,' he tried to deflect me, 'you must be fully occupied with that man who visits the bawd from Diana Aventina.'

Accepting the distraction technique, I explained that she looked like a loan shark, not a bawd. 'When you are next nuzzling up to your crony, you might ask Morellus whether he has a note of where Laetilla lives.' Usury was illegal, at least at the interest rates a shark would demand. The vigiles ought to have such a woman in their records.

'Of course. Anything you need, my darling.' This was a blatant put-off.

Tiberius did remind me that one tradition of Saturnalia is that the law against public gambling was suspended. My quarry might be addicted to dice; this could be the time of year when he went overboard with debts. Oh, joy! If I wanted to spy on Gaius Murrius, I would have to search for him among the inebriates who quarrelled over Soldiers and Twelve Lines in disreputable bars. I grumbled that I must remember to borrow my sister Favonia's beaker and weighted dice to give me cover.

Tiberius corrected me: gamblers would never choose to play Duodecim Scripta. If they wanted a race-and-strategy game, they would prefer Tabula, which was much faster.

Almost the first time I noticed this husband of mine, he was outside a wine bar with their draughts board in front of him. On that occasion, I now believed, the only strategy in play was a hope of seeing me pass by. As I went about my business locally, I had caught his eye. The draughts board was bluff.

Even so, he seemed to have a striking knowledge of games. This is something any wife should be aware of.

As a magistrate, Tiberius Manlius always seemed very straight, but I liked to think there was a rapscallion underneath. A man with a past is less likely to feel that life has eluded him, and be more able to resist sudden urges towards excitement.

Perhaps Nephele's husband used to lead a boring life. Perhaps his trouble now was a middle-aged yearning to explore all the wickedness he felt he had missed. So, when he gamed, was he stupid? Was he being conned? Had too much Tabula against better players, probably swindlers who kept raising the stakes, kept him away from home and drawn him into debt with Laetilla?

If so, it made me despondent. I knew there would be little hope of Nephele reforming Murrius. Divorcing him might be her only escape – though my chance of fees might trickle down the drain along with his debts.

23

In early evening, when losers would start coming out to play, I set off to track down Murrius. We still had two days before the big Saturnalia feast. Of course, if this was Moon Day, with Mars and Mercury before the festival started on Jove's Day, it would probably be called three days by inclusive Roman date counting. Such craziness reverts me into a stroppy barbarian: we had two working days by my system.

When I set out at twilight, the atmosphere was already lively. In some ways most riots occurred publicly in the festival run-up; once the official holiday started, people would be trapped at home. Now, in anticipation of being stuck with their families for five grim days, men in particular were out on the loose. There were women too, and those women were intent on having a high old time. Both species were loud, though the girls tended to scream and totter more.

I called the Vicus Armilustri our Street of Shame. It was a long, straight route across the top of the hill, easily used for an evening saunter or stops at the many drinks outlets; they were mainly guarded by bare-armed bouncers, some in colourful ethnic costume (rarely the costume of their home province). Paraded along the street were eye-watering party clothes. Most revellers had no idea of matching their dress to their maturity or status. The young threw themselves into shocking behaviour. The old had skin like dried leather and the dead eyes of habitual drinkers. The middle-aged men were looking around, wondering where all the good parties were and whether they could shed their wives, while their women, in silly shoes that hurt their feet, gradually realised they should not have come, as they wished that they lived with better men. Once in a while we would hear next day that someone had been fatally stabbed or a young girl dragged down an alley and viciously raped.

If this was the normal beat of Gaius Murrius, it need not brand him as seedy. Ordinary people walked down the Vicus Armilustri for genuine reasons. We kept up the pretence that for locals it was harmless. We just made sure we walked carefully to avoid being bashed into. We never showed fear. Or stared. Or giggled openly. We never made eye contact.

I had looked through the notes Nephele had written for me. She had named a couple of wine bars Gaius Murrius liked: the Ephesian and the Syracusan. I knew them; they would not have been my choice for meeting friends. In these, customers could go inside to sit down at rough tables, but the prices were twice as much as at street-side stand-ups. The snacks might be more sophisticated (that is, smaller), but the wine would be the same.

I took Paris. He brought knucklebones. Neither establishment we visited viewed this well; they wanted us to use their gaming boards, for which an addition would appear like magic on the bill. Neither was pleased to see us at all, really. One place decided I was a straying wife and Paris must be my honey-boy. The other thought Paris was there to lift purses, using me as his glamorous decoy. Not glamorous enough, Suza would have said.

I was reluctant to ask if they had a customer called Murrius because if he was a regular they were bound to tell him. That would put him on the alert. Instead, at both bars we listened in to other people, straining to pick up names, eventually deciding he was not among the groups around us. Although Nephele had implied she had told me everything I could need, her details about him were witness banalities: he was of normal height, with dark hair, brown eyes, no marks, nothing remarkable. Rome's inhabitants must number a million, half of them male, most fitting that description.

'This is hopeless. What now?' asked Paris. 'Do we keep coming every day until we strike lucky?'

'I don't think so,' I mused, feeling bored by failure. 'No, I reckon the Ephesian and Syracusan are places Murrius tells his wife he goes to. Is he being sneaky, though? What we want is the favourite bar that he never mentions to Nephele – the one he really calls home.'

'He's probably sitting in it right now!' Paris agreed glumly.

The slippery one might be fooling his wife, but I still had ways to track him down. We gave up for that evening. Tomorrow would be another day.

We came home to a strangely quiet house. Glaphyra had successfully put the boys to bed. Bliss. Well, a short-lived respite. They heard our voices, eluded her and came scampering down to see us while Tiberius and I were talking, but they sat with us quietly and we said they could stay. Tiberius was touched that they wanted to be with us; I thought they were simply playing up, but I let it happen. Soon they became drowsy; we carried them up to their beds again.

Next morning Nephele called on me for a report, as I had instructed. I hid. Even if things had been going well, it would have been too soon.

Suza was to tell her I was working on the case and see her off, while Paris, whom Nephele had not so far encountered, was to follow her. Even if she dawdled on other errands, he had to stick with her. Once he discovered Nephele's home address, he would park himself nearby until at some point the husband emerged. Then he would change over and tail the husband.

To our surprise, this proved unworkable, for a curious reason. My runabout did what was needed. Nephele called on a friend in Dolichenus Street, went shopping, had a pedicure, but with her fondness for the ritual of lunch at home, home she eventually went. Paris identified her house in Greater Laurel Street as we had planned. Straight away he realised this was no use. After a few checks with neighbours, he came home to tell me: 'That house is not going to give up Murrius. You and I have been there, Albia. Murrius is no longer allowed in. You and I saw her chuck him out the other day. It's the place with the parrot.'

24

I had stopped caring who had custody of that parrot. If it had any sense it would fly away from both of them and make a nest in the plane tree grove.

I blame the face pack. No wonder I had not recognised her. Whether it was home-made bean-meal, standard Egyptian clay, or some pricey turmeric-and-frankincense goo she obtained on special order from Silk Road importers, when Nephele was pampering her skin prior to screaming out of a window at her husband, only her eyes showed. Anyway, we had only glimpsed her.

'Good excuse!' grinned Paris.

'Not one I've ever used before,' I commented wryly.

I could see it would be an unlikely coincidence if there were two suspicious wives on the same street, whose husbands were both wandering off for lunch elsewhere. Mind you, being cynical, behind Greater Laurel Street's veneer of respectability, it wasn't unlikely and there could even be more culprits. We were very close to the Temple of Diana, which Laetilla patrolled, and it has been known for a single predator to run through all the susceptible idiots in a neighbourhood. For one thing, the men tell each other where to find her.

'At least if we see him, we'll know him now,' I said. 'No

one can miss his trashy shoes, or the dodgy look in his eye. But, Paris, has Nephele permanently locked him out?'

Paris looked troubled. 'Now that was strange, Albia. I couldn't tell. I did my best. None of the neighbours were keen to talk.'

'Weird! Usually a few people are discreet, but most are thrilled to gossip about a scandal. Especially when it's fresh – and we do know their marital upset erupted only three days ago. What do the locals say, Paris?'

'One person thought they had seen him around, apparently same as normal. Then a shopkeeper reckoned they hadn't set eyes on him lately. Another person said he might be staying with his brother. But when I asked where this brother lives, they shut their trap and rushed away.'

'We do know he has a nasty brother,' I told Paris. 'Maybe this brother lives nearby, which explains why there has been a sighting of Murrius. I'm not going to waste time on that, in case it's just a theory. If we really get stuck,' I suggested, 'we'll use the trick of sending someone fresh to knock on the door of the house we do know and ask for him.'

'Suppose he's not there?'

'Here's where we try to find out, Paris. Our messenger will say he has a message for the master but cannot repeat it to anybody else. If Murrius does respond, the knocker-boy pretends he is from Laetilla, who needs to see Murrius urgently. You follow him, Paris, then we discover *her* address. But if they say Murrius is not at home, the knocker just runs away, like a neighbourhood menace.'

Paris was impressed. 'Good game!'

'Yes, but I can only do it when I have a team. My father used to be all right: he had so many scruffy little nieces and nephews he could always find a messenger with a clean face. Well, a grimy face with fish-pickle sauce all around its foul mouth, but someone new to the recipients.'

Paris was fired up to experiment. He spent the afternoon coaching Dromo, who was to knock on the door. To me, that was bound to go wrong. But the wife had failed to win me over, so I was losing interest. I didn't care enough to stop them.

I said there was no point attempting the trick around midday. The main complaint about Murrius was that he stayed out when his wife wanted him back for lunch. Ideally, Paris should have waited until next morning, but he was too impatient. He and Dromo went off at what Paris thought was the time before dinner when a man-about-town might go out to the baths if he was living at home.

Hopeful, they hung around in Greater Laurel Street, but no one emerged. The Murrius house stood on a corner beside a narrow entry called Cowrie Court, so Paris worried there might be a side entrance. He walked around the corner to look. He found no discreet door for tradesmen, only the next house along the lane. The size and painted columns on its formal porch advertised neighbours with status.

Paris stayed long enough to see this significant house had a variety of people coming and going. There were so many callers, it was either a brothel or an after-hours meeting place. He even went into a couch shop to ask about the residents, but a shifty assistant pretended to be busy, which they never are, and claimed not to know. I said upholstery is always a dead-end source. 'With fringes on it.'

Paris decided the house in Cowrie Court was too discreet to be a brothel, since no one thinks twice about such places and, anyway, brothels need to be visible to attract customers.

It must be the secret haunt of a trade guild or a dodgy religion.

The lads plucked up courage for their real task. Dromo sidled over to knock at the Murrius door. He was rejected by an aggressive porter. Surprise! That's why people have them. Even Rodan would see Dromo off, if he didn't know Dromo lived with us.

Paris and Dromo hung about, discussing what to do. While they were still loitering, a small group of large toughs appeared from Cowrie Court and surrounded them. Unsmiling men suggested they were casing the Murrius house for burglary and should immediately leave. Paris quickly apologised. The men began smiling, which Paris said felt even worse.

Paris and Dromo scuttled back home.

25

Dromo had a swollen eye. This had nothing to do with being seen off from Greater Laurel Street: revellers had been throwing nuts. When he turned to see who, he copped for it hard. That might only have bruised him, but he rubbed his eye with a grimy fist. Now it was bloodshot and watering. I told him to wash out the dirt, but he took no notice.

I wanted to know more about the incident with the threatening men. 'Who were you bounced by? Did a nervous householder summon the Urban Cohorts, thinking you were suspicious characters? Who could blame them, by the way?'

'No.' Paris was grumpy. New to this work, he had yet to learn how to weather setbacks. 'No one military.'

'Well, I suppose that's a relief. Were you followed back here afterwards?'

'Probably not. I thought it best just to put my head down and scarper.'

'I had a look, I didn't see why not,' Dromo breezed, too gormless to appreciate the danger. 'They all just stood on the spot and watched us.'

'What were they like, Paris?'

'Very tough household security – long tunics, heavily bunched over wide belts with big buckles. Boots you wouldn't want a kicking from. Athletes' strapping for show, on various arms and shins.'

That could have been my father and Uncle Lucius, spruced up in their favourite gear to go out on a tour of welcoming bars. 'Proper athletes? Gladiators?'

'Sham. But they looked scary.'

'Liberty caps?'

'Bare heads. Very short haircuts.'

'Sharp snipping? Playboy-style?'

'Arena followers. "Shave it close and skip the lotions, barber." Pimply chins.'

'Ugh. So, this barber of theirs skimps on hygiene! Cloaks?'

'No cloaks. All too hard, no fear of the cold. No fear of any damned thing, we could tell. Coordinated,' Paris listed. 'Same expressions. Menace. It was assumed we would not argue.'

'I follow. Jewellery?'

'Knuckle-rings the size of figs. One had an amulet depicting a skull.'

'A lot of bad scars,' Dromo put in, though he had appeared not to be listening.

'Like old soldiers, Dromo?'

'No, like brutes who had been in many knife-fights,' Paris spelled out. 'You know that saying, "You should have seen the other one"? They hadn't come from Nephele's house but someone there opened the shutter and called out, "Get rid of them, will you?" or something. One raised an arm, to signify obeying orders.'

'Woman's voice?'

'Male. Youngish.'

'Not Murrius, then. And what did you think these men were?'

'Villains.'

It was bad news. Even Dromo was quieter than normal, while Paris had been shaken up. He must have had confrontations before, but not in this class. It was only recently that he had witnessed a violent home invasion, in which his old master was murdered. Although his character was steady, he still suffered from anxiety. He tried to conceal it, but I knew. I said quietly that I was sorry I had let the pair of them go out like that.

'We wanted to go,' the runabout assured me.

'Yes, and now you don't want to do it again, Paris! I won't allow it.' This, I hoped, offered reassurance. There was no point pretending that working on my cases would involve genteel secretarial tasks or watching mild-mannered witnesses from elegant colonnades. Closer supervision was needed. And when there seemed to be a threat, I must take it on myself.

Later that evening, while Tiberius was still out following up the warehouse murder, a visitor came for him. 'It's that man who sells the statues,' Rodan announced. 'You had better want to see him, because I've let him in and said I'd tell you.'

Mental jot: training needed. Further comment: you'll get nowhere. Final note: tell Gratus this is his job!

Agemathus shambled in, though this time he had felt no need to bring his brother as back-up. The evening was not too cold; our boys were on hands and knees in the courtyard, playing marbles. They had brought Merky in from her stable to watch. 'She's keeping score!' She was eating my pergola climbers.

I spoke to the *sigillaria*-seller there in the open. He wanted to ask about payment for information he might supply to Tiberius and Morellus.

'Vigiles standard rates,' I said inventively – I had no idea. Any handout would be pitiful, that was sure; the vigiles have no real funds. Agemathus seemed satisfied, however. 'What do you have for them, Agemathus? Tell me now you're here. I work with them a lot. I will pass it on.'

The tall African wriggled his thin shoulders shyly. His manner was quiet. He was smiling, which he did most of the time; it meant nothing significant.

He had seen a man threatening the nut-sellers. After that body was found in the warehouse, others had started muttering together that they refused to be cowed. One had jeered at an agent who came from the new supplier, trying to recruit him. The defiant hawker refused his stock, turned his back, then walked off.

'What did the agent do?'

'Oh, he just stood there looking mean.'

'There was no violence?'

Agemathus shook his head slowly. 'The nut-seller was fired up and ready for a fight. He knew how the other one was murdered. He knew that man. He was grieving for his comrade and ready to hand out punishment. The agent let him go.'

'I am glad the seller avoided trouble, but I hope it lasts. Is he known to you, Agemathus?'

'Rosius.'

'Well, Rosius defying the new supplier could have repercussions. These people are very dangerous. Tell me, has there been any attempt to lean on you, Agemathus, to change where you obtain your *sigillaria*? I presume you get your statuettes from someone who actually makes them. Has there been anything different this year?'

He smiled at me gently again. '*Nooo.*'

'Any idea why not?'

Perhaps he writhed uncomfortably. 'The *sigillaria* come to us from the Campus Martius.' It made sense that the Campus, which I had seen crammed with stalls, would also act as the central distribution point for outlying districts. Night-time on the Campus would be hectic with wagons bringing in Saturnalia toys and trinkets, plus nuts, which runners would then carry to the hawkers, ready to flood Rome with them next day. Agemathus added, 'The producers who bring the little statues to Rome are big men, very strong and sure.'

'They've been doing it long enough! I suspect nobody would enjoy trying to weasel into their cartel. Tell me, have they always been good to you?'

'Not very good. But they need us to sell the little men. We argue, they argue back at us, but they give us figurines and we give them money, and this year it is the same as always.'

'You're saying the new suppliers won't try shoving them aside? They are afraid to upset your traditional source?'

'Those new ones will come after us one day.' This sense of foreboding explained why Agemathus wanted to see Tiberius and Morellus. 'Rosius has told me who the agent is: a newcomer, a very bad man. His name is Greius.'

I promised to pass on the details. I asked for a description, but all he would say again was 'Bad! Very bad!'

26

When Tiberius arrived home, he managed to avoid discussing whatever he and Morellus had been doing. Refusing to be petty, I passed on the Agemathus message nevertheless. Tiberius wrote 'Greius' in his note-tablet to follow up next day.

'You haven't encountered him?'

'Not crossed our paths.' He pulled a face. 'Yet!'

He did reveal that while he was out, he had dropped in on his uncle. Tullius was preening himself that he had bought hugely expensive toys to give to the boys for Saturnalia.

'He would not say what,' Tiberius groaned, 'but I know he raided the Emporium. The presents must be frights, something the children will adore but we shall loathe – he admits it. After scouring imports from all over the Empire, Uncle Tullius has grabbed the biggest, loudest, newest toys he could find. He will appear with them before we can stop him, crying, "What are rich uncles for, if not to spoil the little dears?" They will think he's wonderful.'

No, I thought, they would be torn, because they already knew he didn't like them. 'Oh dear, if he does this once, they are bound to expect it every year . . .' I winced. 'Is that how he used to treat you?'

'Of course not. I was sixteen when I came to Rome. He only ever asked me what books I would like, then sent out for those.'

'I had the impression he always kept his distance?'

'No, no. He certainly liked to run the business by himself, then as now, but he was always a decent guardian.'

I considered possibilities for presents, bearing in mind what my brother Postumus had chosen for himself when small, before he nagged for herbs and crucibles when he was ten, because he had decided to become a hired poisoner. This year he planned on being a gladiator, so had merely demanded gym lessons (plus exercise equipment, a protective belt, two different helmets, arm padding, leg padding, a shield and a trident; I was buying the trident). 'I bet Tullius has bought miniature soldiers' uniforms, with weapons that could actually kill someone.'

My loved one, a pacific man who had never done army service, shuddered. 'Oh, please not! Remember Caligula. He started his descent into madness being dressed up as a little legionary and toddling around the German camps.'

'Are we bringing up two mad emperors? Perhaps Tullius will think armour's too ordinary. Perhaps he's got a shrieking pet monkey they will be frightened of.'

'Could be. Plenty of exotic animals come into the Emporium. Would a dangerous snake be worse?'

'No problem at all. I know an exotic dancer who would take it off our hands. If it's an animal, I bet it's a crocodile.' I sighed. 'Hey-ho. Better start rehearsing our act: "Oh, darling Uncle Tullius, that is wildly generous. You really shouldn't have!" Then we just have to hope the present dies, or at least breaks.'

'Either can be arranged,' promised my calm, tolerant husband in gravelly tones. 'Larcius has left a really big hammer in the tool store.'

Nobody seemed to have noticed us talking quietly together, which was a rare treat. Something about two people enjoying private moments normally drives other people to interrupt.

If possible, I would have withheld what had happened in Greater Laurel Street. I would have plied the old excuse of not worrying Tiberius; that really means you want to avoid being pounced on for some foolish deed. I knew Paris might have the nous to keep quiet, but Dromo had no such sensitivity so I owned up sweetly.

Tiberius Manlius gave me the shrewd grey-eyed look he normally kept for persons who were using doctored weights in markets. 'I am surprised at you!'

'Why, darling?'

'For not keeping this mad adventure to yourself!'

I feigned amazement. 'Who, me? We are married. There ought to be absolute trust between us – and there is.'

'Thank you, sweetheart.' Since he had made his point, he subsided. Instead he pensively proffered a theory as dark as any I would hold: 'Have you noticed that when people bleat on about all parties sharing trust, it really means there is bitter suspicion between them?'

'Generally deserved,' I answered, thinking of many clients.

'Yes, it usually means severe doubt is already there. Besides, if you really trust someone, there is no need ever to mention it.'

I chuckled. 'I think a carefully composed contract with multiple clauses will cover most failings.'

'The secret about contracts,' Tiberius disagreed, 'is that

while everything is working, no contract is needed. If things go wrong, no contract in the world will solve it.'

'Like marriage! Fortunately,' I suggested, 'you and I have a true Roman pact: no written terms. I agree to live with you. You agree the same with me.'

My husband fell silent. 'So – do you trust me?' he then demanded suddenly.

'I do.' Fact. I never even had to think about all the times he had already saved me from desperate trouble. 'Tiberius Manlius, that is why I am here with you.'

He thought about this for slightly longer than required, although that was simply his way. 'Me too,' he responded eventually.

This was the kind of awkward conversation where you do wish somebody *would* interrupt. It was all unexpected, though I felt confident it came out of nowhere and no problem was festering.

I sat there with him quietly in the lamplight, considering how firmly I believed Tiberius would never cheat on me in the way he had once betrayed Laia Gratiana. He certainly had no need to find another bed for lovemaking. He was mine for sure.

I do know that every woman who is ever surprised by the break-up of her marriage falls into this trap. The error happens even when everyone around her has seen trouble coming – seen it from the start. I could be making the same mistake, and yet – like all the rest – I convinced myself we were different.

We were. I was right. *He* was right too. Time would prove it.

Sometimes in life you reach a point when all you want is to stop the struggle. We were both ready to be satisfied with what we had and, Hades, what Tiberius and I had together ought to satisfy anyone.

Inevitably I began to contrast that against the unhappy strife experienced by my current client. Tiberius had one last point to make, one that turned out to be relevant: 'I think about you all the time, Albiola. We may be working separately, but I do not forget you. So . . .' Tiberius had a hint of a tease '. . . you asked me whether Morellus knows anything about the woman Laetilla.'

'And he does not,' I prophesied.

'Correct.'

'He should. Trust the vigiles! Never mind. But, Tiberius, after today's incident with Paris I shan't continue working for this client. I only took her on to make you and Morellus think I was leaving you alone.'

'We never asked that!'

'Hah! A typical client will suddenly dump their informer, but as it's Saturnalia, I can reverse the process. I'll cite safety reasons, since those bouncers were so menacing. Nephele may protest that she had told me not to visit her house. But if her husband has been thrown out, why not? And Paris and Dromo thought the men who put frighteners on them had a connection with her home.'

Tiberius pursed his lips, looking downcast. 'I wasted my time, then.'

'What time?'

'Doesn't matter.'

'Stop teasing.'

'No, you don't need to know.'

'I do,' I said, gently enough. 'Never keep secrets from me, Legate! Tiberius, if you know something, tell me for my own satisfaction.'

A broad beam lit his face. 'That's my girl. Well, think about aediles' duties. Public games, markets, streets, baths, taverns – and . . .?'

'Poking your noses into brothels? Capturing dangerous animals?'

'No, no. I corralled one of those, brought her home and married her. Once is enough . . . What else do we do for the community? We stamp out illegal gambling!'

'Killjoys.'

'Forces for good. I said I always think of you. I looked up my past conviction lists.' Given his enthusiasm, it cannot have been easy to wade through so many scrolls. Hardly a stallholder on the Aventine had escaped my husband's scrutiny; there must have been chortles when news flew around that the aedile Faustus had been given a free sheep but bad people stole it. 'Your Murrius was in there. I once imposed a fine on him.'

'You fined my client?' I whooped.

'No, be accurate, girl. I fined her out-on-the-town, rule-flouting, social-nuisance husband. By the way, I do feel your mistake was taking on Nephele. You really should be acting for their tug-of-love parrot.'

'The birdie deserves rescuing. You fined Murrius for gambling?'

'For gambling in a public place. He and his cronies were clearly betting on their game. Gaius Murrius had his elbows on a table in a courtyard at a drinking place, so I could see him from the street.'

'Well, that shows I deduced his vice correctly.'

'You know your craft,' Tiberius flattered me. 'The man is a hopeless dice addict. He would barely pause long enough to reach for his purse and pay me. For a moment I thought it would turn nasty, but he coughed up. That means I, happily, can help you out, love. Murrius drinks at a bar called the Cosmographer. It's off Dolichenus Street – you can easily find it: the sign is a map, though in my opinion they have the two Mauretanian provinces switched around. From memory, that was what caused me to stop by the bar in the first place.'

'Disaster! Misplaced Mauretania Tingitana? Outrageous Caesariensis gaff? That was bound to attract your attention.'

'Too right. I'd have fined the bar-keeper for it, if only I could have brought to mind the right statutory misdemeanour.'

I always liked the way my husband acknowledged that he was pedantic. He dug me in the ribs, grinning with me. He was a lovely man to talk to; it refreshed us both. 'Now you're stuck, aren't you? You had decided to cancel on your client – but I've given you something unignorable. A lead has jumped out and you will never be able to let go.'

I pretended to find a limp excuse. 'You are right. I have to look into this for the parrot's sake,' I murmured.

Io, Saturnalia!

27

This was another thing I liked about my husband: he gave excellent tips.

Even a dedicated gambler was unlikely to start at breakfast, so waiting for tomorrow was no good. Now was the time. I was as bad as Paris.

Aware that I had better not tell anyone or I would be stopped, I pulled on a cloak and slipped out of the house. It had drizzled with rain so the pavements were as slippery as if tiled with fish scales. Watching how I placed my feet, I nevertheless dodged the few active revellers. I found the Cosmographer from the directions Tiberius had given me. I wondered if he had realised all along that I would bunk off.

I stood in the side-street, gazing at the bar's painted wall-sign as if checking up on some remote province where my soldier boyfriend claimed that the army was stationing him. I tried to imagine how a woman would look if she suspected her untrustworthy beau had really been discharged or if he'd absconded, so she felt sure he was living back at home incognito, while fathering children on an asparagus-seller he met at the vegetable market when he was shopping for his elderly mother . . . At least this invention of mine was exhibiting thoughtful and dutiful filial behaviour. I quite liked him.

Gaius Murrius was no figment. I could see him in a

brick-coloured tunic with a black leather belt: long sleeves, neck-and-cuff braid, thumping great buckle. Now that I inspected him, he had an oval face with an unpleasant mouth, receding hair and, if he pulled himself upright, he could not be tall. He was among a seated group playing dice. All old pals, good-humoured and in it together. Theirs was not, as far as I could see, a collection where hardened fleecers were applying dubious pressure to a foolish mark. Murrius was no victim, but one of the boys.

They were a matched set, all with the same style and similar accessories. At the table were, as my father would say, more buffered torques and multi-strand necklaces with dangling coins than you'd find in a tart's jewellery casket. An auctioneer might bundle their flash into a job-lot but potential bidders, ever a canny species, would shake their heads. Modern tat, not even stylish repro. No resale value. Barely good for scrap.

As I watched, a man who stood beside him was nagging at Murrius, who abruptly made a gesture of capitulation, then pulled out his purse and handed over cash. It was counted, they shook hands pleasantly and the creditor left. A standard scene, especially at this time of year. Murrius said something to his mates then stood up. He tossed a few remaining coins into a pottery saucer towards the bill, then shook an empty purse to show there was no point in detaining him. The friends let him go, with cheery goodbyes; they seemed used to him.

He left the bar then walked alone, with a jaunty step for a man who had been publicly cleaned out. He might have had cash at home, packed into big iron-bound chests. Of course I knew Nephele would give him problems getting at it, but this man was showing no anxiety.

I peeled myself away from the bad map, to saunter after him. Leaving the Cosmographer's murky side-street, he cut out through Dolichenus Street, which was no better, into the Armilustri, then hiked along the main road to Greater Laurel Street. He spoke to no one; nobody hailed him. At what I knew to be his house, he thundered on the door, then yelled to be admitted. The upper window flew open as before. From deep within, Nephele's voice shouted at him to get lost.

'Let me in! Open up for me, you skanky bitch!'

His wife did not bother to answer. Before shutters slammed to, I heard their parrot squawk. The bird had learned to mimic 'Skanky bitch!' Hardened to that, Nephele cooed, 'Naughty, naughty!' clearly to annoy her husband.

Murrius seemed to expect rejection. Perhaps he had yelled as a matter of principle. He was ready to move on somewhere else, though he glanced up and down the street, as if embarrassed for anyone to hear him having this fruitless exchange with his wife. He looked my way. I had to sidle quickly in front of a shop, like a time-waster eyeing the stock. Fortunately, the hole-in-the-wall sold footwear; my charade would look feasible. I spent rather too long inspecting a pair of looped sandals with tiny flowers on their big-toe straps. When I turned around again, Murrius had vanished.

I nipped along to look down Cowrie Court around the corner, where he was not to be seen either; no other side-turnings were near enough. Could he have gone in somewhere?

I might have cursed but saw no need to waste my efforts. I went back, sat on the fitting bench and tried on those sandals. Always make surveillance useful.

I was acquiring my parcel when Murrius reappeared

unexpectedly, apparently from Cowrie Court. I wondered if that was where his brother lived. It made sense: families often snuggled side by side. Murrius had picked up a couple of retainers; the large, swaggering, acned characters fitted the description of the men who had bounced Paris and Dromo. I carried on paying the shoe-seller while they passed; they took no notice of me. Sometimes you win on the hazard, Gaius Murrius!

I followed discreetly. One of the bouncer types was carrying a number of flat satchels over a shoulder, obviously empty. I tailed them across the Thirteenth into the Twelfth District, to the edge of the hill, overlooking the Circus. They went to a house near the Temple of Mercury. Murrius knocked, a fairly relaxed summons this time. No yelling. A woman came to the door. It must have been a pleasure for him to be greeted without insults, then to be invited in. Though I had to keep my distance, I was sure his obliging hostess was Laetilla.

I stared at the closed door, thinking this was a dangerous way to spend an evening. The Aventine was growing darker, while its revellers were increasingly looking for trouble. Chasing women happens a lot at Saturnalia. To be out alone is asking for it. The south-eastern slope was not my area either. Here I could only identify Mercury's Temple. Its three steps led to a portico where flat-backed herms supported an architrave picturing the trickster god's animal attributes; I remembered a serpent and a fox, but there might also have been a parrot.

Laetilla's street was normal and residential: pottery shops, smelly fish stalls and ladies who gave lunch to friends. I had no desire to hang about until Murrius finished whatever fun she provided. Since he was homeless, she might actually offer him a bed for the night. But just as I decided to retreat, like a sensible woman, the door opened again. Out he came. Out swaggered his entourage too, now sharing fattened-up shoulder-bags among them. Even Murrius himself was lugging one. Though not large, the carriers were substantial leather, firmly buckled up – and I could see that they were dead-weight heavy.

That meant one thing: cash. If Murrius had asked Laetilla for a personal loan, his borrowing must be stupendous. I suspected something else, though, something much more intriguing: if Laetilla gathered in loan repayments, it looked to me that Murrius collected the takings from her. Juno with jaundice. He was certainly not a victim of pressurised lending, but directly involved in running it. This man was the banker.

I followed the guard party back. Now I took even more care to keep my distance. They walked with purpose. They kept in a pack, though not ostentatiously defensive; they felt confident they could move their loot around at will. They had done it before, they would do it again. Nobody would trouble them.

In Murrius's home street, they turned through ninety degrees, like soldiers, and wheeled into Cowrie Court. Most of the byways hereabouts trickled through to join the Clivus Publicius, although this was a dead end. I reckoned they were going to the large house Paris had noted. It confirmed my idea that the Murrius brother lived here. Now I had some idea why Paris had seen so many people coming and going. It was certainly not because of a religious sect holding prayer meetings!

As the group arrived, a couple of other, similar, men seemed to be waiting. They moved across the junction, barring anyone else from the cul-de-sac. They owned the place. Civic records would be silent on that, but I guessed no locals ever argued the point.

I walked on, still carrying my shoe parcel. I continued quietly from Greater to Lesser Laurel Street until I reached my own house.

For a few moments I was denied entry, though nobody shouted abuse from a window. My problem was just Rodan, pretending to be deaf. I was too preoccupied to berate him when he finally answered. I was staring at a new Saturnalia present.

Standing upright on our front doorstep was a single human leg.

28

?

29

For two beats I felt genuinely terrified. Finding Sheep's head had affected my brain. This must be another appalling threat against us.

Saturnalia. It was some new mad prank.

I made myself throw a proper glance over the object. It was a left leg. Unlike the severed head of Sheep, it was not bloody. With huge relief I took in that it was not flesh and bone either, but a good representation. This must be a special delivery, perhaps a gift for someone in my household who, unknown to me, had a human-limb fetish. Or muggings do occur when a lone person returns home, fumbles for their latch-lifter and fails to spot doorstep thieves coming. The leg could be an unusual distraction. I looked back over my shoulder, but common sense told me muggers were never this sophisticated.

Right. I have never been a person who stands around fretting. *What is going on, who put that there, shall I scream? Or should I just take it inside with me in case somebody wants it?* My brother Postumus, for one, would like the macabre limb for his cabinet of curiosities. I had better not leave it standing around for a passing thief. When gingerly lifted, it felt heavy. I quickly turned my key, gripped the leg under one arm and went indoors.

'Good grief,' observed my husband, mildly. 'Here is Albia, with a spare leg.'

He was sitting in the courtyard, a small boy on either side of him, reading them an Aesop's Fable before bed. The scroll had been his reason for visiting Uncle Tullius earlier. Tiberius had hunted it down among old books of his own that he had left behind in the library.

I went over and leaned the leg up against a movable table where Gratus had placed a beaker of wine and a water jug for Tiberius. I had to be careful, or the weight would have pushed over the furniture. Tiberius peered at the leg, saying it seemed to have a wooden core, sheathed in bronze. 'The man it belongs to would be about five feet seven,' he declared, acting the expert. 'Maybe five eight, if slim.'

'You don't say! Is it custom-made? He's a muscly boy, from the modelling,' I replied, making it salacious. 'Superb thighs. That is, thigh.'

'Is it a Saturnalia joke? Or are you collecting all the parts, intending to weld your own living statue like Pygmalion?'

'I think it has dropped off a mythological marvel. There will be a magic bronze giant somewhere, searching for a piece of himself.'

Gaius and Lucius jumped off the bench. Plucking up courage, they walked the leg around the courtyard. I told them not to break it so they soon lost interest.

Tiberius had his eye on me. 'Where'd you go, scallywag?'

'The Cosmographer.'

'You could have told me.'

'You would have stopped me.'

'I might have tried!'

'You knew I would go.'

'I suppose so. Learn anything?'

I told him. He said that settled it: on safety grounds, I had to drop my client. Her connections were too dangerous.

Her separation from Murrius made working for Nephele no safer: when he discovered my involvement, Murrius could turn on me, bringing his aggressive associates. Merely smiling, I sat down with Tiberius and finished off the contents of his beaker. He let me.

The boys clambered back onto the bench, demanding Tiberius complete Aesop's Fable of the Wolf and the Crane. Wolf gets bone stuck in throat, begs for help, other animals all refuse, only brave crane puts long beak down his throat, extracts bone; crane asks wolf for reward, he snarls that survival after putting head down a wolf's throat ought to be reward enough. Like them all, it is a short story, though Tiberius was padding it out by inventing encounters with various other creatures, which he mimicked finely.

'Are you reading that?' demanded Gaius, deeply suspicious. 'Is it the proper story? I think you are making up the animals.'

'It's the story that my father, who was your grandfather, always read to me. Just like that. With lowing and growling and really loud roars.'

Gaius backed down. We moved into general questions like why do lions roar. I said Tiberius would have to answer, because he owned an encyclopaedia. He said only the Index and Book One. (Book Two would be his Saturnalia gift, with Book Three as an extra surprise.) I joked, but all men are clever, aren't they? He bantered, no, men are wise, it is women who are clever. This went over the boys' heads, though I could see that the five-year-old suspected they had missed something.

When the boys were collected by Glaphyra and taken off to bed, Tiberius Manlius gazed at me. 'You don't want to live with a moralist, but let me say this, please. You have put your head down the wolf's throat, Flavia Albia. Be satisfied to escape alive. Please don't risk any more with Nephele and Murrius! It cannot be worth it.'

I answered that I had scruples about taking a fee that I knew was financed by loan-sharking. I saw it as blood money.

We sat in thought, staring at the false leg. I pulled it closer to investigate and found that straps to attach it were pushed deep down inside. One might go around a stump of thigh, the other around a wearer's waist.

'Marcia's fellow,' I deduced.

'Where does that random thought come from?'

'Not random. Corellius had a bad limp, from falling off a horse, he claims, though Marcia told me it looked as if he was hit by some kind of combat missile. Gone to see a medic. Must have had his crushed leg amputated.'

'Brave man.'

'Corellius was in more pain than he let us see. He works for the Emperor so presumably he has access to specialist military docs. He has had an operation, she has gone to nurse him, and now nobody has bothered to tell us, but they may arrive back here for the festival.'

'Meanwhile his prosthetic has been delivered ahead of him,' Tiberius concurred. 'Steaming hot from a workshop. We can let them stay here. We have room, and you get on with her.' He did not say that getting on with people was rare with me. Perhaps I could see him thinking it.

'The leg looks rather good. I hope he survives to wear it.' I was acutely aware of the danger of amputation. My first husband had had a badly damaged thigh, but after I made enquiries about what could be done for him, Lentullus chose to struggle on as he was. That decision later caused his death in an accident when he lost balance, but at least we had had a couple of years together. 'I hope Corellius doesn't struggle back to Rome, then die at our house.'

'Fortunately you are a forgiving woman,' Tiberius joked.

A forgiving woman with a lot to do, I thought. Such as further checks on the Murrius-Laetilla financial association, with its implications for Nephele. And now I must do so discreetly, to stop Tiberius being anxious for me.

To satisfy my own curiosity, I would continue investigating, despite his qualms. I might have felt guilty about refusing to listen to him, but I was sure he fully understood.

Of course, I was well-placed to know how many wives find their husbands deny there was any such understanding!

I did not ponder guiltily for long. Someone came knocking and they were not enquiring whether their leg had been misdelivered here. It was a messenger sent by the vigiles to tell Tiberius about a disaster.

Once the man had persuaded Rodan to let him in, he staggered into the courtyard. He was covered with smuts and an aura of smoke hung around him. He pushed the leg aside, barely aware what strange article he was displacing, then leaned heavily on the table. Even before he croaked out his message, we could see that what he had to tell us must be grim. There had been a bad fire in which people had been killed.

30

I fetched his cloak for him and Tiberius went out straight away.

When he came home again, he would be whacked. He had already spent the good part of a day patrolling with Morellus. In large doses Morellus was a trial.

This second trip out would be much more upsetting. By the time Tiberius finally returned from the fatal fire scene, I had sent everyone else to bed. I was waiting up with a couple of oil lamps. I hugged him in silence, then took him into the room he normally used as an indoor study. He was chilled through; he kept his cloak on. I crouched to pull off his outdoor shoes for him. Knowing her duty, the dog came in and lay where he could warm his feet on her.

'Wine?' No. Nothing. Seated beside me on a couch, he leaned forward, elbows on knees, head down. 'Tell! Tiberius, let it out or you won't sleep.' He nodded for me, but even after he straightened up, it took him a while to speak.

He was grey. I had not seen him so drained since the worst period after that lightning struck him.

He managed a factual start. The fire had been in an apartment block where one of the traditional nut-sellers lived. 'Rosius.'

A familiar name: Agemathus had muttered it, while giving information about the agent, Greius. After the previous nut-seller's death at the warehouse, Rosius had taken a stand, Agemathus had said. He had turned his back on Greius in what had sounded like a very public rejection. Organised crime never allows that. They were bound to have come for him. He must have known they would do something. 'Remember, Tiberius. When Agemathus came earlier, he was talking about this man being leaned on by the nut-suppliers. He refused to knuckle under.'

Beginning to speak more freely, Tiberius confirmed it. 'Retaliation. Morellus learned Rosius had been a target before because he wouldn't play. The gangsters tried attacking him then, beat him up with staves, but he remained adamant.'

'Agemathus said Rosius knew that other man they murdered at the warehouse. It had made him even more defiant. They couldn't budge him. Tonight they burned Rosius's home as a last resort?'

'Final reprisal. Disgusting crime. He died inside.' Tiberius had to force it out: 'Seven dead. Rosius, wife, his sister, her husband – and three children, one a baby.'

'You said the fire was in apartments?'

'Yes, a large block – but only one family died.'

'Targeted!'

'Had to be.'

He sat rigid, with clenched fists. Into my mind came a picture of him here earlier tonight, happily miming animals for his own two young nephews. I gripped one of his fists between both my hands; it was no comfort for a man who had seen the Fourth Cohort carrying out burned bodies.

Tiberius began again, more fluently sharing awful facts and sights: 'It took ages before the red-tunics could even get inside. Heat too intense. They drained the siphon-engine over and over. The poor men were distraught, but they could do nothing.' Tiberius was stricken himself, even though he had arrived after the worst was over. 'Couldn't go close, couldn't force a way in however brave they tried to be – and those men are brave, Albia . . . It had been set up to look like a travesty of a Saturnalia accident, but the disguise was minimal. Candles dropped in the street – nonsense. Wicked. No one in those apartments can afford wax candles. Besides, we also found wood-tar and straw discarded.'

'Arson,' I stated, as he stumbled, too emotional. I needed to encourage him to keep talking. I wanted to know; he needed to debrief.

'Arson. No bloody doubt. From all the times the vigiles have attended genuine accidents, they can recognise a fit-up. They knew immediately this one was not right. Morellus was called, Morellus sent for me. Afterwards, we found the evidence. There was no serious attempt to make it look good or to hide what had really been done to those people.'

'No, there wouldn't be. They want their involvement known – it's a scare tactic. And nobody escaped?'

'No – and why? Because the bastards came to the building when everybody was asleep – of course such a family goes to bed early, they *went* early tonight. They always turn in as soon as it gets dark. The arsonists must have known there were young children and the menfolk had to work. They routinely had to leave at dawn, so everyone would be deeply asleep. Setting the fire must have been done silently, stealthily. Intruders went in, quickly dumped combustibles, and then – Albia, Albia, can you believe this? – the door, the only door to the outside, was blocked up. It's a well-built apartment block. They lived on too high a landing for any escape from windows, and there were none onto the corridor. The vigiles could not reach any windows from outside either. Their ladders are not long enough.'

'A lot of other people live there?'

'Yes. They all had miraculous escapes. Well, that proves this fire was deliberate. One apartment burned, it went up fast and furious, while everyone round about, next door, immediately below, even above, had time to flee before their places caught. By comparison, no other rooms suffered much damage. This one apartment had been made into a sealed firebox.'

'Lethal! A normal tenement fire is never that concentrated. Were other people given warnings?' I asked, suspiciously.

'Can't be certain. Alarms were raised, but probably by chance. One of the Fourth lives on the top floor. He was going for his shift tonight when he smelt smoke. He did what he could, sent a message for the Cohort to come running, and I suppose he yelled his head off, organised people from the building to hammer on doors and bring occupants out to safety. But he couldn't get into the Rosius apartment – nobody could, because the door was blocked like that, wedged up, with fiercely burning materials piled outside. When the crew did clear a path to break the door down, a firestorm blew out at them.'

'There! Stay calm, love, or it doesn't help, you know that.'

Tiberius slumped back, holding his head again. 'I know, I know, but, oh, sweetheart, it was horrible. Morellus hopes the end came fast for the poor victims – he thinks they would all have been overcome by smoke quite early on . . . but onlookers had heard screams initially. I was there when the bodies were removed. They were seared toast, no soft tissue, all unrecognisable. The only way we knew there was a baby was when one of the men found the charred wood of its cradle. He wept. It will haunt him. They kept him on duty, but only to provide him with colleagues' support.'

'What's to be done?' I asked quietly.

'I don't know. It's hopeless. Morellus will appeal for witnesses, but we saw what happens, saw it after the warehouse murder. People are too scared to talk. Our only hope is it's so abhorrent that this time someone will come forward out of pity.'

'Let's hope.'

I stayed with him until I could persuade him up to bed. He did sleep, eventually. I found less rest, as I worried for him.

31

I was growing accustomed to being first up. There was no point in hankering for my old life, when I could let sunlight squirm in through shutter cracks, like a randy god coming to ravish me, while I buried my head under a blanket. This was it nowadays. The matron. Domina Albia. The deserving one, chaste, modest and frugal, who loves her husband, his house and all his possessions: pleasant conversation, keeps the keys, works in wool (no chance!). Unto death. Albia the domestic queen . . .

Rubbish to that.

I had slid out from alongside Tiberius, holding my breath while I pushed my feet into slippers and groped on a chest for what felt like a stole. I left our room in darkness. Barley squeezed out along with me; she followed me downstairs like a honey-coloured wraith, although when we reached the courtyard she sought out her kennel. She lay down, nose on paws, watching me in the hope of food.

While I was making mulsum with wine and honey warmed together, Gratus joined me, openly yawning – a rare unprofessional slip. He too had been drawn into early household manoeuvres. Cradling beakers, we leaned against the kitchen cooking-bench and did not bother to speak.

Astonishingly, I had a visitor. That was me: Domina Albia – chaste, modest, frugal . . . and runs a list of annoying clients.

Snapping alert, Gratus loped quickly to answer the knocking, to avoid disturbing people. The caller was Terentia Nephele. Gratus and I were taken aback, though she seemed oblivious to her timing.

I am a grouse when disturbed in the morning. My brain likes to fire up at its own sullen pace. I like to rinse my teeth, ready to gnash at people.

We moved grudgingly to open the small salon for use, Gratus bringing a brazier, me organising a drink for Nephele so I could continue mine without seeming impolite. Really, I needed adjustment time. I had not expected to see her again, let alone before my family was astir.

Well, one was up: little Gaius hopped down, barefoot and in his sleeping tunic. He plonked himself in front of the visitor, staring. 'We have a false leg. Do you want to see it?'

She was not a woman to engage with a five-year-old.

I managed to prevent him dragging the leg across the courtyard. 'Not now, Gaius. Don't be rough, it's not yours. Go back upstairs, please, darling. You can come down when you have washed your face and are dressed. And *proper shoes!*' This one had a footwear antipathy. I could see him deciding to resist, so I picked him up, set him on the bottom step up to the balcony and gave him a slight push on the rump. 'Up you go.'

I wondered whether to explain the prosthetic limb, but Nephele had no interest, lost in whatever had compelled her visit. *Hello! What's up with her?* Her face was set more than usual.

My visitor was given a breakfast drink since mulsum was already made. I let her stir it herself. Hell, I gave her a spoon. That was enough; I wasn't a serving wench. I folded myself into my stole, preparing myself.

This is why informers live in uninviting alleys. At Fountain Court only emergencies brought call-outs so early, but when you live on a respectable street, clients and customers start cluttering up the neighbourhood along with the market traders. In Londinium, at least everyone hibernates in winter. In Rome, people assume if they are up, you should be too. They go out for bread and bother you at the same time.

Juno. But I felt curiosity stirring: *What have we here?*

Gratus popped his head in to say he was going out – for breakfast rolls – a clear hint to Nephele to hurry up. I would be needed. Breakfast with infants requires a full posse.

I sat with my client, perplexed but allowing myself to be hostile. 'If you are sent to find out how the aedile is faring after last night's incident,' I rattled off irritably, 'you can go straight back and tell them it has only made him angrier!'

Nephele looked blank.

'There was a fire.' Now I was shooting facts at her fiercely. 'Arson. People dead. Children. A baby. A gangsters' gesture – it had better not be from your relatives!'

'Oh. People are talking about that locally. Nobody I know would be involved!'

I gave her a look to say we would see about that.

Once again, Nephele had arrived alone: no maid. She looked neat, though evidently had left home unaided by her girl. Gone were the complex ringlets, waves and interwoven loops of hair – though her self-pinned chignon, of course, gleamed with past applications of topical shine. A silk gown is a silk gown, whether a factotum lifts it reverently over your head or you throw it on quickly yourself. The previous necklace group was reduced to one chain, with its clasp showing at the side instead of being centred out of the way at the back. Her skin was as clear as ever, no lines showed, yet Nephele now subtly gave herself away: she knew life. She seemed older than I had thought previously.

She stayed silent, as if waiting for me to lead. Finally, I told her that I knew she had not been frank with me, that my people had called at her house and been moved on with threats, that my insight into her husband's position had led me to end the commission.

'You are dropping my case?' She looked briefly thrown.

'That is my decision. Can you suggest why not?' Yesterday I had intended to continue, but the fire had hardened my attitude. She belonged to a despicable family; for all I knew they were behind the recent troubles. 'Nephele, I first thought your husband had a gambling addiction – but what he really does in the community is worse. If his only flaw was spending money unwisely, I could have advised you like any client. But if he is what I think . . .' I left it there.

She said nothing.

I spelled out that Laetilla was not, or not primarily, her husband's lover. 'She assembles the proceeds of illegal money-lending. People can pay her direct, or I presume a bunch of collectors goes around leaning on debtors. Such enforcers tend to be brutal. Laetilla holds their takings at her house across the Aventine. Gaius Murrius then collects the loot. She may give him lunch, as you suggested, but I saw him go there in the evening. He didn't take love-gifts, he took heavies to carry the money-bags. I presume you know all this, Nephele? You understand what business he is in?'

'I know nothing about his business.'

'If that's true, you're an idiot!' I snapped.

'The men in our family never discuss what they do.'

'Listen to me, then. Loan sharks move in on desperate

people. They act very friendly at first, but they charge sky-high interest rates, with no proper contracts so they can never be sued. When the time comes to pay, they turn nasty, use threats, use violence, drive women who can't repay their loans into prostitution or force men to engage in criminal activity on the gang's behalf. It's usury. It's illegal, but nobody dares report them. Your husband belongs to an organisation like that. I suspect he is high-placed, a key figure. He runs it.'

'It is news to me. I am only his wife.'

'No, no. You are more astute than that, Nephele. Perhaps it's a new discovery and that is why you threw him out. Incidentally, I do know you have barred him from your house – rejected the taxidermy, spurned the stepchildren. But you certainly know Murrius derives his income from a filthy occupation. You can't *not* know – he has a group of strong-armers who work with him. You cannot imagine they are there to read him poems while he picks his nose. I myself have seen him boldly bringing cash back to what I presume is his brother's house. Don't pretend. You understand what is going on, where his money comes from, how your husband operates.'

She refused to concede this. She either knew, as I said, or more likely she chose not to accept the truth. Plenty of women are happy to spend dirty money, while acting blind to its source.

'I had to lock him out,' she protested, dodging the real issue. 'I want to leave him, but he won't allow it. I need a life of my own, but he and his relatives just pretend everything must carry on the same as usual.'

I chewed at my beaker bitterly. 'Come clean. Why are you here today?'

Nephele placed her cup on a side table, folded her hands, stared at the floor. I noticed a small spider running away to a corner.

I said firmly, 'I cannot work for clients who are dishonest with me.'

At last, Nephele seemed to give up. She accepted what I had said. She stirred, ready to leave. It all felt oddly negative.

I stood up, ending the interview. I would not willingly tangle with a gangster's wife. As with other clients who were voiding their commissions, I tried to ignore my disappointment. Once she was gone, I knew of old I would be glad. It was time to ditch this, shake my skirts free, move on.

I led the way out to the courtyard. Fornix must be up; I could smell the first sizzles of stew-preparation. We were eating a lot of mutton, all well disguised.

Nephele stopped. I paused too, politely.

She burst out, 'I have to get away from him!'

I stopped too. *Hello, hello!* Then she muttered, as I was already half expecting, 'I am terrified what he will do to me. I have to escape.'

32

Everything altered. Time to regroup. That was the moment when Terentia Nephele truly became a client of mine.

I must have shocked her into action, saying I would dump her. It happens. I turned back, holding open the salon door again.

Behind me, I was aware that Tiberius had appeared on the balcony and paused, watching, while Gratus returned from the bakery with a covered basket; seeing us reactivate our meeting, they would either hold up breakfast or carry on quietly without me.

Nephele came past me, back into the salon. I sat her down. Once she obediently resumed her chair, I took charge. 'Right! Let's do this properly. So you really do want to leave your husband, and he and his brother are very unpleasant characters. One important question first: you told me Murrius has never resorted to violence. Was that true?'

'He does not need violence. He gets what he wants in other ways.'

'I understand.' Mental stress and family pressure.

That must have been right because she added, 'His brother is the dangerous one. And mine's worse.'

Noting her anxiety about these brothers, I extracted more

history. 'Tell me about your marriage. How did you first meet Gaius Murrius?'

Quietly, she obeyed. Her story contained few surprises. The couple came from similar backgrounds; their union was arranged for them by relatives. He was older, not as old as he might have been, though he had two infant children from a wife who had died. Anyone would say the arrangement was suitable. The orphans needed a mother.

Clean goods, I thought. Never been with anybody else. Never would do, once he had her. To be sure, I demanded, 'Do you have a lover, Nephele?'

'No.'

I believed her. For one thing, if she had, the lover would lead in helping her escape. Well, he would if he had anything about him. Plenty are useless, but she did not strike me as someone who would take risks for a man like that. Not even if he drove a quadriga and had all his own teeth.

In many ways the match with Murrius was promulgated in classic Roman tradition, the ghastly linkage of two bodies for financial and political reasons that still occurred in extreme senatorial circles. I had been brought up by Helena and Falco to view this with horror; professionally I made no judgement. The only difference with Nephele and Murrius was that their connection came not from having consuls among their ancestors, but from basic criminality. She still tried to be vague about it, as they had trained her to do, but I had already realised that both her own and the Murrius family were classic, old-style, deep-dyed racketeers.

As I had thought originally, they might have slavery in their backgrounds, typical for the Aventine, though Nephele glossed over it: 'They all came from nothing. They used their wits until now they have something.'

'When people say, "using their wits" it tends to mean finding ways around the law.'

'Our people have a respected profession within the community.'

'Ah, yes!'

As Nephele paused, I considered her coming to spy on Tiberius so I put in a direct question: whether she knew anything about the nut-wars. Had Murrius anything to do with that? She said she had heard about trouble on the streets, but her husband and his brother only gave people loans. She made it sound like a charitable act, so I was drawn to argue, 'What about all the victims who are terrorised when they cannot pay?' She gave no response to that. The question about nut-wars was also left hanging.

I let her continue describing her personal life. Once she and Murrius were married, they lived in a closed circle, mainly mixing with their own. If this circle ever widened, that was because the family were seeking to expand their reach through new links to other businesses. In social situations wives, in their finery, might be paraded to add lustre to functions where deals were being fixed, particularly when the wives were good-looking. I understood. That is no different from what happens among groups of civic dignitaries, in trade guilds, or in restrictive religions. You dress up so he looks good. Don't get tipsy, go home as soon as he's ready, don't complain about the other men who flirt.

Such wives led lives of privilege. There was money available. They kept good homes, for which they were allowed funds. If they had children, they lied to them about their fathers' occupations. In return for comfortable lives, they conformed to group standards.

'Good behaviour? Because you are a sign of your

husband's power – and because you are bringing up his children?' Nephele let that pass.

I could see how closely she was tied to the group code. That, too, followed the supposed model of marriage in the high Roman establishment. But in both it also went with husbands having mistresses, fathers quarrelling volcanically with sons, spirited daughters eloping with rival clansmen or, worse, getting pregnant by menial staff members who had overstepped trust. Children would tend to be difficult if their fathers were away a lot (in exile, say) or if they were dead (due to the high mortality rate in their operating field).

Traditionalists will feel I can only mean the murky world of criminals. However, if you want patrician parallels, take a quick stroll through the history of the Julio-Claudian imperial family.

A key difference was that in the upper classes unhappy women or restless men were allowed divorces. Indeed, divorce could be a handy device to further ambitious schemes. Repositioning was a well-used social tool.

In the criminal community that never occurred. This was Nephele's problem. 'Murrius wants to carry on. His brother insists we are together for life. My own family won't help me.'

I supposed there were deep fears that gangsters' wives knew too many secrets. Wives had to be told enough to be able to run the business if their men were forced abroad, the Roman punishment for capital crimes committed by free citizens. Wives of men who did terrible deeds also shared the enormity with them. A criminal's wife has her own lifelong punishment. Wives signify much, count for everything, yet are invisible.

Among Nephele's family, and that of Murrius, divorce

never happened. She could think of no one who had done it. When she said to me, 'I have to get away from him', this was a dangerous decision.

'Well! Now you want to leave your husband.'

I reached into a wool basket, which certainly contained no wool-working kit; it was my handy canister for writing equipment. I picked out a note-tablet, then deliberately replaced it: shorthand for assuring the woman that all we said would be in confidence.

I folded my hands. 'Sometimes,' I mused, 'people toss that phrase out in the same tone of voice as "I have to buy winter pears on the way home." But occasionally, a client speaks so intensely I know it is the first time she has dared to voice the words. *I have to leave him.* She has faced a terrible truth. As a result, her world will change for ever.'

Nephele lifted her chin. 'Then?'

'Then I spell out the consequences. She decides whether she is strong enough for what has to be. If so . . .' I braced myself to describe the process. For me, the challenge now was one of logistics – and, hell, I could handle detail.

'If so?'

'I make the arrangements.'

'Can you?'

'I have done it before. But, Nephele, you must want it. You cannot be squeamish. You cannot compromise. It is vital to be taken right out of the man's life. If a woman is frightened enough, she has to break away utterly, move somewhere nobody will ever come to look for her, take a new name, start a new life, contact no one, never look back.'

Nephele did not flinch. Perhaps she had already thought this through; perhaps she simply needed help to organise. 'It has to be for a long time?'

'For ever.' I paused for her to absorb it. 'For women in trouble like yours, it must be, I'm afraid.' Nephele was staring. She reached for the cold beaker of her half-drunk mulsum, as if her mouth had suddenly gone dry. Low-voiced, I emphasised what I meant. 'Listen. I had one client who returned home. Her children had to be left behind when she fled. After a few years she could no longer bear never seeing them.'

'What happened to her?' Nephele asked quickly.

'She died.'

'How?'

'Guess. He killed her. It was inevitable. I had warned her, but she knew anyway what would happen. To him, her sin in leaving was unforgivable, so his retribution was the most extreme. It was nearly a year before anyone found her body, but it happened. Then she was at least given a funeral. Hardly anybody came.' But I went. 'To many of her relatives, even when dead she remained untouchable. They would not speak her name. She was a non-person.'

'What about the man?'

'Ah, him!' Nephele looked startled by the force of my contempt. 'There was no trial, of course, the evidence was circumstantial – he had fixed that. He was sure he would get away with it – he thought he could get away with anything. You must be familiar with that boast!' Nephele looked rueful. 'Still, justice caught up with him. She was my client. I did all I could for her. I believe he was last seen heading for a gold mine, in a line of shackled convicts. If you know the right people, well . . .'

'You do know the right people?'

'I know some.' I could see Nephele assessing all this. 'Nephele, you must have seen the attitude: live with me or

189

live with no one – live with me or die.' I paused slightly. 'I presume that is why you need to leave your husband. And why you came to me for help.'

She nodded. 'What would I have to do?'

I gave her the facts plainly. 'First admit to yourself that you mean this, mean it absolutely. Then leave him, leave him right now.'

She blinked.

'It has to be unexpected,' I explained. 'It must happen very fast.' She understood me at last, yet looked astounded. 'I mean literally this: do it today. Start from sitting right here. Never go back to your house. Walk away in what you are wearing. Shed everything else, family and possessions, abandon your wealth—'

'How can I live?' She had the answer herself: 'I had brought some money to pay for your commission . . .'

'Keep that, then.'

'I have a friend—'

'Don't tell your friends.' With hindsight, I should have pressed her for an identity. I was too concerned with what she had to do. 'Go without planning, so you are dropping no clues. Do not discuss anything beforehand, never contact your husband afterwards. Go far away. I can help you with that. Become a different person, have no past, only make whatever you can of your future.'

'He will try to find me.' She was a hardened realist. 'He and his brother.'

'Yes. I imagine they will search maniacally. Follow my instruction, stick with it. They will be thwarted.'

'He will guess that I came to you.'

'Perhaps. By the time he arrives in a rage, you will not be here.'

'He will not give up.'

'No. He won't. That is why *you* can never waver. Walk away and do not look back for a moment. Never weaken.'

'Even if he dies, he will leave a charge with other people. His brother. My family.'

'You must remember that always.' I could see one possible flaw. 'You told me you have a sister, a sister you are close to?' Nephele nodded miserably, anticipating what I had to say. 'This may seem impossible, but you should not contact your sister.'

'How can I tell her where—'

'You cannot. You must not.' Murrius would see the sister as the weak link. So did I! 'Your husband will find ways to make your sister tell him what she knows – she must, for her own sake as well as yours, know nothing.'

Nephele considered it, acknowledged it, then nodded again. 'I have a brother, but he will be looking for me just as furiously.' She asked me again: 'How can I survive?'

'You will. First, the kindness of strangers – I will arrange that for you. Then, believe me, any resourceful woman can support herself. You must learn to live very simply. Stretch every denarius.'

'Can I not go home quickly to collect a few important things?' she quavered. I hoped this was her last tremor of weakness.

'No. Somebody will see you. It is bound to happen. If anyone does see you, they will spot your intentions from your expression or the way you act. Eventually you will be tracked down. No one observed you this morning? Or heard you?' Nephele shook her head. 'What about your maid? Was she awake?'

'I had allowed her to go out last night to a party with

her girlfriends, for the festival. As I left, I could hear her being ill.'

'Excellent! She will be in no condition to answer questions.' If the maid was still drunk enough, when Murrius thrashed her – as I was sure he would – she would feel less pain. 'You let yourself out of the house?'

Nephele nodded. Of her own accord, she now made a deliberate gesture: she unhooked a key from a chatelaine ring at her belt, then placed it firmly on my marble-topped table. I could dispose of it. She would never go back.

I spoke quietly. 'It will be hard. But at least, unlike my other client, you do not have children.' I had already heard her tell Murrius the stepchildren were his concern.

'I have a pet!' she exclaimed. It sounded as if she had only just thought of this and was on the verge of mind-changing. 'My Beauty! She is doomed if I leave her to him. He wants her, but he will kill her out of spite against me. You must let me go to fetch her.'

'No.'

'Yes!'

'No! That would be fatal. I hear your pain. You must live with it. You have to be anonymous,' I instructed her relentlessly. 'Live quietly, look uninteresting. Beauty will make you visible, remarkable – and traceable.' With its crazed croaks of 'Skanky bitch!' that bird would make her *audible*. 'Nephele, this is your Rubicon. Save yourself. Forget the parrot.'

33

By the time I sat down for my breakfast, Nephele was already gone from our house. By noon, quietly secreted amid the bustle of pre-festival boat traffic on the Tiber, my client would have left the city. By tonight she would be in Ostia. Tomorrow a trusted contact of the auction house would see her on her way by road to an ancient city south of Rome. Everyone involved would immediately forget what they had done. There would be no trail.

In fact, I had breakfast at my parents' house. I had arrived there with a maid, who was not Suza; later I left alone. I had stayed there until one of the household told me the traveller had boarded her boat safely.

I had devised a plan. My mother corresponded with a priestess at a shrine in Latium; she wrote to this woman rarely, but always at Saturnalia. It was the anniversary of when they had met, an occasion when Helena Justina, with various people she dragged into helping her, had preserved the life of this foreign priestess even though it had been claimed by the state. That had been when Rome was ruled by the benign Emperor Vespasian. Overturning a political death-penalty would not happen, these days.

Helena made me write a letter of introduction, since it was for my client. 'You want it, Albia, you do it!' I might be almost thirty years old, but I felt about thirteen.

I grumbled that I was assisting out of good nature: as this client's exit was abrupt, I would earn no fee. That made no difference. Mother had always been a stickler for doing your own homework. No cheating happened on her watch. She had brought up four children, very different from each other, yet under her rule we were all intellectually tough as old whelks.

I gazed at her fondly, while I capitulated. Helena was still tall, though perhaps now losing some mass from her bones. Her hair was dark, yet silver had sifted through it, so she seemed to be growing into her natural age: mature, experienced, essentially wise, like a sybil at an oracle. Sybils who met my mother tended to cringe, I'm afraid, then opt for immediate retirement from their caves. She still had her wit, the abrasive, inventive comedy that made my father growl and leave a room as if in a huff – yet if you ran after him quickly enough, Falco would be laughing in the corridor. Her eyes were still the eyes he loved. Compassionate, missing nothing, speaking her thoughts even when she had not spoken.

This was my mother, though we shared no blood. Once, when I was living in misery, Helena Justina had made a mercurial decision to pluck me out of it: after a childhood of expecting the worst, I experienced that one tumultuous crash of true good luck. Falco supported her. There was no one in the Empire I would rather have had adopt me. My father had trained me to conduct investigations, while I also learned from him how to buy, sell, evaluate and love antiquities and art, and to scoff at everything as rudely and roundly as I could. This was my mother, though. She had taught me that if someone was in trouble or desperate danger, saving them was your duty. You strode straight in and you kept at it until the job was done.

'Stop prevaricating. Start writing.'

'Yes, Mother.'

I loathed being diplomatic. Since the banished priestess was of Germanic origin, I had to pretend fellow-feeling as one who might also originate from the northern tribes; that never came easily. At least since she lived at the shrine as a punishment, I could call on this woman for sympathy with someone else who had been forced into a kind of exile.

The priestess herself was not entirely a stranger. I had met her. My family had given her refuge briefly during that long-ago Saturnalia; I had carried her a bowl of broth because she was unwell. When my mother and grandmother swept her off in a Vestal Virgin's carriage to bully the Emperor, there was no room for another passenger, so I had had to stay at home. The priestess never came back, because those strong-willed women secured permission for her to live out her days in a temple, instead of having a date with the public strangler.

She had once had an affair with an uncle of mine. Nobody talked about that.

'Should I tell her how he is, Mama?'

'Only if you lay it on thick that he has six children whom he loves dearly.' Within the family our feeling was 'and a wife whose money he loves even more'. Darling good-looking Uncle Quintus, always the charismatic one.

'Right. I'll just put *All the family send regards and hope you are not yet sick of cleaning out that scruffy old temple.*'

'She is a revered elderly lady there,' Helena scolded. 'Anyone who can make wild warriors believe she has the gift of prophecy, enough for them to pull their big bottoms off their feasting benches and roar into war against Rome, can charm spotty acolytes in Latium. I believe she has revamped her temple, making it a very popular sanctuary.'

'Sausage-sellers and festive lanterns? Not too popular, I hope. I want this hideaway to be discreet.'

It would be. Nephele had vanished off the map. The German lady, who owed my mother her life, would safeguard my refugee. The only problem for me was that, once again, I was left staring at the crumbs in my breakfast bowl. It was a good bowl, as fine as the best Italian Arretine redware, though one that my parents had been given in Germany. But it was empty. Thank goodness I despise symbolism.

My client had left Rome. I had no reason for further enquiries into her evil husband. Worse, I had put myself out for her with no payment. My own man was off investigating an absorbing case, but I had no work.

I did wonder whether to seek guardianship of the tug-of-love parrot.

Settle down, Albia.

'You will find something,' my mother consoled me. 'You have built a reputation. Just sit tight and someone in need will come to you. Do you want me to ask Falco if he has anything you could help out with?'

'No, thanks,' I said. 'I'm not that desperate.'

Helena and I laughed together gently.

34

One place I did not want to be hit by flying nuts was halfway up the Stairs of Cassius. As a shortcut from the Embankment, where my parents lived, to the top of the Aventine, where my own house was, those steps were a tough climb even normally. When idiots were tossing missiles, the narrow, worn stone treads became deadly. To stop for breath made me a target. To plough on doggedly helped the nuts sting more. I could hear giggling, but it's never possible to see who the flingers are.

Just as nuts have been debased from a cheap festival gift to high-velocity missiles, so liberty has changed from new life given to slaves by their masters into a licence for appalling behaviour. Once in their freedom caps, ex-slaves and troublemakers did as they liked, and they liked annoying others. Horribly for me, using the Steps of Cassius meant passing the Temple of Liberty where the worst culprits gathered. The holiday had yet to start but they were out in force, with their unbleached round headgear keeping their mindless skulls warm. It might be mid-morning, but they all had sour breath and dry mouths from drinking to excess and beyond the night before. Unfortunately, they never quite managed to kill themselves with over-indulgence.

'Give us a smile, darling!' these half-wits cried, like roofers who knew they were well out of reach or pot-bellied painters way up on scaffolds. 'Hasn't anybody told you it's Saturnalia, and being serious is banned?' This, inevitably, was followed by offers to liven me up in various disgusting ways.

I don't know the answer. Ignore them, they only shout louder to get your attention. Retaliate, and renewed ribaldry billows back at you, like a volcanic cloud. Ask don't they have mothers and sisters? Their answers will tell you how gruesome their mothers and sisters are. Complain to the authorities and be blacklisted as a prude. Make a gesture— No, never make gestures.

They are beyond wit. They probably won't follow you. You have to walk on as fast as possible and know safe places you can dive into.

Mine was Prisca's bath-house. There, the proprietor was ready with soft towels, sweet oils and sane conversation. 'Can't you get that girl to do something about your hair for a change? And don't ask for cakes – it's too early.' Nobody else was bathing at this time of day so I had the place to myself. The water was not yet truly warm, but the floors were clean. I needed to rid myself mentally not only of the revellers' catcalls but my client's troubles.

After a slow pass through the suite with a borrowed bone strigil, I revived. I joined Prisca in a tiny colonnaded court outside. She was talking to Zoe and Chloe, a pair of female gladiators who practised there. Luckily, I had missed them biffing and banging; the two hearties in their hipster mini-skirts were now sprawled on the ground, recovering. They were short, wide specimens, all mighty thighs and filthy banter. They tended to gorge on sausages, which were always being sold from trays in their hangouts. As combatants, they were not as good as they thought, though they made a big noise about it. As romantic partners they felt compelled to be loud about lesbian sex, just in case any short-sighted men thought they might be available.

They were all with a man today, in fact, though he was a small one.

'Have you met Spendo, Albia?'

'Never had the pleasure – but if you are the legendary estimator, Spendo, I believe my husband knows you?'

Spendo had been described to me. He was a dwarf, not unique in Rome, but his face had been called 'like molten rock', which was a novelty. The public regard dwarfs with curiosity and even affection, but it would take a strong will to cuddle Spendo on your lap. I could not tell whether he had suffered some terrible event, like being seriously burned, or if he had been born like that. Bad manners to stare, my mother would say – before she came right out and asked him.

I knew he was ace with an abacus. All our builders spoke of his estimating with awe. They had told me they sent Spendo to price any job they did not want; he was so thorough that the customer would reel away from his figures and drop the idea.

Today I learned something else interesting: in his spare time, and despite being twisted to one side, Spendo was a keen amateur gladiator. I had never met anyone who looked less suitable – though I was assured by Zoe and Chloe that their fight enthusiast was good because he had to be. Not only small, but physically disadvantaged, he had mastered every arena style and was an obsessive weaponry expert. He made his own arms, so they would be the right size; he had a forge at his house.

'A forge? I assume you're not married, Spendo?'

'Oh, the wife uses it too. She does glass-blowing – and

our daughter makes artisan jewellery. Her enamelling is beautiful. She has a line in Gallic cockerels that are extremely popular. But you were asking about armour . . .'

Having just left Helena Justina I continued to be polite, but even she would admit that politeness can be a mistake. Conversation with this crazed hobbyist entailed him explaining all the technical reasons why a secutor's helmet would be round and smooth, with two small eyeholes to avoid trident thrusts, though limiting vision, which was partly why Spendo himself liked to fight as a Thracian: he showed me in detail his own helmet's upturned griffon head, his visor and his double side-fastened plume-holders . . .

'Then what's the damage, estimator? Is the unit price for these casques expensive?'

Spendo gave me a look as if he thought I was being mischievous, though he solemnly assured me his precious helm was custom-made, high-spec and value-for-money.

'Cut it out, Spendo! I didn't let you in so you could badger my best customer,' ordered Prisca, finally rescuing me.

Although Prisca's was a women-only baths, Spendo had been given access for rehearsals with Zoe and Chloe: they had all been invited – ordered – to be the entertainment at a Saturnalia feast the Emperor was about to hold. I reminded them that our ruler had only just terrified senators – at least all who were mobile enough and not too demented – when he made them endure his notorious Black Banquet. The new dinner, said Zoe and Chloe, would be Domitian's seasonal gift for everybody else, much less funereal. 'Gifties and exotic grub – well, for people who manage to secure invitations. Bootleg tickets are selling at the back of temples, we hear, for as much as if they are written with gold leaf instead of ink.'

'Officials will have passes. Poets can go, if they promise to write up enough slush afterwards. "Oh, oh, Our Master has graciously asked me to dinner – me and a thousand nobodies he calls his friends". I've never been a fan of soggy finger-food,' I sneered.

'Free wine!' shrieked Chloe.

'Chance to wear see-through party robes!' added her girlfriend.

'Extraordinary light show,' said Spendo, single-mindedly. 'They have had military technicians setting up in secret for three days.' He looked modest. 'I myself have been advising them. I have been suggesting they could make a big impression with a flame-throwing implement used at the siege of Delium, as reported by Thucydides . . .'

'For the Undying Sun?' I asked, to show I did have expertise.

'Sol Invictus – that could work!' he confirmed, as if excitedly inventing ideas as we spoke. 'Enormous sun and other effects to be hurled over the venue – the battery of fire enhanced by use of viscous asphalt from the Dead Sea, King Herod's heliotherapy health spa. Extremely imaginative.'

'Sounds unsafe,' quipped Prisca.

'That's the thrill,' I assured her. 'Spendo, you'd better have the vigiles standing by with buckets of water. And during this stunning lights pageant, you three crazy combatants will scamper among the diners, bashing each other to bits?'

Prisca and I agreed it was almost worth going to see that.

Time to move. I said I had better go back and see what my husband was up to.

'He's not there,' I was at once informed by Spendo. 'I

called round at yours to see if he has any jobs lined up for me after the festival. Faustus has gone out.'

'He is down by the Raudusculana Gate,' Zoe filled us in, 'interviewing witnesses for his nutty inquiry.'

I was surprised; Tiberius might be alarmed that everyone here seemed to know all about his efforts. In an investigation it is too easy to suppose you are quarantined from public view; you keep your moves out of sight because so many witnesses try to run away or because you don't want to throw your dice too soon. Besides, beating your head against a brick wall is a solitary pursuit. 'He won't be pleased to hear half the neighbourhood is keeping tabs on him.' Neither he nor I would normally give out details, but I confirmed it was about the nut inquiry and said he was taking statements after the fire that had killed Rosius and his family.

'That's right,' agreed Chloe, nodding at me impatiently. 'He has been talking to the grandmother, who is too upset to tell him anything. Then he's gone to see the dead brother-in-law's brother.'

'Who had been at the apartment last evening, having a bite with them. He might have seen something as he left,' Zoe continued. 'He's a real pain in general, but he's fired up by grief, and will help if he can – at least, if he believes Manlius Faustus is asking questions independently. He won't talk to the vigiles because they are official.'

'Stupid punk!' Chloe commented. 'That warehouse killing was terrible but what happened to Rosius is utterly awful. The arsonist has got to be stopped.'

'They do their best,' Prisca put in. She had vigiles' wives among her customers. 'It's not their fault they are hand-picked idiots.'

'Under-resourced and under-valued.' I sympathised gently with the Fourth.

'Under-skilled and over-confident!' Spendo disagreed. 'Show them a fire and they can throw water on it, if it happens by the river, but this situation needs a much more sophisticated approach. It's a puzzle – which won't be their strength. We all know who the villains are, if anyone could find them, but someone tough needs to tackle the whole problem. If Faustus is up for it, he should be the right man. Energy and attack.'

'Well, he's modest, Spendo, but he will be pleased when I say you commended him. What's the word on the street about these villains?' I asked. I was surprised by the local level of knowledge, and the degree to which the nut-war gangsters and their actions seemed to be subjects for discussion.

'Relics of the old Balbinus gang,' Spendo answered at once. Morellus had muttered this suggestion to Tiberius and me as if it was a deadly secret. Either the Fourth Cohort was harbouring a mole, or more likely Morellus just told everyone.

'Really?' I played dumb. 'Balbinus Pius died years ago, didn't he? So who is controlling his crew, these days?'

'Well, his wife died, that mad hag Cornella Flaccida, but the daughter is still a key participant.'

'Her husband was called Florius?' As mentioned before, I had a personal loathing of that man. It was a bitter grief I had brought with me from Britain. I wanted to hear of his movements and who was supporting him in Rome. 'Wasn't he forced into exile to avoid charges of racketeering?'

'Florius Oppicus – a classic case of "gone abroad for his health",' confirmed Spendo, drily. 'Fast exit for avoidance purposes. He has to control his forces remotely, but there are couriers, and his men must be skilled at evading censorship. He still wields plenty of influence. His wife, the old crook's daughter, Balbina Milvia, lives where she has always lived, down near the Circus Max. She may not be seen about much, but anyone will tell you she is still holding the reins for Florius.'

'Always acted the innocent but is a dyed-in-the-wool associate,' I contributed: family lore.

'Your uncle once played around with her.'

Indeed. That was how we knew about her. 'True, I believe.' My aunt never let him forget it. 'I thought it was a family secret! How do you come by these details, Spendo?'

The little man laughed, almost to himself. He was silent for a while, then came out with his nugget: 'Even the wives and daughters of gangsters need a new roof sometimes.'

'You price their tiles?'

'They have tame builders on their payroll, brickmakers who give them free bricks – but, the cost of a roof being what it tends to be, every nice new pantiled area calls for a detailed estimate. My quote is always high, because I am careful. But the ladies in question give their builders the go-ahead, once they finish gasping at my figures. I get my fee. The wise ones even hire me as a project manager.'

It made sense, though I was amazed. 'You have been in the house of Balbina Milvia?'

He was showing off with glee. 'Met her. Must have been pretty once. Nice woman. Well, nice enough. You wouldn't want to upset her. She knows some very nasty people. *Husband* wasn't there, of course. Sad for her, but she seems to endure it. No doubt the money helps. And there is no doubt, the moolah still keeps rolling in. Paying for her roof will be no problem.'

'Well, that's good to hear!' I gazed at him, letting him enjoy his story. He looked about fifty, under the gnarling. Curly hair on the wild side, but neat dark blue tunic with white braiding. Good mind, wry sense of humour, not as bitter as he might have been, though perhaps an untrust-worthy maverick.

'Yes, I have been in her home. Lovely,' said Spendo, with real appreciation. 'Beautifully appointed, high-fashion décor, tasteful drapes. Everything money can buy, from the day she was married until today. I say "buy" though I don't expect she ever pays for much. Balbina Milvia was dandled by thieves and killers as a baby. Respect for her villainous father and her scary husband must bring her many, many presents. Her bank of treasure chests was formidable, even prettified with Spanish doilies. I have been in her house, I certainly have done – and, if you are interested, I have been on her roof, Albia.'

I saw no immediate use for this, but I promised to make a note.

'The main roof will be tight,' Spendo carried on doggedly. This man did adore specialist information. 'She will have it fixed up to a decent standard, if she follows my advice. I think she will. She commented that I obviously know what I am talking about. The main truss could be salvaged, but her soffits have gone and half her battens are shot, because the old tiles were too crude and too heavy. Probably some job-lot they pinched in the past, or got on the cheap.'

'Never worth it,' I managed to put in sagely.

Spendo careered on by himself, like a runaway wagon. 'Building maintenance is straightforward enough. You just need to find the true cause of your problem, then don't skimp on your repairs. All anybody needs to do is listen to me. There is a weak point by a turret, incidentally, at Milvia's; it only leaks in heavy thunderstorms. She's going to be too mean to continue the remedial works along that far. She will be sorry. Couple of large boys with axes, soon knock a useful hole through, drop in and surprise them.'

'What?'

'Tell your father, Falco, and that ex-vigiles mate of his. Your uncle. They'll never give up chasing the Balbinus mob so this might be a useful tip for them.'

'Oh, you know Father?'

'Doesn't everyone? Falco sold a set of *lorica squamata* for me once, republican scale armour, very rare piece. He got me a good price for it. I'm sorry I had to part with the suit, but we needed the cash.'

I decided not to wade into a tussle about how Father and Uncle Lucius were now too creaky to engage with old enemies, though I knew they would love to make a surprise descent through a roof. The oldies would never retire – they still talked about the Balbinus mob. The rest of us were supposed to discourage them. 'I am more concerned about my husband and the Fourth Cohort taking on the nut-distribution trouble.'

'They been given any leads?' asked Spendo. He never bothered to drop his voice, which was a loud one.

'Keep it down a bit! Agemathus, that *sigillaria*-seller, toddled along last night. It seems they have to find a man called Greius.'

Spendo nodded wisely. 'Once they pick him up, they can batter him until he croaks.'

'Tiberius Manlius prefers to be subtle,' I murmured, trying to be more discreet. 'I don't imagine you've heard anything about this Greius?'

This time Spendo shook his head, though it was a gesture of sorrow not a simple negative. 'Flavia Albia, Flavia Albia, what did I tell you about meeting Balbina Milvia?'

'I'm sorry, Spendo?'

'You need to listen more!' announced Spendo. 'Milvia has no secrets from me! I have been on her roof, Albia.'

35

My husband would say it was obvious what I should do next: be a good meek wife and tell him this, then he and Morellus could debrief Spendo officially. Tiberius would immediately add, 'But I suppose you have asked him for me?' Exactly, understanding spouse!

While I began talking to the estimator in earnest, Zoe and Chloe lost interest. They picked up their bucklers and wooden practice swords, then wandered indoors. Prisca followed, after a slave signalled to her that customers were in the changing room.

I made myself more comfortable, transferring to the seat Prisca had occupied, which had a battered cushion. 'Tell me, this roof you priced, Spendo, when did you inspect it?'

'Last week.'

'Amphitrite's armpit! No wonder you are up-to-date.'

Spendo touched his eyes and his ears with a forefinger to show he kept them open. He had old forge-burns along his wrist and arm. Blacksmithing is notoriously dangerous. His short stature must have meant he had to stand closer than was wise to the heat and the hammer.

He repeated that Balbina Milvia had called him in to price her leaky roof. While Spendo was up there measuring, she had a visitor. He, as a courtesy, stayed put, so the ladies could talk. He waited on the roof, rather than coming down to interrupt Milvia with points for customer consideration. I guessed he would have many such points, each needing its mini-lecture.

The women were served lunch in a room off an upper veranda, pushing the shutters wide open to let in light. They came upstairs to be private from the household staff; this brought them conveniently closer to Spendo. Milvia had forgotten him, but Spendo claimed he was hardly being furtive since he had left his ladder propped up in plain sight.

It was the first time I had heard of a ladder being used as an alibi. To some people they are invisible features in the landscape, but I am a contractor's wife, trained to check whether work is being done by rival builders and whether the position of their ladder could be reported as unsafe. In addition, as an informer's daughter, I had always been encouraged to watch who is nipping in furtively through windows.

Spendo, never in a hurry, took out his own lunch from the satchel where he kept his rules and note-tablets. It must have made an unusual sight, a madly inquisitive dwarf sitting up on a roof tree with his short sturdy legs dangling and breeze-blown curls, munching hard-boiled eggs and onions. Spendo was, I believe, aware of the comedy.

'What if anybody saw you from the street?'

'I would have hurled onions at them. I don't do target practice for nothing.'

'Wonderful! If you are ever short of work, you can come and help me on surveillance, Spendo. So! You could eavesdrop on Balbina Milvia?'

'They were obligingly in range.'

'The visitor was female too, you said?'

'She lives on the Aventine. Her name is Laetilla.'

'Oh, I know of her.'

'You know she is in a dirty business, then.'

'I do. A loan shark. Is she part of the Balbinus organisation?'

'Sounded as if her tribal ties are different. I meet a lot of people. I consider myself an expert judge,' Spendo boasted. 'My impression was she and Milvia knew one another of old but don't work together. Laetilla didn't talk in any way subserviently. If she answers to anyone, it will be other people.'

'What people, Spendo? Could you tell her reporting lines?'

'No names were mentioned. She called her associates "the brothers". That,' Spendo began, 'must be—'

'Couple of bullies based in Greater Laurel Street,' I interrupted, trying to establish credentials for myself in the conversation. 'Murrius and his bigger, supposedly badder, sibling.'

'Well, if you know, I needn't tell you!' Spendo grumbled sulkily.

'I don't know the brother's name.'

'Stuff you,' he reported rudely. 'Neither do I!'

'All right, then.'

'Quintus.'

'Quintus?'

'Quintus is the brother's praenomen anyway.'

'Well, thank you, though it's not much to go on.' There would be thousands of men in Rome with that first name. I had an uncle with it and the only oddity was that I didn't have more.

I calmed Spendo down, saying this set of brothers, Gaius and Quintus, were bankers for Laetilla; someone had said they had a bad reputation, but that was all I had learned. I wanted to hear why Laetilla met with Milvia. Had their meeting been tactical or casual? Just gossip, said Spendo. The women had shared a quick dish of olives and a herb tisane, both said business was good for them, then Laetilla wanted to share the exciting news that Murrius had been thrown out of home by his wife.

'Bit of scandal?'

'Gangland upset. They had a giggle together in a who'd-have-thought-she-had-the-nerve kind of way. According to Laetilla, Murrius is having to submit to it so he has moved in with his brother, at least temporarily.'

'Yes, people nearby have suggested that.'

'Analysing the language used,' Spendo carried on in his pompous way, 'I reached my verdict that Laetilla and Milvia have known each other long-term, but the brothers don't figure much.'

'Not in the Balbinus group?'

'Known associates, not enmeshed.'

I nodded, though I was mainly concerned to find out what might have been said about my now fleeing client. 'And what was the verdict on the Murrius domestic?'

'He asked for it. She is testing him. He won't accept that. His brother will gee him up to retaliate, to show he is a man. The wife will pay for chancing it. The crunch is coming any day now. The women agreed that, once the brothers are ready, they will bring the wife to heel and it will not be nice.'

I screwed up my mouth. Part of my duty to my client meant not telling anyone, even good contacts, what I knew about Nephele's escape. At the moment she must still be on her journey downriver, not safe yet.

I suspected Spendo could see I was holding back. 'Did they mention the parrot?' I asked, as a distraction.

'There is a parrot involved in this comedy?'

'Feathers and bile, but they love it. Bitter custody battle.'

'So they will pretend they are staying together for the bird?'

'Fatal mistake. Same as children – it always goes sour.'

'Parrots can live for many years, though not for ever! The impression I received,' Spendo assured me solemnly, 'is that a reconciliation will occur. Will making-up be forcibly imposed? I wonder. I detected that the Quintus brother rules like a despot. You may have better information than me, Flavia Albia.'

'Not my show. I was just passing the house and I heard them shouting.'

'Laetilla said the wife even threw his mummified leopard out into the street.'

'She threatened it. She yelled she would dump the step-children too – but his precious wild-beast collection was intended to rile him more.'

'The leopard issue is a kick in the balls for Murrius,' agreed Spendo. 'He is going demented over it. According to Laetilla, big bro says little bro's furry friend stinks, so tyrannical Quintus refused to give it house room. But they have now found somewhere to put it.' The dwarf reached a new level of emphasis even for him. For the first time he had even lowered his strident voice.

'Am I interested in where a crime lord secures his tatty taxidermy, Spendo?' I quizzed.

'Mummy,' Spendo corrected me. 'Not taxidermy. This is what makes the puss precious. Its owner spent a huge sum having it made. Laetilla never said how he first got hold of it, but a firm of Egyptian specialists by the new Temple of Isis did the work. It was to be a big feature of a jungle tableau that Murrius was planning to set up in his dining room.'

I said I could see why his wife threw him out.

Spendo, obsessive himself, missed my point. 'It could have worked. I'm envious. Myself, my pride and joy is my own slingshot machine, an *onager* that I keep in the yard, but it's not particularly useful in a city setting – the neighbours don't like me firing it. I would happily make an offer for this beast, but apparently the preservation fails to satisfy close inspection. This is Rome. The Egyptians preserve a lot of domestic-sized cats, but a full-sized leopard is a whole new game of knucklebones. You can't get the natron. That's a drying salt they use for various purposes, but most signifi-cant in funeral ceremonies where pellets are stuffed into corpses to soak up moisture and deter moulds. It is gathered from evaporated lake beds . . .' He was off again.

'I don't care,' I declared frankly.

'I think you will, Flavia Albia,' came the ponderous reply. 'The ladies chattered away about this leopard.' I dare say Laetilla and Milvia were both relieved they did not have the odoriferous thing standing among their own cushioned dining couches. 'Laetilla said the brothers have the leopard in a lock-up until Murrius regains access to his home abode.'

'And where is the temporary leopard lair?'

'That I don't know,' the dwarf apologised. His disfigured face crumpled with disappointment at this failure. 'Laetilla saw no need to specify, which you may find of interest in itself. I am dying to know – I would love to evaluate the Egyptians' work.'

'But you've no gen on where Spotty is stashed?'

'Sadly no. Laetilla mentioned "that old hole-in-the-wall",

as if Balbina Milvia knows. But every street in Rome is lined with those. All Laetilla specified is that the key to it lives with some trusty the brothers must know.'

'New face?'

'Not a new name, though. You should tell Faustus. The key-holder for this lock-up is called Greius.'

36

Yes, it would be useful for my husband to know of an association between Murrius, his brother called Quintus, Laetilla, and now Greius. If Murrius and his brother had just been identified as employers of Greius, it fingered them as the nut-dealing mob. Whether loans and nuts were linked in criminal activity, or how it worked, was an intriguing question, though of course my male associates would hog that question to themselves.

For me, these glimpses from Spendo confirmed that Nephele was right to flee and had chosen her moment well. She had married into a family with rising influence, villains in age-old rackets who were flexing new muscles. If she was lucky, she took off before Murrius and his tyrannical brother gained so much kudos that he would be absolutely unable to tolerate loss of face.

Even so, Murrius would endeavour to punish Nephele. I must hope his network was not yet so widespread that he would trace her despite the screening I had put in place. People said his brother was worse, but Murrius sounded hard enough. To me, his coveting the parrot and the leopard were not signs of a soft heart; they advertised a man who had the money for very expensive luxuries and who thought he warranted such trappings.

He sounded no pushover. When his brother had

complained the leopard stank, Murrius still kept it. They then found a solution together so there must be no serious bad blood. Their lock-up was somewhere Balbina Milvia knew, which suggested her father's organisation had used it, but now the Aventine nut group had taken it over. I must tell Morellus to have his men look for a booth with a big cat peering out. Murrius couldn't hide a leopard in a cupboard. He wouldn't want to shove it in a corner. If the fool dreamed of this beast as a dining-room spectacle, he would mothball it carefully.

Then there was the killer agent, Greius: did he work for one of the brothers, or both? What did he generally keep in the lock-up? More bad nuts? Other materials? At Saturnalia, my bet was candles. I tried to buy some on my way home, but there were none to be had. A pop-up chandlery usually appeared in December, yet I saw no sign of it. This was how criminals operated: they created a shortage, then cashed in when children were pathetically crying because they might have no lights this year.

I was mentally allotting a better business plan to the mobsters than I had myself. I could have run a successful crime network. If I did not pick up new clients soon, that might be a new career. Being married to an aedile would give me a good start: people in your neighbourhood always respect men who buy their way into magistracies, which extends to the women who have snapped those men up.

As I walked the short distance home, I reflected that controlling commodities was nothing new. Emperors did it, not only with critical resources like gold and silver, but corn to feed the masses and, on occasions, wine, olive oil, balsam, rare dyes or silk. In imperial protectionism they used the same strong-arm methods as criminals. The key purpose was to make money. Money and power were equal, inter-dependent assets. Rulers behaved like crooks; crooks aimed to become kings in the community. Rome, thank the gods, had an antipathy to kings.

At our house, someone was about to be appointed King-for-the-Day. As happens with real-life rulers, it was the wrong person.

I came in, unchallenged. Rodan was not in his cubicle. Had he yet sat on his stool for even half an hour? Would he ever? Or had I merely added a pointless hanger-on to the food bill? One extra embuggerance in the general quotient?

I tested the air, as if trying to sniff out our mouldy gladiator. I caught only the slightly damp, decaying odour of green vegetation, as festival garlands started to hum. They were near death already. By the time Saturnalia ended, our home would be decorated with strands of garden compost.

Paris appeared. He told me Rodan was sulking in his hut. 'When Dromo brought over his things for him, some of Rodan's gruesome possessions must have fallen off the handcart. Have you seen that murderous spear he treasures? Dromo insists nothing else was ever on the cart, and Rodan himself loaded it. Anything he missed must have been left at Fountain Court. Rodan wants to go back, but he won't go by himself.'

'Why not?'

'People hassled him. Really put the wind up him.'

'Oh, I remember him saying something. Some gladiator! If he had ever fought in the arena against wild animals, a lion would have picked him up and gently put him in a basket on the sidelines, feeling sorry for him. Will you volunteer to take him?'

'No,' said Paris.

I sighed. Thanks, Paris. I would have liked to cut his festival bonus, but we both knew he had done good work to earn it. I managed not to snarl at him. 'Well, at least that sounds as if Rodan does intend to stay as our porter.'

'Thrills!' Paris was becoming outspoken. Still, he would fit in. Everyone here wore liberty caps all year round. 'You'd better come quick, Albia. Fornix has made must-cakes today, so people are forcing him to give out the bean for choosing the Lord of Misrule.'

In our house, misrule was hard to control even normally. For instance, they had started this little ceremony without me. I was supposed to supervise our cake lottery, to make sure that the bean ended up where I wanted it.

Too late.

Dromo had grabbed the serving tray, determined to help out on the sole occasion I needed him to leave this alone. Cake was his province, he believed. They were all as bad. Everyone had gathered; even Rodan had stopped sulking. The entire crew, including Tiberius, had their spiced treat ready in their hot hands. It looked as if the little boys were already slyly nibbling.

My arrival was greeted with a cheer, not out of love but because they could now let fly with '*Io, Saturnalia!*' and before I could check the position of any cake Fornix had secretly marked, they would sink their teeth in. Fornix was looking helpless. It was going wrong. I knew my mother would never let this happen, so why had I lost control? (Answer: I went out; they did whatever they wanted while I foolishly left them to it.)

There was one crumbling cake saved for me. Tiberius looked guilty. 'I'm afraid you've ended up with the wonky one.' Half of it was missing. I noted the rest had been 'tidied' by someone picking out its pine nuts. 'Oh dear! Is yours too battered? Want to swap with me, love?'

It was a feeble offer. I declined with a long-suffering shrug. This festival was really ramming home that I was a failure in my new maternal role. If we had owned a parrot, I might have told Tiberius he could keep the children while I was going into exile with the bird.

Even though I no longer had a client, Beauty in Greater Laurel Street had glued her foul-mouthed self into a cranny in my mind. What would happen to the poor feathered thing? This is the curse of the freelance. No work, no pay, everyone relying on you and, to cap it all, a bad conscience.

My secret plan was for two beans. I had discussed this with Fornix, who was ready to say he had put two in by accident. Little Gaius and Lucius would have received one each. We would have had two Kings-for-the-Day, called it a special treat, and avoided whining. They would both be excited and happy, then possibly the regal demands they imposed on the rest of us would not have been too crazy. It was a perfectly decent plan. Like all good plans, it fell apart as soon as fools interfered.

Lucius did receive the first bean, but he swallowed his cake without chewing and choked on it. Fornix, a useful kind of chef, upended the three-year-old, held his heels and shook him briskly. I wondered satirically how much call there had been for this when he presided over the lush kitchens and fancy clients at Fabulo's, the famous restaurant. Barley ran up; she wolfed down the regurgitated cake, including the bean. 'Oh, good dog!' I warbled despondently.

Dromo had taken the other marked cake. 'I've got the bean! I'm going to be the King! Oh, I'm going to have a lot of fun with this . . .' There was no longer any point in asking him to generously give up his bean to Gaius, because Lucius no longer had his. I despaired.

Dromo had no idea he had done wrong. 'This is brilliant! Do I have to wear a crown?'

Everyone roared 'No!' (Or, in one surreptitious baritone, '*No, you bloody don't, Dromo!*') Over the racket we could make out a visitor at the door, knocking. Rodan was too busy thinking about why *he* had no bean, then wondering whether there was a dark plot against him. I went myself.

I swept open the double doors with a festival flourish. This might have been a serious mistake, because I realised that Nephele's absence from home must have been noticed there. Outside, her husband and his heavy squad could well have been gathered to attack me. Fortunately, it simply turned out to be the flitter's sister.

37

She told me on the doorstep that her name was Terentia Berenike.

She was significantly younger than Nephele. Right from the start I wondered about that. Nephele had said they were very close, and Berenike behaved as if it were so. But in my own family there were more than ten years between my two sisters and me; I knew it made a difference. They thought we were all best friends, but there were many things I would never say to Julia and Favonia.

I made sure I looked surprised. I let her come in, and the interview salon was called into use again. Outside in the courtyard, the noise quietened, then everyone else dispersed. I'd like to think they were learning polite behaviour, but they had simply run out of cakes.

Berenike was not only younger but prettier and livelier. She was well turned out, in her own style, which involved long scarves to twirl and hair curls to twiddle. A perfume I would have rejected formed a defensive wall around her, driving away anyone with a sensitive nose. For that whiff alone, she seemed less intelligent than her sister, or had a worse personal maid. The women's relationship showed in their build and their facial features.

'Can I help you?'

'I am looking for my sister.'

'Not here, I'm afraid. She did explore using my services at one time, but in the end we parted company.' When you tell lies, use as much truth as you can. Any successful criminal knows that. 'You seem anxious. Why are you looking for Nephele?'

This one was a burbler, letting a torrent tumble out: 'I called on her today, but she was not at the house.' She blinked sooty eyelashes in a dramatic show of anxiety. 'No one knows where she is, or when she left, or why. When her people went to wake her this morning, they couldn't find her. She had said nothing to me. I am terrified something bad has happened to her.'

'Really? What do you think it might be?' Berenike looked vague. 'She has mentioned troubles with her husband,' I suggested patiently. 'Could he have something to do with this?'

She shook her head vigorously and came out with, 'He is as upset as I am.'

'He knows she has gone missing?' I asked, showing my surprise. 'I can tell you, without breaking any confidences, that I do know your sister has barred Murrius from their house.' Face it: all Greater Laurel Street knew that.

'He came this morning while I was there, and because Nephele has disappeared, the servants let him in. So far, he is just striding about, shouting. He is utterly distraught.'

I bet he is! I addressed the sister firmly. 'I can shed no light, I'm afraid. But aren't you all reacting too soon? Your sister has only been missed this morning. There could be a perfectly ordinary explanation. Nephele may have gone somewhere particular and wanted an early start. She decided not to disturb her household at such an hour – whenever it was.' My breakfast time, dammit. 'She should be back. It's too soon for hysterics, I suggest.'

'My sister would never do anything like that.'

'No? Once women start taking a stand against their husbands,' I scoffed, 'in my experience they quickly change in other ways. Are you married?' I asked, jumping on the subject abruptly.

'Not yet,' Berenike answered, with a jangle of her arm bangles. She pushed gold up and down in agitation. 'We are finalising plans.'

'Who is the lucky man?'

She tensed, shy of discussing her engagement. I deduced an arrangement of convenience, without affection. Perhaps she was even an unwilling bride. Quite possibly she wanted someone else.

'Known him long?' I persisted, wondering about this.

'A son of family friends.'

'First time?'

'Yes, for both of us.'

'When is the happy day?' Still curious about her attitude, I kept hauling out the usual trivialities.

'In the New Year.'

'Soon! Are you excited?'

'Of course.'

'Was your sister excited for you?'

'I think so.'

'I would expect you both to be looking forward to you being a married woman as well,' I said frankly. 'So much more to talk about!'

'But she tells me everything!'

Did she? 'She said you were close. Berenike,' I sprang on her, 'is it possible your sister has taken a lover?' I had decided this was good cover to protect Nephele.

Her sister gasped. 'Oh, no!'

'No?'

'Never!'

'You seem very sure!' I let scepticism register. 'I do know the kind of families your sister and her husband belong to. Private clans where loyalty is always strong. Where wives do not abandon husbands because traditional rules forbid any flexibility – and they dare not stray. This could explain a great deal of reticence. In a situation where nobody breaks those rules, a wife with a secret might well say nothing, not even to you.'

The younger sister brushed this aside again. 'Oh, she would have told me!'

I made no reply but I certainly knew Nephele had, after reflection, agreed with me to keep her sister in ignorance about her real flight from Rome.

'So you cannot help me, Flavia Albia?'

'No, I am sorry. I have nothing to tell.'

At that point, I saw a subtle change. As Berenike twisted scarves and adjusted bangles, it was clear she was failing to achieve whatever she had come for. She had no idea what to do next. If she did have a mission, what drove her?

Suddenly I guessed: 'He sent you!' I challenged. 'Gaius Murrius. He believes his wife came to me with her problems, and he has persuaded you to find out!'

'The poor soul thinks she has left him!' Berenike wailed. She seemed relieved I had given her something to say, though she was defending him very unexpectedly. 'He desperately wants her to come home.'

'I am sure he does,' I answered coldly. 'Did he bully you into coming?'

'No! I wanted to come.'

'Murrius made you do his dirty work?'

'No, that's unfair. He loves her.'

'Oh, I am sure he is enraged if he has lost her!' I scoffed. 'I have seen this man. I draw my own conclusions. You ought to be ashamed to act as his spy.'

'No! I am concerned for her. I love her too!'

I stood up. 'If you do, then allow her to make her choices – if that is what she has done. Your sister was never really my client, but as a woman I will speak on her behalf, defending her, as you should do, Berenike. From what I saw, any decision was made from free will. And judging by what I have glimpsed of that marriage, if she were to be reconciled with Gaius Murrius, she would most likely pay for it dearly.'

I was shooing the younger sister out. 'Go back to your brother-in-law – if you really must report to him.'

'You sound as if you are questioning my loyalty to Nephele!'

'Only you know whether you are loyal. My advice is, choose very carefully which party to support. Tell Murrius this from me: if she has left him, he should consider *why*. Would a just husband pursue her, or should he accept an inevitable situation? When a couple have lost all mutual respect, it is time to conclude the farce.'

I wanted to ask what would happen now about the parrot, but I sensibly kept quiet.

38

I was finished with my non-client, let alone her fluttery, jingly sister. My household needed me. Dromo had had time to realise his new role as King-for-the-Day might not be as wonderful as he had thought. He was puzzling and growing nervous. 'Nobody has told me what I have to do!'

'Behave nicely all day and be kind to everyone,' I bluffed airily.

Suza, young herself and envious that *he* had snaffled the bean, explained more bitterly: 'Be in charge, you idiot. You have to make mischief during the celebrations. When guests come, you must insult them horribly. They must only react with a gay laugh to whatever you do, and nobody can beat you for it. You have to wear crazy clothes—'

'Where do I get those?' Usually he wore old cast-offs from his master, mended as necessary, although Tiberius was a careful man. After Dromo had worn a tunic for a week, its patch quota increased fast. After a month his outfit looked like a floor cloth.

'Dromo,' I suggested, 'you can go down to my parents' house. My sisters may be able to find you an old costume we once used.' I didn't tell him it was a carrot.

Suza kept going: '—and chase women around.'

'Chase them where to?' he fretted. One good thing about this slave was that he was not fully out of his pimply adolescence, so he fled if a woman said boo. Which they therefore did on principle.

'*Around!*' yelled Suza, maddened even more. 'You run around after them. You are not supposed to catch them! It's a joke, Dromo!'

The boy found that even more worrying. Although Dromo had desperately wanted to be chosen, it had not struck any of us until then that he would be so anxious. He loathed the responsibility and was terrified of messing up. In a boy I had liked more, it would have seemed sweet.

'Now look!' Tiberius gravely instructed him. 'You have seen it happen plenty of times, Dromo. The idea is that as King-for-the-Day you will rule over chaos, rather than the normal good order that applies in Roman households.'

'Ha! Not in mine!' I snorted. I then remarked loftily that only the uptight Romans could formally organise chaos for themselves. Give it a special day, invent traditions, apply rules, appoint someone to ensure a suitable riot happened . . .

'Oh, Albia!' everyone else trilled. 'You are such a Briton!'

To avoid the Dromo tutorial, I decided I would take Rodan back to Fountain Court to fetch whatever nasty item he had left behind. First, he had to be reminded that he had been making a fuss earlier, and why. In front of everyone he would not say what he had lost, though as he and I walked he confided that it was the purse of money my father had given to him. He had buried it in a corner of the yard for safety; when Dromo brought the handcart to fetch his other things, Rodan had forgotten it existed.

The ridiculous lump was shambling along with me, full of anxiety. Once tall, over the years he had grown stooped and grizzled. His arms and legs were muscular but his belly was far too big, clad in a tunic that looked as if it had been used to rub down a very grimy cow. His battered old boots had never matched; one had lost its fastening.

'Do you think anyone will have dug it up, Albia?'

'Not if you kept it a secret and if you disguised where you had been digging. I hope you locked the gates after you left?' At that, his silence was ominous. 'Juno, what's worrying you, Rodan? Had you told someone?'

'Oh, no!' he said, in a way that confirmed he had blabbed. As we reached the end of the alley, he slowed down and asked whether Falco would be angry.

'If you lost the loot? I shouldn't think so.' I thought my father would guffaw that on the one occasion he was generous to Rodan it had turned into a pointless gesture. 'He won't care – but he won't replace it. It is – or was – your money now. Don't expect another purse if you haven't taken proper care, Rodan.'

Rodan was dragging his feet when he ought to have been rushing to find his treasure. Puzzled at how upset he was, I insisted he tell me the problem.

'I don't want to go down the alley. Albia, will you fetch it for me?'

This big scared hulk was supposed to be my protection. I growled, but it was a time of seasonal rejoicing so I agreed. He could wait near the corner, by the old barber's, which was closed today for the holiday since this was never a district where men paid to look spruce at festivals.

'Confess now, Rodan.' I had had more success in screwing admissions from murder suspects. 'Come on, you've lost your nerve. What happened to you? What was bad enough to scare a tough old fighter?'

My father said Rodan had never been any good. Still, he looked the part – and I now learned that that had caused

228

the trouble. Rodan admitted he had taken some cash and gone out for a Saturnalia drink. Normally he stayed in his cubicle, too mean to buy a round, which meant people had asked him about his unexpected appearance at the Hungry Goat.

'Oh, gods, Rodan, you never chose the Goat?'

Then, as often happens when a man is big and ugly and, Rodan claimed, if he looks able to handle himself, some drunk tried to goad him into a fight.

'What, the old *Who are you looking at? Think you're hard? Want to try it, then?*' Anyone who tackled Rodan must imagine he was well past it.

Rodan looked surprised that I could imagine this scene. He said that with the bar owner wanting to prevent his place being smashed up, together they had managed to calm things.

'What was scary, then?'

'Afterwards.'

On Rodan's way home the same character, with aggressive friends, had surrounded him. He reckoned they had been lying in wait. They tried to persuade him to drink more with them, but even he could tell this was a bad idea.

They continued to pester him. Pushing and shoving him, they showed a big interest in the tenement he was supposed to look after: was anyone left living there? Could people get in to use the space? They had more menace than he could handle. 'Those fellows were planning something. I didn't want to be dragged in. After that, even though I'd said it to the barman, they asked me again whether Falco gave me a Saturnalia pay-off – but I pretended I had already spent it. "He would not give me much," I told them. "He is too mean." You won't tell him?'

I would, because Falco would laugh, though I soothed Rodan. 'Let's hope nobody thought you were dumb enough to leave your money unguarded!' Dear gods, he had done, though. I told him to sit outside the barber's and not move.

'He won't let people use his stool, not unless they want a shave.'

'Rodan, he will today because he's closed. It looks as if he has left and gone to his family, poor fellow. Shut up, sit there, just stay still until I come back.' When Rodan meekly squatted on the stool, I noticed his hair was grey all over. That's Saturnalia: you suddenly notice someone you have known for ever is turning into an old man. He has a look that makes you wonder if he will even survive until next year.

I set off glumly. All the other shops were closed too. Most looked derelict, the favoured decorative style for premises in our alley. There were no garlands on porticos. When the December darkness fell, nobody would put out lamps.

I had lived in Fountain Court for long enough. I won't say it held no terrors for me; I was cautious today. I ought to be safe with a gladiator, though locals would know Rodan was useless. I had brought my dog. Barley knew we were not safe. She was huddling up behind me, so close that her shoulder bumped my calf. When a shutter creaked, I heard a small whimper.

The lane was as dirty as ever. Unidentifiable smells hung above foetid winter puddles. I walked up the centre of what passed for a street, the dark passageway between the looming unhappy buildings. My wariness increased; I knew not to pass close to doorways. We always fooled ourselves that to belong here gave some protection, but that was a travesty.

I had pride that I had survived such a long time in this

hole, yet on returning I felt newly annoyed that the sordid neglect was allowed to persist. When would the Aventine become a refined haven? How could the rack-rent tenements and heartbreak lanes be transformed into something salubrious? Well, watch out: Trajan is coming! They were all in for a shock when they gained a tight-arse provincial senator at the old Eagle Building: Lenia's Laundry, Falco's office, Albia's sad home for over a decade . . .

I passed by the Lumber Room. I thought I heard a door-hinge, but when I looked back it was closed, with the place in darkness as usual. No one was buying Gifts of Charm. No one ever would. On a whim I clucked at Barley and walked back to peer inside. If anyone had suddenly appeared, looking out at me through the shutter, I would have been terrified. No one did.

At our own building, I had brought my key to the lock on the metal gate, which I found Rodan had properly secured. However, when I walked through the entrance and out into the old laundry yard, I saw at once that people had been in. They had smashed open a gate from the back lane. This was not simple vandalism: they seemed to have been industrious. Bits of old line were strung, criss-crossing the open area; new candles hung in pairs from string loops, their wax drying. Typically for Fountain Court, these wobbly, wind-bobbing artefacts looked meagre: one-dip wonders. They would either flare and splutter out, or shrivel down to nothing much too fast.

I was oddly furious that people had invaded *our* building. I had lived here. I married and lost a husband here. Struggled and suffered, then learned to tolerate my situation until I met Tiberius. Now, as my father loved to tease me, the funds from selling up would be my inheritance one day. Well, mine,

Mother's, my sisters', my brother's – plus another score of hangers-on that Falco claimed he had to look after. 'You can have all the loot but take note: it comes with blood-sucking parasites!'

We had our own freeloaders, without giving half-baked Fountain Court artisans unlicensed use of our space. Muttering, I pulled down all the candles, wound up the lines, marched through the back gate into the manured gully that passed for a track, then flung the pathetic lights outside. On a whim I kept a pair to show Tiberius and Morellus, in case they matched the candles left by those arsonists who burned the Rosius apartment.

Whoever owned the rest would need to come before scavengers descended. Given where we were, eyes were probably watching me. In the laundry's old fuel store, I found lumps of charcoal and wrote on the back wall:

DANGEROUS SITE
DO NOT TRESPASS
YES, THAT MEANS YOU, PUNKS
NO PAY-OUT FOR ACCIDENTS

That would be a useful health-and-safety guide for intruders who could read.

Inside the yard again, I piled old props, planks and a holed laundry tub against the back gate. This was my gesture for illiterate ones, or idiots who simply ignored my sign.

I found Rodan's purse. I dug it up easily, since the big booby had left the short-handled spade he'd used to bury it leaning on a wall right there.

232

Quietly I left the Eagle Building, hoping this time was the last time. It was an enduring feature of Fountain Court that you felt you could never escape.

As I came into the alley, a man slipped out of the Lumber Room. He was tightly cloaked against the winter, wearing a liberty cap pulled right down. From behind, he had the familiar shifty lope used by everyone around here, where even people who were managing to get by looked like losers, while anyone who was slightly successful hated anybody else to know.

Now when I went past the shop it had a very faint light inside as if someone had stayed behind there. I carried on and picked up Rodan. He was gibbering in case the man who had emerged had been one of the scary crew who tried to bully him. I offered to go after him to ask him nicely not to do it again. Rodan started to create even more; by then the man had vanished.

I would never have tackled the stranger in any case. We now had the money purse so I wanted to move on quickly. I was still grasping the spade (it was too good to leave), which might have been misinterpreted as a threat – never wise when speaking to a neighbour in Fountain Court. *Who are you looking at? Want to try it, then?*

Rodan and I set off homewards in silence. I was feeling dark nostalgia, a result of visiting the old place again. Perhaps that accounted for my sudden fantasy about the furtive man. Even from behind he had seemed familiar from elsewhere, somewhere a thousand miles from here and many years before . . . He looked like Florius. But I knew it could not be.

Still, people who worked for Florius were in Rome. I should have thought of it before, but the Lumber Room had once belonged to the father-in-law, Balbinus Pius. That was why Balbina Milvia would know about it, as Spendo had said. She and her husband must now be the owners. How could I have been so slow? Well, one reason was that I hadn't lived in Rome then. I did not automatically make a link to a gangster like Balbinus Pius who had died before my time.

'Rodan, has anyone been using that old shop, the one full of junk that's never bought or sold?'

'The place Falco says is for stolen goods?'

'That place.' Rodan looked vague, but I knew he was always nosy and never disturbed by ethics. 'I don't suppose – well, let's face it, Rodan, I *do* suppose – when you thought nobody was there, you broke in for a quick look around?'

'Oh, yes,' Rodan admitted easily. If he'd ever had brains they were pulped long ago. And the clumsy lump was bound to have left behind traces of a nocturnal visit. I bet they realised he had been in – I bet that was why they'd applied frighteners, to stop him going in there.

'What are they up to inside?'

'Some horrible skipper and his boys store a lot of sacks.'

'Nuts?'

'Could be. They bring them in, they take them out again. Then they bring in new ones.'

'Who is the big rissole?'

'What?'

'The horrible skipper you mentioned?'

'I don't know.' Then how can you call him horrible, Rodan? 'I've never seen him and they don't like people asking questions. Those boys of his are the ones who muscled in on me.'

'They probably wanted to keep you out of their shop. Was their skipper with them that night?'

'No. But another one was, a young man who comes along all the time to open up for deliveries.'

'You've seen him? Can you describe him, Rodan?'

'Just a man.'

'Young, you say?'

'Well, younger than the chief.'

'I thought you said you had never seen the chief?'

'Well, maybe. Somebody who made them all jump was in there one day, but I stayed at home in my cubicle.'

'That's so helpful! Was it the opener-upper who just walked down the alley today? Had he been there to shutter up?'

'No, it wasn't him.'

'Sure?'

'Positive.'

'The place used to be deserted. No one used it for years. Extra activity is interesting.'

'Right!' said Rodan, not at all interested.

I was now thinking that if we had not had his purse to keep safe, I might go back and break in myself. Caution took over. I changed tack. 'Rodan, someone is making tapers and drying them in our old yard.'

'Falco won't like that. I bet it's them from the shop. It's for Saturnalia.'

'Badly made rubbish to sell for the festival?'

His voice dropped. 'When they hustled me the other night, they threatened they would set me on fire. The man who opens up said it, the cocky one. He said burning people alive was his speciality.'

'Rodan, that's an appalling threat.'

'I'm not scared.' He was, extremely. 'Afterwards they all made out they were only joking. But I knew they could do it, because when I was in the shop I saw they have a great big container full of sulphur matches.'

'Really? No wonder there's a shortage.'

'They're not any good.' He must have pinched a few and tried to use them. Rodan then told me something else he saw that was crazier: 'They've got a big stuffed lion in that shop. I thought it was a real one – I scarpered out of there when it looked at me, I can tell you!'

Ah! Pardon my pickiness, but I think that lion was a leopard. And not stuffed, Rodan, but preserved by the best priestly Egyptian methods.

So! Murrius was keeping his mummified cat there; Rodan had seen it. Now I had identified the lock-up, I was stunned to realise that the bully who came to open for deliveries must be Greius.

39

As we neared home, we saw someone trying to escape from a friend: Pinarius and the pal who wanted his money back. 'I have to have it, man! The goldsmith has delivered a stinking ultimatum. He must be paid before the holiday.'

I stopped to listen.

'Let go of me, old mucker,' Pinarius suggested, sounding polite as he attempted to free his tunic, which the other man had grasped so hard at the neck it was ripping. It was a good garment, sound cloth with long warm sleeves, a decent fit around the body. The owner was almost suspended. Pinarius might look as if he used his gymnasium member-ship for falling asleep on the massage slab, but his assailant's muscular shoulders and legs were the results of serious weight-lifting. 'Leave off and I'll fetch your cash . . .' He was fibbing in my opinion.

'You said that the last time!'

'Now I'm serious.' No, he was still lying. But the angry debtor loosened his grip so Pinarius had his feet back on the ground. 'I've got it safe, you know I have, Quintus. The goldsmith was stupid. He should never have let you take the chain home.' It was common practice to release goods on approval, though it led to a great deal of non-payment.

'Two chains!' snarled the buyer, Quintus. Still, he released

Pinarius at last. 'Two, in case both desperate ladies wanted one – which the greedy kittens both did, surprise, surprise! I can't hold him off any longer. He's already badgering my uncle for some debt he stupidly ran up, and now he's really got me by the goolies. He'll be complaining to my father next.'

'He may already have done.' Pinarius had stepped well back, brushing down his clothes. He pulled his cloak across, as if to protect his tunic from further ripping.

'Oh, sod him! My old man told me to stop screwing around. You know I gave you the cash to stop him getting his hands on it. He's trying to tie up my funds so I can't hand out girlfriend presents. Has my pater had a go at you?'

'He may have tried,' Pinarius hedged nervously.

'Well, sod him too!' roared the other. 'He can't accept that I live and work in another sphere now. You'll have to choose. Are you more frightened of him – or of me?'

'Oh, you!' admitted Pinarius, straight away.

'Get my cash, then! I'll be in Dolichenus Street.' His friend thrust Pinarius hard against a wall to emphasise the urgency, then went beetling off, as if he assumed it was a done deal.

As Rodan and I passed Pinarius, he was still straightening his tunic and adjusting his cloak brooch, a roundel with a face on it, pudgy and dim-looking. He himself was finer-featured, someone I had regularly seen around our neighbourhood, so I gave him a friendly smile. He nodded back. We were in sight of home; I pushed Rodan on his way, while I stayed to talk.

'He meant that!' I sympathised, while Pinarius rubbed a bruised arm. 'For Heaven's sake, why on earth are you not returning his money, sunshine? Have you spent it?'

'I have not!' Pinarius retorted hotly.

'Give it to him, then.'

'I can't.'

'What's stopping you?'

'I can't tell him why.'

'Never mind him, just tell me! That goldsmith won't give up, you know – they tend to persist. Share,' I wheedled shamelessly. 'You will feel better. What's the story, Pinarius?'

Using his name had an effect; he probably thought I might know his mother. Indeed, this was possible, if she used Prisca's baths. 'It's his venomous father who forbade me to give him back the money.'

'Has the pater grabbed the cash off you?'

'No, it's not his to pinch. My friend earned it working for someone even more aggressive – though that's another story. We were mates once, but Quintus has gone to the bad since he joined forces with new people. His own damned father is never slow to argue, but even he is leery because he farmed out their boy as a business deal – supposedly to gain experience. Which he certainly has, the cocky sod!'

'Experience in what?'

'Hell, I don't know. I close my eyes to the dark arts of commerce.'

His friend had not struck me as someone with an apprenticeship. Basically, he did not look like anyone who worked. Neither did: they were trust-fund tots – big signet rings and dressed in different tunics every time I saw them. They were about the same age, middle twenties. When they grew up, perhaps by forty, they would merge into the crowd as commodity traders, becoming fathers themselves and creating wealth to spoil their own vacuous children. Clean hands, dirty ethics: normal for Rome.

I sighed gently. '"Two chains", he said. Lad about town?

Splurging in wild, exciting ways? Well, two-timing girlfriends is routine in some circles. I suppose his father has learned what he's up to, so he wants to put a stop to it? Reputation. Family honour. Junior will never rise in society if he behaves like a low-grade adulterer – well, not if all the world knows about it. It's time he cleaned up his act, which he has no doubt been ordered to do many times?'

Pinarius nodded mournfully. 'They are making him get married. Supposed to settle him down. Also it's making another link to those people he's gone to work with.'

'Lovely!' My tone must have been drab. 'Then he'll two-time the wife.'

'He'd better be careful! She has a powerful family. I wouldn't want her brother coming after me. He won't cope well with a let-down.' Smiling sadly, Pinarius admitted, 'Quintus is asking for it, I'm afraid. He's fixed up a bachelor love-nest. He's thinking he can juggle any number of conquests. He and his wife will be living with his parents, so his mistress can be kept in his getaway. Mind you, I hear his women are starting to feel suspicious of him.'

'And also his father?'

'As soon as that old bastard can pinpoint exactly how young Quintus carries on, just listen for the war-cries.'

'You are caught in the middle?'

Pinarius groaned. 'Skewered!' the stressed young man admitted. 'His pater knows mine. I could end up in trouble at home for something that was never my fault. I have two fledgling brothers jostling in the nest and I need to look blameless. Besides, I do not want to be anywhere nearby when the Cornelli start disembowelling each other. And the bride's brother is terrifying.'

'Who are the Cornelli? And the bride's brother?'

'If you don't know them, Flavia Albia, be glad.'

He was taking off. As he went, I called after him that this was Saturnalia. At times of joy and reconciliation, in almost every family some war occurs, whether it has been declared or not. Pinarius replied over one shoulder that the Cornelli would not pause for formalities. 'During a war, Rome opens the doors of the Temple of Janus to show there's conflict somewhere. The Cornelli don't bother. They simply go for people. When tomorrow's feast is at its height, pop your head out of a window and listen for the screams.'

I hallooed after him down the street that I hoped it would not be him screaming. Pinarius raised an arm as he went loping off. All around was festival merriment, even though it was still only afternoon.

40

The clamour died behind me as I closed our front doors. Once inside, street noise was muffled. I paused, listening to the quiet of the house. All sounded well.

I left my cloak on a chest in the entrance, then went in to conduct a fast survey. Suza was talking to Paris, with Paris patiently enduring Suza's nonsense. Gratus was talking to Fornix, who was busily cooking since tomorrow was the main feast; Fornix, concentrating, would not talk back. Barley, who had scuttled for home when I stopped to chat with Pinarius, lay in her kennel, hoping for scraps. There was no sign of Dromo; he must have gone to see my sisters, asking them to fix him up with a King-for-the-Day costume.

The yard door stood open; beyond, I could hear Rodan trying not to grow agitated with the boys. He obviously wanted to hide his purse in secret. Gaius and Lucius sensed it, so kept hanging around in the yard. Glaphyra was sitting in the courtyard with her big feet on a stool, finishing a liberty cap that one of the children had messed up. When I appeared, she tossed the second piece of work at me. She knew I could knit. She had taught me. I sat down to do it, unravelling some wonky rows first.

Hearing our voices, Tiberius joined us. He joked that at last he had a house where women worked in wool.

'Put a stopper in it, Aedile!' Glaphyra looked harmless,

but she had worked for my mother so automatically squashed anything daft.

Smiling openly, I told him my conclusions about the Lumber Room. He sent Paris to advise Morellus that I had identified a lock-up connected to Greius; he passed on the candles I'd brought for matching with those at the arson scene. This would be a long shot, but it was good for a raid, or they could deploy the old had-a-report-of-a-fire-hazard method. The vigiles never bothered with warrants. They had right of entry any time they smelt smoke – or when they said they had. Loath to go out again simply to be a sightseer while the troops stormed the property, Tiberius stayed at home. Morellus would send word of any developments.

My lead was welcome. Intense enquiries by the vigiles had failed to turn up anything else on Greius: neither an address nor even a suggested neighbourhood to start their winkling. Everyone was now sure he was the active facilitator, the man in the community, though if Greius was not the gang chief, his commandant was even more elusive. 'When we started,' Tiberius summed up, 'Morellus was hoping to nip this in the bud. He reckons the secretive mobster wants to control the whole Hill. That was why I agreed to help. Now it looks as if the trouble has got away from us. This new outfit has a free hand and is expanding its reach too fast for us.'

'Well, if the lock-up leads to Greius that will be a start.'

I wanted a conference on this, but Tiberius shook himself. He brushed off his gloom and entirely changed the subject. 'Anyway, while I was out this morning, I bought us our first *oscillum.*'

Oscilla were plaques to hang up as festival decorations. The one Tiberius showed me had the mature Saturn with a full beard of ringlets; Suza would say some twisted the wrong way, so perhaps Saturn needed a hand with his curling rod. The hairy god was peering out from foliage full of nuts and berries, surrounded by neatly bound leafy garlands. He had big ears and a squint, but he looked amiable, for a deity who in mythology ate his own children.

I dumped the knitting and, with Tiberius, walked around looking for the best place to hang his plaque. I again tried discussing my theories about Murrius and his brother. 'You can imagine the situation. Greius may be their freedman. The two patrons started out in the loans business, but now they have given him a commission to go into new projects. It is always possible his methods – murder and arson – are harsher than the oldsters really like.'

Tiberius nodded. He agreed the theory sounded good, but told me soberly, 'I'm coming to the conclusion the nut mobster isn't them.'

'Ah! Still, run it past Morellus,' I urged. 'We do know where Gaius Murrius lives. Maybe it's time for an official visit.'

'It would only be fishing,' Tiberius demurred. 'No supporting facts.'

'So? Morellus will say, "Who needs evidence?" My information from his sister-in-law Berenike is that, now his wife has skipped, Murrius is back in the house. He is sitting in there, sweetheart, glowering at her parrot, all ready for you to interview.'

At that point, unfortunately, we had to break off. We were interrupted by the arrival of my uncle, Lucius Petronius, and my aunt Maia. 'Door, Rodan!' No answer. I let them in myself.

'What – no door porter, Albia? Bit of a comedown in a swell pad like this!'

They gave the impression they had enjoyed a good lunch, with Saturnalia drinks.

Petro had brought a barrow, intent on fetching his share of forest greenery. My heart sank. Too many other people had already sent staff to collect what they wanted; my parents had been quick off the mark and Uncle Tullius never held back if he thought he was owed something. Sure enough, when we led Petro and Maia through into the yard, earlier scavengers had carried off everything except a few awkwardly bent cypress boughs amid a carpet of dropped needles. Where once there had been a mound of inviting softwood, little of use remained.

Words occurred.

The critical tirade that followed was pretty rude. It was all the worse because grouping family and friends together to share a special order had been Petro's idea. According to him, *he* then did all the work with a forester (who was a hustler), negotiating price and delivery. The big old warhorse was perfectly aware he ought to have come round sooner; this only made him angrier. Having worked in a public position of authority, he would never admit that anything was his own fault. In fact, I suspected he had always been like that.

Gaius and Lucius swung on the stable door, pretending to feed the donkey while they watched how to rant, and with wicked adult words.

Petronius let rip. Maia backed him up. Even on a good day she would make the Furies look like frightened mice. Her time of life was increasing the aggravation. When Maia and Mother got together these days, my sisters would huddle out of the way with loud groans of 'It's the menopause!'

'I carefully checked what your bloody caupona is decked

up with!' my uncle raged. 'Of course the Stargazer has been allowed everything they want.'

'Even though Junia barely contributed to the whip-round!' Like my father, Maia loathed their bar-keeping sister, whom the younger siblings viewed as a mean-spirited, highly annoying amateur, who should never have been placed in charge of the family bar, or anywhere in the hospitality industry. Also, Junia could not cook, but always insisted on doing it. Plus, she was a snooty, selfish cow (whose meno-pause annoyingly seemed to have slid past without her even noticing it).

Someone new was knocking. 'Door, Rodan!' Rodan was too busy in his hut. 'Grab some branches back off her – just take them from the Stargazer,' I suggested. 'Junia must have sent her husband to pick out the best while Tiberius and I were not here. *Door, Rodan!*'

'That's them all over!' Maia glowered. She had children still at home and Petro's little grandson, all looking forward to decorations they had been promised. 'Gaius Baebius is always the guts who grabs the best sweetmeats off the dish. This is absolutely typical – but I am surprised at you, Albia, letting those hustlers get away with it.'

'Door, Rodan! Oh, I'll go myself.'

'Don't you walk away when I'm yelling at you!' Uncle Petro stopped me, with a relaxation into humour.

I said I wasn't scared of him. My father always maintained Petro was a big softie. Lucius Petronius damned Falco for that, then claimed Falco was a clown, he'd been saying so for thirty years.

We tried shepherding them back out of the yard. 'Mint tea?' I proposed brightly.

Without bothering to answer, they carried on carrying

on. This was family life at a festive time so I knew better than to try soothing them. Tiberius, too, was keeping quiet. His expression implied that once his eccentric wife's crazy relations had worn themselves out, he might come up with a peaceful solution – one he had not yet thought of.

Petronius and Maia continued to give their colourful feelings full rein, so I still could not go to the door. They might have kept it up all afternoon, especially since they now had several hours of free time when they had planned to be at home, putting up their decorations.

I was waiting until they ran out of bombast, then I would apologise. However, I was spared the humiliation. A crisis occurred instead. A commotion in our yard, with screams from our little ones, took us all back there at a run.

41

We had intruders, intruders I recognised: Murrius and his heavies. One man was sitting up high on the wall with his thick, hairy legs dangling, having second thoughts about whether to jump down. Three more toughs, following their leader, had simply walked in through the door from the street. Tiberius had unlocked it earlier, so Petronius could barrow out his branches, had there been any to take home. When we appeared, most of the intruders tried to look like innocents who only wanted to ask us the way to Dogfish Alley.

Rodan had already attacked the ground-level group. He thought they were there to steal his purse. Since that purse was the nearest he had ever come to a winner's trophy, he leaped into action for once. Running from his hut, he had grasped the much-derided heavy spear he owned, then shoved it through the muscly shoulder of the nearest invader.

The wounded man spun round and round, holding onto the spear head as if afraid for his neck artery. He was now adding more blood from cut fingers. I could not tell if he wanted to withdraw the fatal finial himself or hold it there for safe medical removal, but as he circled, the spear's long shaft kept crashing into his companions. These large men were yelling at him to stand still, while they also tried to

fend off the manic Rodan. He had found the spade from
Fountain Court. He was rampaging around the yard,
smashing it on anyone in reach.

Maia and I grabbed a child apiece. We dumped the
stunned little boys in the stable. 'Stay in there. Calm down.
Yes, you can watch.' The donkey had other ideas: they had
to push against Merky for space, while she poked her large
head over the half-door nosily. Gaius and Lucius stopped
screaming. Nothing like this had ever happened during their
quiet country lives in Fidenae. Merky started braying, as if
she wanted to trot out and join in.

Petronius always reckoned to be the first in any ruckus
to knock someone out cold. With his long career of breaking
up street fights and apprehending criminals, he believed
himself the expert. Though clumsier these days, he charged
around the builders' yard. Once Petro began grabbing arms
and cloaks to swing one thief against another, there were so
many circling bodies, our yard looked like a planetarium.

Tiberius sidestepped niftily around Petro, to begin remon-
strating with Gaius Murrius, whom he must remember from
fining him at the Cosmographer. Murrius was standing
bemused, not fighting. The men he had brought were his
usual backing crew, the ones I'd seen fetching the money
from Laetilla's house. Rushing up with Gratus and Fornix,
Paris must have recognised them too. Not really a fighter,
whenever a wide-shouldered, wrist-strapped thug came near
enough to bop he darted in and hit out, then nipped back
to the sidelines again. When one target turned after him,
Maia and I grabbed the man and used his own momentum
to spin him off course. He banged up against Rodan's
battering spade, though Rodan dropped it and turned tail.
Petronius took on the pursuer.

Reinforcements: Suza and Glaphyra peered through the doorway from the house. Suza screamed, which was not helpful in itself, though she had a piercing shriek, like a knife scraping a dish. It caused one man to cover his ears, which left him vulnerable. Glaphyra stomped into the yard. Enraged on behalf of her charges, our nurse came at him, a whirling, hard-breathing, indignant human machine in flapping sandals, which she had undone while knitting because her feet swelled if she sat for too long. In her arms she was wielding her weapon of choice. Grasping this by the narrow end, its ankle, she swung it and viciously smashed the man's head with its muscular thigh. He went down in a soft heap, like a startled pigeon: felled by a false leg.

'I hope you are dead, you nasty fellow!' Glaphyra told the body at her feet, which might still live but showed no inclination move.

'Oh, heavens, he's croaked!' cried Suza, though she too ran up, tore the leg from the nurse, and kicked him with its foot, repeatedly. The fine metal-clad prosthetic made a well-balanced tool. He curled into a foetal position under the onslaught. 'Well, that's cured him. He might have been one of those horrible pigs who came in and stole Sheep!'

To my shame, I had forgotten all about Sheep.

The loud clang of bronze on bonce caused other combatants to pause. In the lull we heard Tiberius, full of hauteur as a householder who happened to be a magistrate (until next week), demanding to know what the hell clause of which ancient statute had given Murrius permission to break into our house through the back gate with a bunch of dingy followers?

To the rebuke, Murrius responded feebly: 'I did knock at the front door, but nobody would answer.'

Though believable, it was hardly the retort of a master criminal.

For Gaius Murrius worse was to follow. Through the open back gate there suddenly entered a jaunty troop from the Fourth Cohort of Vigiles. Fresh from smashing up the Lumber Room, half the red-tunics were carrying stolen items, which, fired up by excitement, they did not bother to hide behind their backs. At their head stomped Morellus, triumphal. Under one arm he was carrying, backside first, a large, once furry animal of the *panthera* genus. It might have been an ordinary spotted cat at one time, but it was a rare black specimen now. It looked so beaten-up it was never more to be classed as what my father derisively calls 'a decorator's piece'.

With care, Morellus stood up the leopard on its long legs in the yard, letting everyone stop fighting and gather round to look at its seared pelt and fixed expression. He joyously informed us that while – following information received – his day shift were proceeding with a raid on an unlicensed chandler's bunker in a bad part of the Aventine, they had found a large number of sulphur matches – long splints of wood tipped with flammable material, which could be lit from a fire or a hot poker, then carried about to light people's lamps. One of his lads checked whether these were viable (that is, items to take home) or worthless goods (to confiscate on 'trading standards' grounds). He burned his fingers, dropped a match, and it landed on the animal with these sad results, despite the ever-caring vigiles rolling the leopard in a dusty curtain to put him out. The once striking feature piece was now pathetic. Most of its fur was singed off, a split had appeared around its middle, from which natron poured out in a caustic flow, and somebody had given the creature a cauliflower ear. The vigiles had failed to find anyone to arrest and the prized leopard was ruined.

Morellus had brought the leopard away, with the dubious hope it would serve as an introduction to questioning its owner. This looked unlikely. Murrius tottered forwards to kneel by his expensive mummy, inspecting the damage. There was no hope of repair. His stylish puss was defunct. Unable to bear touching the remains, he extended his arms over the beast as if in prayer, moaning faintly.

'Murrius,' Tiberius uttered to Morellus. 'Loan shark by heritage. Thought by Albia to be our nut-scam mobster. You would never think a man who can give orders for murder would be so cut up about a big stuffed toy.'

'Diddums,' Morellus murmured, as the distressed owner continued with his grief. 'I'd have told my boys to be more careful, if I'd thought he was so fond of it!'

42

Murrius wrenched himself upright. He looked street-wards, though he cannot have thought he would be allowed to leave. The three men who had come into the yard with him began edging away as if preparing to bolt; the man on the wall had disappeared and must have jumped down into the street. The one with the spear in him had had its shaft snapped off by my uncle so he could run away more easily; Petro was not without kindness. 'Don't pull out the head yourself or you'll die at once.'

My husband took charge. It was his yard. To a building contractor, yard-possession was paramount. 'Manlius Faustus, aedile. I believe I have fined you.'

'Possible.' Murrius had clearly forgotten.

'Public gambling,' spelled out Tiberius, with as much distaste as if naming a sexual perversion. 'You are in my yard.' A worse sin. 'This man is Titus Morellus, inquiry chief of the Vigiles' Fourth Cohort. We would like to discuss certain matters with you, Murrius. We don't need your bully-boys. Send them home.'

To my surprise, Murrius did. The two walking-wounded shouldered their speared comrade. Murrius called after them to tell his brother, though apparently not wanting reinforcements. He appeared unflustered by Tiberius proposing a formal interview. A cynic might think being interrogated was a regular occurrence. 'How can I help you?' he asked, like a good-mannered haberdasher. 'Is there a problem, Officers?'

At the same time as the enforcers left, the vigiles took the nod from Morellus. They also left the yard, and were either going to have further fisticuffs with the Murrius heavies, or more likely would start drinking with them. I waved my household back to their duties. Glaphyra took the boys. My uncle and aunt picked up any greenery they thought fit to use, briefly helped by Rodan, though he quickly disappeared. Petro sent Maia home with the barrow; he skulked behind, yearning to be back in post with the right to conduct the interview.

I went over to the donkey. This left Murrius with Faustus and Morellus, all standing, like three fixed points in a triangle, around what was left of the leopard. Unsupported, it keeled over.

Plenty of crooks are defiant. Most bad men swear and spit, as they refuse to cooperate. A few show more self-assurance, which generally means they have committed such serious crimes they are already expecting justice to catch up. However, such types are often confident that, even with abundant evidence, their crack lawyers will get any charges quashed.

Murrius seemed to be one of these. He dealt with the authorities so politely it was almost as if they were people on the same side in a disappointing world. He called them 'Officer' and 'Aedile' with cloying frequency.

Ignoring this, Faustus and Morellus bluntly put their suspicions: he and his brother were their prime suspects for a spate of vicious crimes, which involved repressive commercial acts, ugly street violence, illegitimate trade tactics, the knowing supply of faulty goods, arson and murder – murder that included infanticide.

A true professional, Murrius pretended shock. Fingering his awful necklace, he replied routinely: they were mistaken. He claimed it was a calumny against honest men of business. Like their father and grandfather before them, he and his brother were upright Romans who lent money to those who needed it; they used entirely legal methods, for the benefit of the less fortunate and the feckless.

He made their established family business sound like a social service, run by kindly do-gooders. He even claimed they had the backing of trade guilds, civic leaders and local temples. I was expecting him to tell us next that the high-minded matrons in the Good Goddess cult thought them wonderful public benefactors, at which point I would have thrown up.

This was not the dangerous tough his wife had described to me, but a much more insidious character. Murrius insisted that welcome financial assistance was all he and his brother ever supplied. He asked whether Faustus and Morellus had anything to back their astonishing theories about nut-scamming. Well, they said, him keeping his leopard among sacks of mouldy nuts for one thing. Of course, he knew nothing of the sacks' contents; they belonged to someone else, in a lock-up where he had innocently borrowed space. Eventually, Murrius suggested that Faustus and Morellus put in writing any points they wished to raise; his brother and he could run matters past their legal team in case they had inadvertently broken rules or edicts.

Titus Morellus, past master of blather, tried tough talk: 'We know what you've done. You had a nut-seller killed and you cremated another alive, along with his whole family.'

'What would be the point of that?' Murrius responded,

with raised eyebrows. 'My brother and I never harm people we deal with. On the contrary, we need them alive to pay us. If we hear of anyone in difficulty, we always try to help them find a workable way out.'

'Forcing them into prostitution and theft! Don't tell me no loan shark ever sends a vicious message, if anyone resists.'

Tiberius stepped in, because this was going nowhere: 'We are looking for the murderous scum who acts as a fixer. An agent called Greius – apparently he works for you.'

'No, he does not,' replied Murrius, still sounding reasonable. 'Greius . . .' The name seemed to amuse him for some reason. 'Greius, I can tell you, has never worked for us.'

'You are aware of him, though? It sounds as if his name is familiar.'

'The young man is very well known on the Aventine, a popular figure locally.'

Morellus fired up. 'He's bloody hard to track down for somebody so popular! Your stuffed cat,' he accused, aiming a kick at it, 'was found snoozing in his lock-up.'

'Where Greius is the key-holder,' Tiberius broke in, sticking to the point that mattered.

'Milvia is at liberty to employ anyone she wants. Yes, my leopard was there,' said Murrius. 'My brother suggested the lock-up as suitable premises. He was helping me, while I had temporary domestic problems.'

'Oh, that's right! Your wife kicked you out!' scoffed Morellus.

Murrius looked pained. 'Unless relevant to your inquiry, Officer, I prefer not to discuss my personal affairs.'

'Stuff your personal affairs. Your home life stinks, of that I have no doubt, but we're not interested in your possessions being tossed into the street. Are you telling us the nuts, candles and other scams are run by some different, more violent, firm – so this Greius is nothing to do with you, but he terrorises the Aventine for them?'

'Sad to say, Officer,' Murrius replied, still so courteous his teeth must have hurt, 'that would appear to be the case.'

'So how come you use his lock-up?'

'The lock-up,' reiterated Murrius, 'belongs to Balbina Milvia, a distant relative of mine.'

'Through her father?' demanded Morellus.

'Through her mother. A strong woman!'

'Cornella Flaccida?' I suddenly recalled. 'So is your family name Cornellus?'

Murrius agreed, looking surprised anyone should query it. 'My brother and I use our last names for preference.'

'Gaius Cornellus Murrius and Quintus Cornellus—'

'Caesius.'

'Does either of you have a son in his twenties?'

Murrius came clean. 'That would be my brother's boy.'

'Another Quintus Cornellus?' I suggested, with a smile. 'Bit of a lad, has had a few family arguments lately?'

'You sound as if you have met him!' agreed Murrius, also smiling. He would not be so happy if he had heard the other Quintus talking. I was starting to suspect a lot about this lad-about-town's love-life. I said, with irony, that I was sure wiser members of his family would soon persuade the younger Quintus Cornellus to drop his wild habits, pay his bills and settle down.

Unaware of my thoughts on Pinarius's friend, Tiberius stepped in. 'I shall ask you one last time to identify the new outfit.'

'Aedile, it would be irresponsible to speculate.'

'You won't break the code of silence?'

257

'Supposition is so crude. Please do not put me in a position where I must refuse to cooperate.'

Tiberius would not give up. 'If you are not behind these crimes, we will get the men who are. You could assist us, if you were a responsible citizen.'

Murrius had his slimy side. 'I report to the Census and pay my taxes dutifully. I cause no trouble. I live respectably.'

'Of course. What criminal was ever convicted of tax evasion? Answer me this, then,' Tiberius demanded abruptly. 'What do you know about a sheep that was stolen from this yard?'

'A stolen sheep? Aedile, it is news to me.'

Tiberius worked himself up to relieve his feelings. 'So, are you planning to take my donkey next? Or was stealing the sheep and leaving bloody evidence on my doorstep just another mysterious action by the shadowy business colleagues whom you refuse to name?' Angrier than usual, he made his final throw: 'Well, there is one crime that you cannot deny, Gaius Murrius. You broke into my house today!'

'The gate was open.'

'You came in with threatening supporters – uninvited.'

'My men were quietly escorting me, which is their job. All I wanted was to ask a question.'

'Questions are our business! What question?' Morellus demanded, furious that a suspect should intrude on his own role.

Murrius looked oddly stricken. 'Can anybody help me find my wife?'

43

Officialdom had got nowhere, as it so often does. Holding up a hand to quash the excited Morellus, Tiberius Manlius took the decision that there was nothing to gain by hammering Murrius further. 'We still have not finished with you and your brother. In due course you will be interviewed again. Please reconsider the answers you are going to give. Anything concerning your wife, Gaius Murrius, lies in the province of mine. If she is prepared to speak to you, I shall turn you over to Flavia Albia.'

Giving our donkey a final pat, I managed to pull my stole, which she was eating, out of her teeth. I indicated coolly that I was prepared to discuss Nephele. Tiberius and Morellus allowed Murrius to step over his leopard in order to follow me through the courtyard door.

He had to pass my uncle. Petronius Longus had remained silent throughout, while men he regarded as incompetent amateurs asked idiotic questions. Now, with clenched fists and a classic air of tired derision, the grizzled old-timer blocked the suspect's path. 'I know you, don't I?'

It was an old line, to which Murrius once more reacted as if this was normal business. Threats in his face did not faze him, let alone when they came from a fading fossil. He stopped, smiled politely, but gave no reply.

'I did for your father,' Petronius sneered.

'My father,' replied Murrius, in the sad tone of a pious son, 'died many years ago.'

'In Phrygia. He should have gone outside the Empire, but Phrygia is a dismal hole to be exiled in.'

'Mistaken identity.'

'Do pigeons crap?' scoffed Petronius. He began an angry movement.

'I am a free citizen,' Murrius broke in. Using this line was in his blood. 'Please do not lay hands on me.'

Petronius stepped back, making an exaggerated hands-off gesture.

I managed to lead Murrius through the door to the court-yard before we hit the next challenge. My door porter came rushing up. 'I am not letting you in!' cried Rodan, showing off. 'I don't like the look of you.'

'I am trying to find my wife.' Murrius spoke wearily.

'This man is with me. Shove off, Rodan.' He retreated feebly.

To Murrius I said, 'Let's get this straight. Your wife is not a client of mine. I believe that when she came here to see me, you sent her. You wanted to discover what we knew about you and your brother's criminal activities.'

'I never sent her.'

'Really? My husband and the vigiles think you were covering your backs. Well, she came. It was a curious experience. She never hired me, I don't know where she is, and nor is she here now.'

'Show me!' he bounced back, becoming more agitated than at any time previously. 'I want to see for myself.'

'All right.' Reaching a decision, I gave a signal to Gratus, who was hovering. 'I want you to feel satisfied. Then you can leave us alone. This is my steward. He will take you around and will let you look anywhere you want.'

On my instruction, Gratus showed him every room, opening cupboards or lifting valances on beds so the anxious husband could kneel in the dust peering underneath. I waited in the courtyard, fighting off bad memories. To me it felt like an occasion with Vespasian's Chief Spy: Helena had had to permit him to search my parents' house. Do not ask me what Falco did to that man after he found out.

Really, don't ask. But assume it was fatal and that there was no comeback.

Gangsters, however, could run free. Even I had been coerced. I let Murrius prowl through my home, peering into all the rooms, opening chests, lifting the ends of couches until the cushions slid off. Gaius and Lucius solemnly marched everywhere after him, mimicking it all. I did not stop them.

'I take it you failed to find her?' I said coldly, when Gratus returned him to me. 'To be frank, I met your wife. I cannot see her hiding under furniture, even to evade you, Murrius.'

I was acting the offended householder. He drooped. All the bombast went out of him, like air escaping from a holed football gourd. He covered his face with his hands.

'Get a grip!' I ordered cruelly.

'I don't know what to do!' he wailed. Either he was a really good actor, or this was true and he was hysterical. Had nobody told him what methods gangland honchos employ against rebellious wives?

I made him sit down, then tackled him firmly. 'I have been told by you and others that you really love your wife. I didn't believe it. Now is your chance to change my mind. But I do not have her. I already told your sister-in-law that Nephele is not here.' Murrius looked puzzled. Again, it seemed genuine. Was this another piece of drama, or should I start worrying? 'I supposed you sent her earlier in the same way you had previously sent Nephele. Your wife's young sister? Berenike?'

'Not me,' he claimed. 'We never use women for errands. If my brother and I have questions, we ask them ourselves.' I gained a dark impression of the way they ran their loans business.

'Stop pretending. Berenike admitted it.' Perhaps I exaggerated.

'The stupid girl is a lying bitch, then.' I wondered if the parrot had yet learned to say that.

'What is happening about your wife's parrot?' I asked him suddenly, seeing this as a test. Nephele had claimed Murrius would kill the bird if she left it with him. 'She mentioned how fond of Beauty she was – in fact, don't you think if Nephele really has left you, she would have taken her?'

'It is not her parrot!' Murrius exclaimed, with a flash of anger. Then he came out with a facer: 'Anyway, the bird is male.' He seemed puzzled. So was I. While I wondered what was going on here, he added a whole row of parrot surprises: 'It was never hers. She hates it. It used to belong to my father, given to him by a sailor who could not pay a debt. My brother inherited it when our father died, but its feathers made his wife sneeze. His son wasn't interested, so he gave it to my own children. Their name for their pet is Squawker. It always has been.'

I felt the ground shift. What had Nephele been playing at? If she lied about irrelevant facts of this kind, what else might be in doubt? 'Why would your wife invent such details?'

'I have no idea. But mixing up minor information, when she is under stress and confused, is not important, surely?'

Great gods, Murrius was defending her. I gazed at him, sizing him up with new eyes. I still deplored his abysmal footwear and jewellery. He was a type. He had the chunky shoulders and big backside of a small man who wishes he were taller and eats too much to compensate. I did not like his unattractive mouth, but he must have been born with that and I am – well, I can be – a fair woman.

He was a loan shark, from a family of predators. That made him a bully with no conscience, who abused the destitute for profit; despite his denials earlier, he probably hurt defaulters and possibly did worse to them. Even so, I now faced a peculiar truth: Gaius Murrius was starting to seem like a loan shark who genuinely loved his wife.

At this point Tiberius came in from the yard. I signalled that he could join us. I sat back in my seat and prepared for a reassessment. 'Murrius, I need to understand this. I myself have heard you shouting raw insults at Nephele. I have heard such exchanges more than once, made publicly in the street.'

He looked shifty, yet confessed readily enough: 'I don't want the neighbours to think she walks all over me. Anyway, whatever I said about her, she deserves it. I know she treats me badly.'

I was beginning to sympathise. Nephele now seemed less an abused woman, more a hard-faced, lying, conniving trollop. Nevertheless, I supposed there were two sides to everything.

'Isn't this the fellow,' Tiberius asked me, 'whose wife complains he is always out to lunch with his fancy woman?'

'Your wife calls her "that bawd from the Temple of Diana",' I reminded Murrius.

'My wife uses colourful language sometimes,' Murrius

scoffed. 'She is twisting the truth. It's ridiculous. I don't see anything wrong in a man visiting his sister!'

'Laetilla?' I asked him, puzzled.

'Laetilla is my sister.'

Oh, joy! It was a three-way family business.

He stared, then insisted, 'We are all very close. My brother goes there most days, now he is a widower. I often dine at her house because my wife is never at home.'

My disillusion reached its lowest point. 'Nephele has not been wilting in your house, wanting you to have lunch with her?'

'I cannot remember the last time we did that,' Murrius complained bitterly. 'She goes out to see people, I never know who.' He sounded as if he suspected. He seemed drained by misery, in which increasingly I believed. His next detail clinched it: 'It's why I never set up my dining room, the one I bought the leopard for. There was no point. We were never going to use it, even if I did.'

Right: the cheating, dangerous husband was a lonely, lovelorn worm. The supposedly mistreated wife went out on the town, enjoying a freedom she denied possessing. Doing what? 'Do you suspect Nephele may have a lover?' I asked carefully. I had tried this on her sister without much conviction; I threw it at Murrius with much more certainty.

'Oh, I'm pretty certain.' He was matter-of-fact.

'Any idea who?' Tiberius put in for me. He might have thought Murrius was unlikely to be frank with us, though I was finding this gangster a tell-all witness. It all poured out easily enough. If this had been a different interview, if he had been a suspect in a crime, I would now be expecting a full confession, plus a thank-you for letting him unload his troubled conscience.

Murrius shook his head. 'For all I know there could be several . . .' His voice faded unhappily. Somehow I felt he did have a particular suspect. 'I don't know how long it has been going on, or where she goes to meet the swine.' As Murrius said this, I remembered when Paris was tailing her, back in the beginning, he'd said she had called in somewhere to visit a friend. Even her husband had attempted surveillance, apparently: 'I tried having her followed once, but she recognised my men and simply went to buy new lamps.'

I was now furious about the trouble I had taken for Nephele. Critically, this was a story I dreaded admitting to my mother. I now believed my disreputable client would never arrive in Ardea; she had never intended to take refuge. I was her smokescreen. I could only hope she had destroyed the begging letter I scratched out for the priestess.

'Gaius Murrius, do you believe your wife has left home in order to join her lover?'

He nodded miserably.

'At least that means she only has one and you will find out eventually who it is!' Tiberius cried jovially. I shot him a look to say he was not helping, though these were good points. Undeterred, he then asked, 'If she went off only this morning, how did you decide so fast that it might be a permanent flit?'

Murrius had yet another surprise for us: 'She told me. She left me a note saying so.'

'*What?*' I screamed.

'A waxed tablet propped on the lararium shrine.' Left it with his household gods? Nice touch, Terentia Nephele! 'She wrote: "I have left you. Don't bother to look for me." But of course,' Murrius moaned, 'I am such a devoted idiot, here I am, looking anyway. My brother says I'm cracked, he maintains I'll regret it, but I badly want to find her. I don't care who says I am stupid, I will forgive her anything. I only want her back.'

He was sad, but I was livid. Murrius was well rid of this woman. As I recalled the touching scene when I gave the 'desperate' Nephele advice on a safe escape, bile burned my throat. She had seemed to be reaching difficult decisions, yet her plans were laid. While she was letting me advise her to walk away unexpectedly, her written farewell was already propped up among their dancing lares and penates. *Leave everything* . . . No chance: I bet a chest of gold and silver had been stowed with her lover.

Never mind what she suggested Murrius would do in revenge. If I ever caught her, I would make sure no one ever found the body.

'Calm down,' Tiberius murmured, though I had not spoken. 'Gaius Murrius, this is a touching tale and, if true, my wife and I are extremely sorry for you. But we have to consider that you could be bluffing, and Nephele is an innocent party.'

'So do you know where she is?' Murrius pleaded, still hopeful.

'No, I have no idea,' said Tiberius.

I was reflecting bitterly how I myself no longer knew where Nephele might be. Certainly not in Ardea. I had no doubt she had jumped off the boat, before it even left for Ostia.

Skanky bitch! I screeched at her mentally, in the voice of the parrot. A parrot that, I now knew, had never even been hers.

44

We had had enough of Murrius. Tiberius and I took him to the door. Gaius and Lucius pinned themselves to us, winding themselves around our legs with fierce little hands gripping our tunics as they perfected their staring-at-a-visitor act. Tiberius reminded him that a formal interview had been promised. Since tomorrow was Saturnalia, he could not say when it would be.

'After the festival would suit. Tonight is the Fourth Cohort's annual splash.' Murrius must possess inside sources. He betrayed a gangster's keen awareness of vigiles' practices. Tonight, the Twelfth and Thirteenth regions would be free of surveillance. If arsonists set fires to homes, any blaze would rage unchecked. Or there could be another reason Murrius had heard about the party. I wondered if the Fourth's tribune, Scaurus, a man of woozy ethics, had even invited regular villains, as 'community relations'. But that would mean Scaurus knew who Murrius and his brother were, and what they did.

'Tonight? Oh, is it?' breezed Tiberius.

'No doubt you are going.' Murrius ignored his feigning. 'I shall expect you and the good Morellus when I see you, Aedile! With sore heads.' The seditious crook then said he was sorry about our sheep, and if he heard anything about who was responsible for the incident, he would let us know.

With our doors already opened for him to leave, Murrius paused. He stooped down and spoke to the children, like a friendly uncle. Tiberius and I were trapped: they were with us; he was being pleasant; objection would look churlish. After giving them a copper each (again we could not stop him), he straightened and told us they reminded him of his own two when they were this age. 'My son and daughter have a parrot,' he gravely informed Gaius and Lucius. 'Do come along to our house and see it, if you like.'

'Perhaps tomorrow,' I jumped in, using the motherly code that means, *not if I can help it!* Like any deluded parent, I hoped that overnight they would forget the invitation, though eager glances passed between them. Fortunately, they were still young enough, and shy enough, to hide behind our legs saying nothing. Lucius was attempting to eat his *as.* Gaius had quickly pocketed his.

We waved off Murrius. Our two immediately went racing to tell Glaphyra they were going to see a parrot.

Surprisingly, Glaphyra flared up. 'Oh no! I know what this is about. Don't you suppose *I* will take those children to that man's house, Flavia Albia! I had enough of this kind of thing with your ridiculous parents. I put my foot down with them and the same goes for you.'

'What kind of thing?' asked Tiberius.

She liked him. She thought he was noble, sensible, and obviously put upon by me, the uncaring flighty one from the untrustworthy province. 'Don't you worry, Aedile. We can sort this out. Flavia Albia knows exactly what I mean.'

'If there is some kind of problem,' Tiberius cajoled, 'I feel I have a right to know. I am responsible for the welfare of you all. Please tell me.'

Glaphyra was burning with indignation. 'I will not be *used* to go into houses and –' she could barely bring herself to say the words '– *find things out for you!*'

I told her I had never even thought of it. That was true although, given my upbringing, the idea immediately appealed.

'Dear Glaphyra!' exclaimed Tiberius, that grey-eyed confidence trickster. 'I would never countenance any such a thing.'

He wagged a finger at me deviously. I looked apologetic, as if Helena and Falco's unscrupulous methods could not possibly be mine. The nurse simmered down, reassured.

When Glaphyra took the boys for their supper, Tiberius and I immediately dived into a salon where we began to plot how we could utilise the suggested visit. The boys were already friends with some vigiles' children; now we would despatch them to cosy up to a gangster's son and daughter. 'You don't think he intends to kidnap them and blackmail us?' Tiberius did have nervous second thoughts.

'No. They are going. Stop wondering about his motives! See it as a friendly offer. Perhaps he simply likes children. A man who remains miserably in love with a runaway wife must be very soft-hearted.'

'But is it immoral? Unfair use of infants?' My husband had been a magistrate much too long: spelling out rules had got to him.

'No, darling. Murrius knows our work. Digging into his household can't count as subterfuge.'

'You or I ought to go with them.'

'Much too obvious. We need one of our staff, who can wheedle *his* staff unobtrusively.' I had in mind one who could do it and who would love to.

'All right.' Tiberius subsided.

At once he changed tack and told me, 'Incidentally, I had a quiet word with your Uncle, Lucius Petronius.'

'Is he happy with us about the decoration boughs?'

'Oh, the thrill of a fight took care of that! He went off for a drink with Morellus and his men, though according to Petro it's likely he'll find them dug in with the Murrius bodyguards too. Maybe not the invalid with Rodan's spearhead stuck in him. Anyway, while Petro was still here, I asked his opinion about Murrius and his brother, since he had made those comments about their father.'

'Petronius knew everyone in his day – he arrested most of them. What does he say?'

'Their loans business goes back generations. He remembers the family – so deeply embedded among the Aventine poor, they are like lichen on the native rock. The father used cruel methods, and the brother is hard, but Petronius reckons once the father was exiled, a decision was taken to keep low, out of the authorities' sight. So he isn't convinced the brothers will have branched out. Trade warfare's not their style and much too visible for them.'

'Has he any ideas who the real nut-scammers are?'

'No. Well, not yet.'

I smiled. 'Uncle Lucius has forgotten he retired. He will be nosing around, I imagine, asking questions for you?'

Tiberius smiled back. 'Morellus got hardly anywhere trying to set up Agemathus and Victor as informants. So, I rather hope Lucius Petronius will do just that!'

He paused. I knew what was coming.

Tomorrow was the first, most important, day of the festival. All decent men must be at home, pretending to enjoy themselves among their families. Everyone would be on holiday, even the vigiles. Tonight, therefore, the Fourth

Cohort would hold their Saturnalia drinks party. Good men were free to be bad tonight and the vigiles would do it with traditions they had made their own: riotously, lengthily, absolutely disgustingly.

Tiberius had been invited, I already knew. He asked again whether I minded, but I gave him the expected answer, 'No, of course not, darling, you go out and enjoy yourself. If Aunt Junia does the catering don't touch her meatballs. Please try to come home sober . . .' He said Petronius was coming back to pick him up, since he knew the way to the venue (always a secret, to prevent gate-crashers).

Even Tiberius, a brave man, looked apprehensive. 'I ought to be sociable, love. I had better go. I won't stay long.'

'Ha! I won't wait up.'

'Just one drink with them.'

And all the others they offer you!

I told him he would know better next year. Then I hugged him as if he was going away to the wars. I said I had been widowed once so I knew how to cope, but I made him promise to be brought back to me alive.

45

My mother had given me succinct advice about husband-management: 'Feed him and listen to him. Choose what he wears, but not so he notices. Always try to stop him going to the Fourth Cohort's drinks.'

Hey-ho. And, indeed, *io*!

Petronius Longus picked up my man for their night of debauchery. Those two would not be seen dead in gauzy dinner robes. Petro had dressed down as if he still belonged in the cohort but with a better shave, since retirement left him all day to sit at the barber's complaining about modern life. I had steered Tiberius into a quiet ochre tunic, one he had owned for a while, so if it came home past laundering, never mind.

On their way out, they passed Dromo returning from my sisters. Julia and Favonia had created a home-made costume in which he would look suitably crazy for his kingly role. He had walked through the streets in it, though managed to escape assault. Were it not for familiar knock-knees, skinny legs and semi-destructed sandals, he was so enclosed he might have been unrecognisable.

He was a gourd. The body came up to his neck with an extra knobble for his head. His gormless face looked out from a circle of marrow vines, into which the girls had pinned home-made large bright white artificial flowers. My sisters could be a wicked pair.

'Good grief, young man, we could hang you up as an *oscillum* and everyone would be impressed.'

Dromo was less sure. I had thought there might be an old carrot costume at my parents' home or, if the girls could still find it, the turnip. Those legendary relics of past Saturnalia events had gone missing, it seemed. Nevertheless, the reluctant Dromo had been grabbed by my eager siblings. Even Postumus had taught him a weird rolling walk to use while dressed up.

Dromo did not want to be a gourd. Heartlessly, we told him that waddling around in a fat-suit as an African calabash was wonderful. 'You wouldn't have wanted to be a cucumber – you'd need to keep bending, and green is not your colour!'

Petro and Tiberius abandoned that tease because a herdsman who had been on the drink all afternoon drove a string of pigs in garlands up Lesser Laurel Street, heading them off to be temple sacrifices. Thinking little of this, the pigs broke free. The subsequent chaos called for strong men who knew what they were doing, or thought so. My husband and uncle strode in with manly cries of 'Hep!' and 'Yours!' Time passed agreeably for observers as they herded the porkers around in the road, while the animals ran into houses through any open doors, doubled back squealing hysterically, then charged in a massed phalanx to knock our gourd's legs from under him. His suit was stuffed with straw and wool so Dromo was unhurt, but encumbered with padding and could not struggle back upright.

Petronius and Tiberius remembered they had an urgent appointment where they were wasting drinking time; they shrugged at the mayhem and made off. Gratus and I pulled

Dromo indoors by his enormous feet. One of his flowers had fallen off, but Barley brought it in. Glaphyra sat him down while she sewed it back on for him. 'Hold still, or it's going wonky.'

'Do I start giving people orders now?'

'Tomorrow, Dromo.' By tomorrow, he might have forgotten any bad jokes that my brother had taught him. Postumus had been King-for-the-Day more times than Tantalus reached for the hostess tray and had it snatched away. My brother loved it. He had exactly the right mix of humour, bravado and cruelty.

'If it's not until tomorrow, how am I supposed to get out of the costume, when I want to go to sleep tonight?'

'How did you get into this ball of rind in the first place, Dromo?'

'They made it on me.'

'Bad news, then!'

'Oh, no!' wailed the King, in horrified misery. 'What happens if I need –' his voice dropped shyly '– a toilet?'

'Settle down, boy.' Glaphyra was starting to treat the daft slave as just another child she had to look after. 'Those young girls are intelligent. Very thoughtful! They have put a nice placket up your back. We can let you out and lace you back again whenever necessary.'

During the fracas, one piglet had somehow ended up trotting all on its own through our courtyard, straight into Fornix's kitchen where it pronged itself onto his meat rod and laid itself ready on his firedogs, pleading for flames. That was my cook's story, one that must have been repeated across the Aventine. It was said not a single sacrificial swine made it to the altar that evening. Local demand for sage and for crackling salt went sky high.

'Why didn't my master want me to go out with him?'

'You're too nice, Dromo. This party will be too wild for you.'

Besides, Tiberius had heard enough in advance to realise what the vigiles, when dangerously sloshed, might decide they could do with a helpless human gourd.

'Won't he need someone with a lantern to help him see his way back home?'

'No, he will be too tiddly to care. You can go out tomorrow morning, looking for him. Take your handcart. When you find which gutter he ends up in, you can load him onto it.'

Dromo looked appalled. Paris explained I was joking. Gratus gave me a look as if he feared I might not be. This all passed some of the time while I stayed at home worrying.

I was unhappy about Tiberius being in bad company, but I set it aside to wallow in personal gloom. Even though I had sworn I would not give up work, there was no work. Every time a situation arose where I might normally be called in, either it turned out that no problem existed, or else people just gave up. Where was the usual whining for justice? Was this the future? Everyone would be saying, 'No thanks, Albia.' They did not need help. They reckoned the authorities were doing a fine job. I was too expensive. They had already hired someone else who worked in the Saepta Julia . . .

That called to mind Naevius, even though he worked from the Forum not the Saepta. I was consoled now by his wise words: there would be clients after Saturnalia, clients who would start feeling the pinch of their personal unhappiness as soon as the festival got going.

Then I remembered an odd remark from Nephele. The first time she called on me, she had looked down her nose at my professional prospectus, but later mentioned having tried out hiring Naevius. With our paterfamilias out taking risks, it was a quiet evening at home. Nobody needed me. Now that I knew her commission was a mirage, I decided to see whether Naevius could shed any light on this odd, deceptive woman.

That presumed I could find him, of course.

46

I took Paris. I am not completely mad. I would have brought along the dog too, but Barley was too wise to venture out. She applied her 'But it's raining!' face and scampered kennel-wards. It was not wet outside but, if I was honest, she had the right idea.

Though fine weather-wise, it was a wild evening on the Aventine. We scuttled downhill at a fast pace, trying not to notice things that were going on. Down in the valley, there were even worse fights and screams in the arcades around the Circus Maximus, with onlookers who stood munching Xero's pies as if this was paid entertainment. That was when they weren't throwing up on the pavement due to drink taken in astronomical quantities.

We turned right. Not even I would try passing through the meat and vegetable markets. They would be sordid. We tramped around the Circus to haul past the Palatine, though when we approached the Sacred Way the Amphitheatre was closed off, perhaps in preparation for Domitian's festival banquet. We dodged revellers by the Arch of Titus and the Sweating Fountain. There were a lot of people around the Colossus, which Vespasian had remodelled from Nero's self-glorified portrait of himself. Now it was Sol Invictus, the Undying Sun, that this festival celebrated. Eventually we squeezed through, to get up and across the Forum. The

Basilica Aemilia had officially closed for the holiday but there were still events in what many considered the most beautiful building in Rome. What was happening in its triple naves and up against its semi-Doric columns was filthy. It was no place for me, passing myself off as a respectable matron. Paris muttered it was no place for him either.

He wanted us to go home, before we were either assaulted or arrested. On the promise of a drink, I managed to drag him around a few back-of-the-Forum bars where Naevius might be. Each time I nipped down an alley, I had to pretend I knew a shortcut home. We found Naevius in the Corinthian, his favourite.

He was dicing by himself. This was partly because, as an informer, he was assumed to be broke. Also, nobody wanted to play with him in case they said something unwise in their cups and he grassed on them to the authorities. Normally he would do no such thing, but tonight he was in his cups too.

While Paris tried to get in drinks from the hectic waiters, I explained what I wanted, spelling out in simple words how Nephele had approached me, then fooled me. I held back on what her husband did for a living.

Naevius claimed client confidentiality. I said she was not his client. She was never even mine. 'Therefore no strings, Naevius!'

Paris came back from the bar, wincing at the noise, bearing goblets that he had filled himself and so far not paid for. Naevius reached eagerly. He was drunk enough to dig in his heels over Nephele, so I grabbed the gambling cup, rattled dice around, like an over-confident amateur, then offered to play him in return for information. He was a patsy, too far gone to object, though I saw that Paris had a knowing smirk. Poor Naevius then discovered that I had learned how to play from my father, then practised throwing with an ex-marine. Dice is a game of chance, Falco and Lentullus had told me. The key thing is, you have to cheat.

Naevius was a pleasant character. Once I had thrashed him, he coughed up his story with a rueful grin. 'You've got me. Look, you know how prospective clients arrive with no real idea of what they want, then try out daft ideas on you? Nephele was one of those. At least, when she finished messing me about, I decided that that was it.'

'Tell me, Naevius.'

Paris went on the hunt for olives.

'I never did any real work for her.'

'Me neither.'

'I could have told you, Albia, she's a time-waster. Her story was, the first time she appeared that is, it was. Let's get it right: her sister was thinking about getting married, to Nephele's husband's nephew – if you follow me.'

Oh, I did. The two-timing non-payer of goldsmiths.

'Nephele believed the young man was playing Cupid elsewhere. She wanted to protect her sister from disappointment. That was what she said anyway. My nose was twitching. I thought there might be more to it. Didn't trust her. But fair enough. I could do that. Standard. I was only supposed to find out if the young fellow was honest.'

'She didn't try out a wonky tale she passed off on me, about her own husband playing away from home with Laetilla, the loan-shark harridan?'

'No.'

'Laetilla is his sister anyway.'

'Incest!'

'Not specified, and not tested – but I don't think so.'

'Presumably the wife would know who Laetilla was?'

'Yes, but I didn't. Pointing me that way was a dodgy try-on. I wonder if she wanted to distract her husband by having me following him around. Then he would not notice her plotting to elope.'

'She eloped? You are too good for such people, Albia!' giggled Naevius, taking in more wine, though in my opinion he was silly enough already.

'Thanks, friend.' I could accept undeserved credit from a man in his condition.

'Nephele was very organised,' he said. 'I told her the usual background I needed, and she sent me details on the nephew same day. Name, age, appearance, haunts, associates and filthy habits.'

'Oh!' I groaned. 'The same as she had to put together on her husband when she was finagling me. Have you still got the notes?' I was eager for facts about that nephew.

'Threw them away when she dropped me.' Damn.

Paris came back, bearing no olives but a small dish of nuts. We were far enough from the Aventine; we sniffed them, inspected them in case of mould, then ate them despondently. They were not actually rancid but dried up and tasteless. Another customer reached in rudely. We passed the dish over.

'What can you tell me about this nephew the sister's marrying, Naevius?'

'Nothing. I never did anything about him.'

'What had Nephele said?'

'Can't remember. Oh, he's twenty-five. He drinks in, well, in a bar somewhere. He keeps a little apartment four floors up on Dolichenus Street.'

'That's a place I keep hearing mentioned, for some reason.'

For one thing, his crony had told Pinarius to bring the money to him there.

'I dunno why. I never bothered to go.'

'Well, what happened over Nephele hiring you? Disappearing act?'

'No. I would not have been surprised, but she did turn up to say sorry, no deal, goodbye. Her sister was determined to go ahead with the wedding in January – Nephele seemed very annoyed over it – so goodbye to me. That was it.'

I told him I had met the sister, Berenike. I had gained the impression she was jumpy about her coming marriage.

'That's families!' snorted Naevius. 'There will be work for someone, then. Once the party is over, it will all collapse.'

Paris brought him a new goblet, from staff who were so harassed they had no idea what anyone's bill should be or who had paid; they were just sloshing liquid into cups, which you had to hope had had a wash after the last drinker. Then they let customers take full cups away for themselves. Offering to settle up caused them too much bother.

Paris and I said goodbye to Naevius, then started for home. I already had a feeling this might turn into a night when I needed a cool head.

As we negotiated the crowds, I was not really thinking as we walked, not to begin with. That is when your brain often takes on the effort of its own accord.

Mine had privately realised that I had done only half the adding up. That young man Pinarius had given me all the clues, but I was so excited about having tied his cocky girlfriend-juggling, debt-dodging friend to Murrius and Caesius, I'd forgotten what Pinarius had also said: the Cornelli had loaned out his friend. Quintus had been given a job. He had a career, one that Pinarius reckoned he had learned all too well. He had no need to renege on the goldsmith: he was apprenticed, trained, given free rein, earning – in fact, he was working for somebody so powerful even his own father was leery of upsetting the man.

I could hear in my head Murrius sneakily saying, 'He has never worked for us.' A wicked technicality. Denying knowledge was a lie. Murrius had lied to us, of course he had – he was a hardened criminal. The young man in question was theirs all right. His nephew. His brother's son. And Quintus Cornellus Junior was the bully, the murderer, the new mobster's agent: Greius.

The only good thing I could see here was that Cornellus Greius might be about to come unstuck. The new wife he intended to cheat on and her sister came from a dangerous family; they had a brother people were afraid of. He, presumably, was the secretive serious criminal Greius was working for.

This was the lead that Tiberius and Morellus needed. Trust me to find it when they were both getting drunk out of their skulls.

47

When we arrived home, buffeted by street merriment, another unwanted visitor had sneaked in. Rufinianus, the vigilis on recall from retirement, had shimmied past Rodan and made himself at home. It was still early evening, but I was ready to relax and unwind. I ground my teeth at the sight of his portly figure lounging on our courtyard bench while he filled himself with dainties from the kitchen. I could not bear the prospect of one of his terminally tedious lectures.

He had the grace to wipe crumbs from that small, straight mouth. He had cleared his *patera* so well, I could not even tell what kitchen treats he had been gorging. Dromo, still dressed in his gourd suit, was sullenly in attendance; everyone else had vanished. Paris promptly followed their example. Dromo grumbled that he was only waiting for somebody to let him out of his costume before he went up to his sleeping mat on the balcony. I unfastened him. He scarpered. I was left, stuck with Rufo.

Rufinianus had dropped in because of his invitation to the cohort party. Some irresponsible joker had told him that Petronius and Tiberius would take him to the secret venue.

'I am sorry, they left together hours ago. The drinks are

supposed to be tonight, but you know how it works. They will have started already.'

'I'm in no hurry. So long as I get there at some point.'

I was terse. 'Listen, I don't know where they went, Rufo. Now I have something I want to think about.'

He stretched lazily. 'Well, I can wait, in case they send a message back for me.'

'Won't happen. Set off by yourself and ask people in the street where the riot is.'

I was growing desperate, but he insisted; he could update me on what he had been doing. I felt tempted to say the nuts inquiry was not my pistachio, but curiosity won. Perhaps he could add to my theory. 'What's new, then?'

He settled in for a long narration. 'How far are you with the story, Flavia Albia?' Even the way he asked that set my teeth on edge.

I tried to speed him up: 'Gaius Murrius and his nastier brother Quintus, plus their dubious sister Laetilla are not who you want. I'm with my uncle's assessment: Petronius Longus, always tops, says nut-scams are not the brothers' style. Murrius and Co are simply long-term traditional loan sharks, preying on long-term traditional futile victims in the long-term traditional disgusting manner. But the key man to capture *is* a Cornellus: strong-arming nut-sellers, causing that warehouse death and setting up the Rosius arson. I presume Morellus has you looking as a priority. He's Greius. The nephew.'

'Whose?' Rufo, never good with names.

'Murrius. Greius is the son of Caesius. Keep up! We had Murrius here today, lying his head off, but I'm certain. Murrius claims to know nothing about Greius and his new activities. I expect the father, Caesius, would say it's not

284

Cornellus business – even Greius will deny everything, of course. Spill!' I commanded.

'Spill what?'

'Greius, you idiot. Usual tips: name, age, appearance, haunts, associates and filthy habits.' I was quoting from my conversation with Naevius. I decided not to confuse Rufo with talk of bachelor apartments. 'I know he's a randy cheat. He's also violent, cold, ruthless and contemptuous of authority. Classic.'

'Well, that would be how he has been taught,' said Rufo.

'Taught? You sound in the know. So what dark tycoon is his mentor?'

'There's a particular firm where the head of household returned from abroad. He had to re-establish. He must have approached the Cornelli to supply a fixer.'

'So whose trusty wingman did Greius become, Rufo?'

I never expected him to answer, but it came out: 'Greius is with Appius Terentius.'

For once, Rufinianus had stunned me. 'You've got his name?' It is always disconcerting when one of the vigiles does something competent. Rufo was matter-of-fact, but I reeled. 'Who is this?'

'The next king of filth – that's what he wants. He is working very, very hard to get there. Word is he acquired Greius as a favour on both sides. *Let us be brothers from now on. Send me your boy – he can be my trainee, my second-in-command, my trusted aide . . .*'

'I originally imagined Greius as somebody's freedman, but that's much higher status. The Cornelli are not to be trifled with. Is Greius with Terentius as a hostage? *I've got him close, so you won't step on my toes, and my own men will leave yours alone . . .*'

'If that was it,' said Rufo, 'Greius soon changed it. Word is, he quickly showed his class, made himself an independent number two, with voting rights. He'll do as he likes now, Albia. Stay or leave, it's up to him. He's bonded with the new group and has become key. Terentius utterly relies on him.'

I sniffed. 'I presume he acquired the necessary pull when he had those nut-sellers killed.'

'Yes, revenge jobs tend to earn kudos,' Rufo agreed, in his solemn way.

'If Terentius enjoys having a baby-burner for his henchman, that's really bad. Does Morellus know who Terentius is? Tiberius Manlius? Or have you only just found out?'

'Just found out. When I see them at the drinks, I'll pass it on – if they want to listen on a social occasion.'

'Never mind the social occasion. They'll rip your head off for this! Recalling you was a dream, Rufo. Even the tribune will tick your bonus without even blinking. Who told you?'

'A man in a bar.'

'What's *his* name?'

'He was a man at the counter; he was trying to get a round in, but the barman wouldn't look at him. We got talking while we waited. That means, by the rules of drinking, he didn't have a name.'

'How reliable was he? Drunk or sober?'

Rufinianus gave me a pitying look. 'Flavia Albia! There is a climate of fear on the Aventine.' He loved clichés. That time when he took my statement about having killed the would-be rapist, this Rufinianus even told me I had been in the wrong place at the wrong time. On the other hand, when he pushed himself, he could manage rational thought: 'If he had been sober, he would never have told me!'

I managed not to say the bleary man must have supposed Rufo was too slow to pass on the information. Luckily, I would now do that.

'Get your cloak, Rufo.'

48

The vigiles had been in existence for more than a hundred years. That was quite long enough for these skilled lads to establish entertainment rules. The first was: no man should reveal the venue to his wife. There were very good reasons for that. For a start, wives were never invited. That, too, was a sensible precaution.

It made finding them tonight a problem. Trailing Rufinianus, a compliant stooge, I first went to see Morellus's wife, Pullia. No answer. Neighbours told me she had taken her children to hear ghost stories. Next I tried Aunt Maia, where I did discover Pullia and the young Morelli, since it was Maia who was hosting the ghost party. Her children were grown and Petro's grandson was still a baby but Maia was clinging to the role of cohort mother, even after Petro stopped working. The tribune's wife was out of the picture (she left him: everyone could see why) and Pullia must have decided it was easier to give way to the stronger woman.

Maia took a swift dislike to Rufo, although as she waded towards me through toddlers she tried to drag me in for must-cake.

'No, thanks. You have too many snotty infants crawling about. You could have invited mine!' I said frostily. 'They know how to blow their noses, but I could have told them to sniff so they fitted in.'

'Too young.' Maia Favonia was ever a frank woman. She added unnecessarily, 'Too whiny!' Before I could return another dusty comment, she fixed me. 'I see you are calling them "mine" now, Flavia Albia!'

'And I see you've hired the terrible Zoilus as your spook,' I sneered. 'How many years has that old fraud been going *whoo-hoo!* in vain attempts to scare people?'

'Too long,' admitted Maia. 'He never tries to fiddle with the little boys, but that is all you can say in his favour. I'm getting a clown next year. Olympus, I'm too busy to chat, woman. Some have already started throwing up – and that's not the children; it's their pie-eyed mothers. What do you want, Albia?'

'Where can I find the men's drinks party?'

'None of us managed to prise it out of them.' Some years the wives did, then flew in like a dark flock of harpies, ready to pick flesh from bones. Maia laughed drily. 'Give it time, then try the Urbans.'

She meant that when neighbours complained about the disturbance, with no vigiles available, the Urban Cohorts would be summoned instead. At the moment, the night-duty Urbans would be sitting snug in their barracks up by the Nomentana Gate, awaiting the customary call. The normal job of these brutes was to dispel riots. They threw themselves into it. But traditionally, when they turned up at a vigiles party to demand less noise, the cohort grabbed them by their fancy uniforms, told them not to be silly, then filled them up with wine until their big-thighed, strong-kneed, hard-booted legs crumpled under them. The Fourth could bring off this feat in half an hour; their boast was that, with the Urbans, it was not even necessary to doctor the wine. However, I assumed they did.

I had no intention of crossing the whole city, south to north, tonight. Forget the Urbans. I had one last place to try: I dragged Rufo, who claimed his feet were hurting, downhill to the Embankment. At my parents' house, Falco had slipped out while acting mysterious, so I knew he was at the Fourth Cohort's bash. Mother had gone to her brother's to take presents for the children. My sisters were at a clam bake. We were greeted by my brother, aged twelve, charging at us, dressed as a gladiator over a lopsided loincloth.

'Bad boy! You opened your presents early!' He had four names already, but told me he wanted his stage alias to be 'Turbo'. I held the so-called whirlwind at arms' length while he writhed enthusiastically. He was a solid child, but untrained. In an arena situation he would have been dead on the sand in minutes.

'I can put all the things back neatly. I couldn't wait. It's not my fault, Albia. Everyone knew what I might do if nobody was here looking after me.'

'Where is your tutor – where's Vitalis?'

Postumus hung his head. 'Lying down.'

I peered in through his helmet visor. 'Oh, no! Have you hurt him with your trident?'

'Only slightly,' admitted Postumus. A slave nodded confirmation. Since Vitalis should have stopped him digging out tomorrow's presents, I wasted no more sympathy on the young man.

Postumus did not know where the vigiles were, but he had been told where the girls had gone in case an emergency happened (they often did, with him left home alone). I took him with us. Julia and Favonia would groan at having to care for him, but he was several years younger and they were always kind-hearted towards him.

He refused to change out of his arena outfit; I accepted it once he said the girls had gone to their party dressed as mermaids. He would not be the only boy in Rome who had found his festival gifts ahead of time, or been given them early to stop him nagging. Luckily it was the kind of night when passers-by barely noticed me walking through the streets holding the hand of a bare-chested, trident-bearing child with a wide leather belt over his underwear, who could not see properly out of a crested helmet and who kept grunting fight cries.

The clam party was full of teenage girls, drinking mock cocktails of water faintly coloured with wine, while they ate big clams and lobsterettes, combed each other's long hair and thrillingly discussed the boys they knew. Or the Adonis they all wanted to know, who disdained to speak to them. And the bad lads they had been ordered never to fraternise with, for reasons they simply could not imagine. Plus Longidius, whose staring scared them . . .

I felt old.

My arrival caused a frisson, but as soon as they saw who I was they all ignored me. I was another generation, though for once, these days, was not categorised as a mother.

Julia and Favonia were in good form since they had the prettiest necklaces and had made themselves the best sea-creature tails. They gathered in Postumus graciously. Of course they knew, being steely wheedlers from whom no secrets could ever be kept, exactly where the vigiles were. They gave me directions, without even needing bribes.

As I left, I heard one of them tell their friends, 'She's Albia. She came from Britannia, but she is all right, really.'

I was still enough of a girl myself to be delighted by this accolade.

49

The vigiles loved a party. I had heard many tales, though had never yet witnessed their annual get-together; the stories did not exaggerate.

They were in a large warehouse. It was the one that belonged to my husband's ex-brother-in-law because, of course, it was known to be empty since Tiberius had burned the mouldy nuts. Salvius Gratus must eagerly have hired it out again, foolishly believing troops were safe tenants. I could have warned him, but since he was Laia Gratiana's brother, I might not have done so.

On the way, Rufinianus had tried to regale me with facts, concerning giant clams found in the Indian Ocean that were three feet across and, he said, man-eaters. At first I humoured him, but soon I gave up. I was in a cross mood when we reached the right place, but all bad temper soon faded.

You could not help but love these men. I knew they dressed up. Sometimes they had crazy costumes. The main dress code for the troops was traditional, which meant a synthesis, or flimsy Greek dinner gown. This is in the Saturnalia rulebook, supposedly. Look it up in your encyclopaedia. Nobody I knew ever did it. Nobody I knew even owned one. The sight of several hundred short, sturdily built, astonishingly hairy men, all flaunting their greasy bits through brightly coloured cheesecloth was mythical. Sweat shone all over them in the hot environment; syntheses that had once been loose were now clinging. Unless you have seen massed buttocks and balls trapped in transparent gauzes, you have not lived.

Some troops had topped off their outfits with liberty caps, though others chose crowns. The crowns were radiant if possible, in honour of Sol Invictus, the Undying Sun; many of their encircling rays were vicious spikes that would eventually cause damage to property or people. To be different, one maverick had a live chicken tied on his head. A lintel had fallen down on him once in a fire so he was never normal afterwards. It happened six years before, but the cohort doctors, being public officials, had not yet got around to assessing him, due to a mix-up with his referral forms.

I had expected trouble at the door, but the party guardians had already reached the point when anyone in a woman's tunic was happily pulled in. They had applied this to three bisexual queens, though now were in the process of removing the rouged beauties. I had wondered if the place would be awash with girls of easy virtue, but it turned out the Fourth were surprisingly prudish, or else had terrifying wives. They were perfectly able to enjoy themselves suicidally without help and, I was informed gravely, their parties never became orgies. It depends how you define an orgy.

The lights were bright, the wine was flowing, good humour was rising steadily, the noise level had reached the point where words were only audible from three inches away but nobody bothered lip-reading. So far, there were no arguments. They had hours to go yet; there would be flailing fights later. These were men whose work was regularly tedious or dangerous, and this was the one evening in the year when they came together to forget their griefs. Their tribune was here, but anyone could slap him on the back and tell him what an idiot he was with no fear of him ever remembering.

They drank; they drank a lot more; they threw into their wide-open mouths pickled beets and mussel-forcemeat sausage. It was no place for prawn mites or frosted canapés with rosehips. While I was there, little old women, who looked like the troops' grannies, came waddling in to massive cheers, pushing enormous cauldrons on wheeled trolleys for the weight, shiny bronze cauldrons that steamed gorgeously with spiced pork dumplings in hearty fish stews, served into huge bowls by the giant ladleful and a whole loaf each for dunking purposes. Nobody at this party would offend etiquette by asking for a simple side salad.

A beaker was forced into my right hand while another found its way into my left. A chaplet of some damp foliage, I could not see what, ended up on my head. Without me needing to say who I was or what I wanted, I was pushed through the crowd, shedding Rufinianus early on by a cunning whisk around a group who were laughing at a lad who had spilled wine: he was bent double, sucking it out of his tunic to avoid waste. I did feel various pinches and slaps on the behind, but generally these were cheeky assaults that I knew had to be taken as appreciation. Propelled by friendly hands, sideswipes from people who hadn't noticed me and an accidental elbow, I floundered through the crush to the men I sought.

'I thought we agreed not to tell her!' roared Morellus at Tiberius.

'You are not supposed to be here,' Tiberius duly said, for

Morellus's benefit. He winked, gave me a winy kiss, then had the wit to swing me sideways, so Morellus would not try to kiss me too. 'I'm overdressed – thank goodness!' he murmured in my ear, his words tickling erotically. Through the plain ochre tunic, his body felt extremely hot, though not unhuggable.

I made an attempt to relate what Rufinianus had worked out about gangster identities. Tiberius looked interested, but Morellus waved it aside. 'It will keep. Tell us tomorrow.'

'You will be drunk tomorrow.'

'We are drunk tonight,' confessed Tiberius. He burped artistically, to demonstrate. 'I believe we shall soon be much, much drunker . . .'

'Show some reaction. This is crucial news about Greius and his mentor! Morellus, do you know the name Appius Terentius?'

'It floats to the surface occasionally. Not associated with nuts but it could be. He fancies high society – our tribune clinks beakers with him on race days. Stop wittering on, Albia,' Morellus ordered. 'We can't deal with anything exciting tonight. Now you're here, grab an olive and enjoy yourself!'

'I don't see any olives.'

Morellus called to a trooper to fetch me olives; the man looked appalled at the idea. I felt myself floundering, as any control I might have had over my companions melted. I had managed to put down both my wine cups, but I needed a bucket of water to hurl over those two.

'Leave it, Titus. I'm easy.'

'No, no, the lady has spoken. The lady wants olives, she shall have them!' Morellus himself lurched off on a vain quest. He would forget what he was looking for the next time a passing waiter filled his beaker. If enough waiters passed him, Morellus would pass out.

My uncle loomed up. He was serving because he had always done it and saw no reason why retirement ought to transform him into a deferential guest. Petronius identified my ditched beakers, into which he poured more, making no comment on me having two. 'Primitivo!' It always was. He himself had collected a whole line of brimming goblets of the warm red liquor from people who had given him drinks to say they were glad to see him. He would work his way through them all before the night ended. By the end of the week he might be conscious again, enough to promise Maia Favonia that he was now too old: he would definitely not be doing this next year . . . He knew the sad rubric from last time.

Petronius gestured to where my father was. I waved one of my beakers at Falco, who raised his own back at me, along with a wild lasso flourish from a long cold meat sausage he was eating single-handedly. I decided against trying to mime across the room that I had seen my brother and sisters or that Postumus had speared his tutor. By now, Mother would have picked them up from the clam party and, after a small tot of the girlie wine and gathering any leftover seafood into a napkin, she would have taken them home safely. Helena would see Vitalis had bandages, though the young man was quite used to receiving unintentional wounds from my brother. No need to struggle across to speak to Father: I was a dutiful daughter, but I would see them all at the big family feast they were hosting tomorrow.

'Uncle Lucius, did you ever arrest anyone called Appius Terentius?'

296

He pondered. 'Mobster?' Through the wine-haze, I thought his face closed. 'Many, many years ago, there was a vicious fraudster called Appius *Priscillus*. I mean, *vicious*. Back while your father was trying to con your mother into living with him, unforgettable period, Priscillus nearly killed Falco. Suggestions were made to bugger off. Being your father, with his ludicrous talents, Falco achieved this.'

'How?'

'He never said. I never asked. If relatives are back in Rome, it needs looking into – but what would I know these days?' maundered the grumpy retiree. 'Ask Falco.' He wandered on his way with his flagon. I looked over, but my father was too happy to be reminded of some near-death experience. I would check with him tomorrow.

Left with me, my husband thought he should be amorous. No one took any notice, luckily. I cannot say I bothered much myself. It was low-grade canoodling, with a wildly missing aim.

'Later, love.'

'You are looking lovely—'

'No, I look like a woman who had intended to stay home, working wool. This crook Terentius, if he drinks with the tribune, is he here tonight?'

'I have no idea. I don't know who anybody is, though I feel they all know me. That's worrying. I have been careful not to insult anyone.'

'It's all right. You are allowed to be a rude drunk, but the system is to disparage everyone equally. The Fourth disapprove of picking on people.'

'They disapprove of very little tonight!' Tiberius marvelled.

'I warned you.'

'You did, you did . . . You always take such good care of me . . .'

Oh, Juno. Taking care of him tonight meant I could not walk away and abandon him to the nightmare. I would just have to persuade him now that he had stayed long enough. Fortunately, Fate suddenly homed in on the party venue. In the dense ceiling of greenery they had roped to the roof, some of the flickering lamps set fire to surrounding pine needles. A cheer went up. Apparently, this always happened. It never made the Fourth reconsider their decorations, nor had the shortage of candles and matches affected their supplies this year. I heard a cry to bring the siphon-engine, so they must have thought a fire was inevitable; at least they had water standing by.

Under cover of the confusion, I hauled Tiberius outside. In fairness, he came willingly. He had to hold onto me hard, because by now the floor was slippery.

As we skated across spillages to the exit, I saw Gaius Murrius. He was with someone else, who had to be his brother, Quintus Caesius: thicker-set, with more miserable features, but similar. Scaurus, the Fourth's tribune, was talking to them: suppositions about his civic invitation list had been correct. I would not speak to the brothers with him there. I would not speak to Cassius Scaurus at all.

A further local grandee was entering, among a small but pushy group of attendants in livery, white tunics with pale green edgings, death's-head amulets. He raised an arm and headed over towards the tribune's group. Even if this was Terentius, it was the wrong moment for me to intervene.

We had to wait while the siphon-engine, minus its towing mule, was manoeuvred indoors, then manhandled tipsily

298

towards the fire. In the street outside, Tiberius stood still, breathing fresh air. I was supporting him. Holding his head, he groaned.

'Cheer up.' I was reasonably kind. These things happen. 'Unless they get that blaze under control, your brother-in-law's warehouse will be burned down. With any luck, he will suspect it was you who suggested they should use it.'

Tiberius shook his head. He had indeed cheered up. 'The bastard won't merely suspect me – he will know!'

50

Even when I had him outside, it was hard to prise Tiberius away from his new pals.

'I must go back in there and help them put the fire out!'

'They can manage. Leave it to the experts, love.' He was still struggling ineffectually, so I suggested he had had enough close contact with flames that autumn. He beamed at me, head on one side, remembering how the thunderbolt at our wedding had nearly killed him. He would suffer for the rest of his life yet had never borne any grudge for it.

Some men batter their wives when they are drunk. Mine became ridiculously loving. It might have been embarrassing but everyone else was rushing to watch the fire. You would have thought the vigiles knew what a blaze looked like.

'What now, beloved?' Tiberius demanded, in a grandiose rostrum manner.

At least I was rescuing my husband. Coming here with news had been pointless. There was no way the vigiles wanted to hear about villains this evening. Even if I had managed to interest Morellus, the relevant gang leaders looked to be here and I guessed there were truce rules: subjecting them to interviews when they had grace-and-favour invitations was out. Once Scaurus was in his glad-rags he became a relaxed host, a save-it-for-next-week man.

'Now? You have been to the party. So, Manlius Faustus, come home and be sociable with your wife.'

Gentlest of drunks, he agreed to be plucked free. He slung a heavy arm over my shoulder, letting me support him. Once I had circled him around to face in the right direction, we set off.

All over the hill, festival music and laughter were spirited. Houses and streets were bright, lit by oil lamps and waxed tapers. The mood was light, though with undertones of menace. It was probably best to avoid jealous old acquaintances. If someone went to their door and uttered the words 'Oh, it's you!' to a dark figure outside, that person might fell them to exact vengeance for a tragic slight years before. This was the night when long-lost relatives would emerge from the shadows without bothering to announce who they were. Old ladies huddled indoors with even older little dogs, muttering about the noise and hoping their happy neighbours would drop dead – which the obliging ones possibly did.

The walk home was not the easiest romantic stroll of my life. We had to cross the main Aventine heights, slow going with a woolsack, who could hardly put one foot in front of the other. He was walking as if his shoes were three inches too big. Battling streets full of whooping and skirling people was difficult enough; luckily, when they bombed us with nuts they were too squiffy to aim. I managed to stop Tiberius stiffly reproving them. He seemed very pleased that his wife was a woman who had helped drunks to their houses before. Using well-tried tactics – manhandling and sweet talk – at last I hauled him home.

'Oh, it's you!' cried Rodan, disappointed. Before I could fell him, like a bitter old acquaintance arriving mysteriously, he let us in.

Once we arrived, I offloaded the master onto Gratus and Paris. Neither of them could claim sobriety, but they had enough in reserve to cover. They laid him on the courtyard bench where, if he threw up, it would be closer to the water tap. By now, he was simply a silent dead weight. I pushed a pillow under his head and spread rugs to keep him warm. He woke up enough to say thank you quite nicely. He then tried to grab me, but it was a purely symbolic gesture.

'Albiola! . . . I love you!'

'I know it.'

'Do you love me too?'

'Mostly, darling.' Not as much tonight. I could have married a hitching post and had wittier conversation.

'I feel rather peculiar.'

'Sleep it off, Aedile,' I advised.

He had had to find out for himself. Even for a man who had been struck by lightning, the vigiles' drinks party was a thumping great test.

I stayed with him until he had no idea where he was or that a caring nurse watched over him, then went to bed. On my way I checked in on the boys. They had reverted to restless night-time crying. Children who experience a tragedy gain an instinct for new risks. I tucked them in neatly; the necessary gestures and murmuring reassured me too. In case they cried again, I thought I would lie down in a nearby room we had prepared for Marcia and Corellius if they came to stay.

Oops!

'What's happening? Get out of here!'

'Sorry. Accident.'

'Oh, piss on the Pantheon, Albia!'

Marcia and Corellius had arrived. They were exhausted

by travel, and in his case by illness. Being jumped on in the dark turned them into very stroppy guests.

'Nobody told me. By the way, your leg arrived.'

'Scram, Albia!'

'I'm going.'

Glaphyra called a question from her room, so I told her that everything was fine.

I fled to my own room, where I crawled under the blanket with only Barley for company. The dog was restless. She kept standing up, digging in her paws as she edged about. She wanted the master here. I made her go on the floor. She whined frantically. I let her up again.

Wakeful, I thought about those men I had seen, Murrius and his brother, then the frowning thickset one with the superior attendants. Though preoccupied with Tiberius, I had registered them. As we left the warehouse, I mentally filed an image of the tableau around Cassius Scaurus. Now I was free to evaluate what I had seen.

I knew how this worked. The Fourth's idle, bullying, skiving, ex-centurion commander would have compiled a short list of dignitaries who lived on his patch. He had invited them to be social tonight; he called it professional courtesy and his list included regular criminals, those he had failed to prosecute. Others whom the cohort had managed to deal with were in exile abroad, of course, their foot-soldiers condemned to death in the arena or the mines. Under Scaurus there had been a few, though never as many as my gloomy retired uncle thought there should have been.

Scaurus must have given his favoured guests an arrival time. Rome was a clock-free city once the courts were closed, but everyone could gauge appointments roughly; that was how we lived. I had seen the tribune provide his invitees with a short burst of generous hospitality, after which I guessed he would ease them out. Thanks for showing up, you must have a lot of other calls to make, see you next year and goodnight. Duty done, Scaurus could bellow, 'Jupiter, thank the gods they've gone. I need a proper drink!' before he became even more rat-arsed than his happy men.

Disclaimer on legal advice: I do not say any crooks presumed his invitations were a signal to send in their annual bribes.

Honest, Judge. I have absolutely no evidence that gold cups, cash, streamlined racehorses or exotic comestibles ever passes into cohort tribunes' warty hands. There are anti-corruption rules, and anyone in that position is well aware of them. We all know that.

What I will say is that, as I hauled my wavering husband out of the smoky warehouse, my brain nevertheless found time to note that Cassius Scaurus had chosen not to wear a synthesis. The troops' party robes mostly looked home-made, sewn by their wives and girlfriends. Scaurus had no access to that because (snigger!) his wife had left him. Instead, over a smart bruised-berry-coloured tunic, with rich bands of contrast, he had been wearing a wide new black leather belt and one of those tawdry gold necklets that I had already witnessed as favoured by Gaius Murrius and his gambling friends. There was a goldsmith on the Aventine trying to gather his payments for twinklers like that.

Well, you add it up on your abacus.

What else could I remember? When I first noticed them, Murrius and his presumed brother were talking together, with Scaurus almost primly listening. The fraternal pair looked tense. Had Murrius relayed his conversations with Tiberius? Were they growing nervous? As they spotted the presumed Appius Terentius, both stiffened. The way they straightened up was not a routine salute to the newcomer. What was he doing there? How would they all handle it? Perhaps they wanted to talk to him about Greius, though of course not in front of Scaurus.

Scaurus himself was tossing mixed nuts and olives into his mouth through his thin lips and what remained of his brown teeth. He had these titbits in a dish he cupped close in one hand. Murrius and his brother had each taken a single stuffed vine leaf from a platter a slave brought round, though they held them without eating. Scaurus kept making fast, greedy movements, as if unconscious of what he was doing, though in retrospect, I wondered. While he munched, had his eyes been, if not narrowed, at least rather still? Was he in fact observing what the crooks all did?

If the third man was Terentius, his only companions were an escort, identically dressed, accompanying their master to show his importance. None was his henchman, Greius. I knew that. I had seen Greius, seen him more than once, haranguing Pinarius. Presumably tonight he was off pursuing his complex love-life.

If Greius didn't show, the vigiles need take no action. They would not tackle an associate, not even the secretive leader whose attaché Greius had become. No point. Organised crime is structured deliberately: no orders that Greius had given would be traced back to Terentius. In fact, we would be lucky if arson and murder could ever be linked evidentially to Greius himself.

At midnight we entered the five-day break. Public business was suspended. The vigiles were off duty and, if asked, they would claim that crime had a holiday as well. That, they knew perfectly well, was untrue. Crime never sleeps.

They would make no new enquiries tomorrow either. Tomorrow, and halfway into next week, those fire-fighting law-and-order troops would be famously out of it. While they all slept it off, it was beginning to look as if everything would be up to me.

Next morning, I was first up again. Was this to become my routine? I fed the dog, then went to see the donkey. She was not in her stable. Trying not to panic, I returned from the yard to find Gratus. Rubbing his eyes, he said Fornix had visited his brother on the Quirinal last evening; he had taken Merky and her panniers; he would come home this morning via any markets he could find open. I had previous reason to think that when the fraternal cooks had a night out together it would be a hard one.

The boys ran down, squealing that it was Saturnalia at last. I put them into their new knitted liberty caps, then, since nothing was happening, they quietened down. Dromo was still snoring on his mat up on the balcony, but Tiberius roused himself. He sat up on the bench, very slowly. While many Romans were holding vacuous hangover discussions – how about crunching a fried canary or, for the really brave, a sheep's stomach and owl's eggs? – we gave him half a cup of goat's milk and nobody tried to talk to him.

'You missed a bit of an incident out in the street last night,' Gratus told me. Tiberius opened one eye to listen but closed it again. 'All good fun. A goldsmith apprehended a customer who owed him money. He'd waited too long and finally given up. Jumped on the debtor with a bunch of slaves, tied his hands behind his back, then carried him away, with everybody yelling.'

Thoughtful, I asked, 'What were they yelling?'

'The goldsmith was declaiming, "I am sick of your whole damned family!" Word on the street says he had trouble over pieces that were commissioned by Murrius.'

'And the one he's snaffled?'

'Bawling up the street as they dragged him off, "Tell Pinarius to bring me bail!" Seems unlikely to happen, now the holiday has started.'

'Perhaps not.'

'No, it won't,' Gratus assured me, grinning. 'It is known on the street that Pinarius Senior has taken his whole family to a lakeside villa, so they can spend Saturnalia playing at sailors – someone has lent the father a rather sleek monster yacht.'

'Being out on a lake is such good fun! Especially in December. Gratus, do we know what the goldsmith is called?'

'Hieronymus.'

I fixed Gratus. 'Any reason you can say that?'

My steward pulled his discretion face, but after a swift glance at Tiberius, he muttered anyway, 'I went on an errand to his workshop.'

I too glanced at Tiberius, who was holding his milk beaker with both his eyes closed, probably waiting out the moment when he would feel safe to move. 'Buy anything?' I schmoozed the steward.

'Don't get your hopes up!' Gratus chuckled. 'Hieronymus was too busy to take on new work for husbands who are leaving things too late.'

'Story of my life!' Untrue. When your father is an auctioneer, you never lack for jewellery. All you need is someone who can mend fastenings and glue back stones. 'Since you know the shop, run on another errand, please,' I instructed Gratus. 'Tell this goldsmith to keep his prisoner

307

locked up, even if bail is provided. The young man may have powerful forces looking after him, though. He is called Greius. His father is Cornellus Caesius. If Heironymus can just keep hold of him for us to collect him later, that would be useful.'

I knew a lot more about the 'two chains' debtor now. I was on to him. His criminal activities would soon be under scrutiny, but he had other sins to explain. By the time his old mucker Pinarius returned from sailing on his father's yacht, his two-timing friend Quintus Cornellus would be in serious trouble. That was not only with us: he had to negotiate the women he was two-timing, plus his and their dangerous male relatives. Worst of all, I thought he might have to extract himself from a gangland eruption of his own deadly making.

51

Like a good wife, I went to my husband. I prised his clenched fingers from the milk beaker, then took his hand. 'Why don't you go up to the bed and sleep some more?'

'I must see that man. The man whose name you brought.'

'Terentius? Love, Appius Terentius is a serious operator. You are in no condition to interview a man like that.'

'Then I'll have to arrest him without bothering to ask questions. Do it the Morellus way. On spec. Him and his murderous sidekick. Gerius.'

'Greius.'

'Greius.'

'Greius is a Cornellus. I told you and Morellus last night but you weren't up to listening.'

'*Io*, Saturnalia!'

'*I*-diddly-*io*. If he's ever at home, Greius lives in Cowrie Court with Caesius. You can pick him up when you feel better – though currently a goldsmith has him in custody.'

Tiberius stood up, but quickly sat down again. He rubbed his forehead with two fingers, groaning. I said he would feel better soon. 'Soon' was pushing it, but I had seen him recover even after he was taken out to a bar by my father, when he had first presented himself as a son-in-law. Tiberius groaned at me again, and agreed to stagger upstairs for another lie-down. Left behind, I sat by myself: thinking time.

I supervised at breakfast, making a claim that Tiberius would join us later.

'Tomorrow?' suggested Paris, grinning. 'Your guests are missing too.'

'Travellers' dispensation.'

'And the fellow may need to work out how to fit his leg on!'

'Have I got to wear the gourd suit yet?' demanded Dromo.

'That is for you to say, Dromo. The King decides everything, then tells the rest of us.'

'I'm not going to put it on. Everyone will look at me.'

'Whatever you say, Your Majesty.'

Suza and Paris were sniggering. The boys were agitating to run upstairs and watch Corellius trying on his leg, so I told Suza to go along to the Murrius house – Paris could tell her where it was. Suza was to ask politely whether it was convenient to bring the boys to see the parrot as their festival treat.

I gave her instructions, saying that while the boys were looking at the famous bird, she could peel off to ask Nephele's maid about hairstyles. She was thrilled. 'Then see what else you can find out.' She cantered off eagerly, holding hands with Gaius and Lucius. Glaphyra remained at home, grimly knitting.

I had kept Paris with me because I had plans. In the event, we acquired an extra. While I was gathering note-tablets, Rufinianus arrived.

'How is the aedile this morning?'

'Poorly.'

'Did he survive the merriment?'

'He should live.'

'Can I see him?'

'No. What about you?' I was surprised to find Rufo bright, breezy and deeply annoying.

'Oh, I never have much of the wine. I learned my lesson over that. I go to those dos for the company, really. By the way, it all kicked off after you two left: they nearly burned the warehouse down.'

I whistled. 'How come? They seemed prepared. I saw them take in the siphon-engine.'

'Oh, yes, they had it,' agreed Rufo, with a laugh, 'but the lads had to scout around neighbouring buildings for water.'

'Forgot to fill it?'

'That mad dwarf Spendo had been doing experiments. He's full of ideas for a big spectacle of light he wants cohort help with. The crazy fool had emptied the tank for some reason. Don't ask me. Once he starts talking, it's all gobble-dygook to me.'

I managed not to laugh at Rufo being outdone by another self-opinionated expert. 'Is anything left of the warehouse?'

'Walls. Blackened walls, with a furious owner jumping up and down among the cinders this morning.'

'I take it the party must have been cut short?'

'Oh, no. We carried on. It only smelt a bit, though most of the lads were coughing while they got their drinks in.'

'What kind of state,' I ventured, 'will Titus Morellus be in today?'

Rufo looked solemn. 'Same as your own man, I should guess. Worse, because he stayed longer.'

311

'Oh, hell.'

'So,' he said, with his usual complacence, 'that's it for now. Neither will be up to hauling Terentius in. They're stymied anyway,' he concluded. 'We need an address. Still, we should roust him out eventually.'

'You reckon? Was that him I saw bringing his dinner napkin to munch olives with your lovely tribune yesterday?'

'I heard it was. I never spoke to him.'

'Now could be your chance!' I said.

I waved my crucial notebook. Paris stood smirking beside me because he knew what I meant. We had both remembered that scene way back: how when Agemathus the *sigillaria*-seller played his great trick on his brother, Paris and I had interrogated that ghastly slave, Sagax. Sagax wore a runaway's collar that named his master as Terentius. If it was the right man, then if the slave had told the truth, the address where the crime lord lurked had been snugly residing with me ever since. While Tiberius and Morellus were suffering, I could at least go there, make local enquiries, and identify the right house.

I threw his cloak at Rufinianus, while I fixed a brooch on mine. My husband and his crony might be taking a breather, but when the men need respite, the women take over. This fine edict is probably enshrined in the Twelve Tables of the Roman legal system.

Cassius Scaurus had known where to send his party invitation. Rufinianus had not thought of that. But no need to disturb the tribune if he had a sore head today. Appius Terentius had no hiding place from me.

I set off briskly, my companions scurrying alongside. Paris was well up for this, though Rufinianus was horrified.

312

In fairness, he was probably right: the exploit might be incredibly dangerous.

'Should you do it, Flavia Albia?'

'Absolutely. Seasonal role reversal. While Faustus is out of action, I adopt his authority. If the Empress Livia could rule the whole Empire for Augustus while he was travelling, I can take a few preliminary notes. Let's get there and move along the casework.'

'You can't deputise for an aedile!' The shocked Rufo meant because I was female. I was female enough to ignore that. 'You had better not try to arrest a suspect.'

'No, you're the vigilis. I shall let you do that.'

Rufo nearly wet himself. He was probably still wearing his party loincloth from yesterday, so that would be doubly unfortunate. 'Oh, no!'

'Only joking, Rufo.'

'Anyone who wants this man to talk needs to know what they are doing. Titus Morellus plans big interrogations carefully in advance.' That was the first I had ever heard of Morellus being thoughtful and organised.

'Me too. My plan is, march in on Terentius and rattle him.'

'I don't like it.'

'I shall start an initial probe, then the lads can crawl along there officially once they're fit again. You can protect me if he turns nasty. He won't be expecting anyone today – and he will be totally stunned that it's me.' Stunning him was the only reason I dared to go anywhere near. The closer we came to his house, the more I began to regret my bravado. I had not really intended to knock on his door and announce myself, but even being spotted in the vicinity asking questions could be a fatal error.

Rufinianus perhaps sensed me weakening. He stopped arguing and produced a rejoinder. 'By the way, Flavia Albia, I don't know if anyone has told you, but a tragedy was discovered this morning. That *sigillaria*-seller died last night. That Agemathus.'

52

Well done, Rufinianus! It worked. I stopped dead in the street.

Immediately I rallied. 'Oh, this is more festive fun, Rufo. Agemathus has already been "dead" once this week. Last Saturn's Day he committed mock-suicide with a fake knife. He always plays tricks with his brother, you know.'

'No, he is dead,' insisted Rufo, at his most humourless. 'I've seen him.'

'Like I saw the "corpse" last time?' I threw back. 'Then he went missing mysteriously, didn't he, Paris? We found the pair of them afterwards, celebrating how well the trick had gone, while they laughed themselves silly about it.'

'He's not laughing. Agemathus is dead, Flavia Albia.'

I cooled the satire. Suddenly this was serious. Now I thought the *sigillaria*-seller must have met with genuine misadventure: foul play, the foulest. He and his brother had been informing on the nut-scammers. Agemathus had given us the name of Greius; so had Greius found out and taken revenge?

Rufinianus sounded sombre as he told his tale. He had been out and about early, since he wished he was still working. He hung about the cohort like a pompous limpet. Being recalled from retirement had made him award himself extra status. Knowing no one else in the cohort would be active, Rufo had taken all their responsibilities upon himself.

He was coming through that fountain piazza this morning when he heard someone shouting. He went into the building to investigate. He found the corpse on the bed. It was too late to revive Agemathus, but Rufo sent to ask a vigiles doctor to come and pronounce. When I knew him before, he would never have done that. Yet now while the troops slept off their wine in their cribs at the station-house, like big smelly babies, Rufo behaved like a legate.

'Then what?'

'Then I carried on to your house, where I had been coming in the first place. The doc will attend. I know he's available. He's at the station-house for when the lads start rolling in, too sickly for duty. I called in there myself and he was mixing up a big vat of headache linctus, all ready to dose them. None of them will be awake for hours yet, though.'

'Never mind that. When you found Agemathus what was there to see? Did he have a knife between his shoulders and a lot of home-made blood?'

'No. He was just lying there.'

'Face down again?'

'Face up. Mind you,' said Rufo, 'that could have been because the person who found him had turned him over.'

'Who was it?'

'Some weasel the two brothers have lodging with them. He wanted the bed – they give it to him in the daytime if they are out working.'

Paris was anticipating me quizzically. He knew what I was bound to say. I duly said it: 'Come along, then. I shall have to go and take a look myself.'

★   ★   ★

316

We marched across the same piazza with its dribbly fountain, up the same sour stairs and in through the sticking door to the brothers' bare room. Agemathus was truly dead. Even in December, flies were finding him. There was no knife, no blood, no sign of injury by other methods. He looked like a man who had died in his sleep. Of course, in my line of work nobody does that, but it was, after all, Saturnalia when all rules are broken.

The empty *sigillaria* tray had been leaned against a wall. The lodger, shaken, sat on the stool. He was a thin, charmless workman in an extremely sweaty tunic, who stoked the furnace at a bath-house near Prisca's, though not actually hers. She would never have taken him on because he looked likely to make himself a spyhole to stare through at the naked women.

He was genuinely too upset to invent or to lie when I questioned him. 'I was asleep yesterday evening.'

'On the bed?'

'On the floor. I heard somebody knock. Agemathus opened the door, then he sounded off with "Oh, it's you!" and he went out.'

'And it was who? Any idea?'

'Yes. His brother.'

'Victor? I thought he lived here. Why was he knocking?'

'He was messing about. He did a loud rap, like a debt-collector.'

'Right. Do you know where they went?'

'The Orion's Dog.'

'They like that bar, I know, but how can you be sure?'

'Agemathus called over his shoulder to ask would I like to come along with them.'

'Did you go?'

'Yes.'

'That's good. You can tell me how they spent their evening. Then what happened?'

'Agemathus started to complain he was feeling unwell. Then he came home.'

'By himself?'

'No, Victor told me to bring him.'

'Which you did?'

'Yes. He lay down on the bed, but he seemed all right, and I went out again. I trolled around some other places, having a drink or two on my own. I came home in the dark, a little bit merry.' He was, in my opinion, still totally paralytic. However, he gave the impression that was normal for him. He would say stoking was thirsty work. I would say he wouldn't have been so thirsty if he hadn't got so drunk.

'Did you speak to Agemathus?'

'No. I was trying to be quiet. I just curled on the floor, thinking he'd go out in the morning.'

'Was his brother back at the room?'

'I didn't think so. Agemathus never said anything, never made a sound. I passed out. When I woke up this morning, I found he wasn't even breathing. Agemathus was lying dead.'

'And Victor?'

'Not here. Still at the Orion's Dog, I bet. It wouldn't be the first time he just stayed there and kipped behind the counter.'

Rufinianus asked officiously about the cohort medic he had sent for. The stoker confirmed the doc had already been. He'd inspected the body, snorted, then gone to the Orion's Dog to tell the brother what had happened. I led my group downstairs, then we went to the bar ourselves, followed by the stoker who was hoping for another drink.

318

The Orion's Dog was open, because it was the kind of bar that never closed. Customers were trying to buy their breakfast, though somewhat hampered. The small counter was taken up by someone lying upon it. They persisted, managing to stretch over him, while the dogged barman passed across their orders, placing cups and bowls on the counter man's chest while he took the money.

Deprived of anywhere to lean, the customers stood back in the street, in strangely calm contemplation, as they consumed their purchases. The doctor was there too; he must have finished his new examination because he was having a small tot of something. It looked like a courtesy gift from the bar keeper.

The person laid on the counter did not require first aid. Nothing would revive him. He was dead. It was Victor.

53

Victor was not acting. The doctor confirmed he had really passed away. No one said, 'Agemathus did it.' Even in unruly festival times, being dead first was an alibi.

The cohort doc was a lean, humourless man who riled me just by standing there. I may be prone to taking against people, but be fair: this man, though attached to the Fourth Cohort, had actually volunteered not to attend their drinks party. Not even for the proverbial 'just one drink'. I could imagine the kind of sanctimonious advice he would give the troops about their hangovers.

I never asked his name. The swine might be competent, but he followed the rule that a medical man should do no harm – only give me heartburn. He enjoyed himself at the centre of attention, as he pronounced that both brothers had died in exactly the same way.

My first question was 'Had they been eating nuts?' Even the barman sneered as he informed me the Orion's Dog never served nuts. Well, seeing what a dump it was, I should have worked that out.

I asked whether the brothers had eaten anything else, then: no, they had spent their entire *sigillaria* proceeds, but none of it on food, only drink. The doctor boasted how he had sensibly ascertained that no other customers last night had felt even slightly ill. None were deceased. Most had even returned here for breakfast, in their normal health. They had phlegmy coughs, limps, piles and psoriasis between them, but nothing terminal.

I mentioned in an undertone my fears that by acting as informants Agemathus and Victor might have suffered a vicious reprisal. Without dropping his voice, the doctor replied that they may well have angered the crime agent. 'But Greius did not cause their deaths.'

'What then?'

'They both had the same symptoms.'

'That seems an odd coincidence.'

'Family history, bound to be. Same effects, same conclusion, same manner of death. Classic. Witnesses report they complained of feeling seedy. They had pressure in the chest, which they called indigestion. It spread down their arms, they felt terribly tired. Agemathus went home but Victor did not bother. Even so, he expired in the same way not long after. Their hearts gave out.'

'Verdict of natural causes?'

'Drastic over-indulgence by people whose poverty normally made them abstemious. If you want to call that a "natural" event, then yes.'

'But they died happy?' Paris supplied, being the optimist.

'No, they died unhappily,' snapped back the doctor. 'Heart attacks are sometimes sudden, but for the victim, being struck down in that way can be frightening and painful.'

'Agemathus appears to have died in his sleep eventually,' I protested. 'When I looked just now, there was nothing to suggest that, once he lay down on his bed at home, he had any idea what was occurring.'

'And Victor had drunk too much wine to feel anything.' The barman supported me. He was keen to advertise that customers of the Orion's Dog enjoyed themselves even while dying on the counter. 'Victor was asking me for another, when he just stopped and passed out. Nothing would revive him. We did try fanning and shouting at him. After a bit I decided to keep him here while the rest of us carried on being festive. This was his favourite place. It was what he would have wanted. If I had known Agemathus had passed away too, I might have sent someone to fetch him, then propped them up together for their last night on earth.'

'Leaning against an amphora?' suggested Paris.

The barman thought this was such a good idea, he nearly did it even at this late stage. That misery the doctor stopped him, pointing out various unhygienic aspects, legal obligations, and the possibility of being fined for disrespect to corpses. Undaunted, the barman rapped back, 'Well, they will have to be kept somewhere. Nobody's going to give them a funeral until the holiday ends, are they, Aesculapius? They both adored the festival – it was when they made their money. I thought they were lovely customers. Everyone else who came here always enjoyed meeting them. The best! What could be wrong in showing our love for them by letting them join in the celebrations for one last time?'

I smiled sadly and saluted him with '*Io Saturnalia.*'

54

My mission to spy on Terentius was permanently delayed. I decided to turn back for home. Tiberius and Morellus could check out the house, taking a posse. Rufo was relieved, Paris more regretful.

I was full of sadness for the two brothers. They had been part of the festival locally for many years. When Mother had first recommended Agemathus, she told me she had bought *sigillaria* from him since Postumus was adopted. When family festivals continue through generations, human nature dictates nothing should ever change.

In my work I was more used to death by foul play. Simple misadventure upset me more. Natural causes seemed just as pointless as murder, yet nothing I could do would achieve any form of justice for these victims. Nature had struck them down. There was no solace.

When I reached home, Rodan took a look at my expression and just waved me in.

Tiberius had a bowl of pearl barley; he was sitting with Fornix, who must have made it the night before (he was a *very* well-organised chef); he had another of the same for himself. They just listened, while Gaius and Lucius gravely told them about the parrot. It was a serious, educational conversation, perhaps pitched too high for men with sore heads who could barely dip their spoons. When reaction was needed, they took it in turns to nod carefully. Dromo was kicking his heels nearby, not contributing. His King-for-the-Day suit still lay unused beside him.

I decided to talk to Tiberius when he rallied. First, I cornered Suza.

'Tell me all about your visit. Start with the house. I want to imagine life with Murrius and Nephele.'

'Clean and comfortable. Best of everything. Good staff. Smarter than here!' Suza said darkly. '*New* stuff.'

'Gaius Murrius loves his wife and is a very rich loan shark. He wants to keep her, so he has bribed her with furniture.'

'Tiberius Manlius loves you, though,' Suza answered, frowning. 'And you have hardly anything.'

'Suza, we have only been married a few months. Murrius and Nephele were together longer. She knew her spending limits, he knew her taste. Was Murrius there?'

'No. Gone to see his sister. Everyone said he has got her a *lovely* neck chain for Saturnalia.'

And perhaps even paid for it, I thought drily, remembering the creditor at the Cosmographer who had made him cough up. I assumed that was Hieronymus. 'Tell me about his children.'

Suza must have harboured set ideas about criminal homes, because the two young hosts were a surprise. 'Well! Twins, a boy and a girl. Ever so nicely brought up. Beautifully turned out. Educated by tutors. They spoke politely and were sweet to your boys.'

'That doesn't fit with their stepmother yelling down the street that she was dumping his horrors back on their father.'

'Well, I don't expect they liked her either!' Suza countered angrily.

'Oh? Did they talk about Nephele?'

'No. Should I have quizzed them?'

'Better not put them on the spot.' Twins have enough adventures traditionally. 'Did they strike you as happy?'

'*Very* happy now their stepmama has gone.'

'And what about this parrot they have?'

'His name is Squawker. He can say it himself. *Shut up, Squawker!*'

'A big birdie?'

'He can sit on your hand, though he weighs quite a lot. He was too big for our boys, who were frightened of his nibbly beak, so the girl held him. He is grey, with a dark red tail and fluffed-up feathers. He can talk well. He says rude words.'

'Do the twins encourage him?'

'No, they apologised.' These were not like any children I ever knew! 'Squawker does come inside the house, but he lives in a big area outside in a garden, which has a tree he can go in and netting, so he won't fly away.'

'The Murrius children didn't mind you coming to see him?'

'No, they don't meet many other children, so they were quite glad. They spent a lot of time with ours, because as well as seeing the parrot, they showed off their toys – they own a lot. Then I'm afraid ours told them about the joke turd.'

I winced. 'How did that go down?'

Suza chortled. 'The twins want to know how to obtain one.'

'Ha! As my mother used to say, *Well, that's another nice home where we won't be asked a second time!* So' – crux of tale – 'have you learned any new hairstyles? Did you get a chance to meet the maid?'

My girl threw back her head, spread her arms wide, puffed her cheeks, assumed the air of one who could be trusted with a simple task. 'Did I? You bet I did!' I smiled like one who had known she could be trusted while I waited for the story. 'I shall definitely try out a few things on you.'

'I've been warned! What's she like?'

'Thinks a lot of herself.'

'No! Really?'

'Well, Albia, she was dying for some attention. She's pretty narked that she was left behind with no warning, *simply dumped like an old neckerchief*. She has nothing to do now her mistress has vanished. None of the other staff will talk to her because they all think she must have been in on it, and even the girl twin has her plaits done by her own special nurse. Murrius keeps grilling the maid – his brother next door nastily told Murrius to thrash the truth out of her.'

That made me nervous. 'Has Murrius hurt her?'

'No. Even she said he is not like that.'

'Then what about the mistress leaving home? Does the maid know how it happened?'

'It was a complete surprise – she could hardly believe it. And she definitely cannot say where Nephele has gone.'

'Really?' Suza's face darkened. From being ebullient she closed in. 'Now look,' I explained, 'the whole point was to find things out for me. It's no good you going there if you then keep secrets. I dare say this girl, or woman, made you promise that anything she whispered must never be imparted to another soul—'

Suza's eyes widened. 'How do you know?'

'I have met enough fancy maids! This will shock you, Suza. I bet she claimed she has never told anybody else, and you are her only confidante. Be warned, though: the next person who takes an interest will be given the full story just the same as you.'

Suza was indeed shocked. 'She would tell you?'

No, she would *not* tell me because I was an informer and she would be afraid of trouble. That was my reason for sending my poor innocent Suza.

'Well, then!' My own maid soon ditched this untrustworthy friend. 'That's not very nice, is it? She swore I was the only person she could trust and how relieved she was to tell somebody what had been going on. I felt glad you sent me, since I could do her so much good by listening!'

'I am sorry, Suza. The world is full of people who are not as honest as you.'

'A complete crook!'

'Well, she works in a crook's household. I expect she has learned from example.'

'Actually, she thinks Gaius Murrius is a good man. It's his wife who was getting up to things.'

'Doesn't deserve him?'

'Absolutely not.'

'Has been playing around with a boyfriend?'

'Horribly!'

'For long?'

'Some time.'

'Murrius knows?'

'He does now!'

'And does he know who the lover is?'

'He doesn't want to believe it.'

'But the maid knows?'

'Nephele seemed to end up not caring.'

'Flaunting?'

'Flaunting dangerously.'

'Dangerous is correct. This is adultery,' I spelled out. 'You know the penalties? A married woman who cheats is not simply disgraced. The law demands much more of her. If Murrius finds out his wife has slept with someone else, he has to divorce her – no choice – which, if he loves her as much as he says, he will not want to do. Plus she could lose all her personal property – well, all she has failed to carry off to her lover's secret hideaway. Who is this lover, by the way?'

'Quintus,' said Suza. 'Well, I was puzzled at first.' Suza had learned how to spin out information. She cannot have acquired that from me: I hate withholding. 'I felt amazed because the twin boy is a Quintus and he is only ten.'

'She's not a cradle-snatcher. Whatever she's done, it's not that bad.'

'No, but I still think it is awful.'

'Why, Suza?'

Suza was still playing for effect. 'Quintus is a family praenomen. The stern brother of Gaius Murrius is Quintus too – but it's not him,' Suza hastened to assure me, finally taking in my irritation.

'Caesius not adultery material? And surely much too close to home?'

'Oh, Nephele didn't care anything about that. All the time nobody realised, but it was going on right under their noses. Nephele's affair is with his son. What about that, Albia?'

'Juno!'

I responded with a theatrical gasp to please her, though I felt less surprise than Suza really wanted. But to be kind, I kissed her and cried, 'Oh, Suza, you have done so well! And, yes, it is a very bad situation. This young man is not simply a close relative but he has behaved abominably: Nephele has been carrying on with her own sister's intended husband.'

55

I took Suza into my confidence to reward her for her work. 'Suza, we can see what caused recent events. Nephele had been having an affair with her nephew, which would have made both Murrius and his brother furious.'

'But Murrius loves her!'

'Not enough, believe me, to like her sleeping with his brother's son! It may well have happened under his own roof too.'

Suza told me excitedly, 'Quintus lives right next door – at least, he does when he is at home. The brothers' houses are joined inside by corridors. That helps them run their business more easily. So the wicked seducer was always around.'

'And a looker?'

'The maid says he is lustworthy. All the women in the household hanker, but now they realise Nephele was the one who quietly went about getting him.'

I nodded. 'Yes, but her sister Berenike was to marry him. From a talk I had with a colleague' – I was remembering Naevius – 'while this liaison was still being brokered by the families, Nephele must have suspected her desirable lover began relations in advance with Berenike, who we know is much younger and prettier.'

'And not married to his uncle!' Suza giggled. Her eyes were widening.

'Quite! What a family entanglement. Nephele dreaded that she was about to lose him. Then everything grew worse because the wedding was fixed.' Thanks, Naevius: *she did turn up to say sorry, no deal, goodbye. Her sister was quite determined to go ahead* . . . 'Crunch time for Nephele. The wedding is in the New Year, Berenike told me. Nephele's dilemma was urgent. Time running out? She must have challenged the lustworthy Quintus, no doubt demanding that he should choose which sister he wanted. Since she's run off to be with him, we can assume he picked her. At least, that's what he's promised her.'

'Why?' demanded Suza. 'He has agreed to marry Berenike. Why would he want an old bird who is already married instead?'

'Not instead. The love-rat wants her *as well*!' This young man was greedy – I had heard him say so to Pinarius. Even so, I suggested reasons for him to continue with Nephele: 'She's experienced? Richer? More grateful for attention? Probably more forceful.'

'She bossed him?'

'Seems likely. Perhaps he caved in, Suza. For Nephele, it would be intolerable that her lover would soon be sleeping with her sister – if he wasn't already – and right next door, if the new couple live with their in-laws. The only bearable option for Nephele is to leave Murrius.'

'Then she won't have to think about Berenike and Quintus bonking?'

'Yes, Suza – plus she can put one over on her sister. Berenike thought she'd got him. Nephele knows different. They were supposed to be "close" but I suspect rampant jealousy.'

Suza joined in, thrilled: 'So, when that Berenike toddled

along here, whimpering over her sister, she really was very upset! She realised Nephele has run away with Lustworthy, and so she's lost him!'

'Exactly. This explains Berenike's anxiety over her marriage. She sensed her sister's affair. She feels she has no grip on Quintus. Her own life will go wrong if they marry, with a husband who is already cheating. I thought Murrius had sent her here, but she desperately wanted to know the truth for herself.'

Suza was still pondering. 'So, why has Nephele pretended that she must escape from Murrius because he's horrible? Her maid says he isn't at all.'

'Smokescreen.'

'What will happen about her now? Where has she gone?'

'Quintus is keeping a bachelor apartment. A friend called Pinarius told me.'

'A nookie-nook? Do you know where?'

'I've heard what street it may be in.'

'How? He could have it anywhere in Rome.'

'That is possible, Suza.' But I had a reliable informer source. *Oh, he's twenty-five. He drinks in, well, in a bar somewhere. He keeps a little apartment four floors up on Dolichenus Street.* 'If I'm right, Suza, he's playing with fire, because it must be very near where Murrius, poor deluded man, goes gambling. This nephew is a real chancer! It wouldn't surprise me if he and Nephele are snuggling up in a room right above the Cosmographer, filthily enjoying that Murrius is tossing dice with his cronies, unaware they are right upstairs. All very unpleasant!'

'Isn't it true love?' Suza had her standards.

'No, pet, I don't think so. But true lust counts as highly with some people.'

'I don't like that!'

'No, and Gaius Murrius won't like it either.'

'Why doesn't Quintus just say he doesn't want to marry Berenike?'

'Other than he doesn't want to tell his uncle and father about Nephele? I bet he does like the marriage. Is he cynical about business? He's cynical about everything. He sees this as professionally useful, the way his father and uncle view it. Remember, the Cornelli have already made one alliance, when Murrius married Nephele. Presume business reasons lay behind that. Now Caesius, the nasty moneymonger, wants his son to strengthen ties again.'

'But when the affair is exposed, everything will go wrong!' Suza protested, with justice.

'Yes,' I agreed. 'Caesius must already suspect. Soon Murrius will know. And young Quintus is really stupid, because any moment now Nephele's own family will find out. He works for her dangerous brother, in a position of enormous trust. Any time now, his love affair will blow up in his face.'

'Hmm! Now that's all sorted neatly,' hinted Suza, 'I'll nip to fetch my beauty things. Then I can work on you.' I glared. 'No, Albia. That was the point of me taking the boys to see the parrot – so I could find out how to do fashion!'

When I still wanted to escape, she reminded me I had better look smart, or at least as if I had made some effort. Today we were going as a family to my parents' house for a Saturnalia gathering.

56

Io? Io Saturnalia?

'Do not say those words!' muttered Mother in my ear, as she hugged me, like a fellow conspirator. 'Farting Furies, Albia! I don't know why we subject ourselves to this vile comedy every year – I am sick of the whole hypocritical paraphernalia! Come in and have one of your cook's lovely cakes – but spare me that sodding salutation!'

This was a woman who taught children that swearing is only allowed in a terrifying emergency. That would be defined as a loaded wagon running over your foot, or your favourite confectioner running out of honey.

'Should be a great party!' chortled Father. After the Fourth Cohort's drinks, Falco appeared much less fragile than Tiberius, having had more practice. 'Hostess blowing her magma plug before anybody even sets a foot in the door!'

'I just want to say,' Helena Justina drew herself up, 'if the Sun is truly Undying, there can be no point in pretending we all have to thrash around hysterically in case feckless Sol bloody Invictus forgets the planetary rules and accidentally turns up his toes at the end of the Winter Solstice.'

My sisters, gorgeous in new violet stoles, exchanged winks with me to say tots had been taken. Well, it is a festival of excess.

'Take vocabulary notes!' I mouthed at Suza, while Julia

and Favonia clustered round to inspect my hair. I was pulled about while Suza gave a lecture on her new pinning, but at least they all rushed off to try out styles upon my sisters.

Because Gaius and Lucius were so young, we had been invited at midday rather than the classic dinnertime. When we first arrived the atmosphere was fraught because my mother, supposedly helped by my father, had been cooking all morning on her own – honouring the tradition that all household slaves just lay about expecting to be waited on. The joke in our family had always been that Falco was so hopeless at acquiring slaves there was little difference between normal days and Saturnalia. Some extremely old souls who lived here on sufferance and occasionally tottered about with trays went right back to my grandfather. Nobody, however decrepit, was ever dumped to die on Tiber Island, not by my family. As Father said, we insisted on keeping the poor worn-out things, even if they piteously begged to be released from the madhouse.

Any special tension was because the ageing parents had tired themselves out. Holiday role-reversal suited Helena, who from choice would always wear a simple gown, no jewellery, and her hair speared up with three old ivory pins. She enjoyed preparing the meal, while Father stood handy as a taster, acting like a slave in a play, spouting cheeky commentaries and forgetting errands. In between he smooched my mother. Or if there was any threading on skewers or basting needed, he took that over. To watch how this pair worked together, with constant banter yet no quarrelling, had been my first serious life-lesson.

Today everyone wore their liberty caps, while as an extra gesture Father brought out his busts of Brutus and Cassius, each with a knitted *pileus* deposited on his stone head. They had turned up for an auction once (minus hats), but nobody bid because possession of historic conspirators was illegal. Falco loved to point this out, as if daring someone to report him. No one ever did. Nevertheless, in a period when real conspiracies were being contrived against Domitian (we hoped), bringing out the Liberators carried an extra frisson.

Whatever Mother said about it, in a speech she made every year in fact, Saturnalia at our house was wonderful. All the rooms we used for feasting had been decorated by my sisters, who were both artistic. Once festival food was safely steaming in pots on the cooking bench, and a tincture finally taken to celebrate not burning the kitchen down, my parents threw a fine party. After my grandfather died and left us a fortune, there was always enough money, for one thing. At least, on the first day, neither food nor wine ran out. Our customs were quaint, present-giving could be fitful, outside guests tended to look baffled, but the family mucked in and the staff felt appreciated. Even the peculiar ones.

On this occasion the parents had decreed no relatives outside my household could come. They had told the numerous Didii we had seen them all much too recently; we wanted a quiet occasion because Tiberius and the boys would be missing their mother, who had died only this month. 'We only do Saturnalia for the children, really.'

My mother had decided she would also do it for Tullius Icilius. She had a theory that every party should include a charming old buffer, a role my father would never fulfil since his charm was of a specialist nature. Some people put him on a plinth as a romantic icon; others thought him a clown. According to Helena Justina, that was because he possessed, as his mother once described it, 'a smile you could crack nuts with'. Besides, not many heroes can whip a traitor or a multiple murderer into line and drop any bodies down a sewer while making the best jokes you have heard all year.

Uncle Tullius arrived, bringing his special presents. Mother was kind to him; he was even polite to her. Tiberius and I were still convinced he would come with miniature military uniforms, ignoring the risk of tiny fingers being painfully pinched in segmented armour, or with heavy wooden swords that would be so unwieldy they knocked things over by themselves, or dangerously sharp sidearm daggers. Not so, however. Next year, promised Tullius.

We had had an early exchange of gifts because Gaius and Lucius could not bear to wait. Some families save presents for the fifth day of the festival, but ours was never like other families. The little boys had been showered with small treats, sweets, tops, dolls and clay horses to pull along, while Tiberius gave them each a *bulla* to ward off the evil eye. They looked like gold. I knew they were only lead, covered with gold foil, because of the high chance of them being lost. They are round medallions hung on thongs, to show children they are cherished. Postumus suddenly decided he would wear his own, which he normally hung on his ferret, so we all joked that the evil eye would take one look at Postumus then flee.

Father had produced (from an auction: he did not deny it was a fortuitous find rather than the result of devoted searching) an automaton: a mechanical man was placing food for a crocodile that would run for it, though this came with no provenance and no instructions. Gaius and Lucius were already having arguments about who could work the man and who the hungry croc, while I foresaw that those strings working the movements were doomed to snap. The

336

boys soon dropped the automaton (literally) once Tullius came.

The old grump had brought them musical instruments. It could have been worse – a drum, say – but it was bad enough: child-sized legionary horn and trumpet. Small but desperately loud. The *cornu* was the most dramatic: shaped like a letter G, with a crossbar to support a huge encircling tube. The *tuba* was extremely long and straight, with more prospects for hitting things. Both were liable to run painfully into the tender roofs of little mouths. They were accompanied by bearskin headdresses that must have been made from a pair of tragic cubs. My sister Julia sniffed one and mimed violent vomiting.

Gaius and Lucius soon mastered how to blow through the mouthpieces, which Tullius solemnly demonstrated were perfect copies of real sized ones, 'Fully detachable!' He nodded at me, suggesting the critical parts could eventually be 'lost'.

As we had rehearsed, Tiberius and I exclaimed, 'Oh, darling Uncle Tullius, that is wildly generous! You really shouldn't have!'

As Tiberius had prophesied, Uncle Tullius answered back, 'What are rich uncles for, if not to spoil the little dears?'

The spoiled little dears marched around for the next few hours being *bucinatores* with their red cheeks puffed out, blowing military signals to which people had to respond or there were tantrums. My parents were good people: they endured the racket and never complained. On the other hand, they knew we were taking the terrors home at some point.

Orders should really have been given by the King-for-the-Day, but that role had been awarded to my brother's tutor, who was too polite. Instead, the tutor was being taught a complex board game by Postumus. Glaphyra, who knew him of old, woke from her nap to scold, 'Postumus, when you are playing against a novice, it is kind to let him win.'

My brother looked up, with his sweetest expression. 'Of course.' He looked down at the board again, muttering, 'Once!' Though a passable intellectual, Vitalis was not sharp enough to avoid playing for real money against our dangerous twelve-year-old. His entire Saturnalia bonus was sliding away into my brother's slick hands. Postumus, naturally, knew exactly how much the bonus was. He stopped playing as soon as he'd grabbed it all.

I asked why Vitalis had not been allowed to spend the festival with his own family. 'Of course he could go. He has quarrelled with his mother – he ran away from home. She just let him. You will find,' warned Helena, 'as soon as you have children, that you decide everybody else's have received a very poor upbringing.'

'Will people think the same about ours?'

'Probably.'

We had brought half our household. Dromo kept sitting silent by himself, with the unworn gourd suit. Suza was keeping very still, afraid to dislodge a towering head of imperial court curls that my sisters had now woven for her. The rest mingled cheerily with my parents' oddball staff. Falco and Rodan were chatting like brothers. Nobody would realise Rodan had acted for years as a rent enforcer for Pa's old landlord, Smaractus, and had on at least one occasion beaten up my father so badly he almost died. Saturnalia is a *very* peculiar time.

The girls were looking after Gaius and Lucius, tirelessly marching around for them as they played their horrid instruments. Uncle Tullius might have been expected to make an early departure, but had stayed, working his way down a flagon of fine wine that he had brought as a gift.

When the hired ghost arrived, my father decided to embarrass Tiberius and me. He whispered loudly that we could slide off now, if we wanted time alone together. He meant— Well, we knew what he meant. We pretended not to understand, while losing all interest in the subject.

The ghost was Zoilus. A whisper went around that this was for the children. Further commentary said, no, Falco always felt sorry for Zoilus. Zoilus was a tradition. We had to keep the undead alive. Every year this ghastly ghost was allowed to earn money from appearances at family parties. Under his elderly shroud, the spook was papery from poverty. Once, he had been able to glide around as if suspended above floor level, zipping himself into fabulous hook-shouldered movements while throwing his voice in such a way that his eerie *whoo-hoo* sounds seemed to reverberate from behind the furniture. Now the shroud really did look as if it had been dug out of an ancient grave. He could still say *Hoo-hoo* in a wavering tremolo but was far too arthritic for more athletic haunting.

Postumus pointed out loudly that ghosts were not supposed to age.

Zoilus was offended. The supernatural actor floated off to find something to eat. He knew the way to the kitchen; he had materialised there to sate paranormal hunger many times before.

Postumus declared that spirits should not need human food. Vitalis, his tutor, was unexpectedly fired up to discuss the afterlife, reminding us of how many people feasted beside their ancestors' graves, some posting food and drink down tubes for the festering corpses buried below. My brother immediately wanted to go to a necropolis; he would dig down to see whether any food and drink had been consumed. We generally encouraged his pursuit of knowledge unless it involved roadkill with maggots. On this occasion, quick-thinking Favonia told him every necropolis was closed for the festival.

'But I want to go and see!'

'Well, you can't.' Vitalis for once sounded stern. 'Now do not ask why not, Alexander Postumus. I am King-for-the-Day and I say so!'

We were all impressed. I noticed Dromo sat up, watching jealously.

Zoilus had disappeared for such a long time that Tiberius and I were sent to resurrect him. We found him staring into space, even more miserable than usual. We asked him why. After renewed *hoo*ing, he told us. He was a scavenger. Most of the time he earned nothing; this month he had ended up in debt because he had found a place to sleep but had had to bribe a man to let him. Someone told him how to get a loan. He would never be able to repay it, not even after he'd worked here tonight and at various other parties.

I said I would ask my father if he could think of anything that might be done. (Falco would probably cover the debt).

Tiberius, in magistrate mode, then asked the spook who had given him the loan.

'Bad people,' answered Zoilus, trembling. 'Hard men. A hard woman. She will come for me.' He must have seen Tiberius glance at me. Sadly, he added, 'The Cornellus brothers. One seems kindly but the other is entirely cruel. And the woman who must receive the repayments. Laetilla.'

'*Whoo-hoo!*' exclaimed Tiberius, very gently.

57

We could have left it there, but I asked Zoilus however he had come to use Aventine loan sharks. I thought he lived out among the tombs on the Via Appia. That necropolis beyond the city boundary was where really destitute beggars lived, beggars who were too squalid even for the streets of Rome. Some old tombs stood empty; others had been broken into. It was a cold, lawless, violent environment but a few beggars preferred it to crouching in Rome's hostile doorways, behind bloody stalls in the meat market or under bridges. There they would be robbed and raped by other vagrants or moved on by cruel paramilitaries, whose method of persuasion was to kick and cudgel them half dead.

Zoilus told us that this autumn my soft-hearted father had let him squat at the Eagle Building, although once it was sold, he decamped voluntarily before the demolition squad decided it was their turn to kick and cudgel him. At one point he found himself a doss in a warehouse. It was undercover and dry, but he had to pay bribes to the building manager. The amounts might be small, but he had nothing. That was why he listened when somebody talked to him about loans.

'But you have to pay them back, Zoilus. And with horrible interest.'

'What can they do to me, Albia?'

'A lot!' muttered Tiberius.

Zoilus was looking forward to his fees for parties – though not because he could repay the Cornelli. Ignorant of what he had got himself into with them, he intended only to buy drink. That should ease his pain. Afterwards, he would have to vanish back to the Via Appia, hoping the loan sharks would not recognise him when he came again (if he was alive) next year.

'I'm afraid they will. They are used to debtors who try disappearing. Who put you on to these terrible lenders, Zoilus?'

'A man in Fountain Court.'

'Oh, no!'

I began gently questioning Zoilus as a witness. When he stayed at Father's building, had he seen anything of the people who were using the lock-up called the Lumber Room? Zoilus was an unreliable source; to screw anything out of him I had to suggest it myself, which is a poor way of obtaining evidence. He knew the old shop was being used for storage, though people there issued threats against anyone who seemed nosy. Like Rodan, he had had a run-in. Greius had threatened to burn him alive, saying being undead would not save him. Unlike Rodan, Zoilus was physically grabbed – though they let go abruptly when they smelt how he stank. 'Death and corruption – *whoo-hoo!*'

He hastily pointed out that he had been to the baths today. Some premises made no charge. If slaves could use them, then ghosts, too, could strigil off their spectral dirt.

'Zoilus, we don't mind a pong. Tell me about the old shop. Was it being used for Saturnalia nuts?'

'I don't *know-ho!*'

'Ha, ha. Did you see any waxed tapers hung up to dry in our courtyard?'

'*No-o.*'

'Would you recognise any of the people there?'

'I don't want to see them. Never again!'

'All right, settle down, you don't have to.' There was little to gain: legally he was useless, far too weird to use for formally identifying anyone. Anyway, he would clam up from terror if we tried a face-to-face.

He seemed afraid of the gangsters, yet he was obsessed by them. 'I am a ghost, I am bodiless – those beings are faceless.'

'No, they are men. They just keep their hats pulled down and burrow into their cloaks, Zoilus.'

'Yes,' he agreed. 'They are men, Albia.' He could be sensible, though he enjoyed being a spirit so much you could never rely on normality lasting. Anyway, he was always so hungry it made him light-headed.

He was nibbling now, a flat round cake made by my own cook, Fornix. Suddenly he put it back on the platter, pulling a face. 'Nuts!'

'What is wrong with nuts?' Tiberius asked casually, leaning against a cupboard.

'Nuts make you sick,' Zoilus muttered.

'Some do,' Tiberius agreed, as if conversing generally. 'I heard of a warehouse that was full of bad ones. They were taken out and burned, so no more people would be poisoned.'

'Nuts!' mused Zoilus again, his pale face showing up amid folds of his shroud even in the kitchen gloom.

'The men who keep nuts in the old shop are wicked people,' I said. 'They use fire, and fear, and fight with planks that have vicious nails stuck in them.'

'Fire and fear.' Zoilus turned over the words as if tasting them. 'Planks with long nails. The man comes with his key so they can bring their bad nuts.'

'We know about the man with the key.' Tiberius was grave, but unthreatening. 'Cornellus Greius. There are spirits now in Hades because of him. Zoilus, he kills people. I know he does. You are quite safe to talk about it with me.'

'He kills people,' repeated the ghost, then added almost soundlessly a confirmative breath of '*Whoo . . .*'

Tiberius straightened up off the cupboard. He told Zoilus quietly: 'Greius organised a fire where an entire family lost their lives. Before that, he had a man murdered in a warehouse. Somebody, and we know this, was sleeping in a colonnade. That person must have seen what happened, the night Greius and his people brought a nut-seller to the place and shovelled him into a walnut sack.'

The spook-impersonator stared at him with dead eyes.

'Was that you, Zoilus?' Tiberius kept his tone level.

'No-how.'

'Anybody hiding there,' I joined in gently, 'must have been terrified. They must have run away. Now they hope Greius and his foot-soldiers never find out that they saw what happened.'

'Somebody saw,' murmured Zoilus.

'Will you tell us?' I pleaded.

Suddenly the ghost spoke out: 'They hauled a man into the warehouse. He was screaming. They kept shouting. I ran away then.'

'Before you ran, did you recognise anyone?' Tiberius asked.

Despite his ethereal aspects, Zoilus grasped what we needed. 'I knew the leader. I knew him again, that man from the lock-up who threatened to burn me alive. When he came into the nut warehouse, I knew where I had seen him. That was why I ran away – so he would not see me.'

'Greius was in charge of the people who put the nut-seller into the walnut sack?'

'He was,' confirmed Zoilus. Then, to our surprise, he added, like any normal witness, 'He told them to kill him. He is Cornellus Greius. He does not work with the brothers and the woman. He acts with another man, whose name terrifies everyone. Those two are going to take over everything, so all things will have to happen in the way they say. Do you know what it means?'

'Murder,' listed Tiberius heavily. 'Extortion, corruption of public officials, illegal gambling, infiltration of legitimate businesses, labour racket schemes, tax fraud and investment manipulation.'

'All kinds of racketeering,' I continued. 'Smuggling, fraud, robbery, bribery, assault, weapons, poisons, fencing stolen goods, prostitution, pornography and theft.'

'Terentius and Greius,' Tiberius stated.

'Appius Terentius.' Zoilus shuddered, not from the chill of the Underworld but real fear. 'King For Ever. It will happen soon. He is going to take over the Emperor.'

58

We let Zoilus return to the family. Soon, candles would be lit ceremonially, festive decorations seeming to dispel fears. But bright lights always make the shadows seem darker.

Tiberius and I stayed together in my parents' kitchen. We pulled out battered stools from under the counter. The permanent fire on the cooking bench enabled us to see each other's troubled faces. Its glow shone on copper and brass, even the iron tools, deep-cleaned of rust this week, with the smallest dried-on sauce traces scraped out of knives' and strainers' deepest handle crannies. All the silver was upstairs being used. Otherwise comports and craters, often collected in distant provinces, would have sat with this shining battery on old stone shelves.

The wafts from cooking had died down or been fanned out of the room. Only rich scents surrounded us. Herbs hung from strings, among hams that were kept on hooks to absorb smoke from below. There were pervasive undernotes of olive oil and spices, sun-dried fruits and fish, stored grains and vegetables, currently in much larger quantities than normal. There was the inevitable hum of fish-pickle from its sticky-rimmed amphora. When people who have known poverty are suddenly able to stock their pantries, they tend to buy everything they see. Equally, we never threw away blunt meat-shears or a chipped pestle because once things that broke or went missing could not have been replaced. This was the hub of the house, which would service large numbers of people through many rich meals this month.

My mother was a senator's daughter but, even so, the legend went that she came to my father with only one chest of possessions. He himself had had almost nothing at the time. Nowadays I could understand that they had taken on undesirable clients and dangerous commissions purely because of financial pressures. Falco joked about it. Joking was his only way to cope. My method was different: I would be morose.

I might have seemed morose now, but my brain was active. Thoughts chuntered, falling into working patterns. When I was ready, I said, 'Talk about this? I can see how it is.'

Tiberius nodded. He listened, clearly with me.

'The Cornellus brothers, Murrius and Caesius, with their sister Laetilla, are old-school money-lenders, descended from others. They have a well-worn format for their business, with guaranteed clients or we can call them victims, the kind of destitute people who will always exist. These Cornelli are relatives of the old Balbinus Pius gang. Laetilla knows and gossips with Balbina Milvia – visits her house down by the Circus.'

'Keep going,' said Tiberius.

'The Cornelli work on the Aventine. They show no signs of wanting to expand their range. They are rich enough, they are powerful enough within the sphere they occupy, and they have chosen not to attract attention from the authorities. However!'

'However!' echoed Tiberius, giving me a slight smile.

'They have ties with another group, the Terentii. That clan leader is a secretive figure, but a man who impresses on everyone how cruel he is. *He* has a different attitude to expansion. And he has two sisters, sisters he deploys to strengthen his place in the underworld.'

Tiberius joined in: 'Terentia Nephele and Terentia Berenike.'

'Right. Then there's Greius. With three siblings all active in the loans business, the Cornelli may have had no room for anyone else with ambitions – and, dear gods, he is ambitious in so many ways! So his relatives gave up their promising scion to work with Appius Terentius.'

'Perhaps,' suggested Tiberius, 'Terentius was threatening to shove in on their operations so, rather than have a territorial battle, the Cornelli reached an accommodation. They could keep the loans, while leaving Terentius whatever else he wants. Greius is the mutual pledge to honour this. Sending him across bought Terentius off, and ensures boundaries are respected.'

'He also grew into a dangerous love-rat, though only we seem to know that!' I exclaimed. 'The Cornellus brothers work with their sister. Women connected to Balbinus Pius always were powerful figures in the old gang. But I think Terentius may be more old-fashioned. His sisters are merely ciphers to him.'

Tiberius laughed. 'Big mistake! Comes along a handsome lover and chaos erupts.'

'Right! So Appius Terentius returned to Rome,' I mused, 'and needed a reliable leg-man. Thanks to the Cornelli, he obtained a treasure. Quintus Cornellus Greius: born with all the confidence of his own heritage, but now gaining added punch. Perhaps unintentionally, he became an ideal field agent. Greius helped create a new racketeering structure, mainly through violence. It looked the perfect partnership.'

'And yet Greius, with his love-life, threatens family disaster,' Tiberius concluded.

I had thought of something arising from that. 'Nephele – remember her odd first visit to me? She kept harping on about how we had lost Sheep, telling me how dangerous the situation was? I thought Murrius had sent her to spy and issue threats, but it's more likely to have been her lover, Greius.'

'Seems right,' Tiberius agreed. 'The threat from Terentius will be against them now. An internal bust-up must be coming. Might that help us smash the rackets?'

'Yes,' I argued, 'it will, because you can't eradicate organised crime using normal methods. Gangsters are too well set up for avoiding prosecutions. My uncle learned the only hope is to trick them into some technical offence – or, as a last resort, fix your jury.'

'How soon will full revelations hit the family?'

'Nephele's maid will let something slip. Greius has a friend who told me Caesius already suspects what's going on. He has begun trying to impose control. I wonder whether Caesius, tough as he is, feels nervous about upsetting Terentius?'

'Greius has moved over,' Tiberius suggested. 'Caesius may be afraid he could reject his own family.'

'Not if Terentius explodes over Nephele and Berenike. And other trouble looms over Greius when his uncle faces how Greius has been harping on the wrong lyre.'

'Murrius knows *someone* is her lover,' said Tiberius. 'I think he guesses who.'

'He and his brother were muttering at the vigiles' party,'

I told him. 'When Terentius arrived, it looked to me as if they might be anxious in case he already knew of the affair. I made a bad mistake with Nephele,' I admitted. 'Now she's stuck, I'd say. All that talk of how she was terrified of her husband may have a grain of truth – but it's her brother Terentius she's really afraid of. What will he do, when he's devastated that she has bust up all the links he arranged to the Cornelli – and, moreover, committed this sin with his trusted agent? This is the worst personal betrayal.'

'My hope,' said Tiberius, 'is that if we charge this stupid young man with the killings and arson, Greius will find himself out on his own. Neither the Cornelli nor Terentius will give him the classic resources that protect gangsters from justice.'

I hoped he was right, but warned, 'Don't rely on that, love. He will get his bent lawyer. Bribes will be laid out for young Greius. Witnesses will fade away and evidence will be tampered with. They may even spring him and conceal him. His relatives and his chief may decide that, whatever he's done, he is one of their own.'

Tiberius understood, but grumbled, 'If they rescue him, I hope they still punish him. I can live with seeing his corpse turn up in a salt pan by the Via Ostiensis.'

We fell silent. Both of us knew we were preparing for action. Then we were interrupted.

59

Still enjoying his holiday role as a slave, my father swung into the kitchen to collect a large platter. He did have to pretend we were enjoying a romantic tryst after we'd sorted out Zoilus. We let him carry on about it.

'You're not drinking!'

'Tiberius is feeling he can never face a wine cup again.'

'You married a wimp!'

'He was all right until he went partying with you and Petronius.'

Falco paused. I waited.

'He had a word with me last night.'

Unsurprised, I replied easily, 'I was asking about Appius Terentius. Petro said someone called Appius Priscillus once nearly did for you. But you did for him?'

For a moment I thought we would get nothing. Then the holiday slave could not help himself: he turned back into Didius Falco, anything legal considered, good refs, cheap rates. 'Priscillus: a rat-faced, heartless property tycoon who made all the other stinking magnates smell as sweet as Paestum roses. He left,' said Falco. 'He left when I told him to. He won't be coming back. Petro believes he's dead, incidentally.'

'Trial?' asked Tiberius.

'No trial. But he was guilty. Without him, his personal hoard was broken up. His best house, of many spectacular mansions in a fabulous portfolio, the house he actually chose to live in, had the best views in Rome. From the first time I saw it, I coveted that house. Up on the Janiculan and, I'm delighted to tell you, it ended up with me.'

'Grandfather's villa?' I was surprised. 'Were you given it as a reward?'

'No, simple daughter. Vespasian never filled the Treasury by handing out free gifts. I paid good money,' Falco said. His voice was sombre. 'If relatives of Appius Priscillus have returned to Rome, having had a proper purchase ceases to be galling and becomes a good idea. If your suspect is half as bad as mine, I advise you never to tell them that we've got the house. Don't upset such people. I was all right. I knew what I was doing. I'll tell you what Petronius Longus told me: wear a body-belt under your tunic and keep a dagger down your boot. Since you're just a couple of amateurs, take back-up.'

He took his leave, but immediately reappeared. The platter swung dangerously on his hip as he posed in the doorway, a practised move. 'Don't mention to your mother anything about this chat.'

He was gone. As always, the room felt smaller and less interesting once he left us.

Peace descended. Tiberius threw back his head and addressed the smoky kitchen ceiling. 'So! Tradition – this is the moment at the height of a great family occasion when my beloved wife drops her ceremonial duties. *Sorry, an interesting clue came up. I have to rush* . . . Flavia Albia scampers off into the night to confront a suspect!'

I smiled softly. 'Saturnalia,' I reminded him. 'Role reversal. Your turn this time.'

'Ooh, I am a good family man. I could never do anything like that!'

'Try it!' I mouthed, seductively.

Old Grey Eyes rose to his feet from the potboy's stool where he had been sitting. He held out his hand to me. 'We have been working the same case, it seems.'

'I had nothing else to do. And I like to keep an eye on you.'

'You were always with me,' he promised. 'I did everything your way, with you in my thoughts.'

'I can live with that.' I shrugged.

'Time for resolution,' Tiberius confirmed. 'You may be surprised that Morellus and I have discussed what to do and planned it. Let's hope the vigiles aren't as hung-over as they bragged they would be. Today's the day. We both believe that on the first day of Saturnalia, none of them will be expecting us.'

'You're skipping from my parents' feast?'

'Oh, yes – and, being a good son-in-law, I even warned your mother earlier. I want to seize Terentius and Greius.'

'Agreed,' I said promptly. 'I will let you go – but only if you take me.'

You may think he could have refused me. But Tiberius knew that if this was a climax there was no chance I would stay behind. Besides, to spring his surprise he needed me. I was still the person whose note-tablet contained that record from Sagax of where Appius Terentius lived.

60

Right at the start of all this, I had learned something about our chief suspect: he locked inscribed metal collars around his slaves' necks. *I've done a runner. Grab me and take me home to Terentius to receive your reward.*

Nobody I knew ever did that. We sent our staff out looking like normal people. If they ran away we might try to find them, but on the whole we sighed and left them to it, generously hoping no harm befell them. Most slaves sensibly stayed with us. They were humans, whom Fate had treated unkindly. We would treat them better. We dressed them for warmth and decency, we fed them the same food as us, we provided education, training them up to support themselves when eventually we freed them. Appius Terentius, we could be sure, had never freed a slave in his life.

We knew we were going into a different world from ours. Our aspirations were to survive and to work hard for a good life; the gangster's intention was to gain wealth by preying on others, never satisfied by what he battered out of them. We had skills and social position: personal strengths, but with responsibility. He was gaining a much cruder power, unhampered by ethics. We respected regulations, even when we satirised them. He broke the rules as if there were none. What drove him was greed. Greed, plus belief in his own right to dominate. We had private hopes; he had terrible public ambitions. Tonight, as we were about to learn, he would begin acting on those. It would be up to us to stop him.

We went with back-up. Even to visit his house, we took a small armed guard. Weapons are banned within the city, but I could tell that our men were carrying. In his position as an aedile, which did not give him powers of physical punishment, Tiberius Manlius was never accompanied by lictors. No wide-shouldered men carried bundles of rods ahead of him, walking single file and shouting, 'Watch out!' to the public. He had to clear his own path through crowds and find his own bodyguards. Rome is a pragmatic city, though. When he needed security, security materialised.

From the parents' house, he had led me up the hill past the Temple of Ceres, the aediles' official base, where without fuss he collected a group of staff who appeared to have been waiting there until he needed them. They looked well trained, willing to be called upon and, despite the season, hardly at all drunk. If they had taken wine, they could handle it. They followed us quietly.

One of them had a message from Morellus. He could not be with us; he was tied up with a vigiles exercise ordered from on high. But his men watching the Cornellus homes in Greater Laurel Street and Cowrie Court had reported that the two brothers were in; Laetilla was with them, a family celebration. Greius had not been seen; amused locals reckoned he was in trouble with his father and his uncle, while another rumour claimed a determined goldsmith was holding the great Greius to ransom in a chicken shed.

First, we concentrated on Terentius. I provided the

address, taken from Sagax before I even knew why I needed it. I admitted a qualm that the slave might have lied. But as Paris said, while he came along with us in case we needed a messenger, Sagax had thought there was no risk because his master's reputation meant I would never dare visit.

The streets were quiet. Behind their shutters, homes sounded livelier than usual. Businesses were closed; stalls either stood deserted with their awnings dropped or had been completely towed away; shops were locked. A few bars served customers who had nowhere else to go, but these were places that lacked character, with drinkers who barely looked up to notice us march past. There were occasional lights, but most lights were indoors.

From the outside his house was like so many in Rome: it offered no clues to its significant owner or his grand facilities. A dark, industrial-looking wall on the street-side had relatively small, high-up windows, all with bars. A forbidding door seemed unlikely to open to knocking. There was a stone ledge for waiting clients to perch on, but it looked dirty and unused. Anyone could see this was not a tenement, yet the place gave no impression that behind its plain exterior there would be spacious, luxurious living quarters. The building sounded deserted. It was not.

Our arrival was quiet. No bombast. No advertisement. Our men lined up on either side of the entrance where they would not be seen through the squint. Someone knocked, as mildly as a sad travelling salesman who expected a no-sale. We waited. Surprisingly, after not too long, someone answered.

As soon as the door swung open, spilling out light and sound, our sturdy men piled in. They moved aside the boy who had acted as porter. Their actions were sure; he made no resistance. We all went straight past him, then crossed an empty atrium as a single party.

Indoors, it all looked masculine: a sybarite's mansion. Noise hit us. Lights were everywhere, regardless of the cost of lamp-oil. Fringed curtains swooped around, in places mismanaged and sagging off their hanging-ropes. Stone couches in a winter dining room were currently upholstered with splayed figures in stages of collapse. They were slaves but had had food, and much wine from cellars they had raided. Chaotic celebration was occurring and would presumably continue for as long as they dared. The harsh ruler of this palace had gone out to a different party.

In the absence of Terentius, his slaves had been rioting around courtyards and salons. Left at home, his mob of unsavoury staff were enjoying their rare opportunity for excess. They were ruled over by a familiar figure. Red in the face, sweating in his master's toga but wearing little else on his grubby body, their liberty-capped King-for-the-Day was Sagax.

Our men began a cursory ground-floor search, met with very feeble protests. There were more people in that house than we had, but most were absorbed in guzzling the best wine Terentius owned before he came home to stop them. A few engaged in more sordid acts. No doubt they could bugger each other in broom cupboards even if he was here, though quietly, in case it gave him the same idea.

In general this household must run more smoothly than today, but it was barely domestic. Female influence was absent. This was a crime headquarters, always a haunt of men, men with no claim and no desire to be fashionably civilised. No one who visited was meant to feel comfortable: they were kept nervous. The master would probably be

357

served lavishly off massive silverware, but his bearers would not put neat napkins on hospitality trays for other people. The latrine would be unspeakable.

We never saw Terentia Berenike, the sister still living at home. Perhaps she was locked in her room on some upper storey, reading or writing letters to take her mind off the commotion downstairs. I presumed she had no rights of protest, even outside the festival of riot. I could understand why she was ready to be married off, to end what must be a bleak existence here. I could see why the thought of Nephele destroying that hope made her desperate.

Sagax, who must have been swigging like young Dionysus ever since Terentius left, made one banal attempt to act out his role as King. It was completely predictable. He instructed me to stand in a bucket of water and sing, naturally while naked. He did not know who I had with me, though I doubt it would have made any difference.

'I am Manlius Faustus,' he was told. 'Flavia Albia's husband. I can endure seasonal licence, Sagax, even such a time-worn old cliché. I am always up for a bit of fun. Let's have a bucket, shall we?' He told a boy to fetch one, which the bemused factotum did. Then it was Sagax himself who was suddenly seized and stripped. 'Turn him upside down. Now, Sagax,' said Tiberius. 'A wise man once told me a good ruler should never give orders unless he is willing to follow them himself. So, King-for-the-Day, you must set an example. We are going to put your head down in this bucket, Your Majesty – then you are going to sing for us.'

They made the plan seem real. Swung upside down by sizeable men with eager grins, the slave screamed. As his head neared the water, I stepped in. 'Hold on, lads. Perhaps we can manage without cruel water play. I think Sagax is going to sing for us anyway.'

And Sagax did. He told us all we needed to know. Terentius had gone out earlier, along with Greius.

'Cornellus Greius is in captivity!'

'That's bollocks. He soon managed to escape.'

Hightailing from the goldsmith's custody, Greius had dared not go to his father's house but came here, pretending that nothing was wrong. I knew that his disputed debt had been for jewellery, intended for both Terentia sisters, but of course he did not reveal it to their frightening brother. Mobsters never expect to pay their way, so Greius could simply laugh off his situation with Hieronymus; in any case, chief and sidekick had been too concerned with their plans for tonight.

Terentius and Greius had bathed and been barbered. Then they put on suitable outfits and were taken off in chairs this morning. They had gone to the all-day religious rites and banquet that were being given to Rome by the Father of his People in his unaccustomed role of a fun-loving host. They must now be at the Amphitheatre.

Terentius and Greius intended to begin slithering in among the establishment. This was the start of a major exercise to grapple important figures close to them. Soon the great and the good would be put under pressure. The mobsters would be smiling, acting as if they themselves were prominent people; their moves would include supporting athletes, chariot faculties and gladiators, giving helpful offers and cynical gifts – use my villa, let me send my musician, borrow my yacht . . . (I thought of the Pinarius family: had they already been suborned?) Top of their list to be drawn into a mesh of corruption was Our Master and God, the lord of the civilised universe, chief god Jupiter's sinister rival on earth: Domitian.

Tiberius and I looked at one another. 'Let's go!'

'How's your sheep?' the cheeky slave Sagax yelled after us obnoxiously, after he had been turned right way up. He assumed any personal danger was over.

'Cooked,' answered Tiberius, stopping and turning back. It sounded as though he had accepted what had happened to the beast, but anyone less drunk might have noticed his tone grew ominous. 'Sagax, what do you know about my sheep?'

Sagax then showed he was really stupid. 'It was me!' boasted this soiled, slurring, ridiculous King-for-the-Day. 'I was the one who grabbed it and I cut its woolly head off. What are you going to do about that, Aedile?'

'Not sensible to tell me.'

'I am a slave. I can't give evidence.'

'You just did, boy! Take him,' said Tiberius, to the men who had accompanied him. 'March him to the aediles' office – and keep him in fetters until I come to deal with him. This one's day of liberty is ended.'

With that, he and I set off again, still intending to find Terentius and his companion Greius. Paris ran to the station-house in case Morellus was there.

We faced some problems. Crossing the top of the hill, we discussed options. Even if we could ever locate the pair, in the biggest amphitheatre in the world, once they saw us coming for them, they were bound to flee. That assumed we even managed to arrive: getting down to the end of the Forum on foot would be difficult and exhausting. We had to expect merrymaking crowds, unless the whole of Rome had gone to the Emperor's party.

I am not the adopted daughter of jokers and chancers for nothing. First, I told Tiberius we should drop back down to the Embankment. At my parents' house, we should borrow his litter from Uncle Tullius. By now he would have emptied his flagon of extremely nice wine and would agree to anything. Taking his luxurious transport, bearers would do the hard work, so we could arrive at the Flavian Amphitheatre with minds and bodies rested. As well – and this in my husband's opinion was my craziest idea – inside its capacious curtains we could change into disguises that would hide our identities. I knew just the costumes we could pick up at the house to use.

'You're mad!' said Tiberius, but Saturnalia was getting to him. He went along with it.

61

If your father and brother have left you the best amphitheatre in the world, you may as well play with it. 'Oh,
oh,' I had joked a few days ago, pretending to be one of the
imperial hacks who greased up the Emperor. 'Our Master
has graciously asked me to dinner – me and a thousand
nobodies he calls his friends . . .'

I was wrong. The fabulous Flavian Amphitheatre had
seating for fifty thousand. What was more, some of the
guests were definite somebodies. Friends and general freeloaders included not only senators and middle-rankers, who
were quietly dying in their hot woollen togas or freezing in
fragile Greek syntheses, but also women, children and the
labouring class. *Now everyone, whether rich or poor, can boast
they have dined with Our Leader.*

They could boast, but would they bother? Even with
perfect eyesight he could only be a tiny figure, many, many
yards away. A vague purple dot, not too tall, never as
handsome as he wanted, overweight, balding under his wig
and wreath, yet the centre of attention amid the clutch of
courtiers and favoured toadies who had special permission
to muscle in and praise him. Even if they were interested
in his crabbed opinions, most other people would have
heard nothing he said. That was if he deigned to speak:
Domitian was famous for gloomy silences while he stared

362

and let everyone assume he was privately planning executions. This host was better at a distance. Anyone who risked approaching tonight to thank the solitary tyrant for his hospitality would find twenty-four lictors and massed Praetorian Guards in their way, sneeringly ordering, 'Back to your seat, sir.'

Why was he doing it? He had held the notorious Black Banquet, where he petrified senators in order to demonstrate his tyrannical control. Now he was winning over the rest of Rome by seeming free-hearted and convivial instead. He was neither. But he would play the host – and, by Jove, this bash of his would have everything.

Everything, and even a court poet, up in the stands, scribbling it all down. *Let them come cluttering up my new note-tablet – unfettered Saturn and wine-soaked December, Laughing-boy Jokester and Impudent Rudeness – I am recording our blithe Caesar's holiday of drunken feasting.* Tumptity tumptity hendecasyllables.

> Watch out: here comes imperial poetry!
> Oh, no, I've got a pain in the fundament.
> Get him: and then stuff that tiddly old Statius
> Where he can scribble no ghastly versicles . . .

Never invite a poet to free drinks; he will get hendecasyllabically blotto.

By the time we arrived, events were at their height. Full-throated noise said the seats were all filled. The Amphitheatre can famously be emptied in only a few moments, via its well-engineered easy stairs and corridors. Less often remarked is that packing in citizens, who never know the time and never care that they don't, takes hours. Announcing the start with trumpets won't help Romans arrive properly; it only makes them remember they left their handkerchiefs at home, so they have to go back for them. This is vital when travelling to a big feast, because you need something to carry away any goodies you can pinch.

Even when properly equipped with their serviettes, the laid-back Romans amble through their streets having discussions with neighbours they may not have seen recently, dodging their accountants or their mistresses or their mothers, after which their children demand toilet facilities (closed for the festival), and everyone stops to watch a dog fight (it always happens: the little black terrier tries to take on that one-eyed scraggy lurcher who hates anything else that moves). Visiting foreigners do not know the way: they cause blockages while havering over their upside-down street maps, even though the entire popula-tion is obviously heading there so they need only to walk along with us. In recognition of the problem, for Saturnalia the arena had been open since morning. Our way here had been fairly unimpeded: districts were sucked dry of popu-lation. The celebrating Romans were finally all in the stands, where much had already been happening.

Rather than run out of food before Domitian even turned up with his festive entourage, people had been bombarded with treats to keep them happy. Allegedly the showers of nuts were first-class hazels from Bithynia and Pontus, although for those of us with an interest in Saturnalia nut-scams, this claim rang hollow. Tiberius and I may also have doubted the luscious Judaean dates, Damascan plums and Balearic figs. But if it's free, who quibbles? Whenever the atmosphere dulled there had been more pastries, spiced cakes, baked figures, apples and pears and berried biscuit fancies, all hurled down by mysterious processes from overhead at the crowds, who happily and stickily reached for them.

Eventually, hundreds of waiters materialised, walking through the tiers of seats with gigantic bread baskets, pure-laundered white napkins, and at last the long-expected and extremely lavish trays of food. Despite being held for hours in the outside corridors, this all seemed exquisite to people who normally ate much more plainly. With almost as many waiters as guests, the effect was of true generosity. Service had been slick: Domitian was famed for his well-drilled, well-mannered staff. The waiters were not only good at their jobs, every one of them looked beautiful. We could see that, even as they milled around the service areas while we were still looking in from the street.

From the moment we got there we knew that the wine-waiters had a bottomless budget. They were serving as fast as they were asked: the people drank the Emperor's health in many refills. Now the hubbub from the arena announced that everybody was pie-eyed and even the waiters were growing wobbly. No wonder Saturnalia was Rome's most popular festival.

Unfortunately, even the ushers on the gates were merry.

Each of the eighty entrances had a reception committee to vet people. Stuck at one of them, Tiberius and I hit trouble. We had to persuade our usher not to have hysterics that we were late, we wanted to arrest someone – and we were an aedile and his wife who seemed to think the invitation specified fancy dress.

I proffered the truth: 'We are hoping to be accepted as part of the entertainment.'

'If you are an aedile, *sir*, you should have your tickets for the front rows.'

'Rather foolishly perhaps,' murmured Tiberius gravely. 'I felt shy to accept after I previously had to turn down Our Leader's kind invitations to his Triumph and the banquet for the Dacian dead.'

'Medical advice,' I burbled. 'Manlius Faustus is the aedile who, you may have heard, was struck by lightning. It was fully reported in the *Daily Gazette*.'

'As an excuse,' snorted the usher, 'that is about as convincing as the schoolboy who cannot produce his home-work because a puppy ate his note-tablet.'

'Lame!' admitted Tiberius. 'It is true, however. Would you like to see my scars?' he offered gamely.

'That's going to be difficult!' At least the usher was now laughing as he pointed at the tightly laced, non-magisterial costume. 'So, Aedile, today you rose from your sickbed to bravely fulfil a mission for justice – but the only garment your wardrobe slaves had left you was a bright green knobbly gourd costume?'

'My personal body-slave is our King-for-the-Day,' agreed the aedile, humbly. Like most masters, Tiberius was taller and sturdier than his slave, so although my sisters' lacing would accommodate some size differential, Dromo's gourd suit was a tight squeeze. This caused him to fidget, which is not the mark of Roman authority.

Nobody bothered to ask why his wife's maid had disguised her under a ghost's shroud. I was feeling desperate. Any moth who flew near the haunting costume would die of its miasma. Underneath it, I could hardly bear to breathe, zapped by the smell of tomb dirt, plus years of Zoilus sweating in a shroud he never laundered.

The usher was a low-grade tipsy prune, who now seized his festive chance to be difficult. He suddenly declared the

366

Amphitheatre full, even to aediles. He had been given no orders about admitting vegetables, and in this situation, Legate, his best recourse to keep his job safe was to have us two flea-bitten tryers-on arrested.

That might have been embarrassing. Fortunately, he called to the nearest law-and-order group – which turned out to be the Fourth Cohort. They even recognised us.

'I thought you lads were all laid low after last night?'

'Oh, we're working through the pain.'

All the vigiles had a presence here, they told us. It was partly to check faces at the entrances, taking note of any people who featured on their many watch-lists for disreputable professions. At the Amphitheatre, grave-diggers, actors and ex-gladiators were specifically banned. Others could be. I was relieved I had only announced myself as 'wife of Manlius Faustus' or as an informer I might have been stopped. Those suitable for admittance were shooed inside; dodgy characters were either rejected or at least had their place noted.

Tiberius and I would have no trouble finding Terentius and Greius. Our fears died. Everyone admitted had been given a token: their designated staircase, their row in a set wedge of seating, and their specific seat number. After getting us in, the Fourth told us, winking, they had special targets. The targets were here. The Fourth were observing.

Morellus was around somewhere, awaiting our arrival, though he had just wandered off to talk to the dwarf, Spendo, who was organising a display. We heard all the cohorts had been commanded to bring their siphon-engines, perhaps in case a lights display went wrong, though the troops said Spendo had been trying out some big idea for later, with a special contribution from the Fourth. I said I hoped they had brought enough water today, not like yesterday at the party; this caused rather strange laughter.

Response: the scruffy form of Titus Morellus advanced upon us, grimacing under his monumental wine headache – and bringing a new difficulty. His tribune came too. The last thing an investigation needs is a high-rank visitation, with embuggerance from an office-dweller who suddenly takes an interest. Even Tiberius groaned under his breath: Cassius Scaurus had decided to direct the operation personally.

His presence in charge indicated how far the mobsters had grown in importance. As a result of Tiberius and Morellus unpicking their scams, Terentius was viewed as a rising criminal organiser. Greius was a major nightmare. Scaurus might have been playing footsie at the party; in reality he wanted to pluck both from his patch and launch them into exile.

'We know where they are,' announced Morellus, proudly, although he was his pessimistic self: 'Pulling them out won't be simple. Happy people are having the best free buffet of their lives. We can't just squash along into the middle of their row, whispering, "Can we have a private word outside, sirs?" Imagine.'

'There would be a riot.' Scaurus liked the idea.

'They will see us coming,' mourned Morellus, 'and they'll skip.'

Tiberius explained we had thought of that: hence our ludicrous costumes. Looking like an innocent part of the entertainment, he and I, gourd and ghost, would dance up to the two men. We would lure them from their seats as if claiming them to take part in a tipsy frolic, so the vigiles could grab them.

'Let's just think about this . . .' Scaurus took a moment

while his brain churned through whether a cohort tribune was outranked by a civilian magistrate, and if it still applied when the aedile was cavorting in a home-made gourd suit.

We had to move. Waiters were now returning from the seat tiers clattering empty bowls and well-picked platters. Colourful members from every field of entertainment were pressing in past them for the next stage of the evening. Scaurus decided: time to act and he would let us play our part.

62

The air was cold, colder than in the corridors, though not as nippy as it had been in the streets. A wall of sound hit us, like a battle. The city all around outside hummed with low-level festivity, but the real noise was here. Thousands of people talked and laughed loudly, all of them at once. Thousands of clashing perfumes – unguents, wine, foodstuffs, vomit and various body odours – were trapped within the great four-storey travertine oval. Cloudy grey skies hung overhead, but the night was free of rain.

We had hurried around under the huge vaults to the correct vomitorium; its staircase was signalled by vigiles on surveillance. Once out in the stand, we reeled. Tonight, the usual all-in experience was increased by huge gusts of sheer pleasure. Rome feasting. Rome fully feasted in fact, now belching and farting. Romans, utterly joyous on holiday, freed from constraints, flush with their ruler's personal generosity. It was more than bread and circuses; it was hand-formed fine rolls in pure white napkins and endless free wine, accompanied by every spectacle the Empire could supply. The fancy entertainment was now starting.

High up above in the darkness, where the velarium could be pulled out for shade in the dangerous heat of summer, I was aware of some large, unfathomable, circular construction. But all eyes were drawn down to the sand-covered floor of the arena, where a whole troop of women gladiators bounded out with bare thighs, shrieks and wildly tossed shining hair. As they wielded their weapons with panache, they played up their notoriety. When women fought, the crowd loved it. Those girls were doing it for real, too, unless that was fake blood. Next, running out like little bundles of furious energy, a line of fighting dwarfs came to join them.

Guided down the steps by vigiles, Tiberius and I were unnoticed, even in our costumes. As the fighters all went at it, the moves looked good, the skills perfected. If it was choreographed, so what? People said that even about professional gladiators. They needed real talent, even in fixed fights, or one slip and that real weaponry could cause real death.

We had to dodge around wine-waiters, while new entertainers were appearing on stage: plump belly-dancers from the east with unexpectedly sinuous movements, the cracking castanets of stylised Spanish dancers, Syrian jugglers, actors and rope-balancers. All were in multicoloured costumes that might be shoddy when close up, but looked jewel-rich from high above. Right here in the stands came more actors and gymnasts, among whom I noticed blatant working-girls, openly available for hire at the Emperor's expense. (He had made himself Censor for life: what kind of moral judge was he?) They offered sex to takers who, on their way outside, had to dodge among men doing tricks with lit sulphur matches. The gangsters must have left some available for these amazing fire-eaters.

At the end of a row, like one of the audience, a vigilis nodded to us. We had come quite a long way down. I spotted Terentius, the man I had seen at the vigiles' party last night. He sat barely a few rows up from the platforms where senators and equestrians had their elegant thrones. There was an empty space beside him at that moment; after some visual searching, I recognised Greius, firmly identified now as the thuggish friend of Pinarius. He had got himself down to the walkway behind the marble seats and stood chatting confidently to notables as if the imperial arena was his personal domain.

It had started. Next year, if no one stopped them, this pair would be positioned down there among those special seats, schmoozing the snooty ranks with all kinds of corrupt propositions, setting their sights on untold political fixing. I touched Tiberius on the arm, warning him to wait. With a cheery wave to his fine new pals, Greius began clambering back to his own seat beside his mentor. He was light-footed and bursting with self-assurance.

Terentius looked like what he was, if you knew his trade; otherwise he could have been any unlikeable businessman. He had the build of too heavy an eater, grey-haired, clean-shaven, square head, pouchy eyes, a straight, thin-lipped mouth when he stopped laughing, though today was for presenting himself as big-hearted and sociable. Even while he was joking with his young hopeful as Greius came back, or with other people in earshot, he had an intent stare. At rest, his inner stillness was chilling.

As he flopped back beside Terentius, Greius casually shoved his expensive ankle boots among people in the row in front; though visibly irritated, they were not protesting. Still in his twenties, his facial bones were good enough and he was sufficiently well-built – no wonder women chased him – but I could see how with more years and looser living he would flesh out into another version of Terentius. He had crude intelligence and total daring. Now I knew what

372

crimes he had committed, I could imagine him bursting into violence.

Tiberius and I set off. As we moved down their row, apologising with silly quips as we stepped over people, Terentius had slung an arm man-to-man across the younger one's shoulders. This was their relationship: the hard master and his willing pupil, the rising star valued by an honoured warlord who had given him independence. Now they were out together in public. The older was showing off the younger – *This is my boy, my trusty, my hard fixer* – his own position boosted by possession of his clever cadet.

Playing two theatre comedians, we reached them. 'You!' cried Tiberius, grey-eyed and moon-faced from inside his vegetable foliage. As he beckoned to Terentius insistently, I echoed the call with Greius, adding mournful *whoo-hoos.* 'Zoilus!' cried the crowd. For a famously dud performer, Zoilus had an impressive customer portfolio. I was proud to be impersonating him.

We deployed that embarrassing game, where hapless members of an audience are dragged out to be humiliated. The crowd eggs them on. Refusal is impossible. Once picked for the ritual, the sheepish victims must oblige. They have to rise and go along with it, looking as if they are enjoying every moment.

We hooked our pair out. The rest of their row cheered, standing up to help push the victims along with us. The people in the row below, whose garments and hair Greius had kicked, enjoyed it particularly. Tiberius bobbed back to the stairs hand-in-hand with Terentius while I swooped around his younger companion, pulling and beckoning.

As we all reached the row end, they spotted our back-up and realised it was a set-up. Their bodyguards had been sitting behind them and were still there, roaring at this comedy. While Terentius began signalling angrily to his men, I continued the drama. Audience members could not tell whether it was truth or fantasy: 'This poor man is mad and does not know it! We have come from his family to collect him for his own safety.'

I whipped off the shroud (unlike Tiberius in the gourd suit, I had on a decency tunic underneath). I flung the material around the astonished criminal, rapidly binding Terentius's arms and fashioning it into a very smelly strait-jacket. Vigiles then gripped his trussed body in a fire-fighters' lift and bundled him up the stairs out of the stands before his bodyguards were even on their feet. Meanwhile Tiberius simply skittled Greius, knocked him over and sat on him.

Troops were supposed to help us. Those I could see were squaring up to the row of bodyguards who, after feasting for hours, were only sluggishly responding to the situation.

'Tiberius, be careful!' I stood on one of Greius's arms, which was flailing on the stairs.

'The lads will come back,' Tiberius mouthed at me, over the crowd noise. Greius was ten years younger and clearly well-exercised.

'Don't let him up. He'll get away.'

'No, I'll hold him.'

That was not easy. I gave the vigiles an urgent shout but too much was going on. The Emperor's banquet had reached the exotic-birds stage. Enormous flocks, whose cost must have emptied the Treasury, were being released for the audience. The flamingos were extremely pink. Someone must have been going to the fish market and feeding them bucketfuls of shrimps. Masses of pheasants and guinea fowl, bemused in the lamp-splattered darkness

374

and stunned by the noise, soared up to roof level, flew short distances among the looped-back shade canvas, knocked into the fixing poles, then fluttered down to be stuffed into folds of dinner outfits. Game birds from distant provinces were crazily flying everywhere. People stood up trying to catch them, teetering and stumbling off balance into lower seat rows. Applause erupted, drowning out yells from Greius, as the people shouted adoration for the Emperor, calling Domitian their Master and God.

Tiberius, my strict traditionalist, hated that. No man could be a living god. Even emperors are 'first among equals', only called divine after death. He cursed, so angry he lost his grip on his violently struggling captive. Political protest was pointless in so large a crowd – and a bad idea anyway. Worse, Greius, who must have been very fit after all his love-making, bucked himself free. I made a grab; he knocked me almost off my feet.

He headed down the stairs. As I staggered into a man with an armful of pheasants, Tiberius was concerned for me, but I cried, 'Run!'

He furiously flew after Greius. Rebalancing myself, I followed. We all ducked our heads as a massive new shower of treats and trinkets was released, along with coupons for prizes, some of which would be high-value. People reaching frantically for Domitian's gifts scrambled in our way.

Beyond, in the arena, came greater activity. Now darkness had fallen, the large metal structure I had half noticed earlier, was brought into action. All the waiters in charge of seat rows simultaneously quenched lights throughout the stadium tiers. Then dim figures ran along ropes in the open roof with torches – the sailors who managed the velarium – as, slowly, a huge chaplet of flickering stars

375

was lowered towards us. The whole effect was magical: it became a single monstrous sun. I vaguely remembered Spendo talking about asphalt and knew it had been planned for days. Who knows how they really did it, but the light was so bright it filled the arena and must have been visible from the Forum outside.

Most attention was on the great sun, but mine followed Greius. As best I could, I was stumbling down the steps, following Tiberius. Around the great arena ran a wall to keep spectators safe from gladiators and wild animals. Greius had hurled himself onto and over it. He took a flying leap down. Tiberius and I balked at following him over, but we leaned and looked. There was a layer of sand on the wooden floor, not deep enough to break his fall. He was strong, athletic and, though he staggered badly, somehow he managed to regain his legs. Then, while he struggled to get his balance, he found himself apprehended unexpectedly. Two sword points pinned him.

'Stop!'

'Hold it right there, Lover-boy!'

He was trapped between two women, normal business for Greius. But Zoe and Chloe would never be playthings of his. I remembered them at Prisca's baths, gossiping with Spendo about the nut-scams and what Tiberius was trying to do, bitterly deploring the warehouse and arson deaths. Zoe and Chloe belonged to the colourful part of the Aventine community that despised all authority – including the power of criminals. If Terentius and Greius thought everyone would roll over and be preyed on, they had miscalculated.

'Cornellus Greius! We know who you are!'

'We know what you've done, you bastard!'

The flaming sun allowed me to see from the stand that

the girls were sweating and bloodied; they had been seriously fighting. Greius, too, realised these Amazons meant business: he kept very still, risking nothing. Zoe and Chloe gestured for him to start walking. They herded him towards one of the gladiators' entrance gates.

Crisis. The huge burning ball that was Sol Invictus must have been suspended on ropes. Had its fiery heat burned through them? It lurched, then abruptly fell. With a sudden roar the fireball sank down as if plunging below some ocean horizon in a dramatic sunset. Parts disintegrated, sending blazing shards in all directions as they hit the ground.

Zoe and Chloe looked as if they were expecting something, but they ran for cover. Greius took to his heels too but was stopped in his tracks. Rollicking out from the gate he wanted to use came a line of vigiles siphon-engines. Their well-trained mules put on a spurt. With a fireball to quench, they were practically galloping. Six cohorts' water carts rumbled across the sand and began pumping furiously to douse Sol. Their presence was more than a general safety measure. I knew there was a planned exercise; from the precision moves, it looked as if this was all part of it.

Greius turned a different way but met a seventh engine. As its team began to push down on its two operating bars, I saw an ecstatic figure, still dressed in his armour as a fighting dwarf, encouraging them to haul the handles faster up and down. Bouncing on top was Spendo, joyfully screaming, 'Go! Go! Go, boys!' He was waving the hose nozzle.

My hand flew to my mouth. I remembered again talking with Spendo about his plans for today, then vigiles telling me he had been working on something special with them. I saw what was about to happen. Whether Spendo intended

377

to aim straight at Greius as he lit up is a big question, but it happened.

The Fourth's siphon-engine had been adapted to use in the light show. It was no longer a water cannon. Spendo had turned it into a battle-winning implement: *used at the siege of Delium, as reported by Thucydides* . . . He had made a flame-thrower.

Nothing like this had happened in Rome since Nero had tied his Christians to stakes and burned them with bitumen as human candles. For today's crowd, civilised by twenty years of Flavian restraint, it was thrilling yet horrific. A silence fell, broken only by Greius screaming.

He stood no chance. Once the stream of molten fire struck him full in the belly, he was done for. The force knocked him over. He dropped to his knees shedding great blisters of skin. One of the kinder cohorts turned their engine his way but water made the chemical flames burn even more fiercely. Vigiles sped up with other equipment, big ex-slaves not needing orders, efficient men who knew their job. A huge esparto grass mat was raised by its corners, flollopped like a giant jellyfish, then slung sideways to cover him. Men stood on the edges to keep out the air. Eventually the fire was smothered. But when it was safe to raise the mat without reignition, Quintus Cornellus Greius was past saving. He had died underneath it in agony.

The Fourth Cohort's engine had trundled on across the sand. Now we saw what that flame-thrower was for: the others had pumped water on Sol Invictus, leaving the great disc completely dark. Then a fierce blast of fire relit it. Once the whole apparatus was burning once more, the Undying Sun slowly rose again in symbolic triumph.

63

Tiberius and I left the stand, holding hands as we tried to steady one another.

'I'm sorry.'

'Not your fault.'

'No, but I am sorry to make you see that.'

I did feel sick. To watch anyone die is difficult, let alone in such a terrible way. Greius had killed the nut-sellers by suffocation and fire, but it would take some time to accept how apt his punishment had been.

At the bottom of the vomitoria there are wide spaces under the Amphitheatre carcass. Where we exited, key figures were gathering. The public and serving staff were being kept out of this area by barricades and by the vigiles. By the time we descended unsteadily, the Fourth's siphon-engine was racketing back from the arena. As Spendo strutted along beside it, I could hear him yammering about the fiery sun: 'Those ropes are going to give way any minute. We can't relight a second time if it crashes. They ought never to have dropped it down from the top. I was for hauling it up from the ground on A-frames . . .' I could not bear listening.

A guard party surrounded Terentius. He had been allowed to shed the constricting shroud I had put on him. He did not bother to threaten reprisals, though the air was heavy with his confidence that this would go badly for the authorities.

He was facing out the tribune. 'We meet again!' This, from the gangster to Scaurus, was his reference to their presumed colluding friendship.

Cassius Scaurus set him straight, however. 'I don't know you!' So much for his party guest-list. The hoary ex-centurion, with his career-long silken capability for lies, bluntly denied any connection. For Scaurus – as for a gangster – the truth would be whatever he said it was.

Even so, the warlord still believed he could control the situation. His expression stayed austere and derisory. However, the tribune set about formally announcing a list of crimes on which he intended to interrogate Appius Terentius. I could see Morellus grinning. Terentius stayed calm. He would blame everything on Greius – knowing Greius would have set up all his foul deeds to avoid leaving evidence. He remained unaware of his trusty's fate.

We held back. I had signalled to an attendant, who ran outside to Uncle Tullius's litter in which we had arrived earlier. Tiberius was struggling out of the gourd suit. He had brought full formal dress, in anticipation. The attendant came with his toga and, as I had done outside Xero's, I began the lifting and pleating process. 'Terentius is sure nothing will lead back to him,' I murmured. 'Have you thought up a technicality to pin him down?'

'I don't suppose,' Tiberius said ruefully, 'we can slam him with false Census declarations.'

'Tax fraud?'

'He will have crooked accountants. Don't worry, I have something in mind.'

Meanwhile official law-and-order plodded on. 'What was

your purpose in coming here?' Scaurus demanded of Terentius.

'Enjoying the bounty, with socialising thrown in.' Terentius was shameless. 'I did hope,' he boasted blatantly, 'there might be an opening for us to pay compliments to the Emperor.'

Now the first shock: 'Forget it!' Morellus snarled. 'Wrong place, wrong time, sir.' He spelled it out with crabby triumph: 'The Emperor loves his people, but he loves his peace and quiet more. His Saturnalia will be in his citadel: Alba Longa in the hills. Sorry, Terentius! Domitian is not here.'

Terentius kept the thin smile of a man who could accomplish what he had wanted another day – and who intended to do so. His complacency was short-lived. Tiberius placed a hand on my arm to warn of a new arrival.

'Let us through – we are family!'

A horrible confrontation was about to happen.

The rest of us stood rapt, ready to watch the families confront each other. Members of the vigiles crowded in, hoping for a cat-fight. Spitfire women would be all the better with a garniture of betrayed men.

The Cornellus brothers, Caesius and Murrius, rushed up to attack Terentius, their sister Laetilla tottering with them in her platform soles. She was chinking with gold chains, as if the fine products of Hieronymus's workshop had been lavished on her from several directions. They must have discovered where Greius kept his love-nest, his apartment in Dolichenus Street. (Word afterwards was that they found it because Greius, like any spoiled young bachelor, had had his father paying the rent.) They had hauled out Terentia Nephele – so she was here – then set off to her brother's house. With him not at home, they had all plunged down to the Amphitheatre, gathering up Terentia Berenike.

The sisters raged at each other. As soon as he learned the Cornelli were throwing his women back at him, and why, Terentius looked thunderous. Berenike screeched at Caesius for not stopping his son. Nephele blamed Murrius for neglect. Laetilla slapped her and told him not to listen. Murrius finally forgot how much he had loved his wife, and with no more compunction dumped her.

Two brothers and their sister, two sisters and a brother: all of them now realised their pact had failed. In this adulterous disaster, damnation would fall on Greius. None of them knew yet that Greius was dead. They must have been wondering where he was. Then they found out.

We heard shouts to make way. We all saw an officious arena squad, hauling by the heels the young man's corpse. As if it were planned – though it could not have been – they dropped his blackened body at his relatives' feet.

Fatal burns are horrible to see. The sisters screamed. The brothers clung together. Terentius stood immobilised. Tiberius and I knew what to expect and looked away.

The squad-leader asked Scaurus whether they should take the body to the Spoliarium. That was a building outside the sinister exit called the Gate of Death. There, dead gladiators were stripped and their corpses prepared for their funerals.

Most of those who knew Greius were unable to react. It was Laetilla who stepped forward. She alone had command of herself. 'Leave him to us. His family will take the body. He can lie on his bier in my house.'

She half knelt, to drape her own stole over him. She spread the fine, fringed material over the top part of his body, letting it fall on him softly.

As she straightened, clinking with her gold, our eyes

382

met. Watching her, I decided something: her two brothers visited Laetilla for ordinary family reasons. She took home other men at other times for other entertainment. One did not care whom he seduced, how many he juggled, how dangerous the risk, or whom he offended. She said nothing. I never asked her. But I was sure: not content with his sister-in-law and his intended wife, Quintus Cornellus Greius had been sleeping with his aunt.

64

No one else seemed to pick up on it. They had enough trouble ahead of them. The survivors' lives would be different, shaken into patterns that were too new to contemplate. Terentius had lost his hard-hitting agent, but he would recruit another – if he survived. He had been betrayed – yet robbed of his retribution. His women would struggle to overcome what had happened, probably bitter for ever against each other. Caesius had lost his son. Only Murrius had any consolation. In years to come those twins of his, those nice children diligently looking after their parrot, would come into their heritage. For them there would be wider roles in the old family consortium, as the old extortion rackets went grinding on in perpetuity.

Standing there in the Amphitheatre, Appius Terentius believed himself untouchable. He had stuck to the code: every tier of his organisation was kept separate; nobody knew what the others were doing; nothing anyone else did could ever be traced back to him. He gave orders to people who gave orders, but no final act would ever lead back to his instruction.

He stated his position to Cassius Scaurus: 'I have done no wrong, Tribune. There is no crime that you can link to me. You have no proof of anything.'

Scaurus was a normal, ploddingly adequate tribune; he

therefore thought the same. Apprehending his villain had been bluff. This was how it had to be. Appius Terentius was unfinished business but crime is a plague that grips all cities. Greed for money and power never abate, fuelled by warped sex and intolerable violence. It continues as long as blood flows in the veins of habitual criminals. Even if he ever managed to manoeuvre the villain into court, an age-old slew of missing evidence and smart lawyering would clear him.

Scaurus was looking unhappy. Morellus was in despair. Time for Tiberius to act. He murmured, '*Domina,* thank you for coming with me.'

'*Domine,* thank you for bringing me.'

I thought very briefly of the home we loved. Our staff would already have returned from my parents' house, travelling back up the Aventine with its frolics and frenzied hand-clapping, bringing our two weary little boys, in the donkey's panniers. Now the donkey was secure in her stable, better protected from vile intruders. Fast asleep in their beds, Gaius and Lucius must be flushed after their exciting day, with a row of new toys lined up, though each of our ducklings was clutching his simple rag doll, home-made by Glaphyra. Our staff would be waiting for us. The candles among our festival greenery represented reassurance: the solstice was coming, when the earth would seem to pause in indecision, yet warmth and light would be restored. Tonight, slaves and freeborn, we would as equals together raise our toast to the Undying Sun.

Tiberius was ready. He and I stepped full into the circle of criminals and vigiles. I smiled gently. He was entirely serious but I felt him squeeze my hand. We were a partnership. In sombre moments, Roman women do not stand back to watch. Though he was clad in his robes of office, it was me who spoke first: 'Restrain this man, Tribune.'

Tiberius, perfectly togate, took control. He raised a hand, the formal gesture. 'Appius Terentius, I am Manlius Faustus, plebeian aedile. I speak for the Senate and People of Rome.'

Terentius laughed bitterly. 'What's your charge? Whatever, I deny it! There is no link to me regarding anything you ever claimed about a few mouldy nuts.'

My husband took that quietly. 'It's true, my witness for that activity accused your dead trusty. *You* are taken on a different charge, one you brought upon yourself. You have, using a slave who admits his crime, offended against a sacred Mother Goddess. You stole and butchered, then dumped like common garbage, a sheep that had belonged to the Temple of Ceres, destined for religious sacrifice.'

Ah, Sheep!

Morellus caught my eye, highly amused that a magistrate should bend the truth and use that age-old apology: *It wasn't mine, sir, I was just looking after it for someone . . .*

'A slave?' Sneering, Terentius made the defendant's usual protest. 'Don't rely on a slave, even if you torture him. Whoever he is, or says he is, I deny he is mine!'

'He is yours.' Tiberius was at last showing satisfaction as he punched in his elegant fatal charge: 'You labelled him with a collar that names you as his owner, a collar you have had permanently welded onto him. Cassius Scaurus, arrest this man. Terentius, prepare yourself: you have committed a capital crime. The penalty is death, for temple desecration. Appius Terentius, I am charging you with sacrilege.'

RECEIVE THE LATEST NEWS FROM LINDSEY DAVIS

Go to
https://www.hodder.co.uk/contributor/lindsey-davis/
to sign up to Lindsey's email newsletter

Visit Lindsey's website at www.lindseydavis.co.uk

Or head over to the official Facebook page
f /lindseydavisauthor

HODDER &
STOUGHTON